HIGH PRAISE FOR
GRAHAM MASTERTON!

"A mesmerizing storyteller!"

—*Publishers Weekly*

"One of the most consistently entertaining writers in the field."

—*Gauntlet*

"Graham Masterton is the living inheritor to the realm of Edgar Allan Poe."

—*San Francisco Chronicle*

"Graham Masterton is a first rate horror writer."

—*Midwest Book Review*

"Graham Masterton is always a lot of fun and he rarely lets the reader down....Horror's most consistent provider of chills."

—*Masters of Terror*

"Masterton is a crowd-pleaser, filling his pages with sparky, appealing dialogue and visceral grue."

—*Time Out* (UK)

"Masterton is one of those writers who can truly unnerve the reader with everyday events."

—Steve Gerlach, Author of *Rage*

"Masterton has always been in the premier league of horror scribes."

THE IMPOSSIBLE VISITOR

The figure made a whining noise, as if it were trying to protest, but Dan switched on the light and said, "Okay, friend, let's see who the hell you are."

He was so shocked that he shouted out *"gahhhh!"* and his legs felt as if they were going to buckle underneath him.

The figure in front of the window was Gayle. His dead fiancée Gayle—not wearing a nightgown, but the cream satin dress that she had been wearing to Gus Webber's wedding. Her blonde curls were gingery with blood—but worse than that, she looked exactly as she had after the accident. The end of one of the scaffolding poles had struck her directly in the face, just below the bridge of her nose, stoving it in. She hadn't been killed immediately, and the fire department had tried to remove her from the wreck of Dan's Mustang by sawing through the scaffolding pole about two inches in front of her face.

Her blue eyes were both open, either side of the sawed-off pole, like a fish's eyes. The pole itself formed an *O* of surprise. Around the pole, her breath was whistling and bubbling with blood....

GRAHAM MASTERTON

THE
5TH WITCH

LEISURE BOOKS NEW YORK CITY

To Wiescka, who has always been magic,
with all my love.

A LEISURE BOOK®

May 2008

Published by

Dorchester Publishing Co., Inc.
200 Madison Avenue
New York, NY 10016

ISBN 10: 0-8439-5790-5
ISBN 13: 978-0-8439-5790-7

The name "Leisure Books" and the stylized "L" with design are trademarks of Dorchester Publishing Co., Inc.

Printed in the United States of America.

10 9 8 7 6 5 4 3 2

THE
5TH WITCH

"Of all the fearful things that beset us in our early days of settlement in Hartford—disease and crop blight and madness and the bitterest of winters—none inspired greater dread in our community than the Five Witches."

—Rev. John Whiting
Pastor of the Second Church,
Hartford, Connecticut
February 1660

Chapter One

"Here he comes, the bastard," said Cusack as three shiny black Cadillac Escalades drew up outside the Palm Restaurant, nose-to-tail. The doors of the first and the third car opened, and five enormous black men in black suits and black glasses climbed out, blocking off the sidewalk so that a party of Japanese tourists had to step onto the road to get past them.

"Speedy?" said Fusco into his microphone. "The Zombie's coming in now. Give me a test."

A crackly voice said, *"You seen the prices in this place, man? Thirty-eight dollars for a steak! I'm glad you guys are picking up the tab."*

"Okay, we hear you," said Fusco.

The doors of the middle Escalade opened, and out stepped a slightly built man in a black velvet suit and mirrored sunglasses. He was wearing a floppy beret, black velvet to match his suit and almost ridiculously large, and his beard was trimmed to a pointed goatee. He carried a silver-topped cane.

He waited on the sidewalk while a girl stepped out of the car behind him. She was very tall—at least four inches taller than he was—and her clinging gray dress showed how thin she was. She was obviously not wearing a bra because her breasts were flat and her pointed nipples were visible; her dress showed off her bony hips, too. She had a profile as sharp as an axe, with slanted eyes and high cheekbones, and her hair was plaited like a nest of black snakes.

Around her neck she wore seven or eight silver necklaces, and on each wrist she must have carried at least a dozen silver bangles.

"Never seen *that* particular piece of tail before," Knudsen remarked, leaning over from the backseat.

"She looks like she could eat you for lunch," said Cusack.

"She looks like she *needs* to eat me for lunch."

"Okay, Speedy," said Fusco, "the Zombie's out of his vehicle, and he's heading for the door. Don't forget—you need him to make a clear admission that he was responsible for torching the Fellini Building. But don't make him feel like you're pressuring him. We'd rather you stayed alive and we set him up another time."

"Ten-four. Is it okay if I order the lobster?"

"For Christ's sake, Speedy. Order whatever you like. Just don't stuff too much into your mouth at once. We need to hear what you're saying."

The Zombie was just about to enter the restaurant when the tall girl in the gray dress looked along Santa Monica Boulevard toward the three detectives sitting in a battered bronze Crown Victoria. She frowned; then she caught hold of the Zombie's shoulder, said something to him, and pointed. He looked toward them, too.

"Jesus," said Fusco. "Has she made us?"

"How the hell could she make us? We're just three overweight guys sitting in a car, minding our own business."

"She's made us," Fusco insisted. "Look—she's walking this way."

"She hasn't made us, for Christ's sake. How could she?"

But the tall girl in the gray dress kept coming, and when she reached their car, she stepped out in front of it and stood with her hands on her hips, staring at them through the windshield with undisguised contempt.

"So she's made us," Cusack admitted. "What's she going to do about it?"

"I think we need to tell her to stop eyeballing us and be on her way."

"You think she knows what we're doing here?"

"How *can* she know what we're doing here?"

"She knows we're here, doesn't she? And she looks pretty pissed about it."

The tall girl in the gray dress was carrying a soft gray leather purse. She loosened its drawstring and reached inside.

"That's it," said Cusack, hauling out his gun. He tugged at the door handle, but the door wouldn't budge.

"Did you lock this thing?" he snapped at Fusco.

"Of course not," Fusco protested. "Anyhow, it's not locked." But when he pulled at his handle, his door wouldn't open either. Neither would Knudsen's in the back.

"Get the hell out of here!" Cusack shouted. "Get the hell out of here—*now!*"

Fusco twisted the key in the Crown Victoria's ignition, but the starter did nothing but whinny, then groan, then die.

The three detectives watched in horror as the tall girl in the gray dress took her hand out of her bag. She wasn't holding a gun, however, but a small black box, very glossy, as if it had been enameled.

"What the Fred Flintstone is that?" asked Knudsen.

Fusco tried to start the engine again, and then again, and then again, but all he could rouse was a regurgitating noise.

The tall girl in the gray dress opened the lid of the box and tipped a small heap of gray powder into the palm of her right hand. Cusack watched her with his eyes narrowed, and he began to feel deeply apprehensive. Being trapped in a car that wouldn't start was reason enough, but the haughty expression on the girl's face disturbed him even more—and why hadn't the Zombie's bodyguards come to help her? Three of them were still standing outside the Palm, their hands cupped over their genitalia in the standard pose of bodyguards all over the world, and the other two must have taken the Zombie inside.

Cusack yanked at his door handle again. When the door still refused to open, he turned his gun around and hit the window with the butt. The first time the glass didn't break, but then he hit it again and it shattered. He put his hand through and tried to open the door from the outside, but even when he slammed his shoulder against it, it wouldn't move, and he was too big to try to climb out.

"Call for backup!" he told Fusco. But when Fusco switched on the radio, all that came out of it was a thick fizzing noise punctuated with disorganized thumps, like somebody jumping down a flight of stairs, three and four at a time. He took out his cell phone and punched in the number for police headquarters, but when he put the phone to his ear, he shook his head.

"Same thing. It's totally kaput."

Knudsen started banging at one of the windows at the back until it smashed and glittering glass was scattered across the sidewalk.

Meanwhile, the tall girl in the gray dress had lifted her right hand in front of her face, palm upward, and now she leaned toward them a little. Cusack reached through the broken window, around the windshield, and pointed his gun at her. "Back off, lady! You hear me? Drop the bag, and step back on the sidewalk! Kneel down, and lock both your hands behind your head! Do it now!"

The tall girl in the gray dress gave no indication that she had heard him. Instead, she blew on the powder in her hand so that it floated up over the hood of the car, like very fine ash. She made a complicated sign in the air, as if she were drawing an invisible picture, and at the same time she shrieked at them in a high, shrill voice, "*Ravet pa janm gen rezon devan poul! Ou pa konn kouri, ou pa konn kache!*"

"I said kneel down on the sidewalk!" Cusack yelled. But she stayed where she was, drawing more pictures in the air and shrieking out the same words over and over.

"Give her a warning shot," said Knudsen.

"Don't do that," said Fusco. "You'll have the Zombie's bodyguards on us, and we're sitting ducks if we can't get these freaking doors open."

"I said—kneel on the goddamned sidewalk!" Cusack repeated.

But at that moment he felt his stomach churn over. His insides were *rattling*, too, like a washing machine filled with dried beans. He burped, and there was a foul brown taste in his mouth. It wasn't bile; it was something sweeter than that.

"For God's sake," he said and burped again, and this time the brown taste was even stronger. He felt his midriff, and it was actually *moving*, in the same way that his wife Maureen's stomach had moved when she'd been six months pregnant. He drew back his gun and put it on the seat.

"You okay, Mike?" Fusco asked him.

"I don't know," said Cusack. "I suddenly feel like puking."

"Well if you're going to puke, puke out the god-damned window," said Knudsen. "The smell of puke makes me puke."

Cusack's stomach churned again, even more violently. He felt a tickling right in the back of his throat, and he couldn't stop himself from letting out a cackling retch. He spat into his hand and spat again, and when he opened it three live cockroaches ran across his fingers and dropped onto the floor.

"Shit, man," said Fusco, staring at him in disgust.

But Cusack was gripped by another hideous spasm, and this time he could only stare back at Fusco with his eyes bulging as a huge gush of cockroaches poured out of his mouth and into his lap. They scuttled blindly in all directions, hundreds of them, dark brown and glistening, their antennae waving. Fusco screamed as he tried to beat them off his coat and his pants.

"Christ!" shouted Knudsen. He stuck his head out the smashed window in the back of the car, then one of his arms, and tried to force his shoulders through.

"Help us!" he screamed. "Somebody help us! Call nine-one-one! Call nine-one-one!"

The tall girl in the gray dress pointed at him with an extravagantly long gray-polished fingernail and shrieked, *"Ou pa konn kouri! Ou pa konn kache!"*

Outside the Palm, the doorman and two of the parking valets were staring at the detectives' car in bewilderment, while the Zombie's bodyguards remained where they were, placid but threatening. A few passing drivers slowed down to look, too, but none stopped. If this was a movie shoot, they didn't recognize any of the actors, and if it wasn't, something seriously weird was happening and they didn't want to get involved.

Knudsen was still screaming when he started to spew up cockroaches, too—a thick rush of brown insects that flooded across the sidewalk, all of them hurrying to escape the sunlight and hide in the nearest dark crevice. In the driver's seat of the Crown Victoria, cockroaches started to pour out of Fusco's mouth, and when he clamped his hand over his lips, they dropped out of his nostrils two and three at a time.

The three detectives gripped their stomachs with both hands, trying to force out more cockroaches. Cusack was gasping for breath and shaking his head wildly from side to side so that the bugs flew out from his lips in all directions. There was no sound in the Crown Victoria but choking and gagging, and the creaking of the car's suspension and the rustling of hundreds of insects as they were vomited out onto the upholstery.

The tall girl in the gray dress reached into her purse again and produced two thin sticks, about nine inches long with hanks of hair knotted at one end. She rubbed them quickly together and at the same time called, "Sa k'genyen, mesyés? Ou byen? Ou pa two byen? Ou anvi vonmi?"

As she rubbed the sticks faster and faster, smoke began to pour out of them. They caught fire, and the hanks of hair began to burn. She pointed the sticks at the three detectives and shrieked, "Dife! Dife! Ti moun fwonte grandi devan baron!"

In spite of all the cockroaches in his throat, Cusack roared with pain. He was suddenly ablaze, with flames engulfing him as if he had been soaked in gasoline. Fusco caught fire next and then Knudsen, until the three of them were burning like religious effigies. All around them, the cockroaches were crackling and popping as they burned, too.

The three detectives desperately tried to escape. Cusack managed to wrestle himself halfway out the

passenger window, but he was too fat and too shocked
and too badly burned. He tilted out the side of the car,
his face sooty, his coat burned through to his red-raw
skin, with a few flames still flickering in his hair like a
coronet.

Fusco pulled at the door handle with his burning
hands, even as he was tugging the flesh off his fingers
in blackened lumps. Knudsen tried to kick the back
door open, but the harder he kicked, the fiercer he
blazed, until he was nothing but a mass of flame.

A crowd began to gather as the interior of the car
burned out, although they kept a respectful distance in
case the fuel tank blew. Two blocks away, from the
West Hollywood Fire Station, came the honking and
wailing of a fire truck.

A middle-aged black man in a brown checkered
sport coat came out of the Palm and peered worriedly
toward the burning car. When he saw what had happened, he started to walk quickly away, his knees
slightly bent, in the half run that had earned him the
nickname Speedy.

But Speedy wasn't fast enough for the tall girl in the
gray dress. She turned around as if she had heard him
hurrying off, even though he was fifty yards away now
and wearing soft-soled loafers.

Out of her purse she took what looked like a dried
chicken's claw and pointed it at his narrow back. She
uttered a single high scream, and Speedy staggered
and fell sideways. He tried to get up, but the tall girl in
the gray dress waved the chicken's claw three times,
calling out, *"En! Dé! Twa!"*

Speedy collapsed onto the concrete, his thin legs
shivering like a fallen pony. Two teenagers on bicycles
stopped and stared, but nobody made any effort to
help him.

The tall girl in the gray dress walked back to the

Palm with an elegant long-legged lope, as if she were a fashion model. The Zombie's bodyguards opened the doors for her, and she disappeared inside.

The Crown Victoria with the three incinerated detectives inside continued to smolder. Billows of black smoke smudged the sky over Hollywood like an omen of strange and uncertain days to come.

Chapter Two

Dan had that nightmare again. It was early evening, and he and Gayle were driving south on the 101 very fast, heading back to Los Angeles from San Luis Obispo. The warm breeze was buffeting their faces, and Gayle was singing the Scissor Sisters song "Comfortably Numb" in a deliberately screechy falsetto.

"When I was a child I had a fever! My hands felt just like two balloons! Eee—eee—eee—eee!"

"That's one thing you didn't inherit from your mom!" Dan shouted. "Her singing voice!"

"I sing like an *angel*," Gayle retorted.

"Sure you do—an angel with her wings caught in her zipper."

The sun had just been swallowed by the ocean, and over the dark outline of the Santa Ynez Mountains the sky looked as if it had been flooded with blood. Dan couldn't remember if it had really been that color or not. He remembered that Gayle's blond curls had looked scarlet, but maybe that was after the collision and not before.

In his nightmare, his Mustang didn't sound like a car at all but more like the rumbling of a thunderstorm, and when other cars passed in the opposite direction, they were silent until they were right alongside, and then they made a noise like a massive door going *slam!*

In his nightmare, he didn't feel drunk, as he had been in reality. He and Gayle had been to the wedding of one of his old friends from the police academy, Gus Webber, and he and Gus had always been competitive drinkers. Between them, they had finished off three bottles of champagne and more than twenty bottles of Coors. One for the road! One for the Los Angeles Police Academy! One for the Dodgers! Another one for the Losh Angelesh Poleesh Acamedy!

In his nightmare, drunk or not, he felt as if the world were slowly winding backward. The highway was flashing past them at nearly ninety miles an hour, but over the shoreline the seagulls were suspended in the blood-colored sky, motionless.

"You're driving too French," said Gayle.

"What?"

"I told you that it was time to leave. I told you. Now what are you going to do?"

He frowned at the clock on the Mustang's dash. 9:59 P.M. Gayle was right. They were going to be late now, so by the time they reached Santa Barbara, the highway would be rolled up for the night. He put his foot down even harder, and the Mustang topped a hundred miles an hour.

Another car slammed past, then another and another—more and more of them, until it sounded as if somebody were hurrying in a panic through a huge house, slamming every door behind him.

As they approached Isla Vista, Dan saw taillights ahead of them, as he always did, and he had to brake, hard.

"God," said Gayle, as she always did.

It was the same in every nightmare, and it had been the same in real life on the night it had happened.

A recreational vehicle in two-tone brown, driving at a crawl, with oily black smoke billowing from the back of it. On the rear bumper it bore a sticker that said *Jesus Is Suspicious*.

"What do you think that means?" he asked Gayle, just as he had asked her on the evening she was killed. "Do you think they're trying to say that Jesus kind of, like, *suspects* something, or do you think they mean that Jesus is acting kind of strange?"

"Maybe both," said Gayle.

"Well, whichever it is, I wish in the name of Jesus this guy would move his wreck of a camper out of my face."

He made a signal and pulled out to pass. As he did, a truck came toward them with its lights ablaze and its horn blaring, and Dan had to swerve back in again.

"Dan—be careful. Please."

He blinked at her, still dazzled. "How long do you think I've been driving? Eighteen years and only one accident, and that wasn't my fault. Some Hell's Angel with a death wish."

He pulled out again. The highway ahead looked clear, so he put his foot down.

The Mustang rumbled louder and louder. Lightning crackled across the sky, and all of a sudden the air was filled with a blizzard of paper and dust and seagulls that thumped against the windshield, leaving it splattered with blood.

"Dan—!"

"It's fine! We're going to be fine!"

But then he realized that the camper was being towed by a long black tractor trailer and that it was going to take him much longer to pass than he had calculated. What he had thought to be smoke from the camper was pouring out of the tractor's exhaust stack and blowing across the highway in front of them so that he could barely see. And still the seagulls thumped against the windshield, bursting apart and spraying blood and feathers.

Dan, something's coming the other way.

He switched on the windshield wipers, and the glass was immediately smeared with two opaque crescents of blood. But he could see the lights approaching, four main headlights and a whole rack of floodlights, and they were growing brighter and brighter at a terrifying rate. A bus maybe, or a truck. He could hear its horn blowing, like three discordant trumpets.

There was nothing he could do but jam his foot down even harder. They had almost drawn level with the tractor's front wheel, although their windshield was filled with blinding white light, and Dan thought: *I never imagined that I was going to die like this.*

There was a fraction of a second when he believed that it was too late. But then they pulled ahead of the tractor, and he twisted the wheel to the right, and a huge Amoco tanker blasted past them, still blowing its horn, so close that its slipstream sent the seagull feathers whirling up inside the Mustang's interior.

"*Shit,*" he said, looking in his rearview mirror at the tanker's disappearing taillights.

And it was then that they collided with the rear end of a truck loaded with scaffolding poles, and one of them smashed through the windshield and hit Gayle directly in the face.

That was when he always woke up—with that last picture of Gayle in his head. It was so grisly that he would have to limp to the bathroom and lean over the sink, his mouth filling with bile, his stomach muscles clenching and unclenching, his eyes tightly closed until the image faded away.

Then he would raise his head and stare at himself in the mirror—a lean, haunted face with angular cheekbones and a sharply pointed nose and eyes the color of washed-out denim. Scraggly black hair and an unshaven chin.

"You again," he said that morning. "You sorry-looking bastard."

His doorbell chimed. He kept staring at himself in the mirror until the bell chimed again. Then he shuffled into the living room and called out, "Who is it? As if I didn't know!"

"It's Annie! You were shouting in your sleep again. I brought you something."

Dan went over to the front door and opened it. A girl was standing on the balcony outside, holding a tumbler covered by a beaded cloth. She was slightly Hispanic looking, with glossy black hair and wide brown eyes and pouting lips that made her look sulkier than she really was. She was wearing a green silk headscarf, a patchwork dress, and a necklace made of big brown wooden beads. Her hands and her feet were decorated with henna designs.

"Oh God, Annie," said Dan. "Not the myrtle tea."

"Myrtle tea is the best thing for bad dreams."

"I know. But it also tastes like tomcat piss."

"You've been doing it much more lately. Shouting. Well, *screaming*, to be truthful."

"It's a bad dream, that's all. I'll get over it."

"It's been three years now, Dan—longer—and you're getting worse."

He went back into the living room, and Annie followed him.

"It's still hot," she said. "You should try to drink it while it's hot."

"Why? I don't like *hot* tomcat piss any better than I like *cold* tomcat piss."

Annie put the glass on the kitchenette counter. "Tomorrow I'll make you up some more essence of nettle. That should help."

"Annie—"

"What?"

"I don't know. Maybe I *can't* get over it. What then?"

She went up to him and laid her hand over his heart. He was six-foot-one and she was only five-foot-four, but there was no doubt who was comforting whom. "She's still here, Dan. You won't ever get over what happened. But for your own sake, you have to accept it. You can't go on blaming yourself for the rest of your life."

"Maybe you can mix me up some hemlock."

"Don't joke. Hemlock would give you a horrible death. It swells the lining of your throat so that you can't breathe."

"Is that less horrible than being hit in the face with a scaffolding pole?"

"It's one hell of a lot slower."

He went to 25 Degrees for lunch, in the Hotel Roosevelt on Sunset, and took his usual stool at the corner of the bar. He ordered the three-cheese sandwich and a Bloody Mary, and sat popping olives into his mouth and looking around the diner to see who was ensconced in the big, circular leather booths.

25 Degrees was glitzy but casual, and there was always a watchable mix of directors, agents, tourists, and chiselers, as well as out-of-work actors saving money by sharing a burger and a milkshake among three of them.

"Late again, Detective," said Pedro, the smooth-faced barman, looking up at the clock. It was a joke between them. It meant that Dan was starting to drink early for today but late for yesterday.

"Slept badly," said Dan. He spat out a small handful of olive pits.

"You know what the cure for that is?"

"I have a terrible feeling you're going to tell me."

"Always go to bed with a very ugly woman, so that you *pretend* to sleep. You close your eyes, you breathe deep, you don't do none of that tossing and turning—and before you know it, *zonk*, you really *are* asleep."

"Well, thanks for the advice. But I don't *know* any very ugly women."

"Hey—you can borrow my wife."

Dan was halfway through his cheese sandwich when his cell phone warbled.

"Dan? It's Ernie Munoz."

"Ernie, I'm off duty this week, remember."

"I know. But we just lost three guys from the Narcotics squad. Cusack, Knudsen, and Fusco."

"Jesus. When did this happen?"

"About forty-five minutes ago and in highly frigging peculiar circumstances. They were outside the Palm on Santa Monica, surveilling Jean-Christophe Artisson. Their vehicle caught fire, and all three of them got cremated."

"When you say 'caught fire'. . . ?"

"Eyewitnesses say that it just went up like the Fourth of July. The poor bastards tried to get out, but for some reason they couldn't."

"They weren't attacked? Firebombed or anything like that?"

"There was some woman standing nearby, and apparently she was making gestures at them, but nobody saw exactly what happened."

"*Gestures?*"

"Don't ask me. That's all the witness said, gestures."

"What about the Zombie? Was he anyplace close? Him or any of his goons?"

"Unh-hunh. The Zombie was inside the restaurant, ordering the tuna. A couple of his goons were standing outside the door, but they were at least fifty yards away when the car went up."

"They couldn't have planted a timing device?"

"If they did, nobody saw them do it. But here's the thing. Speedy Lebrun was inside the restaurant, too, wearing a wire. He was supposed to talk to the Zombie about the Fellini fire—get some kind of confession. When the car went up, he made a run for it, but before he'd even gone a block, he dropped down dead on the sidewalk."

"What the hell? Somebody shot him?"

"Not so far as we can tell. He didn't have no visible bullet holes in him, and there was no blood on the sidewalk. Maybe it was a heart attack."

Dan was silent for a moment, thinking. Then he said, "Okay, Ernie. I'll meet you down there. Give me five."

He tipped back the dregs of his Bloody Mary, folded his sandwich into a napkin, and climbed down from his stool.

"Hey, Detective!" called the barman. "What time do you want my wife to come around?"

Dan gave him a dismissive backhanded wave, like Columbo, and walked out of the diner onto the street, taking another bite of his sandwich as he went.

Chapter Three

Almost at the same time, five men and a woman entered the reception area of Peale, Kravitz, and Wolfe, entertainment lawyers, on the thirty-fourth floor of Century Park East.

The men were all wide shouldered, with faces that looked as if they had been roughly sandblasted out of reddish-brown granite, but they were all immaculately dressed in tailored suits, colorful silk neckties, and highly polished shoes. The woman was in her mid-thirties, with feathery white-blond hair. She was wearing a balloon-shaped dress of bright yellow satin, very short, and very high platform shoes.

The reception area was walled with mirrors so that everything was multiplied three times over—the frondy tropical plants in their cube-shaped marble urns, the modern stainless-steel statuettes representing art and music and acting, and the six people making their way to the wide marble reception desk.

The elegant black receptionist was pecking with inch-long fingernails at her computer keyboard. "If you'd care to wait, gentlemen—ma'am—I'll be with you in just a second."

One of the men leaned forward a little. He had

iron-gray hair tied in a pigtail, a broken nose, and two fistfuls of heavy silver rings. "We do *not* care to wait," he told her in a hoarse Russian accent, almost as if he were pretending to be the villain in a James Bond picture. "You will be with us *now*."

The receptionist said, "I'm sorry, sir, I really have to log in this calendar entry."

"You do not have to log in anything," the man replied. He turned to the woman in the yellow dress and said, "Miska!"

The woman in the yellow dress flapped her hand as if she were throwing something at the receptionist's PC. There was a sharp crackling sound, and the screen instantly went blank. Baffled, the receptionist rattled at her keyboard, but the PC remained dead.

"We wish to speak to Mr. Morton Kravitz," said the man with the pigtail.

The receptionist was bending under her desk to see if her computer had somehow come unplugged.

"I said, we wish to speak to Mr. Morton Kravitz, and we wish to speak to him now."

The receptionist reemerged, looking flustered. "Mr. Kravitz? I'm sorry, sir. Mr. Kravitz never sees anybody without an appointment."

"Mr. Kravitz—he is here, yes?"

"Yes, sir, he is, but he's in a meeting with clients right now, and like I said, he never sees anybody without an appointment."

"He will see us. Where is his office?"

"This way," said the woman in the yellow dress, without any hesitation. She pointed to the turquoise-carpeted corridor on the right-hand side of the reception area. She circled around the receptionist's desk, and the five men began to follow her.

"Stop!" said the receptionist, rising to her feet. "You can't just walk in!"

"Of course we can."

"No, no. You hold it right there. I'm calling security!"

"Of course you will call nobody."

"You want to bet?"

The receptionist reached for her telephone. None of the six tried to stop her. Yet, as she started to punch the number, there was movement in the mirrored wall behind her. The reflection of the woman in the yellow dress covered her face with both hands so that only her eyes looked out from between her fingers. And then two of the reflected men walked around the reflected reception desk, and one seized the reflected receptionist by her hair, twisting her head around.

The real receptionist's head was twisted around, too, and she dropped her telephone and shrilled out, "Aaahh—ahhhh—*ahhhhh!*"

But none of the real men was anywhere near her, and she appeared to be staggering and bending her head to one side by herself, as if she were having an epileptic fit.

One of the reflected men caught hold of her wrists and wrenched her arms behind her back. The other reflected man kept hold of her hair and slammed her head onto the marble desk, facedown.

Even though there appeared to be nobody holding her, the real receptionist slammed her head down, too, and her nose broke with a crack like a turkey's wishbone.

The reflected man hit her head against the desk again and again, seven or eight times. The knocking of her forehead against the marble changed to a crunch as her skull was fractured, and then the crunch changed to a slushier sound. Blood sprayed across the desk, then pinkish lumps of brain.

Eventually, the reflected man lifted her head and looked dispassionately at her red, smashed face. Her real self levitated as if she were a life-size marionette. She stared at the woman and the five men, her eyes wild, even though she was dead. Then she dropped back onto the desk.

"What did I say?" asked the man with the pigtail. "I said of course to call nobody."

The six of them pushed their way into Morton Kravitz's office.

Morton Kravitz himself was sitting at the end of an oval mahogany table, a tall patrician man wearing a red-and-white striped shirt and red suspenders. He had an orange suntan and a gray hairpiece that sat too high on his head, as if he were hiding his wallet underneath it.

Three other entertainment lawyers were sitting around the table—Russ Pepper, a big, gingery-haired man in a yellow sport coat; Dominic Serrantino, who had black slicked-back hair and a nose like a predatory hawk; and Grace Trilling, a hard-faced brunette with lip gloss the color of freshly spilled blood and a black Rick Owens jacket.

"Sorry, people," said Morton Kravitz. "Think you took a wrong turn somewhere." He smiled expansively and said to his companions, "That's the trouble with having such goddamned labyrinthine offices. We ought to give our clients a handful of beans when they come in to reception, so they can find their way back."

"Of course this is the correct room," said the man with the pigtail. "You are Mr. Morton Kravitz?"

"That's right. But I regret that I can't see you without a prior appointment, my friend, and some idea of why you want to consult me. I only handle corporate business, not personal."

"You handle Coastal Productions, yes?"

Morton Kravitz looked uneasy. "I'm sorry, but I'm right in the middle of a very important meeting here, and I can't just—"

"You can. I assure you. I am Vasili Krylov."

"Oh. I see. I'm sorry, Mr. Krylov, I didn't recognize you. The last time I saw you—well, you looked altogether different. You were sporting a—kind of a luxuriant mustache, if I recall?"

Dominic Serrantino blinked in obvious anxiety. "Mort, I think we need to call security."

"You call *nobody*," said Vasili Krylov. "If you call somebody, that will be the last somebody you ever call."

Russ Pepper stood up and said, "Come on, Mort—this is intolerable! You can't just let this guy waltz into your office without so much as by your leave."

He flipped open his cell phone, but Morton Kravitz laid a hand on his arm and said, "Don't, Russ. Just don't. This gentleman is Vasili Krylov."

"I don't care if he's frigging Tchaikovsky."

"You like Tchaikovsky?" asked Vasili Krylov. He turned his head like a shark that has just tasted blood in the water.

"What the hell is that supposed to mean?"

"I ask you, sir, if you like Tchaikovsky."

Russ Pepper was confused. He looked to Morton Kravitz for some indication of how to respond, since Morton Kravitz obviously knew who this man was and Pepper didn't.

Morton Kravitz said, "It's okay, Russ. Just sit down, okay?"

"No, no, you should answer me," said Vasili Krylov. "I ask you if you like Tchaikovsky."

"I like any kind of music," said Russ Pepper uncertainly.

"Of course this is a pity," Vasili Krylov told him.

"Miska . . . show this gentleman what happens to people who insult the name of Russia's greatest composer."

The woman in the yellow dress covered her face with her hands, as she had done before in the reception area. There was no mirror in this office, but Russ Pepper was clearly reflected in the light-sensitive glass of the windows. As he stood there, a reflected image of one of the men walked around the table toward him, although the real man stayed where he was with his arms folded.

"Any way I can help you, Mr. Krylov?" asked Morton Kravitz. "You obviously came here with something on your mind."

Vasili Krylov raised one finger to indicate that he would answer in his own time. As he did so, the reflected man took hold of Russ Pepper's right wrist and forced his arm sharply upward.

Russ Pepper stared at his own arm in shock. "What the *hell?*"

He turned around in bewilderment, his arm still upraised. "Somebody grabbed me! Who the hell grabbed me?"

In his hand he was holding a gold mechanical pencil. But he suddenly gripped it tighter, as if somebody were squeezing his fingers together so that he couldn't let go of it.

He began to move the pencil slowly toward his right ear, although his arm was shuddering with effort, and he bent his head to the left as if he were desperately trying to keep away from it.

"Russ!" shouted Morton Kravitz, getting up from his chair. "Russ, what the hell are you doing?"

He turned to Vasili Krylov. "What is this? Hypnotism? Put a stop to it, *now!*"

He tried to take hold of Russ Pepper's arm, but the

reflected man in the window pushed him away so that he stumbled backward and fell against his chair.

"Oh my *God*," gasped Grace Trilling. "Oh my God, what's happening?"

Russ Pepper grunted like a hog in his efforts to stop himself. There was a moment of high tension when his fist was trembling, only two inches away from the side of his head. But then he stabbed the mechanical pencil deep into his ear, and a narrow jet of blood spurted out all over the collar of his lemon-yellow shirt.

He gave a high-pitched *eeeeeee!* of pain and dropped to his knees on the carpet, wrestling to pull the pencil out. For a long count of five, the reflected man in the window wouldn't let him, until the side of his neck was smothered in blood, but at last he allowed Pepper to take his fist away from the side of his head.

"*Russ!*" said Morton Kravitz.

Russ Pepper fell sideways, kicking his loafers and shrieking, "No! *No!* For Christ's sake! *No!*"

But even while he was struggling and shouting, he bent his arm around and started jabbing at his left ear. He missed two or three times, but then, with a crunch of cartilage, he plunged the mechanical pencil straight into his ear canal.

Again, the reflected man in the window forced him to keep the pencil in his ear for five or six seconds. At length, however, the reflected man stood and let Pepper slowly extract it. It came out with a bloody string of connective tissue attached and a flap of skin from his eardrum.

Russ Pepper lay on his side, his breathing harsh, his florid face blotchy with shock. Grace Trilling knelt beside him and loosened his necktie, while Dominic Serrantino passed her a clean white handkerchief.

Morton Kravitz looked at Vasili Krylov, and he was shaking with anger. "I don't know how you made him do that, but that was the most sadistic act that I have ever witnessed in my entire life. This man is my friend, as well as my associate. Do you seriously think that I would consider doing *any* kind of business with you after that?"

"I think that you would be a fool not to, Mr. Kravitz. That was only a small demonstration of what I can do."

Vasili Krylov smiled down at Grace Trilling as she dabbed the blood from Russ Pepper's ears. "You should see what I can do with women, Mr. Kravitz. You think you have ever heard a woman cry? Believe me, I can make a woman cry."

"You creep," said Dominic Serrantino. "I'm going to see you locked up for this for the rest of your miserable life."

"Miserable? My life is not miserable. My life is very joyful. It will soon be even happier, when you and I make some arrangements together."

"Do you have any objection if I call the paramedics?" asked Morton Kravitz.

"You're asking his *permission?*" said Grace Trilling. There was blood spatter on her cream-colored skirt and on her knee.

"I said before you call *nobody.*"

"He could die."

"Of course, yes, he could die. But first of all, you and me, we have to talk about business."

"What the hell do you want from me?"

Vasili Krylov turned and smiled at the woman in the balloon-shaped yellow dress. She had perfect bone structure, with high Slavic cheekbones and a squarish jaw, and if she hadn't been so white skinned and her eyes so colorless and cold, she could have been beautiful. But she had a frigidity about her that made Morton Kravitz feel deeply unsettled, almost as if her icy hands were sliding all over his body under his clothes.

Vasili Krylov said, "You are the legal representative for Coastal Productions, yes?"

"That's right. What about it?"

"Coastal Productions make big new movie with David Link, yes? Columbus discovers America, only America is just like it is today—buildings, automobiles, McDonald's."

Morton Kravitz looked down at Russ Pepper, who was holding his ears and weeping in pain. "Hold on, Russ. Hold on. We'll get you some help as soon as we can."

Grace Trilling said caustically, "I don't think he can hear you, Mort. He's pierced both of his eardrums."

Morton Kravitz turned back to Vasili Krylov. "The picture's called *The New New World*. What of it?"

"Twenty-five percent of gross profits." Vasili Krylov smiled.

"What?"

"For Coastal Productions, seventy-five percent. For Vasili Krylov, only twenty-five percent. I am not a greedy man."

"You're out of your mind."

"I don't think so."

"What on God's earth possesses you to think that Coastal will give you twenty-five percent of its gross?"

"Easy. Either they agree, or David Link will stub out his cigarette on his own eyeballs."

Chapter Four

Dan could see thick gray smoke billowing up from seven blocks away. He pulled his grimy black Pontiac Torrent to the curb behind the fire chief's truck and climbed out. A pink-faced female officer approached him with her hand raised and called out, "You can't park there, sir! Move on, please!"

He showed her his badge.

"Oh," she said. "Detective Fisher. I've heard of you."

"Nothing good, I hope."

She blushed even pinker, and lifted the police tape for him to duck underneath. Santa Monica Boulevard was crowded with fire trucks, squad cars, ambulances, and TV vans. A police helicopter was clattering overhead, so low that Dan could hardly hear himself think.

Ernie Munoz was waiting for him beside the charred wreckage of the Crown Victoria. The blackened bodies of the three Narcotics detectives were still sitting inside it, with Cusack's head protruding from the passenger's window. Their arms were held up like monkeys begging for a treat, and they were grinning from the heat.

"Christ," said Dan. "What the hell went down here?"

Ernie patted his shiny bald head, then the folds of fat around his neck with his bunched-up handkerchief. "So far," he said, "we don't have the least idea." Ernie was short and big-bellied, with bulging eyes and a heavy black mustache, and a liking for glossy green mohair suits. Dan always called him El Gordo, the Fat Man.

"Like I told you on the phone, the eyewitnesses are pretty confused. But they all agree on two things. One, there was a woman standing close to the car, waving. Two, the guys appeared to catch fire first, before the vehicle."

"So what are you trying to say? This was, like, spontaneous human combustion?"

"Well, no," said Ernie. "But nobody saw a firebomb or a can of gasoline or nothing like that. Although one witness said that the woman was holding something that was smoking."

"So where is this woman? Have you talked to her?"

"She's still inside the restaurant with the Zombie. I was waiting for you to show up before I interviewed her. You know—you and the Zombie having so much history and all."

"She's still inside? What, *eating*? After three guys got cremated right outside?"

Ernie shrugged. "I don't know about eating. But I told them to wait, and they said they weren't in any kind of hurry."

Kevin Baleno, the fire investigator, came waddling over in a bright yellow Tyvek suit.

"Any ideas?" Dan asked.

Kevin Baleno shook his head. "We'll have to get the bodies back to the lab. There's no odor of accelerants, and the pattern of burning is very unusual. In fact I don't think I ever saw a vehicle fire quite like this before. It looks like the eyewitnesses could have been right and the detectives burst into flame before their vehicle did."

"Is that possible?"

Kevin Baleno shrugged. "If it happened, Detective, it must be possible."

"What about Speedy?"

"Don't know yet. They took him away a couple of minutes ago. No visible injuries. My first guess is that he suffered a heart seizure. You'll have to ask the ME."

"Okay," said Dan. "Keep me in the loop, will you? I'm just going inside to have a word with my old friend Jean-Christophe. El Gordo, you coming?"

He and Ernie went into the Palm. Under the rows of globe ceiling lights, the dark wood-paneled restaurant was almost empty. Most of the usual lunchtime crowd must have left after the blaze outside, but there was still an air of subdued hysteria, and the white-aproned waiters were hurrying from one side of the restaurant to the other, whispering to one another.

Three Lithuanian movie producers had remained, crowded into their brass-railed booth in the center of the room, with beers and four-pound lobsters; as well as a party of five overdressed women who looked and sounded like department store executives from some city in the Midwest.

Jean-Christophe Artisson was still there, too, and so was the emaciated girl with the face like a fire axe and the clinging gray dress. The Zombie was sitting at his favorite corner table underneath the signed caricature of Fred Astaire, with his floppy black beret hanging on the chair beside him.

When Dan and Ernie came across the restaurant toward him, two of his bodyguards sitting at the next table rose to their feet, buttoning their coats as they did so. The Zombie waved them both to sit down.

"*Bon jou, mesyés,*" he said, as Dan came up to his table. "*Ki sa ou vié?*"

The Zombie was very delicate-featured, almost pretty, although his nose was more bulbous than his friends would have dared to tell him. He wore his shiny black hair in ringlets and a diamond earring like a miniature chandelier. He smelled strongly of some floral perfume, like gardenias.

"You can cut the Creole crap," said Dan. "We just lost three good men out there, and I want to know how."

"You don't think I had anything to do with that, Detective Fisher? I have always been very good friends with the police, as you know. Even with vice and narcotics."

"Who's this?" Dan asked, nodding toward the girl in the gray dress.

The girl lifted her head and looked at Dan with defiance.

"*Ki non ou?*" Dan asked her.

"She is a cousin of mine from Haiti. She has come to Los Angeles for a vacation."

"What's her name?"

"My name is Michelange DuPriz," said the girl, haughtily. "You want to ask me some question?"

"*Wi*, Ms. DuPriz. We have eyewitnesses who saw you waving or making gestures at our detectives shortly before their car caught fire. Is that true?"

The Zombie smiled, pushed his plate a little way across the table, and held out his fork. "You feel like something to *manjé*, Detective? Sesame-seared Ahi tuna with field greens and soya vinaigrette. You should taste it."

Dan ignored him and said, "Well?"

Michelange held his stare. "I felt that something bad was about to happen to your friends."

"What do you mean—something bad?"

"I saw a dark *loua* over their heads."

"A *loua*? What the hell is a *loua*?"

"A spirit."

"A spirit? You mean like a ghost-type spirit?"

"That's right. Not a *rada*, not a sweet spirit. A bitter spirit. A *petro*."

"You've lost me. You saw a dark spirit over their heads, and that's why you were waving at them?

"*Sekonsa*. I warned them to get out of the car. But it was too late. They catch alight."

"I don't get it. The spirit set them on fire?"

Michelange nodded.

"So what are you? Some kind of medium? Is that what you're saying? You can see spirits?"

The Zombie said, "Michelange is a *manbo*. But, yes, you could call her a medium if you like. She connects between the physical world and the spirit world."

"Oh, really? Sounds to me like she's been watching too much TV."

The Zombie forked up more tuna. As he ate, he kept grinning at Dan, so that Dan could see the brownish flakes of chewed fish between his teeth.

"I'm so glad this hasn't affected your appetite," Dan told him.

The Zombie said nothing, but grinned even wider.

Michelange said, "It is true, *mesyé*. Who knows why the *petro* wanted to burn your friends. It did not speak. It gave me no sign. Maybe it was the spirit of some bad man who want his revenge."

"This is bullshit," Ernie retorted.

"You think so?" asked the Zombie. "That is not a wise way to think."

"Oh, no? Let's forget about spirits for the moment.

One witness saw you holding up something that was smoking."

Michelange looked away. "Different people see different things."

"Maybe they do. But why would anybody say that?"

"Maybe they saw my cheroot. I am always smoking a cheroot."

"A *cheroot?*" said Ernie. "Who are you trying to kid?"

Dan leaned close to the Zombie's ear and very quietly said, "Jean-Christophe, I want to know what the hell this is all about. Don't try to tell me that there's no connection between you and those three detectives who died out there. Or Speedy Lebrun either. And don't tell me this has anything to do with spirits."

The Zombie wiped his mouth with his napkin. "You always believed in magic, didn't you, Detective?" He turned to Michelange and said, "Detective Fisher is a very talented magician in his own right. He could have been a professional if he hadn't decided to become a policeman."

"I am very impressed," said Michelange, although she didn't sound it.

"Show her, Detective. Show her your famous jackpot trick."

"Your jackpot trick?" asked Michelange.

"You should see it," said the Zombie. "He swallows a quarter, then pulls down his arm like a slot machine and spits out a whole handful of quarters. Isn't that right, Detective?"

"Forget it, Jean-Christophe. I'm investigating four suspicious deaths here."

"Of course you are. But you asked me what the hell this is all about, and I'm trying to tell you. This is all about magic. This is all about *radas* and *petros* and maybe jackpot tricks, too. Haven't you sniffed it in the air? Haven't you *sensed* it? Magic has come to town, Detective, and believe me, everything is going to change."

"This is double bullshit," said Ernie. "Those guys out there, they all had families—wives and kids to take care of. I ought to run you in for depraved indifference."

Jean-Christophe held out his wrists, as if he were offering himself up to be handcuffed. "Michelange, she was nowhere near your friends when their car caught fire. Neither was she anywhere close to Speedy Lebrun, when he collapsed. As for me, I was in here enjoying my lunch. There was nothing that either of us could have done to prevent these unfortunate events. What, exactly, do you think we're guilty of?"

Back outside on Santa Monica, Ernie said, "What do you make of that?"

"What, the spirit story? She was trying to make fools of us, that's all. She knows why that car went up, and, believe me, it wasn't torched by any goddamned *loua*. The question is, how *was* it torched?"

"I'll run a check on her," said Ernie, taking out his notebook and scribbling in it. "At the very least we could have her deported back to Haiti."

They walked back to the burned-out Crown Victoria. The bodies of the three detectives had been carefully pried out of their seats, although fragments of crisp black flesh remained stuck to the seat springs. Ernie crossed himself and said, "Rest in peace, Detectives. We'll find out who did this to you, trust us."

Dan checked his watch. "Listen, I have a couple of errands to run. But I'll drop into the station later and see what CSU has managed to come up with. If forensics can work out how these guys were burned, my feeling is that it won't be too difficult to work out who did it."

He opened the door of his SUV and was about to

climb in when he became aware that Michelange DuPriz had stalked out of the front door of the Palm, with the Zombie close behind her. She stopped, took off her sunglasses, and shaded her eyes with her hand.

"She's looking this way," said Ernie.

"You're right. She's staring at us."

Michelange was saying something to the Zombie, but she was too far away for Dan to hear her. Whatever it was, though, it made the Zombie laugh.

"You know what I'd like to do to that bastard?" said Ernie. "I'd like to cut off his *cojones* and make him eat them raw with *salsa ranchera*."

"You'll get your chance one day," Dan told him. "I'll see you in maybe a couple of hours, okay?"

"She's still staring at us. What's she doing?"

Michelange was reaching into her long gray purse. She was calling out to them, too.

"What's she saying? I can't hear her. That god-damned helicopter."

Dan took off his sunglasses. Michelange was making a flicking gesture with her right hand, and he could see something sparkling in the air. A coin. It looked like she was tossing a coin.

"That is one strange woman," said Ernie.

"No . . . I think she's trying to tell us something."

"What? Heads she wins, tails we lose?"

"I don't know." Dan kept staring at her, and she kept tossing the coin, over and over, and mouthing some words that he still couldn't distinguish.

"I'll tell you what," said Ernie. "I'll go back and ask her what the hell she thinks she's doing."

But at that moment Dan felt a lurching sensation in his gut. His stomach tightened, as if he had eaten far too many shellfish and needed to bring them all up. He leaned against the side of his SUV.

"I'll tell you something for nothing," Ernie declared.

"There's no Haitian bag of bones is going to make no rainbow-assed monkey out of me." But then Dan couldn't stop himself from letting out a sharp, high, retching noise, and Ernie turned around and stared at him in alarm.

"*Dan?* You okay? What's wrong, *muchacho?*"

Dan's stomach convulsed a second time, and his abdominal muscles knotted up so painfully that he couldn't speak. He pointed to his gaping mouth and blinked his watering eyes, but he simply couldn't get any words out.

"Jesus!" said Ernie. "Hold on there, Dan! I'll get you a paramedic!"

He stuck two fingers in his mouth and let out a piercing whistle. "Hey! Paramedic! Got a man sick here! Hurry!"

Clutching his stomach, Dan slid slowly down the side of his SUV, until he was kneeling on the sidewalk. He was shaking with cold but sweating profusely, and his mouth was flooded with metallic-tasting saliva. He had never felt anything so agonizing in his life. He had been shot once, in the shoulder blade, but even a bullet hadn't doubled him up like this.

Ernie knelt beside him and put his arm around his shoulders. "It's okay, man. Look, the paramedics are coming. You're going to be fine. What in the name of God did you eat for breakfast?"

Dan coughed, and something hard hit the back of his teeth. He spat it out, and it rolled across the concrete paving and into the gutter. A quarter. A bright, shiny quarter. He coughed again and again, and suddenly a deluge of quarters poured out of his mouth and were scattered across the sidewalk.

He turned over onto his hands and his knees, and crouched down like a dog, heaving up the last few coins. He felt as if he had been beaten up from the inside out. His stomach ached, his gullet was sore, and all he could taste was nickel.

A Greek-looking paramedic hunkered down beside him. "You okay, man?"

Dan nodded, wiping his mouth. The paramedic picked up a handful of quarters and frowned at them.

"You been eating *money?* Why the hell you been eating money?"

"Did it—for a bet," Dan coughed.

"A *bet?*"

"Not with me," Ernie put in hastily.

"You know how *dumb* this is?" protested the paramedic. "Don't you think we have enough to do, taking care of people who are genuinely sick?"

"I'm sorry," said Dan. He reached out for the paramedic's shoulder and used it to lever himself up. "You're right—it was totally stupid."

"So how do you feel now? You still feel nauseous? Maybe we should take you to the ER, have you checked over."

Dan shook his head. "I'm okay," he lied. "I'm much better now." In reality he felt shaky and very cold, and his stomach muscles kept tightening up into sickening little after-spasms.

"Well, you take it easy, okay? And if you start feeling nauseous again, go see your doctor."

"I will. And thanks. And sorry for wasting your time. I don't know why I did it. I guess I've never been able to say no to a challenge."

"You cops. As if you don't take enough risks without turning yourselves into human savings banks."

"I know. Very stupid. Sorry."

The paramedic walked back toward his ambulance. Dan could see him talking to two of his colleagues, who both stared at him and frowned. He could imagine what they were saying, and it almost certainly included the word "asshole."

Outside the Palm, Michelange DuPriz stood smiling in Dan's direction for a few more moments, her hand still raised to shield her eyes. Dan was tempted to go back and confront her, but the Zombie said something to her, and she nodded, then climbed into his Escalade with all the long-legged elegance of a gray gazelle. The Zombie climbed in after her, and the entourage drove off.

Ernie said, "You really okay, Dan? How in the name of the Holy Virgin did *that* happen?"

Dan bent down and retrieved a single slimy quarter. He held it up, and squinted at it closely. However these coins had found their way into his stomach, there was no question that they were real. God, yuck, he could still taste them.

"You didn't really swallow all of this money for a bet, did you?"

"El Gordo, I didn't swallow any of it."

"Hey, I get it! This was your jackpot trick!"

"Are you serious? We just lost three good men. You think I'm in the mood for doing tricks?"

"Well, no. But all this money—where did it come from?"

"I think *she* put it inside me somehow. That Michelange DuPriz."

"But how? She wasn't nowhere near you."

"I know. But I'm still sure that it was her. And I think I was wrong about Cusack and Fusco and Knudsen. I'll bet she burned them, too. No firebomb. No gasoline. She did it by magic."

"Come on, *muchacho*, you're talking crazy. There's no such thing as magic."

"You saw all of this money pouring out of my mouth, didn't you?"

"Sure, but—"

"What was that, if it wasn't magic? Or the paranormal or the supernatural or whatever you want to call it."

"And you really think she burned those poor guys?"

"*And* stopped Speedy's heart. And she wants me to know it. Not just know it either. She wants me to *believe* it."

Dan spat again and wiped his mouth with the back of his hand. "Making me bring up all those coins, that's her way of showing me how much mojo she's got. How much power."

"Okay—if she has that much power, why didn't she burn you, too, instead of making you puke up money?"

"Maybe she could have. But I'm guessing that she had a good reason not to."

"Which is?"

"I don't know yet. But the Zombie was right. Believe me, El Gordo: magic *has* come to town."

Chapter Five

"Friends—between us, we're going to transform this city. We're going to root out every criminal racket, from drugs to prostitution to money laundering. We're going to purge the streets of gangs and violent crime. We're going to change Los Angeles into the kind of place where everybody feels safe and secure and proud of their neighborhood, whether they live in Beverly Hills or Boyle Heights."

There was a light smattering of applause, and Chief O'Malley raised one hand to acknowledge it. His petite blond wife, Charlene, came up to him and linked arms and smiled proudly at all their guests.

This was their first reception since Douglas O'Malley had been appointed chief of police. He had taken over six weeks ago, after the sudden resignation of Paul De Souza, following his heart attack.

Chief O'Malley was stocky, white-haired, with a broad, pugnacious face, half Irish. Before he moved to California he had spent five years in New York, where his policing policy had become known as "subzero tolerance." He had set up special task forces to tackle crime on every level, from mugging and vandalism to organized drug trafficking. His motto was: "Never give an inch. Period."

It was early evening, and the guests were assembled on the wide flagstone patio at the rear of the O'Malley's mock-Elizabethan house on Woodrow Wilson Drive. The mayor was there and several city councilors, as well as police commissioners, church dignitaries, social workers, and media. They were drinking champagne cocktails and balancing plates of barbecued chicken satay and sashimi and salad. The peal of self-satisfied laughter carried across the lawns.

Mayor Leonard Briggs came up to Chief O'Malley and shook his hand, making sure that he was smiling toward the cameras. Mayor Briggs was black and enormous. The *Los Angeles Times* had once said of him, "No man is an island, especially Mayor Briggs. Mayor Briggs is a whole subcontinent."

"That was a fine, fine speech, Chief," enthused Mayor Briggs. "And I know that it wasn't just words. If anybody can clean up our city, you can."

"Thank you, Mr. Mayor. If I'm going to be fair, though, Chief De Souza has already done most of the groundwork for me. His drug teams have been outstanding, especially the way they infiltrated the Colombian connections."

Mayor Briggs nodded, his gaze roaming around the patio to see if there was anybody else he needed to flatter. "Damn shame about De Souza's heart. I was sorry to see him go. But I'm sure you'll be able to build on what he started."

They were still making mutually congratulatory small talk when a tall man in a white tuxedo came walking across the patio toward them. He had silver hair that was greased straight back from his forehead, and his face was skull-like and very white, with veins

in his temples like wriggling white worms. He had a
white pencil mustache and thin lips, and his eyes were
utterly dead, as if they were two gray stones that had
been picked up from some isolated beach.

Behind him came two squarish-looking men in black
tuxedos, both of them dark skinned, with heavy black
mustaches, one of them with cheeks that were pitted
with acne scars. They were followed at a short distance
by a small dark woman whose hair was pinned up with
Spanish-style combs. She had an oval face with huge
brown eyes, and she was wearing a silky silver dress that
clung to her heavy bosom and her wide, flared hips.

Around her neck hung what looked like a tiny circular drum with a scowling woman's face painted on it.

Mayor Briggs said, "Mr. Vasquez. Didn't realize that
you were invited this evening."

The man with the skull-like face said, "I'm not." He
spoke in a whisper, as if he had throat cancer. "I just
came to pay my respects to the new chief."

"Chief, this is Mr. Orestes Vasquez," said Mayor
Briggs. "Mr. Vasquez is in import-export, mainly between here and Bogotá."

Chief O'Malley inclined his head in acknowledg-
ment but didn't make any attempt to shake Orestes
Vasquez's hand. "I believe I have a file on you, Mr.
Vasquez."

Orestes Vasquez gave him a wolfish grin. "You are
the chief of police, sir. I would expect it."

"I'm surprised you managed to get in here."

"There are always ways, Chief O'Malley. In fact,
that is one of the reasons I wanted to talk to you this
evening."

"I don't really think that this is the time or the place,
Mr. Vasquez. Good night."

"Please," said Orestes Vasquez, raising one hand. "I
need to speak to you only for a moment or two." He

glanced at Mayor Briggs and added, "In private, if that is possible."

Chief O'Malley could see that several of his guests were staring inquisitively at Orestes Vasquez and his entourage, especially Wendy Chan from KNBC news. The last thing he wanted was an embarrassing scene. He laid his hand on Mayor Briggs' shoulder and said, "Excuse me, Mr. Mayor. Maybe I can talk to you a little while later. This way, Mr. Vasquez."

He led Orestes Vasquez to the far end of the patio, where there was a small sandstone gazebo with a dome-shaped roof. The dark-haired woman in the silky silver dress came, too. The sun had just gone down, and the sky had turned a deep burnt orange color. The cicadas in the garden seemed to be chirruping louder than usual, as if they were excited . . . or alarmed.

"I should introduce Lida Siado," said Orestes Vasquez. "Ms. Siado is my new personal assistant."

"I am so pleased to meet you, Chief O'Malley," the dark-haired woman said in a strong Colombian accent. "I have heard so much about you. How you have sworn to lock up every wrongdoer in Los Angeles, from the naughty street children to the big fat gang bosses."

Chief O'Malley didn't reply, but waited for Orestes Vasquez to say what he had come here to say.

"In a way," said Orestes Vasquez, "Lida is the reason that I have imposed on your hospitality this evening."

"Go on."

"Let me put it like this, Chief O'Malley. I am a businessman, and many of my friends are businessmen. Until Chief De Souza took over, we were able to run our affairs with very little interference from the Los Angeles Police Department. It was a question of mutual respect, if you understand me."

"I understand you. You and your friends bribed a number of senior officers in the LAPD to turn a blind eye to your activities."

"There is a great deal of difference between *bribery*, Chief O'Malley, and showing one's appreciation to amenable friends."

"Oh, yes? I'm sorry to tell you that when it comes to narcotics, illegal gunrunning, extortion, and prostitution, I don't do amenable."

Orestes Vasquez grinned again and nodded. "I know your reputation, Chief O'Malley. You are much less tolerant than your predecessor. Which is why my friends and I have been obliged to seek another way to coexist with the forces of law and order."

"I don't do coexistence either, Mr. Vasquez. Not with drug traffickers."

"Oh, no? When you see the alternative, I believe that you will change your mind."

Lida Siado had a small bag tied to her left wrist, in silver silk to match her dress. She loosened the silk cord that fastened it and took out two clamshells.

"I think it's time you left," said Chief O'Malley.

"No, no," said Orestes Vasquez. "Please give us one second more. You must experience this."

Lida Siado took the clamshells and inserted them into her eye sockets so that she looked as if she were blind.

"Listen," said Chief O'Malley, "I don't have the patience for party games. I'm very busy tonight. I'll have you escorted out."

But Lida Siado raised the little drum around her neck and started to tap it with her middle finger. In time to the tapping, she started to sing—her voice high and breathy, as if she had been running. "Night Wind, come blow for me! Night Wind, bring your darkness here! Night Wind, come sing for me! Night Wind, blind this company!"

Chief O'Malley waved at Sergeant Jim Halperin, who was in charge of security. The sergeant began to make his way through the guests, beckoning to two of his fellow officers as he came.

He was only halfway across the patio, however, when all the shutters in the house suddenly slammed, one after the other. There was a whistling, fluffing noise, and a strong wind sprang up, blowing a blizzard of dust and leaves and debris among the assembled guests.

"*Night Wind!*" Lida Sioda repeated, her voice much shriller. "*Night Wind! Come blow for me!*"

Chief O'Malley had to raise his hand to shield his face from the hurtling dust.

"Stop this!" he shouted. "Whatever you're doing, stop it!"

But the wind grew stronger and stronger, and its whistling developed into a lugubrious howl. Champagne glasses tipped over and shattered. Tablecloths flapped in the air and fled off in the darkness like flying ghosts. Women screamed and held on to their hats and the hems of their dresses. More than one man's hairpiece was ripped off by the wind and spun away.

"Night Wind, come sing for me!" Lida Sioda repeated, over and over. Her voice began to drop lower and lower, until it was almost as deep as a man's. "Night Wind, blind this company!"

"That's enough!" Chief O'Malley shouted at her. He made a staggering move toward her, but Orestes Vasquez stepped smoothly between them. His greased-back hair was unmoved by the wind. In fact the wind didn't appear to affect him at all.

"It is not you calling the shots now, Chief O'Malley. If you have no inclination to be accommodating, then *we* will have to take control of matters."

The wind was blowing so strongly now that some of the guests had to cling to the stone balustrade to stop from being blown off their feet. Even Mayor Briggs was down on his hands and knees. A lime tree in a heavy terracotta urn fell over and rolled across the patio, followed by another and another. Tables tilted, and stacks of plates shattered.

"For Christ's sake!" yelled Chief O'Malley. He could see his wife, Charlene, her hair blown into a fright wig, desperately holding on to the low wall around the barbecue. He tried to walk toward her, his pants flapping like those of a motorcyclist traveling at a hundred miles an hour, but the wind buffeted him against the side of the gazebo, jarring his shoulder. He crouched on the ground for a few seconds, trying to summon the strength to stand up again, but when he tried to get up on his feet, the wind beat him back down, and all he could do was kneel there, helpless, like a religious penitent.

He lifted his head toward Orestes Vasquez, who was standing in the middle of the gazebo, calm and unconcerned.

"What do you want?" he shouted.

But Orestes Vasquez closed his eyes and didn't answer, and it was then that Chief O'Malley heard the first woman scream.

"I can't see! I can't see anything!"

Another woman screamed, and then a man shouted out. "I can't see, either! I'm blind! I've gone blind!"

In less than half a minute, all the guests were wailing and crying and sobbing in terror. "I can't see! Can anybody see? I'm totally blind! Help me!"

"Charlene!" called Chief O'Malley. "Charlene, it's Doug! Are you okay?"

"I'm blind!" Charlene cried out. "I can't see anything, Doug! Everything's gone black!"

"Vasquez," Chief O'Malley demanded. "What have you done to these people? What do you want?"

Orestes Vasquez came across and stood over him, so close that all Chief O'Malley could see of him were his sharply creased white pants and his black-and-white alligator shoes with their almond-shaped toecaps.

"I thought I made myself crystal clear, Chief O'Malley. All I am looking for is a little cooperation. You do your police thing. I will do my business thing. We don't have to be bosom buddies. We don't have to go fishing together or wear matching sweaters. So long as we stay out of each other's hair, live and let live, everything's going to be fine."

The wind began to die down until it blew with nothing more than a sinister, sibilant whistle, and Chief O'Malley was able to climb to his feet. Lida Siado came across and stood very close to Orestes Vasquez, holding his arm. She still had the clamshells in her eye sockets, yet Chief O'Malley had the strange feeling that she could see him quite clearly.

"Can you give these people their sight back?" he asked.

"Yes, if you promise to cooperate with us."

Chief O'Malley looked around. Some of his guests were stumbling around the patio, calling out for their friends and loved ones like lost children. "Mary! Mary!" "Guy! Where are you? Guy!" Others were even crawling across the flagstones, too frightened to stand. Still more were huddled together, clinging to each other in desperation, as if frightened that the darkness would drag them away.

"Doesn't look like I have much of a choice."

"Oh, you always have a choice, Chief O'Malley. It's just that some choices are more palatable than others."

"My wife will get her sight back?"

"Everybody. All you have to do is say the word."

Chief O'Malley nodded. "Okay, then. I'll see what kind of a game plan I can come up with."

"I need your promise, Chief O'Malley."

Chief O'Malley took a deep, angry breath. He had never made any concessions to a criminal, ever, even when his cousin Mike had been ambushed and shot dead three years ago by Puerto Rican racketeers. But what else could he do? How could he leave all of these people blinded?

"How did you do it?" he asked Lida Siado. "Where did that wind come from?"

She lifted the drum around her neck. "I was taught by the Uitoto Indians, in the Amazon Rainforest in Colombia. They know that every drum, big or small, contains a spirit. Sometimes the spirit of one of your ancestors. Your grandmother or your great-uncle. Sometimes a *kukurpa*."

"A very hungry spirit," put in Orestes Vasquez. "It likes to eat eyes. And babies."

"I rouse the *kukurpa* by tapping the drum, and the *kukurpa* calls the spirit of the Night Wind in the hope that the Night Wind will leave it some easy pickings."

Chief O'Malley stared at them in disbelief. "You're talking about black magic?"

"You can call it that if you want to," said Orestes Vasquez. "We prefer to call it *ethnic spirituality*."

Lida Siado said, "You should make your promise soon, Chief O'Malley. If you delay much longer, these people will stay blind for the rest of their lives."

Chief O'Malley took another look around at his guests. "All right," he said. "Goddamn you to hell. I promise."

Orestes Vasquez smiled. "I knew that you would see reason, Chief O'Malley. For my part, I promise you that I will run my business in a responsible way. There will be no random violence on the streets. If I happen to have a dispute with any other businessman, I will settle it discreetly and efficiently, and your people will never have to be involved. You will see how peaceful and orderly this city will become. History will judge you as the best chief of police that Los Angeles has ever had."

"Just give them their sight back, you cockroach, before I change my mind."

"Very well. Lida?"

Lida Siado cupped her hand in front of her face and allowed the two clamshells to drop out of her eye sockets.

At once, there were cries of, "I can see again! My sight's come back! I'm not blind anymore!" People started clapping and laughing and hugging each other. Even Mayor Briggs was weeping with relief.

Orestes Vasquez said, "There! Everything is back to normal, as it should be! I am very pleased to have made your acquaintance, Chief O'Malley. I can see that you and I are going to get along very well."

Lida Siado placed four fingertips to her lips and blew Chief O'Malley the gentlest of kisses. "We have made something out of nothing, Chief O'Malley, just like Father Naimuena made the world out of nothing. He attached an illusion to a dream and held it together with his breath."

"You'd better leave now," Chief O'Malley told her, his voice quaking with suppressed rage. "I wouldn't like to spoil my guests' evening any further by having you shot."

Chapter Six

When Dan returned to his apartment building on Franklin Avenue that evening, Annie was sitting outside under the globe light that illuminated the steps, playing with her fluffy white kitten. She had folded a piece of paper to look like a butterfly and tied it to a length of thread, and was tossing it into the air so that the kitten jumped up to catch it.

"Hey, she's grown," Dan remarked. "Given her a name yet?"

"Malkin. It means a witch's cat."

"Very appropriate. Mixed me up any more of your disgusting potions today?"

"I'm boiling you up some essence of nettle, but it's not ready yet. I have some rue tea, though. It relaxes you and helps you to think more clearly. And it shows you the next person you will fall in love with."

"I'm not looking for love right now, thanks all the same."

"Of course you're not. Nobody ever is. Love always comes looking for *you*."

Dan sat down next to her. "Clear thinking, on the other hand—I could use some of that. Something really weird happened to me today, and the more I think it over, the more I don't understand it."

Annie stared at him closely. "You *do* look kind of washed out, Dan, if you don't mind my saying so. What's wrong?"

"Well, you know how skeptical I've always been about all this witch stuff you do? I think I might have been persuaded different."

Annie allowed Malkin to catch the paper butterfly. The kitten rolled onto her back, biting at the butterfly with her tiny teeth and trying to pedal it to pieces with her hind legs.

Dan told Annie what had happened outside the Palm. He didn't tell her the grisly details of how Cusack, Fusco, and Knudsen had been incinerated, but he described how he had vomited up quarters.

"And you think that somehow this woman was responsible?"

"Like I told you, she was tossing a quarter up in the air only seconds before I barfed. It was like she was taunting me—like she was showing me what was going to happen."

"And you say she was Haitian?"

"That's right. Her name is Michelange DuPriz. The Zombie said she that she's a *mando*, kind of like a medium."

"Hmm," said Annie. "I read an article in *National Geographic* about voodoo *mandos*, and one of the things they can do is punish their enemies by making them puke up all kinds of foreign objects. Usually the objects are related to how their enemies offended them. Like, if somebody trespassed on their land, they'd make them puke up stones or dirt. Or if they stole a chicken, they'd make them puke up a whole bunch of feathers."

"But how the hell did she get all those quarters into my stomach?"

"I don't have any idea. I could try asking my friend Véronique. She lived in Port-au-Prince for three years, teaching English at the University of Haiti, and she was always interested in voodoo. She used to believe that the super in her apartment building was a zombie."

"It's *magic*, though, isn't it, for want of a better word? Not like the stuff I do—not a party trick. Genuine magic."

"You always said that magic was a scam. All done by mirrors, that's what you told me."

"Annie, when you puke up thirty dollars in small change, you become a believer pretty damned quick."

"Well, we can soon find out for sure."

"Oh, yeah? How?"

"We can do a witch test. It's very simple. All you need is some salt and a sewing needle."

"A witch test?"

"Sure. They used to do it in Russia in the seventeenth century to find out if anybody in their village was a practicing witch."

"With salt? And a sewing needle?"

Annie stood up. "Come on, I'll show you."

Dan's head dropped down, like a man defeated. "Today just gets more and more bizarre by the minute."

He followed Annie down the steps to her apartment, which was directly underneath his. The front door was painted maroon and decorated with a sly-looking crescent moon. As soon as she opened it, Dan could smell incense and the herbal preparations that Annie was simmering on her stove. Malkin ran between his ankles, and he almost tripped over her.

The kitchen was straight ahead of them, and Annie went through to make sure that her essence of nettle hadn't boiled dry. The living room was off to the left, a large open-plan room with walls painted midnight blue and covered in hundreds of silver-foil stars. Two large couches were set at right angles to each other, each of them draped in a large beige Indian throw with fringes. Between them stood a low wooden table crowded with tarot cards, books on magic and herbal remedies, pottery ashtrays filled with colored beads, two silver statuettes, a half-empty pack of pumpkin seeds, a bong, and a naked Ken doll with twenty or thirty pins stuck in him.

Dan picked up the Ken doll. "Is this meant to be anybody I know?"

"It's a joke. Well, it's meant to be a joke, but for some reason it freaks everybody out. Especially men."

"Are you surprised? Look where you've stuck *this* pin."

Dan walked slowly around the room, with Malkin following him. He had been in Annie's apartment plenty of times before, but because he had never really believed in witchery, he had never taken the time to examine what was on the walls. A medieval astrology chart, like a wheel covered with stars and plowshares and axes, showing the precise date and time that anybody could expect to die. Seven wands, each enameled a different color, with semiprecious stones set into their pommels, arranged in a fan shape. A three-barred cross cast out of bronze, with a serpent winding around it.

Annie watched him with an amused look on her face.

"Is this stuff simply for decoration?" he asked her. "Or does any of it actually *work?*"

"It depends who's using it. I could never get those wands to do anything, but I just love the way they look. They're supposed to be Egyptian, but I doubt if they are. They were probably made in Gary, Indiana."

She went over to a small desk in the corner, opened the drawer, and took out a folded street map of Los Angeles. She opened it and laid it out on the rug. Malkin immediately walked across it, then walked back again, enjoying the crackle she made.

"Come on, you," said Annie. "You may be my familiar, but right now you're being nothing but a pesky nuisance." She carried Malkin out and shut her in the kitchen, returning with a silver-topped saltshaker.

She knelt on the floor at the edge of the map, and said, "I pour a spoonful of salt onto the map and if it detects a place where a sorceress lives, it will form a little heap."

"Amazing. Who needs GPS?"

"Witches *hate* salt because it's the symbol of purity and cleanliness. In the Middle Ages, women used to make a big show of salting their food so that people wouldn't suspect them of having sex with the devil."

"Where does the needle come into it?"

"You place the needle on the heap of salt, and if it rises vertically of its own accord, then you know that the location is genuine."

Dan sat down on one of the couches. "Okay then, why don't you give it a try? I know where the Zombie lives, so I'll be able to tell if it works or not."

Annie unscrewed the top of the saltshaker and poured about a tablespoonful into the palm of her hand. She scattered it across the map, and at the same time she whispered, *"Show me where the witch is hiding. Scurry quick, and find her lair. Show me where the witch is hiding, so that I can trap her there. Salt so clean and salt so white. Show me where she hides this night."*

"Why are you whispering?" asked Dan.

"Because this is a Russian incantation, and most Russian incantations are whispered. It makes them more magical. At least the Russians used to think so. The word 'whisper' in Russian means the same thing as 'cast a spell.'"

Dan stared down at the map. So far, nothing was happening.

"I don't think this is going to work," he told Annie. "Maybe you're using the wrong kind of salt."

"Don't be so impatient," said Annie. "Even salt needs some time to think."

Dan kneaded his forehead with his fingertips. He felt as if he were developing a migraine. If he had known this morning that he was going to vomit quarters in the street, then try to locate a witch with a road map and a handful of salt, he would have stayed in bed.

"I can get you some powdered moss if you have a headache," said Annie.

"No thanks, I'm fine."

"You know what they used to do back in the seventeenth century? If you had a really bad headache, they used to tighten a hangman's noose around your head. Either that, or they would give you a hard kick in the shins, so that the pain dropped from your head to your legs."

"I think I'll stick to Advil, thanks."

Three or four minutes passed. Nothing.

Dan said, "Either this doesn't work, or Michelange DuPriz wasn't a witch at all."

"Wait! Be patient. This is Los Angeles, remember, not some Russian village with a population of fifteen retards and twenty-three goats."

Dan checked his watch. "Look, I really have to call headquarters. They should have the preliminary results of the autopsies by now."

But Annie lifted her finger to her lips and said, "*Ssh!*"

Suddenly there was a soft, shifting sound. Dan looked down at the map and saw that the salt was swirling across it like a spiral star. It went around faster and faster, and as it did so the spokes of the star spread wider.

"I never saw it do *this* before," said Annie. "Usually, it all gathers at one point."

Instead, the salt separated into four small piles— one in Brentwood, one in Santa Monica, one in Silverlake and the last one in Laurel Canyon, in Beverly Hills.

"Laurel Canyon, that's where the Zombie lives," Dan frowned. "But what are these other piles?"

Annie stood up, went to her desk, and opened a small woven sewing basket. She came back with a paper pack of needles and drew one out. She laid it carefully on top of the pile of salt on Laurel Canyon, with its point in the center of the pile. Without any hesitation, without Annie touching it, the needle rose and stood vertical.

"There," she said. "That proves it. Your Haitian woman is a witch."

She laid another needle on the pile in Brentwood. Instantly, the same thing happened: the needle stood by itself and stayed balanced on its point.

"What does that mean?" asked Dan. "There's another witch there?"

Annie laid needles on the third and fourth piles of salt. They both stood erect.

"We have *four* witches," she said. "And very charismatic witches, too."

"Four? Jesus, the Zombie wasn't kidding when he said that magic was coming to town. Here, let me check these locations."

He took hold of the needle hovering above Laurel Canyon and used it to puncture the map. Then he cleared away the salt and made an *X* with his pen. He did the same with the needles over Santa Monica and Silverlake.

He was about to mark the Brentwood location when Annie gripped his hand. "Stop, Dan—be careful! Look!"

She was right to warn him. The needle was glowing a dull red—and, as they watched it, it began to glow brighter and brighter, until it was white hot. A thin wisp of smoke came out of the map, and the little pile of salt began to crackle and jump.

"This witch knows that we've found her," Annie said.

"What?"

"She knows that we've found her. She can probably taste the salt and feel the prick of the needle."

The salt turned blue and green, and began to jump even more violently. Then, with a flaring noise, the entire map burst into flame and flew into the air. It floated nearly as high as the ceiling before it was burned into nothing but black ash. It fell, crinkling and glowing, back to the rug. Dan stamped on it to make sure that all of the sparks were extinguished.

Annie said, "My God. That is one powerful witch. I never knew that there was a witch with that much influence, not in L.A. I don't know why I never felt her before."

"Maybe she wasn't here before. Maybe she only just arrived."

"This is very strange," said Annie. "It's worrying, too. I can't believe that it's a coincidence, four witches all appearing at the same time. Especially four witches as influential as these."

"Could be that they simply decided to hold their annual convention in L.A."

"No . . . witches are very reluctant to travel to other places except when they're called for, especially if they have to cross salt water. Your Haitian woman must have been specially invited by this Zombie guy. The question is, who are the other three witches, and who invited *them?* Especially the one who set fire to my map. She's the strongest, by far."

Annie picked up the four needles from out of the ashes and held them tightly between finger and thumb. "You know, I feel very strongly that there's a connection between these witches, that they're all in contact with one another."

"Maybe they were *all* invited by gang bosses."

"Did you manage to see where they were located?"

"Two out of them. One was on Rosewood Avenue in Silverlake, and the other was on Ocean View Road in Santa Monica."

"Pretty upscale addresses. Would gang bosses live in places like that?"

"Are you kidding me? As soon as they make any serious money, the bad guys almost always move out of the ghettos and the barrios and into the posh neighborhoods like Bel Air and the Hollywood Hills. I'm only speculating here, but if these other witches have been invited here by people who share anything of the Zombie's behavioral characteristics, they shouldn't be too hard for us to identify."

Annie sat down next to Dan and took hold of his hands. "Dan, you have to be really, really careful."

"Hey, I'm not afraid of mooks like the Zombie. Not much, anyhow."

"I'm not talking about gangsters. I'm talking about these witches. You've seen what they can do."

"Don't you worry, Annie. I never want to go through anything like today's experience, ever again."

"You do really believe in this now? In magic, I mean."

"I told you. When those quarters came up, I was Saul on the highway to Damascus, or at least Dorothy when she landed in Oz."

"You *have* to believe in it, Dan, or you'll never be able to fight it."

"I'll tell you something—when I was a kid, I always wanted to believe that my dad actually could produce hard-cooked eggs out of his ears. But I knew in my heart of hearts that it was only a trick. What Michelange DuPriz did to me, though—that couldn't have been anything but real."

"I think I can guess why she did it, too."

"Oh, yeah?"

"It's simple. She wants you to be scared. She wants to make you realize that she can do anything to you that takes her fancy, *anything*, and there's nothing you can do to stop her. And she wants you to spread that fear to all your fellow detectives."

Dan arrived back at police headquarters at 3250 Hollywood Boulevard just after 9:00 P.M. Ernie Munoz was still at his desk, talking on the telephone to the coroner's office. He looked tired and sweaty, and his desk was covered in reports and scribbled notes, as well as a box of congealed pepperoni pizza and several Styrofoam cups of cold coffee.

Dan perched on the edge of Ernie's desk and waited until he had hung up the phone.

"What's the latest?" he asked.

Ernie lifted out a flaccid triangle of waxy-looking pizza and took a large bite. "The ME still hasn't finished a full autopsy. All he can tell me so far is that the three bodies were burned very quickly at a very high temperature."

"What did Kevin Baleno have to say?"

"No trace so far of any accelerants. No cans of gasoline, no Molotov cocktails. No indication that the fire was caused by any kind of electrical fault in the vehicle itself. He's still analyzing the burn patterns, but it looks pretty certain that his first impression was correct: that the men themselves somehow combusted and that the damage to the vehicle was secondary."

"Have we found any more witnesses?"

Ernie wiped his mouth with a crumpled paper napkin. "I have to say something, *muchacho*. You don't seem to be very surprised."

"What should I be surprised about?"

"Well, maybe you should be surprised that three grown men should spontaneously catch fire and burn so hot that there was nothing left of them but bones and charcoal."

"Like Kevin said, it's impossible, but it happened, so it must be possible."

Ernie looked at him narrowly. "Do you know something about this that I don't?"

"I can't be sure yet. But maybe. How about witnesses?"

"I've interviewed three more drivers who were passing the scene at the time. None of them has been able to add anything much. A van driver said he definitely saw Michelange DuPriz holding something that was smoking—not a cheroot, more like two sticks. But he said that she never touched the car with them. She didn't throw them either, and he said that she was too far away to have set the car on fire."

"Okay. Will you be talking to any of the Narcotics squad tonight?"

"Sure. Sergeant Locatelli, most likely. She's calling me later for an update."

"Good. Ask her if she knows of anybody with heavy-weight criminal connections who lives on Rosewood Avenue in Silverlake, and on Ocean View Road in Santa Monica."

"Ocean View Road? I can tell you that one myself. Vasili Krylov, your friendly Russian extortionist and people smuggler. He just moved in a couple of months ago. He's got himself a fifteen-bedroom antebellum-style mansion, and his own nine-hole golf course."

"Krylov. Shit. I should have remembered that myself."

Ernie said, "You *do* know something that I don't. What the hell is it? Is Krylov involved in this some way?"

"I'll tell you when you've asked Sergeant Locatelli about the other address."

"Sometimes, *muchacho*, you can be a right royal pain in the ass."

Chapter Seven

Dan made himself a messy turkey-and-tomato sandwich, opened a bottle of Goose Island stout, and sprawled on the couch in front of the television. He didn't feel particularly hungry, especially after bringing up all those quarters, but he always slept badly when his stomach was empty. Either it gurgled, which woke him up, or else he had nightmares.

Unlike Annie's apartment, with all its mystical clutter and its arcane wall decorations, Dan's living room was minimalist to the point of being nearly empty. The walls were painted off-white and the floor was pale polished oak. The only pieces of furniture were a black leather couch, two black leather chairs, and a smoked-glass table with stubby chrome legs.

There were just two pictures in the room: a huge silkscreen print of yellow grass blowing in the wind under a thundery sky by the Dutch artist Jan Cremer, and a black-and-white photograph of Gayle, standing on the end of the Municipal Pier at Santa Monica Yacht Harbor in a white yachting cap and a boatneck sweater.

In one corner there was a small stack of books and magazines. *The Yosemite in Winter, Playboy, Guns &*

Ammo, 1001 Hot and Spicy Recipes, The Confessions of Nat Turner with a bookmark only six or seven pages in, and *The World Almanac*. The library of a man who couldn't concentrate.

Dan flicked over to the local news on NBC. The top story was the freak hurricane at the garden party held by the new chief of police, Chief O'Malley.

Reporter Wendy Chan said, "The hurricane was highly localized . . . in fact it affected only Chief O'Malley's property and was not felt anyplace else. It was so powerful, however, that many of the new police chief's hundred and twenty guests were momentarily blinded—including this reporter.

"The cause of this temporary loss of sight? According to weather expert John Mezzo from the UCLA Department of Atmospheric and Oceanic Sciences at Westwood, an extreme drop in air pressure. A similar blinding effect can be caused by sudden blizzards.

"The hurricane lasted only minutes, and nobody was seriously hurt. However, damage to the house and garden was widespread, and the party had to be brought to a premature close."

The second item on the news was the apparent suicide of a twenty-eight-year-old woman, who had fallen from the thirty-fourth floor of Century Park East. "Astrud Mitchell, who worked as a receptionist for the entertainment law firm Peale, Kravitz, and Wolfe, had given her friends and family no indication that she was suffering from depression and was described by her sister Carla as 'the happiest, best-adjusted person I ever knew.'"

Dan managed to eat half his turkey sandwich. Then, with his mouth still crammed, he went into the kitchen and took another bottle of stout out of the refrigerator.

The phone rang, and it was Ernie. "Dan? I just finished talking to Sergeant Locatelli."

"How is she?"

"Pretty upset, naturally. Those three guys were the best detectives she had."

"Anything new from Kevin Baleno?"

"Nope. He told me he's doing some experiments, trying to set fire to pig carcasses, but he doesn't sound too confident."

"Did you ask Locatelli about Rosewood Avenue?"

"Sure. She said that the only serious bad guy who lives in that neighborhood is Orestes Vasquez."

"The White Ghost?"

"That's your man. But did you hear about Chief O'Malley's garden party?"

"Sure. I saw it on the news. Some kind of a hurricane, wasn't it? Sounded like one of those dust devils you get out in the desert."

"Maybe," Ernie said. "But whatever caused it, Orestes Vasquez was there when it happened."

"You're kidding me. Vasquez? What was *he* doing there? Don't tell me he had an invite."

"I doubt it. But according to Locatelli, he came along with two of his heavies and a weird-looking woman. He was talking to Chief O'Malley when the wind started to blow."

"A weird-looking woman? Did Locatelli have any idea who she was?"

"Locatelli didn't attend the party herself, but one of her PR people was there. Apparently the woman was Hispanic looking. Black hair and a silvery dress. Big chested."

"That's it. Now I'm sure of it."

"Sure of what? Come on, *muchacho*, you're talking in riddles."

"Think about it. That's two gang bosses in the same day, both showing up with weird-looking women. One of the women burned three detectives and made me puke up money, and where the other one appeared there was a freak hurricane. They're witches, Ernie."

"Sure they are," said Ernie, his voice heavy with disbelief.

Dan could see himself in the long gloomy mirror that hung in the hallway. He thought that he looked like his own older brother, not that he had one. He was pale and haggard, and he needed a shave.

"I'm serious, Ernie. I know it's hard to get your head around it, but the girl who lives downstairs—you remember Annie?—she did a kind of test for me."

"Yeah, I remember Annie," said Ernie. He didn't sound impressed. "She was the one who told me that I should chew chicory because it would make me *look* thinner, even if I wasn't."

"Annie says we have at least four witches in the vicinity right now. They're all powerful, but one of them is extra powerful. She says that they all had to be invited here, and I think that they've been invited by gang bosses. For protection, probably, and to keep Narcotics off their backs."

"Dan, I saw you puke up the money, so I believe that was some kind of paranormal what's-its-name—but apart from that, where's your evidence?"

"Don't you worry about it. I'm going to *find* myself some evidence."

"Okay. All I can say is, good luck."

Dan finished two more beers, then went to bed. His bedroom was as sparsely furnished as his living room, with nothing but a king-size bed, two ebony-finish nightstands, and a digital clock.

He lay awake for a while. Someone in another apartment was playing samba music, and occasionally he heard laughter and the sound of a door slamming.

The more he thought about what had happened to him today, the less believable it seemed, as if he had dreamed it. Yet he couldn't get the image of Cusack, Fusco, and Knudsen out of his mind, like three charred monkeys; and he couldn't stop thinking about the way Michelange DuPriz had stalked across the sidewalk and then turned to stare at him.

He felt as if she had been able to see right into his soul—as if his whole life had danced in front of her eyes like a flip book. Every aspiration that he had ever had, every weakness, every moment of pride. Nobody had ever looked at him like that before. Nobody had made it so clear that they could see exactly who he was and what it was that haunted him.

Around 1:30 AM, he fell asleep. Almost immediately, though, he opened his eyes again and sat up. He listened, hard. The samba music had stopped, and the night was hushed. Yet he was sure that he had heard something.

He stayed where he was, still straining his ears. He could just about make out the distant sound of traffic on the freeways. For a moment he thought he heard a small child crying, but then that stopped, too.

You're overtired, Dan. Go back to sleep.

He turned over and punched his pillow into shape, but as he did so he glimpsed somebody passing the mirror in the hallway. It happened so quickly that he couldn't be sure if it was a man or a woman.

"Hey!" he called. "Hey—who's out there?"

There was no reply. He waited for a moment, and then he opened the drawer of his nightstand and took out his .38 revolver and cocked it.

"You'd better show yourself, whoever you are! Come into the doorway with your hands on top of your head!"

Still no reply. He waited a little longer, then swung his legs off the bed and stood up. "This is your last warning! I'm an armed police officer, and I will shoot to kill if I have to!"

He crossed the bedroom and looked out into the hallway, holding his revolver in both hands.

It was dark out there, but there was a tall window right at the very end, covered by a white cotton blind. As his eyes grew accustomed to the gloom, Dan saw that a figure was standing in front of the window, not moving. It was silhouetted against the blind, but he could see that it was dressed in something pale, like a nightgown.

"Hey, put your hands on top of your head where I can see them."

The figure remained unmoving.

"Did you hear what I said? Put your hands on top of your head, or I'll shoot you."

No response, except for the whistle of somebody who was finding it a struggle to breathe and the faintest of bubbling sounds.

"Can you hear me?" said Dan. The figure swayed very slightly, but it still didn't answer, and it was beginning to make him feel unnerved. He kept his revolver aimed at it and backed down the hallway toward the light switch.

The figure made a whining noise, as if trying to protest, but Dan switched on the light and said, "Okay, friend, let's see who the hell you are."

He was so shocked that he shouted out, *"Gahhhh!"* His legs felt as if they were going to buckle underneath him. His heart thumped once, twice, three times—so hard that it hurt his rib cage.

The figure in front of the window was Gayle. His dead fiancée Gayle—not wearing a nightgown but the cream satin dress that she had been wearing to Gus Webber's wedding. Her blond curls were gingery with blood—but worse than that, she looked exactly as she

had after the accident. The end of one of the scaffolding poles had struck her directly in the face, just below
the bridge of her nose, pushing it in. She hadn't been
killed immediately, and the fire department had tried
to remove her from the wreck of Dan's Mustang by
sawing through the scaffolding pole about two inches
in front of her face.

Her blue eyes were open on each side of the sawn-
off pole, like a fish's eyes. The pole itself formed an *O*
of surprise. Around the pole, her breath was whistling
and bubbling with blood.

Dan lowered his gun. He tried to say something, but
he couldn't. Gayle simply stood there staring at him,
her eyes occasionally blinking in mute desperation.

*This is a nightmare. I'm asleep. I'm dreaming this.
Wake up.*

He couldn't bring himself to approach her. He
could only do what he had done on the night of the
accident—stand and stare at her in horror.

I have to find a way to wake up.

He took two steps in Gayle's direction, until he
reached the bedroom door. She kept on staring at him
and swaying slightly, but she didn't try to approach.
He edged his way into the bedroom and climbed back
onto his bed.

*I'm asleep. If I shut my eyes and open them again, I'll
wake up, and Gayle will be gone.*

He turned over and closed his eyes for two or three
seconds, but he didn't have the nerve to keep them
closed any longer than that. *Supposing she comes into the
bedroom and I don't see her?* So he propped himself up
on the pillow and sat facing the open door, keeping his
.38 on top of the nightstand.

Ten minutes went by, and he began to calm down.
Maybe he had been hallucinating and Gayle wasn't really there. After all, he had been through a strange and

highly stressful day, as well as drinking four bottles of Goose Island stout. Maybe his mind was playing tricks on him.

But what if he went out into the hallway to look and she was still there?

She was dead; he had been to her funeral. She couldn't be there. But what if she was?

Okay—if she *was* there, maybe it was her spirit, looking for some kind of closure. Maybe she wanted to hear him say how sorry he was that he had killed her. Maybe she wanted to show him that he was forgiven.

Or maybe this was another magical stunt by Michelange DuPriz to show him that she knew exactly what cross he was carrying and to warn him to keep his nose out of the Zombie's personal business.

He picked up his gun and went back to the bedroom door.

"Gayle?" he called. He knew she couldn't answer, but he wanted to reassure her that it was only him.

He hesitated for a moment, then stepped out into the hallway. Gayle was still standing in front of the window. Now, however, her face was miraculously intact and she was unhurt.

"Gayle? What are you doing here? You're not alive anymore."

She was staring at him, but she didn't appear to see him.

"Gayle?" he said and took a step toward her, holding out his hand. God, he had forgotten how pretty she'd been.

She still didn't seem to be focusing on him. Her eyes were fixed in the distance, as if she were looking down a long road.

Under her breath, she started to sing, *"When I was a child I had a fever . . . my hands felt just like two balloons . . . eee . . . eee . . . eee!"*

"Gayle baby," said Dan. His eyes filled with tears, and he had to wipe his nose with the back of his hand. "You have to know how sorry I am. I've never been able to forget you. I've never been able to forget what happened."

Softly, she carried on singing. But then suddenly she stopped and stared straight ahead of her, along the hallway.

Dan said, "Gayle, listen to me—"

As he took another step forward, however, there was a terrible clanging sound right behind him, like a badly tuned church bell. Instinctively, Dan took a step back, just as a twenty-foot scaffolding pole came hurtling along the hallway and struck Gayle directly in the face. He heard her nose break and her cheekbones smash.

She flew backward into the window, and then she was gone, vanished, and the scaffolding pole vanished, too.

Dan stood in the hallway for a long time, breathing deeply to steady himself. Hallucination, no question about it. But what had made him hallucinate? His own exhaustion, his own drunkenness? Or witchery?

Chapter Eight

He stayed awake for the rest of the night, sitting on the couch with all the lights on and the television, too, but with the volume muted in case Gayle came back and he failed to hear her.

Early the next day he drove out to visit his father at the Stage Performers' Retirement Home in Pasadena. It was a hazy morning but very warm, and his father was sitting on his balcony, looking out over a steeply sloping orange grove. He had three decks of playing cards on the table in front of him, and he was obviously trying to perfect some trick. A bright yellow canary was sitting in a cage next to him, twittering and cheeping on its perch. Perversely, his father had named the canary Sylvester.

His father was a small man with a round pugnacious face, a snub nose, and rimless spectacles. His hair was white now, but it still stuck up like one of the Katzenjammer Kids. He was wearing a yellow and red Hawaiian-style shirt with white chest hair curling out of it, red shorts, and yellow socks.

"You don't usually visit me on Tuesdays," his father remarked, as Dan stepped out onto the balcony.

"You don't want me here? I'll leave."

"Of course I want you here. I'm just saying that you don't usually visit me on Tuesdays. Park your ass. You want a cup of coffee? The coffee here is unique. It tastes exactly like yacht varnish."

"What are you doing?" asked Dan, nodding toward the playing cards.

"I'm working on a variation of Dusenfeld's Arrangement."

"What the hell is Dusenfeld's Arrangement?"

"Didn't I ever tell you about Victor Dusenfeld? One of the greatest card illusionists there ever was. He used to perform in Berlin in the 1930s. Hitler loved him."

"That's not much of a recommendation."

"Oh yes, it is, because Hitler believed in magic, and he was convinced that Victor Dusenfeld was the real deal. I've seen some old movies of Dusenfeld's act, and you can see why. The man was a genius. He used to ask some guy in the audience to pick a card. Then this girl would come down from the stage and drop her unmentionables, and she would have the exact same card tattooed on her tush."

"You're not trying to do that, are you?"

"I wish. No, this is Dusenfeld's Arrangement. He took three decks of cards, asked three people to shuffle them. Then he took them back, cut them three times, and all three decks would be back in order, just like they came out of the box."

"So how did he do it?"

"I could show you, but it would probably take the rest of the day, and I'm not sure that I'm doing it the same way Dusenfeld did it. But there was one trick that Dusenfeld did for Hermann Göring in 1932, and I still can't work it out. He was performing at Horcher's restaurant, which was one of Göring's favorites, and he asked him to pick a card without telling him what it was.

"When he went home to bed that night, Göring found the card on his pillow. I mean—that's what I call a card trick. Not only do you have to guess the right card, you have to break into the mark's house before he gets home and plant it there. Either that, or you have to be in cahoots with one of his staff."

"There's a third alternative."

"Oh yeah? Such as what?"

"You could put it there by magic."

Dan's father took off his spectacles and stared at him narrowly. "Something tells me you're serious."

"Yes, I'm serious. Some pretty strange events happened yesterday—three detectives got burned to death, and then there was some kind of freak hurricane at Chief O'Malley's house."

"I saw those on the news. What are you trying to say?"

Dan told him about the money and the witch test; and then he told him about Gayle appearing at his apartment. His father sat and listened without interrupting.

Dan said, "I guess I came here to ask you if this really could be magic. Or maybe I'm making a prize asshole out of myself. You—you're the best magician I ever saw. You remember that trick you used to do when you cut off a girl's legs and they walked around the stage on their own? Or when you stuffed about twenty chickens and a dozen cats into a hatbox?"

"Of course I do. Those were pretty amazing tricks. They were funny, too."

"Three detectives getting burned to death—that was amazing, but that wasn't funny. And puking up thirty bucks worth of quarters, that wasn't funny either."

"I know, son, I know. But the difference is those weren't tricks. And it doesn't sound like this hurricane was a trick either."

"Then you think this could be genuine magic?"

Dan's father leaned forward in his basketwork chair. "Don't sound so surprised. The very first thing you learn when you start out to become a stage magician is that you're not really a magician. You're an illusionist, an entertainer—a con artist, that's all. Even Harry Houdini never called himself a magician, though his promoters did. But you also learn that real magicians *do* exist. Witches, sure, if you want to call them that."

"You believe in them?"

"Sure, I believe in them. I never came across many. But I saw a woman in Louisiana who could heal people who had terminal cancer, and I saw another woman in Pennsylvania who could rise clear off the floor right in front of you—no wires, no pulleys, nothing. I met an old black guy in Florida who could make a glass of water boil just by looking at it, and when I went to France I was introduced to this fellow who could set newspapers alight from fifty yards away."

Dan said, "I don't know if I ought to be feeling relieved because I'm not going crazy, or even more worried because these women are for real."

"Let me tell you, son, you should be *seriously* worried. Everybody who has the gift, they're different, depending on their personality. Some witches do nothing but potter around, mixing up medicinal potions and telling fortunes and helping lonely people find a soul mate. But most witches, they let their powers go to their head. They just love to cause havoc for the hell of it. Even that fellow in France—he used to walk past a café and before you knew it, *everybody's* newspaper was on fire."

A redheaded young nurse came out and gave Dan's

father a plastic cupful of pills and a glass of grapefruit juice. Dan's father peered into the cup and said, "You forgot the Viagra again."

"You don't need Viagra, Mr. Fisher."

"Not right now. But I will tonight when you come creeping into my room wearing those black stockings and that peekaboo bra."

"Sorry, Mr. Fisher, I'm washing my headache tonight."

When the nurse had gone, Dan's father shook his head and said, "You can tell she's Irish, can't you?"

Dan said, "What I need to find out is what are these witches going to do next?"

"Nothing good, I'll bet you, especially since they've teamed up with mobsters. Think about it. A witch could rob a bank simply by hypnotizing the tellers to open the safe for her. Or maybe she could spirit the money right out of the vault and into the trunk of her getaway car the same way that woman spirited all those quarters into your stomach. She could smuggle drugs by making customs inspectors believe that they were looking at something completely different, like cakes, for instance, or boxes of candy.

"Worst of all, though, if you guys go after her, a witch will do everything she can to protect herself. Like setting you on fire. Or making you shoot yourself. Or having you jump off a building. I've heard of a witch who could literally shake people to death, until their fingers and their arms flew off in all directions."

Dan said, "Before I do anything else, Dad, I have to convince Lieutenant Harris that we're up against a bunch of witches and that I'm not a prime candidate for the funny farm."

"I think you'll be able to convince him, son, once he sees for himself what's going on."

"I'm not so sure. You couldn't convince Lieutenant

Harris that his office was on fire until his pants caught alight."

"Well, he'd better take care, or else that just might happen."

Dan stood up and went over to the balcony railing. It was growing very hot now, and the smell of rotting oranges was almost overwhelming. The shadows under the trees were so dark that he could imagine that anything was hiding there—a black cat, a witch's familiar; a gremlin; or a witch herself, able to turn into nothing but darkness.

"So how do we get rid of them?" he asked his father.

"I don't know. Who do you think I am, Cotton Mather? You'll have to ask that girlfriend of yours or look it up on the Internet."

"She's not my girlfriend, Dad. She just happens to live downstairs and have an interest in natural healing and fortune-telling and all that stuff."

"They used to burn witches, didn't they, in the Middle Ages—or women they thought were witches. Roast them over a fire. Or throw them into a pond to see if they floated or not. But most of those women weren't witches at all. They wouldn't have been able to catch them if they were."

Dan checked his watch. "I have to get back. I want to talk to Chief O'Malley about that hurricane if I can. Listen, Dad, you've been really helpful. I'll call by Thursday."

"Dan? You listen to me. I am not kidding you when I say that going after those women could be very, very dangerous. An experienced witch can suck the air out of your lungs without even touching you and suffocate you where you stand."

"Dad—'very, very dangerous' comes with the badge. I'll be careful, I promise you."

His father nodded. "I know."

Dan was about to leave when his father said, "You know something—there's one bit of real magic I wish I could do, and I can't."

"What's that?"

"Stupid, I know. But I wish I could turn back the clock to July 12, 1979, when we were sitting on the beach—you and Katie and your mom and me—and that spotted dog came running up to you and snatched your sandwich. You ran around and around, trying to get it back, and we were laughing so much we had tears in our eyes."

"I was angry. I wanted that sandwich. I'm *still* angry."

"Well, so am I. The next day your mom had her stroke and two days after that the good Lord took her away from us. But we laughed that afternoon."

"I know, Dad. But nothing lasts forever. Especially laughter."

As he drove back to Hollywood, Dan got a call from Ernie on his cell.

"We're not making much headway, *muchacho*. Kevin Baleno has cremated five pig carcasses already, and he says that the fire department laboratory smells like Mr. Cecil's California Ribs restaurant. But he still can't work out how those three detectives burst into flame."

"What about Michelange DuPriz? Find anything on her?"

"Yeah, better luck with that. She came from Jacmel, originally. That's a seaside town on the southeast coast of Haiti, pretty much rural and run-down. Her mother ran a voodoo store, and she got herself a reputation for voodoo, too. She could help people to talk to their dead relatives and curse people who were making trouble, stuff like that."

"How'd you find that out?"

"I have a Cuban friend who has a cousin in Port-Au-Prince, and *he* has a friend in the Haitian National Police."

"Now that's what I call networking. What are you doing now?"

"I was planning on paying a visit to the Zombie's house, ask Ms. DuPriz some more questions."

"Not a good idea, El Gordo. Not yet."

"My friend's cousin's friend said that there's a voodoo ritual in which you can light two sticks and the fire will jump into anybody you want it to, burn them alive. I think I really need to ask her about that, don't you?"

"Ernie, we're not dealing with party tricks here. If you go round there, she could do the same to you. Let's take this careful, one step at a time."

"So what are you going to do?"

"I'm going to talk to the chief about what happened at his party yesterday evening. Then I think I'm going to have a word with Orestes Vasquez. Then I think we need to sit down with Lieutenant Harris and see if we can persuade him to believe in black magic."

"Okay. Why don't you pick me up? I'll come with you."

Dan had arranged with his personal assistant to talk to Chief O'Malley at 12:20 PM, but when he and Ernie arrived at the Days Center on North Los Angeles Street, they were told that the chief had decided to hold an impromptu press conference, and they would have to wait.

The media room on the fifteenth floor was crowded with reporters and cameramen, and Dan and Ernie stood at the very back.

"I went to see my dad this morning," said Dan. "That's the reason I told you not to go see Michelange

DuPriz. My dad believes that she's a genuine witch and that these other women are, too. If you upset them, they'll kill you. Or worse."

"I don't suppose your dad has any bright ideas about how we're going to deal with these ladies."

"No, he doesn't. He's a stage magician, not a witch finder."

"I have to tell you, *muchacho*, I still think that this is all bullshit. There's a logical explanation. There has to be. The only trouble is I don't know what it is."

"El Gordo, the only logical explanation is that it's witchcraft."

"How can you say that? Witchcraft isn't logical by definition. I'm only going along with you because I was trained to be open-minded."

"You? Open-minded? Compared to you, Pancho Villa was open-minded."

At that moment, Chief O'Malley entered the room along with his deputy chief, Walter Days, and three members of the police commission, one man and two women. They posed for a moment, serious faced, while scores of flashes flickered, and then they sat down.

Chief O'Malley said, "Ladies and gentlemen, I've asked you all to come here this morning because this great city of ours is facing a very grave and unusual menace. I am not yet in a position to advise you of the exact nature of this menace or who is responsible for it. But I *can* tell you that it involves organized crime.

"Those of us who uphold the law in Los Angeles have been personally threatened on an unprecedented scale. Not only police officers. Not only judges and social workers and other members of the community who work so tirelessly to keep our city safe, but their friends and their loved ones, too. Even their children.

"To put it as plainly as I can, we have been warned that if we try to interfere in the running of drug trafficking and prostitution and extortion, hundreds of us will suffer a truly terrible fate."

There was a deafening cacophony of shouted questions. "What kind of fate?" "Are you talking about terrorism, Chief O'Malley?" "Are you talking bombs?" "Does this have anything to do with the hurricane at your reception?" "When you say organized crime, are you talking about anybody specific?"

Chief O'Malley waited for a while without answering. Then he raised his hands for silence. "So far, this is all that I can tell you. But I wanted you to be aware that a serious threat has been made against those of us who enforce the law and our families, too, and I appeal for your cooperation in passing on any information that you might consider helpful.

"In order to defuse a highly critical situation, I initially told the individual who made this threat that I would accede to his demands. But he needs to know now that there are some promises that are made to be broken, and this is one of them.

"I will never bow to blackmail, ever. As far as criminals are concerned, my motto has always been 'Never give an inch. Period.' I repeat that motto today."

There was another roar of questions and a blizzard of flashes. Chief O'Malley waited until the noise had died down again, and then he said, "I promise you that I will convene another media conference as soon as—" He coughed, then coughed again. "As soon as I—"

He slapped his hand against his chest and coughed yet again. Deputy Chief Days quickly poured him a glass of water and passed it to him, but he shook his head. He was growing redder and redder, and it was obvious that he couldn't breathe.

"Chief! What's wrong? Chief O'Malley!"

"Loosen his collar!" said one of the police commissioners. "He's choking!"

A black police officer pushed his way around the table and said, "Keep clear! Keep clear! Give him some air!"

The officer tugged Chief O'Malley's necktie loose and unfastened the top three buttons of his shirt. Chief O'Malley was in serious distress now. His eyes bulged, and his face was turning blue from lack of oxygen. The officer opened his mouth and peered into his throat. Then he said, "Help me! Help me to lift him up."

Between them, the officer and Deputy Chief Days heaved Chief O'Malley to his feet. The officer stood behind Chief O'Malley and wrapped his arms around him, making a fist. He punched him six or seven times under his rib cage, but still Chief O'Malley couldn't breathe.

"Paramedic—*now!*" shouted Deputy Chief Days.

The officer gave Chief O'Malley another six punches and another. Chief O'Malley arched his head back, his mouth stretched wide open and the veins on his neck swelling. There was a moment when he stood with both fists clenched, utterly rigid. Then he let out a thin, strangulated *keeeeeeee* sound from the back of his throat. A greasy, yellow toad emerged from between his lips and dropped onto the floor.

There were shouts of shock and disgust from the media. The toad crouched on the carpet for a few seconds, blinking, and then it began to crawl scissor-legged toward the door. A police officer took two steps forward and stamped on it. It burst with an audible *pop*.

The black officer gently lowered Chief O'Malley onto the floor, where he lay on his side, shivering violently, as if he were having an epileptic fit. His eyes were staring at nothing at all, and a long string of phlegm was sliding from the side of his mouth. The whole conference room was in chaos, with reporters shouting into their cell phones, cameras flashing, and police officers trying to hold everybody back.

Ernie turned to Dan, and it was plain that he was stunned.

"You want to give me a logical explanation for *that?*" Dan asked.

Chapter Nine

Dan managed to push his way through the crowds of reporters and TV cameramen outside the emergency room at Cedars-Sinai, and he eventually located Deputy Chief Days in a small side office.

He had to tap on the window of the office door so that Captain Kromesky and Commissioner Philips could shuffle to one side and let him in. Captain Kromesky was bald and pugnacious, and looked like an attack dog in a sharply pressed uniform. Commissioner Philips, on the other hand, was willowy with bushy black eyebrows and could have been the minister of a particularly forgiving church.

Dan maneuvered his way around them and approached Deputy Chief Days.

"Detective Dan Fisher, sir, Homicide, West Hollywood."

"Sorry, Detective, I'm pretty much tied up at the moment, as you can imagine."

Deputy Chief Days was a tall, bony-shouldered man with a face like a grieving gundog. He spoke in a measured drone, his upper lip completely motionless, and when he laughed, which was rarely, it seemed as if whole minutes elapsed between one "ha" and the next. His subordinates, of course, called him Happy.

"How's the chief, sir?"

"Still critical, or so I'm told."

Dan looked around. There were over a dozen people packed into the office—most of them senior police officers, although he recognized City Councilman George Zachariades from the 5th District and Jenna Forbes from the mayor's office.

Dan leaned close to Deputy Chief Days and said, "I wonder if I could have a private word with you, sir? What happened to Chief O'Malley—I have a good idea who could have been responsible."

"He regurgitated a live toad, Detective, on network television."

"I know, sir. But I think I know how it was done and who did it."

Deputy Chief Days blinked at him, as if Dan were speaking in a foreign language.

Dan said, "At least two organized crime bosses in Los Angeles are using what you might call unnatural forces to keep the police from interfering in their activities."

"Detective, I think you would be better advised if you talked to your immediate superiors at West Hollywood."

"Sir—I can explain what they are, these unnatural forces. I know it's not easy to get your head around any of this stuff, but as far as I can see, there's no other explanation that makes any sense."

Deputy Chief Days was about to reply when there was another tap at the window. A wide-hipped black lady in a lilac suit edged her way into the office and said, "Deputy Chief Days? I'm Trudi Belafonte, senior ER administrator. I've just been talking to Dr. Kellogg about Chief O'Malley."

"What's the latest?"

"Dr. Kellogg has been treating Chief O'Malley since he was admitted, and he thinks there's something urgent you should come see."

"It's not serious, is it?"

"Best if you take a look for yourself, sir."

"Sure. Yes. Excuse me, everybody."

Trudi Belafonte led the way along the corridor and Deputy Chief Days went after her, closely followed by Captain Kromesky and Commissioner Philips, their shoes all busily squeaking on the polished vinyl floor. Dan decided to go along, too, and Captain Kromesky must have assumed that he had the right to because he didn't challenge him.

They entered a dimly lit imaging room next to one of the ER operating theaters. A surgeon in blue scrubs was frowning at a series of CT scans on a fluorescent viewing screen, one hand clamped to the back of his neck. The surgeon was only in his mid-thirties, but he was already gray-haired and stooped, and his elbows were dry with eczema. As they came in, he turned around and said, "Damnedest, *damnedest* thing I ever saw. Ever."

"This is Dr. Sam Kellogg," said Trudi Jackson. "Dr. Kellogg is our leading consultant in abdominal trauma. He specializes in any kind of insult to the human digestive system."

"That's right," said Dr. Kellogg. "And what we have here, believe me, is the biggest insult to the human digestive system that you can imagine."

Deputy Chief Days unfolded a pair of rimless spectacles and peered at the scans in bewilderment. "Can you explain to me what we're supposed to be looking at here, Doctor?"

Dr. Kellogg pointed to the shadowy outline of Chief O'Malley's stomach. "You see these heart-shaped objects all crowded tightly together? Well—they look like hearts, don't they?"

"Yes, I see them. What are they? Something he's been eating?"

"If they are, I wish I knew how the hell he managed it. They're not hearts, in fact. They're toads, about fifteen of them, so far as we can tell. The trouble is they're still alive and constantly clambering around, so it's difficult to give you an accurate count."

"*Live toads?*" Deputy Chief Days stared at the scan in horror. "I don't understand it. He couldn't have swallowed fifteen live toads."

"He must have. There's no other way they could have gotten into his stomach."

"Well, however they got in there—Christ almighty— you have to get them out!"

Dr. Kellogg nodded. "He's being prepped for surgery even as we speak. I just wanted to make you aware of his condition."

"What the hell am I going to tell the media? One toad dropping out of his mouth was bad enough. The religious channels are already saying it's a punishment from God!"

"There's something else you have to know," said Dr. Kellogg. "When toads are frightened or attacked, they give off a thick secretion called bufotenine. Depending on the species of toad, it can be highly toxic, and it can affect the brain. Some hippies used to lick toads to give them a psychedelic trip.

"Chief O'Malley already has a dangerously high concentration of bufotenine in his bloodstream, and we have to be prepared for the possibility that he may not recover. Not mentally, anyhow."

"This is a nightmare," said Deputy Chief Days.

"Even more of a nightmare for Chief O'Malley than it is for us, I'm afraid. One of the effects of bufotenine on the brain is to make sufferers feel permanently terrified—whether they're asleep or awake. It doesn't wear off either. They feel terrified for the rest of their lives."

The swing door to the operating room opened, and a nurse in a mask appeared. "We're ready for you, Dr. Kellogg."

"Okay, fine. You got the vivarium, to put the toads in?"

"Yes, sir."

Deputy Chief Days said, "Do your best for him, Dr. Kellogg—please. He's a good friend and a very fine public servant."

Dr. Kellogg laid a reassuring hand on his shoulder, then followed the nurse through the swing door. Deputy Chief Days stood in silence for a while, then turned and looked at the scans again.

"*Live toads,*" he repeated.

Dan said, "What I was trying to tell you before, sir—about unnatural forces—"

But Deputy Chief Days didn't seem to hear him. He turned and walked out of the imaging room and back along the corridor, as erratically as if he had been drinking.

Dan caught up with Captain Kromesky. "Sir, I think I know what's happening here—and Deputy Chief Days really needs to hear me out."

"Go through the recognized chain of command, Detective," Captain Kromesky retorted. "Report to your lieutenant first, and then your lieutenant can assess the value of your information and pass it up to headquarters if it warrants it."

"If it *warrants* it? Chief O'Malley is lying on an operating table with a bellyful of live toads! And you know what happened at his reception when that hurricane got up and nobody could see? This shit is all connected, sir. It's unnatural forces. Or *supernatural* forces."

"Detective, have you been drinking?"

"For Christ's sake, Captain. It's black magic if that makes it any easier to understand."

Captain Kromesky stopped and stared at him, and Dan could see by the repetitious tic in his cheek that the man was grinding his teeth.

"You'd be well advised to leave this hospital now, Detective, before I report you for insubordinate conduct."

"Captain, there are toads crawling around inside the chief's stomach. *Toads.* If he didn't swallow them deliberately, how do you think they got there?"

"That's up to the doctor to tell us, wouldn't you say?"

Dan took a deep breath. He was about to say something more, but he decided against it. There was absolutely no future in antagonizing a man like Captain Kromesky. You might just as well hit yourself in the face with a two-by-four.

He left the hospital and drove back to Franklin Avenue. Even though it was early afternoon, the sky was a dark greenish color, rather than blue, like corroded copper. He switched on his SUV's radio, and it was playing "Comfortably Numb."

"You are only coming through in waves . . . your lips move, but I can't hear what you're saying . . ."

He had a feeling that something really bad was about to happen. Something even worse than Cusack and Fusco and Knudsen being burned to death, or Chief O'Malley vomiting a live toad. He felt as if he were back in his nightmare, the same nightmare in which Gayle had been killed, only this time he was awake.

As he parked his SUV in the driveway, Annie arrived home, too, in her old red Volkswagen Beetle. She opened the trunk and took out three grocery bags. Dan said, "Hey, let me help you with that."

She opened the door of her apartment, and Dan carried the bags through to the kitchen. There was a strong smell of licorice around and a musty, herby undertone.

"What are you cooking up now?" Dan asked.

"It's a cure for arthritis. My grandma gets it in her fingers, so bad that it makes her cry sometimes."

"Did you hear what happened to the chief of police?"

"No. What was it?"

"He was right in the middle of a press conference and he puked up a live toad."

"What?"

"I was there. I saw it for myself. It came out his mouth and plopped right down on the floor. They took him to the ER and scanned him, and they found that his stomach was full of toads. Fifteen, maybe more."

Annie stopped unpacking her groceries. "That was your Haitian lady again, I'll bet. My friend Véronique called me from Port-au-Prince this morning. She said that making your enemies sick—that's a classic *bokú* technique."

"*Bokú?*"

"*Bokú* . . . they're like hired sorcerers. Families in Haiti usually call them in when they want to cast a bad spell on somebody who's hurt them or upset them. Or maybe they pay them to break a spell that somebody else has put on *them*. President François Duvalier used to use *bokú* all the time when he was running the country."

Dan said, "You should have seen it. Well, to tell you the truth, you *shouldn't* have seen it. It would have made you lose your Cheerios."

"Do the media know about the toads in his stomach?"

"Not yet, but they've been going wild. Some of them are saying that it was an optical illusion or a magic trick. But most of them are saying it's an act of God—you know, like the plague of locusts in the Bible, because Chief O'Malley is so intolerant toward ethnic minorities. He doesn't think we should go easy on drug dealers when they happen to be Hispanic."

Annie stacked jars of herbs in her pantry. "Pretty funny, isn't it, how people are always ready to believe in religious miracles but not in witches?"

"I tried to talk to Deputy Chief Days about it, but I didn't get too far. I think he's totally in denial."

"What did you say to him?"

"I didn't mention witches per se. I just said 'unnatural forces.'"

"Not strictly true, really. More like *natural* forces. This Haitian woman is simply using the power of her magic to change the world around her. She didn't create those toads, anymore than she created the quarters that you brought up. All she did was move them out of their swamp, or wherever they came from, and into Chief O'Malley's stomach."

"Like 'beam me up, Scotty'?"

"In a way. Almost all witches can move objects or animals from one place to another. Some of them can even move them from one *day* to another, or one year to another. And they can move themselves, too—incredible distances, sometimes *miles*. That's how witches got the reputation of being able to fly, even though they can't."

Dan said, "There's something else. The doctor said that the toads in Chief O'Malley's stomach had given off some kind of poison that might affect his brain.

He said the chief might end up in a permanent state of terror."

"Bufotenine," said Annie. "That pretty much *proves* that your Haitian woman was responsible."

"How come?"

"Bufotenine is what the voodoo *houngan* use to create zombies. They poison their victims with it so that it numbs their souls, and they have all the characteristics of being dead, even though they're not. It also makes them frightened of everything and everyone, especially the *houngan* who created them."

"Is there a cure?"

"Only one that I've ever heard of. Cut the victim's head off."

Chapter Ten

Dan slid a frozen pepperoni pizza in the oven, opened a bottle of stout, then heaved his damp laundry out of his washing machine. He went out onto the narrow balcony outside his living room and started to pin the laundry onto the makeshift clothesline he had fixed up—a sheet, a couple of pillowcases, three T-shirts, and five pairs of striped boxers.

He was just about to go back inside when he saw a pale shape flickering in the yard below under a wide-spreading fan palm. He went to the railing and peered downward, trying to make out what it was. He could see a light-colored triangle that could have been some-body's shoulder, but the crisscross shadows of the palm fronds made it difficult for him to be sure.

"Anybody down there?" he called. If there was some-body there, he had no compunction about challenging them to show themselves. In the past two or three weeks there had been a rash of petty thefts along Franklin Avenue—bicycles, sunbeds, swimming-pool cleaners—mostly taken by crystal-meth addicts.

"I said, is anybody down there? Come out from under that tree and let's take a look at you."

There was a long silence. A warm breeze stirred his washing, and a California quail landed on the railing at the far end of the balcony and cocked its head at him. Quail had a strange habit of flying down whenever he hung out washing, and sucking the water from it with their beaks.

He thought: *No, there's nobody there. It's just a stray sheet of newspaper that's blown from somebody's balcony or a trick of the light.*

But as he turned away, a figure stepped out from under the tree and stood beneath his balcony, staring up at him. His skin felt as if it were shrinking, and Dan almost lost his balance. It was Gayle. She was unharmed, her face as perfect as it had been in the split second before the scaffolding pole had struck her. Her blond hair was unbloodied, and she was wearing the same cream satin dress.

He looked down at her, and he didn't know whether he ought to say anything or not. After all, she couldn't be real, could she? How could she be real when she was dead? Maybe he was suffering from the long-delayed effects of crucifying guilt. Maybe he was going mad. Or maybe Michelange DuPriz was trying to make him *think* that he was going mad.

But he stood there staring at her, and she didn't fade away. She cast a real shadow across the overgrown grass, and her hair was blowing in the breeze. The look in her eyes was distant and unfocused, but then she had always been dreamy.

"Gayle?" he said, with a catch in his throat.

She didn't answer.

"Gayle, are you for real?"

Still she didn't say anything.

"Gayle . . . if you're for real, I'm coming down. I need to talk to you."

She parted her lips a little, as if about to speak, but no words came out. All the same, Dan thought he saw her give him the faintest of smiles.

He backed away from the railing, still watching her. Then he hurried through his living room, out his front door, and vaulted down the steps. As he was passing Annie's apartment, she opened her door and said, "*Dan?* What's wrong?"

"Nothing! I'm fine!"

He ran around the side of the apartment building and into the yard. There was nobody there. No Gayle, nobody. No footprints in the grass either, to prove that somebody *had* been there.

Annie came around the building behind him and touched him gently on the back.

"Dan? Tell me what's wrong."

"It's nothing. I think I'm more stressed out than I thought I was. Maybe I shouldn't have taken any time off. You know what they say. It's only when the pressure's taken off them that people go to pieces."

Annie looked around the yard. "Did you . . . *expect* somebody to be here?"

"No. Not really."

"Who was it? Was it Gayle?"

"You read me like a book, Annie Conjure."

"That's because I have the gift. But you should be very careful if you're starting to see people who have passed beyond. Especially people you love."

Dan looked up at his sheet hanging on the line. He had seen a movie once in which the outline of a dead woman's face had appeared on a sheet, and he half expected it to happen now.

"I was there, on the balcony. She was standing right here, looking up at me."

"Whatever you saw, Dan, it wasn't her."

"Annie, she looked totally real. Totally solid. The grass—she was throwing a shadow on the grass and everything. Her hair and her dress . . . they were being blown around by the wind. If she wasn't real, how could that have happened?"

"Dan, you can see dead people in your dreams and they have shadows, don't they? You can see dead people in movies and their hair gets blown by the wind. It wasn't Gayle, I promise you."

Dan took a deep breath. "Okay. It wasn't Gayle. But if I see her again—or it, or whatever she is—I'll make sure that you get to see her, too."

"That's a deal."

Annie opened a bottle of zinfandel, and they talked for over a half hour. She explained to him how witches could move solid objects from one place to another— from one room to another, from one city to another, even from one country to another.

"Transportation was discovered by the ancient Druids. They realized that everything in the world is connected by a network of what they called ley lines, and that anything could be moved along these ley lines by using the Earth's own natural magnetism—especially anything made of metal or stone with any kind of metallic ore in it. But living creatures, too, because they contain minerals. People, even."

"How about you? Have *you* ever managed to do it?"

Annie shook her head. "Once I tried to make all my dirty dishes vanish from the dinner table and reappear in the dishwasher, but they wouldn't."

"That sounds like Mickey Mouse in *Fantasia*, making all those broomsticks carry water for him. Maybe it only works if it's something you're passionate about. Or angry. Or vengeful."

"Maybe I'm just not powerful enough," Annie admitted. "Last night, I tried to locate that fourth witch again, the one who set fire to the map. I used salt, and I used needles. I even used a spider tied to a length of thread. I can sense that she's very close. I can sense that much. She could be hiding in my closet for all I know. But she's keeping herself very well cloaked."

"We'll find her. I have a feeling about it. That's if she doesn't find us first."

Annie looked at him, wide eyed and serious. "This is scary, isn't it? I mean, like, this is very scary. It seems like these witches can do whatever they want, and nobody can do anything to stop them."

Dan held out his wine glass for a refill. "Nobody wants to believe in them, that's why."

"But you believe. And I believe."

"Exactly. So it looks like stopping them is entirely up to us, doesn't it?"

Dan climbed the steps back to his apartment. When he opened the door, he found that the living room was billowing with acrid smoke, as if the place was on fire. He pushed his way into the kitchen, coughing. His pizza was burned black, like charcoal. "Shit," he said. He had lost his appetite after seeing Gayle, but this was all he needed.

He opened all the doors and windows to disperse the smoke. Then he went for a shower and washed his hair. He dressed in a black short-sleeved shirt and tan-colored chinos. As he came back into the living room, combing his hair, the NBC news was rerunning its footage of Chief O'Malley vomiting up the toad, over and over. This was followed by a discussion from a panel of experts—a Roman Catholic priest, a veterinarian, a gastroenterologist, and Roland Zod, the famous TV illusionist.

"From earliest times, the toad has had very strong religious associations," said the priest, who had a crimson face and wild white hair. "The ancient Egyptians believed that the goddess Heket sprang out of the wetness of Ra's mouth and that she looked exactly like a toad, as well as having the power to make the Nile flood every year. Even today the Orinoco Indians still beat toads to death with sticks, in the belief that this will make it rain.

"But in the Christian canon, toads have always been associated with heresy, and the devil. It is my personal belief that what happened to the chief of police this morning was a sign from Our Lord that we should return to the laws and morals of the Christian church."

"So where do you suppose this unfortunate toad came from?" asked the veterinarian, blinking at him furiously.

"It was such a totally obvious trick," said Roland Zod. He was thirtyish with a shiny, bald head and a pencil mustache. "It *appeared* that a toad came out of his mouth, yes. But in my opinion, it was a yellow balloon painted with eyes to make it *look* like a toad. The chief put his hand up to his mouth, spat out the balloon, which he immediately deflated and tucked into his cuff, and then dropped the real toad onto the floor."

"Do we know if Chief O'Malley has ever had any training as a stage magician?" asked the gastroenterologist with undisguised sarcasm.

"And why would he resort to such a stunt?" asked the priest. "At best, it could only make him look ridiculous."

"He did it to impress his audience," Roland Zod retorted. "Jesus was always pulling off tricks like that to make his point. Changing water into wine, feeding five thousand people with nothing but a couple of fish, raising the dead. Well, the *allegedly* dead."

"You're trying to suggest that Jesus was nothing more than a *conjuror?*"

"A good conjuror. Maybe even a *great* conjuror. But I'm just asking you, Reverend, what is the most rational explanation for Chief O'Malley bringing up a live toad? Miracle, personal warning from God, or trick?"

Dan switched off the sound. It was plain that the media still had not been told about the toads in Chief O'Malley's stomach, although a streamer along the bottom of the screen said, *L.A. police chief still in critical condition at Cedars-Sinai.*

He was on his way to the kitchen for another stout when the phone rang. It was Ernie.

"El Gordo! How's it going, fella?"

"How's it going? Everything is going loco. That's why I'm calling you. Days is organizing a SWAT team to bring in Orestes Vasquez."

"*What?* On what charge?"

"Well, it's not for casting spells. From what I hear, the DA has managed to get an arrest warrant for some pissant immigration scam. Kitchen staff from Colombia with no green cards, something like that."

"This is nuts. They don't have any idea what they're up against. You know that."

"It may be nuts, but right now the LAPD is looking like a three-ring circus, and Days wants to show the media that he's taking some action."

"Why Vasquez? What about the Zombie? Annie thinks that it was Michelange DuPriz who worked that toad trick."

"Listen, *muchacho*, don't keep talking that black magic stuff, *please*. Days is going after Vasquez because Vasquez is the one who threatened Chief O'Malley if he interfered in any of his rackets. Days believes that Vasquez pulled off this toad thing by way of showing

Chief O'Malley that he couldn't break his promise without suffering the consequences."

"Okay, maybe he's right. But how the hell does he think that Vasquez did it, unless it was black magic?"

"Search me. And I don't think Days has any idea either. Maybe he thinks he's going to find something incriminating at Vasquez's house."

"What? Like a lily pond? This is madness, man. You've seen what we're dealing with here."

"Dan, you know where I stand on this. I'm willing to believe it if you can show me the evidence. But so far—okay, yes, you puked up all that money right in front of my eyes. But I was brought up to believe in God and the Virgin Mary and the Holy Spirit."

"Oh, so nothing supernatural then? Do you know when SWAT is planning to go in?"

"Oh-three-hundred hours. When the White Ghost and most of his entourage are sleeping. Well, that's what they hope, anyhow. They've asked for uniformed backup."

"I'm going to call Days again. I have to. I can't let him do this."

"You think he's going to call this off because of some cock-and-bull story about witches?"

"I have to try, El Gordo. Listen, I'll call you back. If I can't persuade him, then you and me have to go to Silverlake when the SWAT team goes in and see what we can do to keep down the casualties."

"Who cares if the White Ghost gets wasted? Or any of those sacks of shit who work for him?"

"I'm not talking about Vasquez, you dummy. I'm talking about the SWAT team."

"Oh, come on. Those guys, they have helicopters and body armor and helmets and the most advanced weapons you can think of."

"Sure they do. But they don't have the power of the

voodoo, or whatever powers these other three witches can summon among them."

He could almost hear Ernie's jowls shaking over the phone, like a dog that had been swimming in a neighbor's pool. "I don't know, *muchacho*. But call me, yes. I'll come with you if I have to. You need a witness to prove to you how delusional you are. Let's face it, man. Witches? Maybe some other phenomenon. But *witches?*"

He called Deputy Chief Days. A woman with a nasal voice said that Deputy Chief Days was completely tied up and couldn't speak to anybody (especially a lowly detective from the West Hollywood Homicide Division).

"Tell him it's a matter of life and death."

Pause. "Why don't you send him an e-mail, Detective, and I can try to make sure he looks at it first thing tomorrow."

"Tell him tomorrow is going to be too late. This is about tonight. This is about Rosewood Avenue."

Another pause, longer this time. Then a hoarse young lieutenant came on the phone. "Detective Fisher? This is Lieutenant Corcoran. I've been asked to ask what you know about Rosewood Avenue."

"Rosewood Avenue is where Orestes Vasquez lives. The White Ghost. Your target for tonight."

"For God's sake, Detective, this is an open line."

"What do you want me to do, tap it out in Morse code? That SWAT team is in serious jeopardy. You don't have any idea how much. Deputy Chief Days needs to call this operation off until I've had time to talk to him about it."

An even longer pause. "You want to talk to Deputy Chief Days and tell him to cancel a full-scale SWAT operation?"

"Pretty much. That's it. Yes."

"What did you say your name was?"

"Dan Fisher."

"Okay, Detective Fisher. I'll make sure that the deputy chief is aware that you called."

"But—"

The line went dead. Dan thought of trying to call back, but he knew that it was futile. He called Ernie instead and said, "Ernie? We're on for tonight. Wear your vest. Oh, and Ernie? Wear your crucifix, too. The largest one you have."

Chapter Eleven

Orestes Vasquez, the White Ghost, lived in a $3.5 million house screened from Rosewood Avenue by a row of tall, dark cypress trees, but with views from the rear of the property up to the canyons and out over the Silver Lake Reservoir. It was a modern house, faced with prawn-pink brick. It had three stories and three balconies and looked more like a medieval castle than a family home.

Dan and Ernie were already parked across the street when the SWAT team arrived. They were sitting in Dan's Torrent listening to *tamboraza* music on the radio and drinking hot chocolate, which Ernie had brought in a flask. Dan didn't usually like hot chocolate, but Ernie's wife brewed it so rich and so dark that drinking it was like committing a sin, and he felt almost as if he ought to go to church and confess it.

"Here they come, God help them," said Dan, as two black vans pulled up in front of them. Seven other police vehicles were positioned around the immediate neighborhood—squad cars and SUVs—with twenty-one uniformed officers and a dog handler. Less than half a mile away, on Silver Lake Ridge, three ambulances were waiting, too.

"Who's this?" said Ernie, turning around in his seat, as a black Lincoln Town Car came up the slope and stopped right behind them.

Dan checked his rearview mirror. "Jesus. Deputy Chief Days. Looks like he's come to oversee this little operation in person."

Ernie switched off the music. "I hope for his sake that this doesn't go as wrong as you think it's going to go."

The doors of the black vans swung open, and two six-man SWAT teams climbed out, all dressed in black fireproof coveralls and black bulletproof vests, with black Kevlar helmets that made them look like clones of Darth Vader. They were carrying 9mm Heckler & Koch submachine guns and .45-caliber Colt automatics, as well as breaching shotguns for blowing open doors, flashbang and stinger grenades, and rifles that fired bean bags at high velocity.

Dan climbed out of his SUV and made his way across to the SWAT team's senior officer, a grim-faced sergeant who looked as if he had been the model for Major Chip Hazard in *Small Soldiers*.

The officer was waving to two high-grounders who were positioning themselves on the roof of the house next to the Vasquez residence. Dan flashed his badge and said, "Detective Fisher, Sergeant. Homicide, West Hollywood."

"Appreciate your support, Detective, although I don't think we're going to be having much trouble picking these particular clams out of their shells."

"As a matter of fact, sir, I didn't come to give you backup. I came to warn you off."

The sergeant was making complicated signals to one of the marksmen on the roof. When he had finished, he turned to Dan and said, "Excuse me, Detective, you've come here to do *what?*"

Already Dan could hear the deep throb of helicopters approaching over the hills. "You don't fully appreciate what you're up against, sir. It's not easy to explain this, but Orestes Vasquez has some very powerful people to help him."

"Detective, members of our team have been keeping this house under close surveillance for the past nine hours, and we know exactly who's in there, where they're located, and what level of threat they present."

The beat of the helicopters grew louder, and Dan began to grow increasingly worried. "You *think* you know how dangerous these people are, and under normal circumstances, yes, sir, your assessment would probably be spot on. But these are not normal circumstances, and these are not normal people."

"You want to explain that?"

"If I tried to, you wouldn't believe me. All I'm asking is that you postpone this operation until I've had the chance to prove how dangerous it could be."

The SWAT teams were hurrying across the road now, their soft-soled urban boots pattering on the blacktop. They gathered around high, studded gates that shielded the White Ghost's mansion from the world outside. Two officers began to fix a C2 explosive charge to the locks.

As they did so, two black Huey helicopters appeared over the hilltops, shining floodlights down onto the Vasquez house. They hovered only thirty feet over the chimneys, and Dan was deafened by the thump of their engines and the *whack-a-whack-a-whack-a* of their rotor blades. Their doors were already open, and four SWAT officers had fastened ropes to the D-rings at the rear, ready to rappel down to the roof.

The SWAT sergeant was shouting orders into his helmet mike. "Go! Go! Go! Let's breach that gate!

Blue leader, make sure you knock out those security cameras. Go!"

There was a muffled bang as the gates were blown apart, and brown smoke billowed across the street. The SWAT sergeant stalked toward the entrance, taking out his automatic as he did so, still barking instructions.

Dan followed him and shouted, "Sir! You still have time! I swear to God, you need to call this off!"

The helicopter's floodlights were swiveling all around, which made shadows lean at impossible angles, as if they were dancing or drunk. The SWAT teams were yelling, *"Go! Go! Go! Go!"* They ran up the driveway between Orestes Vasquez's five shiny black SUVs and vaulted over the ornamental flower beds and the decorative fish pools.

Dan stayed back by the blown-open gates. Maybe he was totally wrong and Orestes Vasquez would surrender without putting up a fight. But on the other hand, maybe he wouldn't, and before he got too close, Dan wanted to see if the White Ghost was going to retaliate—and if he did, how. Helicopters were beating over the rooftop, police armed with submachine guns were running all over the gardens. Yet nobody had switched on a single light inside the house, and so far Dan hadn't seen a single face at any of the windows.

"Let's have those doors open!" shouted the SWAT sergeant, striding up to the wide porch.

Two explosives officers set another small C2 charge between the double oak doors. At the same time, the four rope-sliders were beginning their descent from the helicopters.

Ernie came up behind Dan and said, "So much for black magic. Looks like we're going to collar Vasquez without even breaking a sweat."

But at that instant, there was a blinding crackle of lightning, right over the top of the house. It was so dazzling that Dan could still see it on his retina after it was gone, like the wriggling, jerking branches of an immense upside-down tree.

The two Hueys dipped and tilted, their engines moaning, and almost collided with each other. Below them, all four ropes were on fire, and the SWAT officers clinging to them were blazing, too. Dan could hear them screaming as they were swung around and around in fiery circles.

There was a bellow of thunder that made the driveway shake underneath his feet. Ernie crossed himself and said, *"Madre mia!"*

There was another blast of lightning, and this time it seemed to split itself into four convulsive snakes—each of which struck at one of the burning ropesliders. The men exploded in a shower of scarlet flesh, with heads and arms and rib cages flying in all directions, as if they had been bombed.

Thunder bellowed, and the ground shook so violently that mock-Greek statues tipped over, and the surface of the fish ponds shuddered. Dan could see the SWAT sergeant shouting into his helmet mike, and although he couldn't hear what the officer was saying, he could guess because the two helicopters abruptly angled away from the roof of the house and headed back toward the hills, each still trailing two burning ropes behind it.

As the beat of their engines faded, the explosives experts hurried away from the front porch, yelling, "Fire in the hole!"

There was a long pause. Then they yelled it again. *"Fire in the hole!"* But still nothing happened.

The SWAT sergeant stalked up to them in fury. "What the hell is wrong here? Blow those goddamn doors!"

Dan said, "I have to stop this. This is insane. It's going to be a massacre."

Ernie said, "Dan—"

"For Christ's sake, El Gordo, admit it! It's black magic! They don't stand a frigging chance!"

Dan dodged his way across the garden and ran across the driveway. Blood and smoking flesh were splattered everywhere. One of Vasquez's SUVs was draped in pale pink intestines, like a wedding car, and there was a Kevlar helmet with a head still in it lying in one of the flower beds.

Dan climbed the steps to the porch. The SWAT sergeant was pacing in agitation while the two explosives experts were desperately fiddling with the C2 charge on the door.

"This was supposed to be a surprise operation!" the sergeant was shouting at them. "A frigging *surprise*, get it? You might as well have sent them a polite letter to tell them what time we were coming!"

"It's the C2, sir. It's changed consistency. For some reason it won't detonate."

"It smells bad, too. Jesus, it smells like something dead."

"Sergeant!" said Dan. "You really have to call this off. What I told you—you've seen it for yourself! Vasquez has the power to wipe out all of us if he wants to, just like those poor bastards on the roof."

The SWAT sergeant ignored him and beckoned impatiently to three of his men trotting up the driveway, carrying a heavy, black breaching ram. "Let's have that baby here, now! If we can't blow this goddamned door down, let's knock it off its goddamned hinges."

"Sir," Dan persisted. "What do you think happened up there with those rope-sliders?"

"A goddamned flamethrower by the look of it, and grenades. How should I know? Now clear the area, Detective, before I have you forcibly cleared."

"There was lightning, sir. And thunder."

The SWAT sergeant looked up at the sky. "Do you see a storm, Detective?"

"No, sir, I don't, and that's my whole point. That lightning was created by unnatural forces."

"Right!" shouted the SWAT sergeant. "Stand back and let's effect some dynamic entry!"

Six of the SWAT officers positioned themselves around the porch, their submachine guns aimed at the doors, while one of them hefted up the breaching ram.

"Hold it!" Dan shouted. "I swear to God, you don't want to do this!"

The SWAT sergeant lowered his head for a moment like a man trying very hard to keep his temper. Then, without looking at Dan, he said, "You have three seconds to give me a three-word reason why not."

"There's a witch inside. Vasquez has a witch. She can kill you as soon as look at you. Or blind you. Or worse."

"A *witch?* As in, The Wicked Witch of the West?"

"Not a fictional character, sir. A real witch. She was the one who caused the chief to puke up a toad, and she was the one who killed those guys on the roof just now."

At that moment, Deputy Chief Days came striding up, accompanied by Captain Kromesky and Lieutenant Cascarelli. He looked around at the lumps of flesh that littered the driveway, and his mouth turned downward in disgust and disbelief.

"You shouldn't be here, sir," said the SWAT sergeant. "We're just about to breach the front doors."

"Oh, *now* you're going to breach the front doors?"

"We had a technical glitch, sir. It's all under control."

"It's all under control, is it? Four good men have been blown to smithereens and the media are starting to show up, and you're standing around here with your finger up your rear end."

"It's my fault, sir," Dan put in. "I've been advising the sergeant to exercise extreme caution. The White Ghost has a woman in there with very dangerous capabilities."

"A witch, apparently," said the SWAT sergeant.

Deputy Chief Days stared at Dan and said, "I saw you before at the hospital, didn't I, when the chief was taken in?"

"Yes, sir, you did, sir, and I was trying to warn you about the same woman then. Or women. There's more than one of them. Four, in fact."

"Are you *on* something, Detective?"

"No, sir. You've seen it for yourself. The hurricane at Chief O'Malley's house. The toads. And now this. These four guys getting blown apart."

Deputy Chief Days closed his eyes for two or three seconds. Then he said, "Get this officer out of here. I'll deal with him in the morning. Meantime, I want those doors open right now, and I want Vasquez and everybody else in that house arrested on every charge you can think of."

"Yes, sir."

"Okay, then," said Deputy Chief Days. "If that two-bit Colombian *traqueto* thinks he can declare war on the entire Los Angeles Police Department and get away with it, he has a very rude awakening in store. I'll have his balls."

"Everybody in their positions?" shouted the SWAT sergeant. "Let's do it!"

"Listen!" said Dan. "You should at least know what you're up against here! Cordon off the house, don't let Vasquez leave—but before you try to break in there, I have a friend who can tell you exactly what these witches are capable of!"

"I said, get this loony tune out of here," said Deputy Chief Days.

One of the SWAT officers took hold of Dan's arm and firmly pulled him away from the house. "Okay, take it easy," Dan told him. "I'm going." All the same, the SWAT officer took him all the way back to the gates and pushed him out onto the sidewalk.

"Just keep back, sir, please? Sergeant Miller's not the kind of guy you need to get riled."

Dan said, "You want some advice? Stay out here in the street. Make like you're having trouble persuading me to go home."

"What exactly are you talking about, sir?"

"I'm talking about saving your life, son. That's all."

"I'm not chicken, sir."

"I never suggested you were. But one day you're going to find out that there's a difference between 'chicken' and 'prudent,' and I just hope it isn't today."

Ernie was waiting for Dan outside. On the other side of Rosewood Avenue, behind a police cordon, a crowd of reporters and TV cameramen had already gathered, as well as local residents in their nightwear.

"I'm sorry, *muchacho*," said Ernie. "You can't explain anything to people who won't listen. We have a saying in Mexico: You can tell a joke to a stone but don't expect it to laugh."

They heard a hollow bang as the ram struck the heavy oak doors. Then another bang and another. Then shouting as the SWAT team poured into the house. Dan could see the lights from their guns rapier fencing with each other in the hallway.

They waited two or three minutes, but nothing happened. There was no more shouting, no more movement. Nobody came out of the house.

Dan looked at Ernie, and Ernie looked at Dan. "What the hell's going on? It's total silence."

Dan waited a moment longer, then walked across the road to the lead SWAT van, where a young communications officer with spiky hair was perched in front of his radio set. Dan showed him his badge and said, "What's happening, officer? It's all gone quiet in there."

The officer lifted one of his headphones away from his ear. "Every channel suddenly went dead on me, sir. I can't get nothing but static. It could have been that lightning."

"Okay. Just keep trying."

Dan looked along the police cordon. Fifteen or sixteen cops had gathered there now, most of the backup, including the dog handler and his German shepherd. They were standing around talking. The three ambulances had been called forward, too, and were waiting at the far end of Rosewood Avenue.

The crowd was very subdued, speaking in wavelike murmurs, as if they were already attending the funeral of the men who had been killed.

Dan went back to Ernie. "Still nothing?" he asked.

"Still nothing. Come on, it's only been three or four minutes. They're probably putting the bracelets on them right now."

As they were standing there, though, a sergeant and a patrolman from Metro came up to them and said, "We lost radio contact. Did they collar Vasquez yet?"

"I have no idea."

The sergeant was big and beefy with sandy hair and tangled eyebrows. He gave a sharp sniff, then he said, "Deputy Chief Days is in there. I think for the sake of our pensions we should make sure that he's not in any trouble. Morales, let's get a half dozen of the boys together. The worst they can do is accuse us of overreacting."

He strode back to the police cordon to assemble his men. As he did so, Dan touched Ernie on the arm and said, "I'll see you later, okay?"

"What do you mean?"

"I'm going back to take a look. I have to."

"You're not going in there by yourself?"

"I'll be okay. Or maybe I *won't* be okay. But I still have to go."

"You're loco! Wait for the backup!"

"Listen, Ernie, if that witch has done what I think she's done, I can't expect any of those other young guys to go in there. They have wives. They have girlfriends. They have children, most of them. What do I have? A recurring nightmare of Gayle."

"Dan—this is one thing you shouldn't do. It's quiet, for sure, but maybe it's quiet because the SWAT team has them all rounded up."

Dan listened. Still nothing from the house. He looked across at Ernie and from the expression on his face, Ernie could see that Dan was going to go anyhow.

"I'll cover you. Any sign that something's gone wrong, you get out of there, pronto. And that's an order."

Dan didn't stop to argue that *he* had seniority—at least as far as length of service and pay grades were concerned. He lifted his gun and entered the gardens, stepping through the ornamental flower beds with the rosebushes catching at his pants. He circled around the fishponds until he could see directly onto the porch.

The gardens were well lit, and the double doors were wide open, but inside the hallway it was unnaturally dark. Dan hesitated for a moment, then crossed the driveway, walking crabwise, his gun held in both hands. He climbed the steps of the porch, peering into the hallway, straining to see if there was anybody there.

"Anybody there?" he called. "Deputy Chief Days?"

He waited. Nothing.

"If there's anybody there, you'd better come on out and show yourselves."

Another long silence. Then he heard a hoarse voice shout, "Hey! Detective! What are you doing?" Glancing over his shoulder, he saw that the gingery police sergeant was stomping up the driveway toward him, accompanied by six or seven other officers, four of them carrying .223 carbines.

He lifted his hand to indicate that the police should stop where they were. When he turned back toward the house, he saw a tall, pale figure in the darkness of the hallway.

"Hey, come on out!" he shouted. "Come out where I can see you! And keep your hands up!"

"Please—it is not necessary to shoot!" called a Hispanic-accented voice, although it sounded amused more than frightened.

Out onto the porch like an actor playing Othello stepped Orestes Vasquez, with his hands half lifted. He was dressed in a white silk robe and white silk mules. His eyes, as usual, were dead and expressionless, but Dan could have sworn that—as Vasquez emerged from the shadows—he was wearing the ghost of a smile.

Vasquez was followed by Lida Siado. She was wrapped in a complicated arrangement of black loose-weave shawls, all overlapping and fastened together with decorative silver pins. Her hair was tied up in a black silk turban with a huge glittering brooch made of emerald and ruby crystals pinned to the prow of it. The brooch was fashioned to look like a green human skull with a red snake sliding through its eye sockets.

Dan could see four more figures behind them in the hallway—the bulky shapes of Vasquez's bodyguards.

"I need all of you to step outside with your hands where we can see them," he called out. "I need you to do it in slo-mo, you understand me? Sergeant, let's keep these clowns covered, shall we?"

The gingery sergeant had needed no telling. He had already fanned his men out around the driveway, with their carbines lifted. Dan thought: *Even a witch must be aware what a 60-grain .223 TAP polymer-nosed bullet can do to the human body.*

"All right, Mr. Vasquez," he said, "you want to tell me what's happened to our SWAT teams?"

Orestes Vasquez leaned toward Lida Siado and murmured something in Spanish. Lida Siado nodded and said, *"Accidente tragico."*

Orestes Vasquez looked back at Dan and gave him a shrug. "You heard what Ms. Siado said? A most tragic accident."

Chapter Twelve

"*Accident?* What are you talking about?"

"I am very sorry. None of them survived."

"They're *dead?* Are you pulling my chain?"

Orestes Vasquez shrugged again. "It was most unfortunate. There was nothing at all that we could do."

Dan lowered his gun. "Mr. Vasquez, there were twelve heavily armed men in those two SWAT teams. And the deputy chief of the Los Angeles Police Department was here, too, along with two of his senior officers."

"I am very sorry, Detective. We were powerless. We had no idea that they were police—they came bursting in before we could warn them."

"Warn them?" demanded the gingery police sergeant, harshly. "Warn them of what?"

"Tonight is a very special night in the mythical calendar of Colombia. Tonight we hold a ceremony to celebrate the creation of the world."

"What is this shit?"

"You should not underestimate it, Detective, or insult it. It is the very power from which the world was first made. Unfortunately, it can be very dangerous to those who do not understand it."

"Where are the SWAT teams, Mr. Vasquez? What have you done to them?"

"I will let you see for yourself. Please . . . follow me."

Dan climbed the steps, and the gingery sergeant followed him with his officers close behind. Vasquez's bodyguards stepped forward to block their way, but Vasquez said, "No . . . let them in. All are welcome to witness the terrible power of Father Naimuena."

"Just keep your hands where we can see them," Dan told him.

Vasquez and Lida Siado led them along the hallway, switching on the lights as they went, one chandelier after another. Like everything else in the house, the chandeliers were strikingly modern, like showers of shattered crystal. The floor was tiled in shiny white marble, and there were abstract paintings on each side in the styles of Pollock and Mondrian and Kandinsky.

By the time they reached the end of the hallway, it was glittering with light from one end to the other. Ahead of them was a pair of cream-painted doors with triangular gold handles. Orestes Vasquez turned around, and for the first time Dan noticed that there were fine speckles of blood on the lapels of his white silk robe.

"In here . . . this is my library," said Vasquez. "In here, we were holding our celebration when your police officers came bursting in. You can see by the marks on the doors where they battered them open, although it wasn't at all necessary. The doors were not locked."

"They *surprised* you?" said Dan. "How the hell could you be surprised? You had two helicopters hovering right over your roof, your front gates were blown open with explosive, and your front doors were knocked open with a breaching ram."

"I don't think you understand," said Lida Siado. "During the celebration of the creation of the world, none of us is aware of anything real."

"Well, you're absolutely right there. I *don't* understand."

"In the very beginning, when there was nothing, the world was created by an illusion. Father Naimuena attached the illusion to the thread of a dream and kept it there by nothing more than his own breath. It was a mirage, a mystery. For a while, we lose our consciousness of the physical world and become part of that mirage."

"Where are the SWAT teams?" Dan demanded. "Where is Deputy Chief Days?"

"Listen. Before you see them, you must understand what has happened to them. When we are lost in the mirage, we are guarded from harm by the spirit of the Night Wind, and the *kukurpa* creatures that always follow in the Night Wind's wake."

"The *what?*" asked the gingery sergeant. "What the frig are you telling us, lady?"

"I have told you all you need to know. Now you can see for yourself. Open the doors."

Without hesitation, one of Vasquez's bodyguards opened the double doors. Inside, it was very gloomy, but Dan could make out a large hexagonal room with a high ceiling that reached right up to the second story. On the far side of the library was a tall window, which must have looked out over the gardens at the rear of the house. The night was still inky black, so Dan could see his own reflection, like an explorer looking into the mouth of a cave.

One of the officers said, "Jesus, what's that smell?"

Dan sniffed. A thick, nauseating stench was rising out of the library, both metallic and sour.

"Let's have some illumination on the subject, shall we?" said the gingery sergeant.

The bodyguard clicked the switches, and a huge chandelier flooded the library with light.

"Holy Christ," said the gingery sergeant.

At first sight it looked as if somebody had emptied out a thousand cans of chopped tomatoes and used a shovel to spread them thickly across the carpet. But there were black flak jackets among the chopped tomatoes, and helmets and boots and bones.

Dan said, "This is *them?*"

"As I told you," said Lida Siado. "When we are lost in Father Naimuena's mirage, we have creatures that protect us. It was always so. Otherwise tribes in the Amazon could have waited until their enemies were celebrating the creation of the world and slaughtered them."

"How the hell was this done?" Dan asked. Everywhere he looked there was crushed flesh with bones sticking out of it, glistening under the myriad lights of the chandelier in every conceivable shade of red. "It's like these people went through a goddamned blender."

The gingery sergeant turned away and spoke on his radio. His voice was low and expressionless. "A dozen officers down, at least. I need medical examiners, I need crime-scene specialists, I need a fire department cleanup crew. I need them *now.*"

To Orestes Vasquez, he said, "You're under arrest, all of you, on suspicion of first-degree homicide. Taylor, Bryman—go search the rest of the house. Anybody you find, bring them down here."

The White Ghost looked unperturbed. "I thought that this would be your reaction, Sergeant. But you can see that, logically, there is no way we could have been responsible. How did we do this and in such a short time? How come your people made no attempt to protect themselves?"

"I'll let the crime-scene people work that out. Meanwhile, let's get you out of here."

Orestes Vasquez and Lida Siado went without any further protest. The bodyguards were quickly frisked for weapons, and then they were led away, too. Dan stood staring at the thick layer of human mush. It was horrifying beyond belief, but Orestes Vasquez was right. A hundred men with machetes in each hand couldn't have reduced two SWAT teams to this condition, even if they had been hacking away for hours. And the police hadn't fired a single shot in their own defense.

Ernie came in. He had obviously been warned by another officer what he would find, and he didn't say a word. All the same, he took out a large green handkerchief and pressed it against his nose and mouth.

"You're still going to tell me you don't believe in black magic?" Dan asked.

"This is impossible," said Ernie in a muffled voice. "How could anybody do this?"

"We're not talking about *who*," said Dan. "We're talking about *what*. Come on, let's get out of here. There's nothing that we can do."

They were just about to leave when Ernie caught hold of Dan's sleeve and said, "*Ssh!* Did you hear something?"

Dan listened. At first he heard nothing, but then he thought he caught a faint whimpering noise, more like a stray cat than a human being.

"It's coming from over there . . . behind that desk."

"Sounds like somebody's still alive."

They looked at each other. The only way to the other side of the library was to wade ankle deep through flesh and blood and human entrails.

"Maybe we didn't hear it," said Ernie. "Like, who could have survived *this?*"

But then Dan distinctly heard somebody calling, "Help me . . . please! Help me!"

There was nothing else he could do. He hesitated for a moment, then stepped into the ankle-deep glutinous ocean of human remains. He took one step, then another, and he found that it was very difficult to keep his balance. Beneath the soles of his shoes, the lumps of flesh were impossibly slippery and strings of connective tissue caught around his ankles like seaweed. He felt bones beneath the soles of his shoes, too, and several times he almost slipped. Halfway across, he began to feel as if he would never get to the other side of the room.

The worst part about it, though, was the noise. Each step produced a thick, succulent squelch when his shoe went in and a hollow sucking sound when it came out again.

He thought: *I can't do this. I have to get out of here.* Every breath filled his nostrils with the smell of blood and bile, and with every step the desk seemed to slide farther and farther away, like an optical illusion.

At last, however, he reached it. It was a large kneehole desk, made of some reddish South American hardwood, like abura.

"Help me," said the voice, weakly, and it sounded hopeless. *"Help me, somebody, please!"*

"Where the hell are you?" asked Dan.

"Under the desk. Please—help me to get out."

Dan made his way around the desk and peered underneath. There, in a fetal position, crouched Deputy Chief Days, his hair sticking up on end and his face smeared with blood.

"Are you hurt?" Dan asked him.

"I don't know. I don't think so."

Dan reached under the desk, took hold of the deputy chief's wrists, and dragged him forcibly out of the kneehole. Once he had emerged, the deputy chief remained on his knees for a while, panting.

"Am I the only one left alive?"

"Looks like it, sir. Don't know how the hell you managed it."

"My God. My God, it was terrible. Those *things*."

Dan helped him onto his feet. "What things, sir?"

Deputy Chief Days turned around and around, as if he were terrified that something was going to come running up behind him. "Those *things!* The SWAT team broke open the doors, and before we knew what was happening they came rushing at us, dozens of them. They started tearing those poor men to pieces. They didn't even have time to scream."

"Come on, sir. Let's get you out of here. Careful where you're walking—it's very slippery."

"Those things—I've never seen anything like them. I don't know what they were."

Dan took hold of the deputy chief's arm and wrapped it around his shoulders to give him some support. "Come on, sir. The sooner we get out of here the better."

But Deputy Chief Days stopped and stared at him. "They were huge—bigger than a man, and they were gray, and they were like insects, and they just came rushing at us, dozens of them."

"Sir, we need to get out of here. You're in shock."

"They had eyes, Detective, and claws and hundreds of teeth. There was so much blood spraying everywhere, I couldn't see anything."

Dan helped the deputy chief across the last few feet of pulpy, tangled remains. The older man's knees were beginning to give way, and when he reached the doorway he almost collapsed. Ernie grabbed his other arm, and between them, he and Dan half carried him into the corridor and sat him on a chair.

Three paramedics were just entering the house, and they immediately took over, wheeling in a gurney, lifting him onto it, and covering him with a crinkly thermal blanket.

They were about to roll him away when Deputy Chief Days said, "Wait."

He looked up at Dan. His face was ashy and his breathing was labored, but he managed to say, "I believe I was spared on purpose. That woman spared me."

Dan didn't know what to say. The paramedics started to push the gurney away again, but again Deputy Chief Days said, "*Wait!*"

He reached out for Dan's hand and grasped it tightly. "You warned me about witches, didn't you? Before we went in there, you warned me, and I didn't believe you. But when the SWAT teams went in and those things attacked them, she was standing there, she and Vasquez, and she was holding up this stick with a little skull on the top of it.

"Whenever one of those things came rushing toward me, she made a pattern in the air, and the thing turned away and wouldn't touch me. But there was so much blood. I tried to get out, but I went the wrong way, and that's why I hid under the desk. I didn't realize that I was the only one allowed to live."

"Don't worry about it, sir," said Dan, trying to pull his hand free. "We'll get them, Vasquez and that woman. They won't get away with it."

"No!" gasped Deputy Chief Days. "If you'd seen those things—you can't! There's no way that anybody can stop them. That's why she spared me, don't you see? I have to give the order!"

"Sir, we have to take you to the emergency room," interrupted one of the paramedics.

But still Deputy Chief Days wouldn't let go of Dan's hand. "I have to give the order."

"What order, sir?"

"To leave them alone. To turn a blind eye. Otherwise, it's going to be a massacre! Give them a week, and the LAPD will cease to exist." He finally released his grip, and the paramedics wheeled him away.

Ernie said, "He's in shock, yes? People say pretty weird things when they're in shock."

"He's in shock, sure. But I think he's right. I think that the White Ghost was giving him a message, and he understood it loud and clear."

"You mean—?"

"I mean that the mobsters and the racketeers in this town are telling us to leave them well alone, or else we'll *all* end up like steak tartare."

"And that's why they spared his life, so that he could give the order?"

"For sure. The only thing is, it makes me wonder even more why that other witch spared *my* life."

Chapter Thirteen

It was dawn by the time he arrived back at his apartment, and the morning was so warm and bright that Dan found it almost impossible to believe that the events of the night had actually happened. Annie's kitten Malkin was sitting outside her door. He bent down as he passed and stroked her, and she mewed.

He left his loafers outside his front door, because they were covered in dark brown blood and he would have to wash them. Inside, he peeled off his coat, switched on his TV, and started his coffeemaker. He was just in time to catch an NBC report that two SWAT teams had stormed Orestes Vasquez's house. Apart from that, however, the story bore no resemblance to what had really happened.

Dan stood in front of the TV, taking off his blood-stained pants and then his holster, and all he could do was shake his head slowly from side to side and say, "What? *What?* How can you—? *What?*"

"The SWAT teams were called in because Mr. Vasquez and his family were being held hostage by a Colombian drug gang that was under the mistaken impression that Mr. Vasquez was running a rival narcotics racket.

"Two SWAT helicopters were fired on by surface-to-air missiles and were forced to withdraw. But two ground teams successfully entered the house and—after a fierce fire fight with the drug gang—were able to rescue the Vasquez family and bring them out safely.

"There were several casualties among the SWAT teams, but no further details are being released until the next of kin have been informed.

"Mr. Vasquez—seen here arriving back at his home—said he had nothing but praise for the SWAT officers who had saved him.

" 'I understand that, regretfully, some of them were hurt in the line of duty. But this self-sacrifice only serves to remind us of the bravery and dedication of the policemen and women who uphold the law in this great city of ours.' "

Dan called Ernie. It took a long time for Ernie to answer, and when he did, Dan could hear a baby crying in the background. "Did you see the news?" he asked.

"I saw some fairy story, just like you," Ernie replied.

"Well, what the hell—it was a total fabrication! Total lies from beginning to end. I'm going to call Sara Brennan at the *Times*!"

"No, *muchacho*, you're not."

"What? What do you mean, I'm not?"

"You're not because you want to keep your job, yes? In a minute, you will receive a call from Sergeant Cutler. Every officer who attended the Vasquez bust has to come in to the station for a full debriefing at fifteen hundred hours. Meanwhile we are absolutely forbidden to say one single word to the media. Anybody who does will be instantly canned and could be looking at a jail sentence."

"A jail sentence? You're kidding me!"

"Something to do with obstruction of justice. Sergeant Cutler will tell you."

"So, telling barefaced lies and letting mass killers walk free—that doesn't obstruct justice in any way?"

"Take it up with Cutler. Meanwhile, I have a very shitty diaper to change. You want my advice? Never have kids. And if you do, never start them on solids."

Dan made himself a mug of blindingly strong espresso and stood in the middle of the kitchen, devouring three-quarters of a pack of Oreos without even tasting them and gulping down repeated mouthfuls of scalding-hot coffee.

He was on his way to the bathroom when the phone rang. It was Sergeant Cutler, ordering him to attend this afternoon's debriefing. "And you won't be making any comments to the media about last night's operations, Detective—regardless of what you might have been seeing on TV?"

"What I saw on TV, Sergeant, didn't bear any resemblance to last night's operations."

"There's a reason for that, Detective. Meanwhile, you're required to keep your lips zipped."

Dan took a long shower, standing with his face raised to the showerhead, and his eyes tightly shut. But he couldn't wash the picture of Orestes Vasquez's library out of his head. And he kept thinking of Deputy Chief Days turning around and around, terrified that something would come up behind him and catch him unawares.

Something larger than a man, something gray, something with claws and teeth.

Eventually, he toweled himself dry, drew down the blinds, and collapsed heavily into bed. He lay there for nearly an hour, motionless, staring at the corner of the pillow, telling himself that he badly needed sleep. He heard traffic outside. He heard somebody singing "It's *amore*" and doors slamming. He heard Annie calling out for little Malkin. "Malky! Malky! Where are you, sweetheart?"

But he also heard the soft, insistent scratching of a yucca branch against his window as it was stirred in the morning breeze, and it eventually took him off to sleep.

At first, he dreamed that he was standing on the ocean. It was a fine, breezy day, and he had discovered how easy it was to walk on water. All you had to do was keep your balance and anticipate the waves as they came rippling in to shore. You bent your knees slightly as a wave came toward you and allowed it to lift you a few inches, and then you straightened your legs as you came down again.

He was surprised how far down the coast he could see—at least as far as Redondo Beach. He could see yachts and sailboards and people swimming, and he could see girls Rollerblading along the sidewalk.

He thought, *No wonder Jesus was happy*.

After a few minutes, though, a bloodred bank of clouds began to roll in from the west. The ocean began to turn bloodred, too, and when he looked down, he saw that there were people floating in the water, just below the surface, staring up at him in desperation.

He started to panic and run toward the shore. With each step, however, his feet sank deeper into the water, and by the time he was thirty feet away from the beach, he was splashing through the waves right up to his knees.

He thought: *I have to get out of here. I have to find Gayle*. He knew that he shouldn't drive, because Gayle would be killed if he did, but maybe this was his chance to make everything happen differently and save her. Yet the sky was almost black, and the wind was rising, and sheets of newspaper were flying through the air, flapping and screaming like seagulls.

People were running for shelter and shouting out in confusion, and he knew that it would soon be so dark that he wouldn't be able to find his way home.

His Mustang was waiting for him, in the parking lot next to the sidewalk café. The red-and-white striped awning in front of the café was flapping wildly and threatening to tear loose. Tables were tipping over, and waiters were hurriedly trying to bring in armfuls of chairs.

To his relief, he saw that the Mustang's passenger seat was empty. He could drive home, even though he was drunk, and this time she wouldn't be killed.

"Gayle?" he called, just to make sure. "Gayle, are you there?"

A hand touched his cheek. "I'm here, Dan. Don't worry."

He opened his eyes. Gayle was sitting next to him on the bed—naked, slender, small-breasted, silhouetted against the blind. He looked up at her, and she was real, her face unblemished. She was smiling at him in that secretive way she always used to smile, as if she knew something about the world and the way in which the world worked that he would never find out.

"Why don't you go back to sleep?" she suggested. Her fingers stirred through his hair and traced the outline of his ear.

"You're *here*," he said, his voice thick with sleep.

"Where else would I be?"

He sat up, blinking at her in fascination and fear. He reached out and touched her shoulder. It was soft and warm and solid and real.

"It *is* you. You're here. How can you be here?"

"I don't know. Sometimes, things can work out differently."

Dan thought: *Maybe my dream really did change everything. Maybe the past didn't happen at all, not the way it did the first time. Maybe I was driving back from Gus Webber's wedding on my own and Gayle was never killed.*

He ran his hand all the way down her arm and took hold of her hand. She was still smiling, but in a different way now, as if she didn't understand why he was so amazed to find her there. But she *was* there, perfect in every detail, down to the pattern of tiny moles on her shoulder, like the constellation of Auriga, the charioteer. She was even wearing the choker she always wore, with beads that reminded him of blueberries.

The yucca branch scratched against the window, and her nipples crinkled in the warm draft that blew through the bedroom. She leaned forward and kissed him, first on the tip of the nose, then his eyelids, and then his lips. Her tongue slid into his mouth and explored his teeth, as if she were making sure that it was really him.

His penis uncurled and began to stiffen. Without taking her tongue out of his mouth, she reached down and encircled his shaft with her fingers, gently rubbing it up and down. He stared into her eyes, even though she was so close that he was unable to focus.

"You're real," he said, with a catch in his throat. "You're real, and you're alive."

She said nothing, but lay back on the pillow and pulled him after her. She parted her thighs, and her vulva opened like a pale pink fruit, overflowing with juice. She guided him into her, kissing his ears and his hair and nipping at his neck with her teeth.

This can't be happening, he thought to himself, as he pushed deep inside her. *She's dead, and her body was cremated.* But he could feel her as if she were real—her warmth and her wetness, her quick, soft panting against his shoulder. He could hear the traffic outside, and *Wheel of Fortune* on somebody's TV. He knew that he had been dreaming about walking on the ocean, but that had been too odd to be real. This was different. He could even see his pale blue bath towel where he had dropped it on the floor.

He tried not to climax too soon, but he couldn't hold back any longer. He made a snuffling sound, and his spine arched, and then he was shaking and shaking and he couldn't stop. Gayle lightly ran her fingertips up and down his back, so that his nerve endings tingled even more.

After a while he lifted himself off her and lay beside her. He reached down between her legs, but she took hold of his wrist and said, "Later, okay?"

"I'm sorry," he said. "It's been a long time."

"It doesn't matter. It was lovely."

He stroked her hair and wound it around his finger. "I need to understand this."

"What do you mean?"

"You were killed, and I went to your funeral."

"But here I am."

"I know. But what I need to understand is, have you come back? Like, are you some kind of a ghost, like that Patrick Swayze picture?"

"I *hated* that movie. It was so sentimental."

"Yes, but is that what *you* are?" He looked around the bedroom. "Or is this like a parallel universe or something?"

"I don't know. I feel perfectly normal. Maybe you had a bad dream, that's all."

She kissed him again, quickly, dozens of little butterfly kisses all over his face. Eventually he said, "Whoa, *whoa!*" and shielded his face with his hand.

"Don't you like me kissing you?" she teased.

"I love you kissing me. But I'm still confused. Tell me this: do you remember driving home from Gus Webber's wedding?"

She frowned at him. "What does that have to do with anything?"

"It's important. I just need to know."

"But that was so-o-o long ago."

"Yes, it was. Three years and twenty-six days to be precise."

"I remember you were very drunk. You were weaving all over the highway."

"And?"

"I was quite drunk, too. You drove me home, and you had to help me into the elevator because I could hardly stand up."

"I drove you home?"

"Sure."

"So what happened the next day?"

"I don't remember. I expect I stayed in bed with a hangover."

"You don't remember any accident?"

"Dan . . . you're being very strange." She climbed out of bed and walked across to the window. He hadn't forgotten how slim and beautiful she was, how pale and radiant her skin could shine. She pulled up the blind, and she was flooded in sunlight, so bright that she almost vanished.

"Hey," he protested. "Don't stand in front of the window. Somebody will see you."

She turned, and she smiled. "Then you'll know for sure that I'm real, won't you?"

They dressed, and went out onto the balcony, taking two frosty bottles of stout with them. Gayle was wearing a plain white blouse with short puffy sleeves, and very tight blue jeans, and Greek sandals. No earrings. She had never worn earrings, for some reason that she couldn't explain.

He said, "I have to go to the station at three. We

had a pretty disastrous night last night . . . two SWAT teams got wiped out."

"That's terrible. How?"

"I don't think I'm supposed to say anything about it, not yet."

She leaned over and kissed his cheek. "Not even to me?"

"You wouldn't want to hear about it anyhow. It was too damned grisly. Listen, I won't be longer than an hour. Do you want to wait for me here, or are you going to go back to your own apartment?" He hesitated, and then he said, "You *do* still live in your old apartment?"

She gave him another of those all-knowing smiles.

"Stay here," he said. "We can order Szechuan tonight, like we always used to. And you can sing along to the Scissor Sisters."

"When I was a child I had a fever," she sang, in a high, breathy voice, and laughed.

Dan went to the bathroom, took a leak, then combed his hair. He looked into his own eyes for an answer to what was happening, but he didn't have an answer, and he decided that he didn't really want one. Gayle had come back to him somehow—as a ghost or as a reincarnation of her dead self. Or maybe his life had been diverted onto another spur, like a train.

He went back out onto the balcony. Gayle's half-empty bottle of stout was still standing on the glass-topped side table, but there was no sign of Gayle.

"Gayle?" he called, going back into the living room.

No answer.

He checked the bedroom. "Gayle?"

Still no answer. She had gone. He went to the front door and looked outside, on the steps. Annie was out there with Malkin, sewing some beadwork.

"Hi, Dan! Everything okay?"

"I don't know. Did anybody pass you, just a few moments ago?"

"Yes. Mrs. Tedescu."

"Nobody else?"

She shook her head. "What's wrong?" she asked. "You look like you've just seen a ghost."

He was tempted for a moment to tell her that he had not only seen a ghost, he had made love to her, but he decided against it. It was too confusing, too inexplicable, and too painful, as well.

He went back inside and walked around the apartment a second time, even opening the closet doors in case Gayle was being childish and hiding. But she had disappeared.

He hesitated for a moment, biting his lip. He picked up the phone and dialed the number of Gayle's old apartment, which he had never had the heart to delete. It rang and rang, but nobody answered. He tried her cell phone number, but that was cut off.

It was ten of three, and he had to go. He took a felt-tip pen and scrawled a message on the kitchen notice-board: *Gayle—if I'm not here by the time you get back, wait for me!! Please!!*

He looked at the message and thought: *You're losing it, fella. You really are.* But he didn't rub it out. Whatever Alice-Through-the-Looking-Glass world he had found himself in, he still needed to see Gayle again.

He collected his wallet and his keys, and drove to the police station for the SWAT debriefing. As he went down the steps, Annie looked up, one eye squinched against the sunlight, and said, "Dan! Come for supper tonight, why don't you? I'm cooking a stir-fry with orchids in it. They're very good for the soul."

Chapter Fourteen

"Hey, *muchacho*, over here," said Ernie, beckoning Dan across to the window. The conference room at the West Hollywood police headquarters was crowded with detectives and uniformed officers and support staff, but instead of the usual laughing and banter, there was an awkward silence, punctuated only by coughs and the shuffling of feet.

Dan elbowed his way along the aisle, and as he did so, several detectives widened their eyes, as if to ask him what the hell was happening. They had all seen the TV news, and they all knew how distorted it must have been. Eighteen cops had been killed in only three or four minutes, including Captain Kromesky and Lieutenant Cascarelli, without any of them firing a single shot. Their bodies had been so mangled and so comprehensively ripped apart that it was going to take the coroner's department weeks to make formal identifications.

"Everybody's been pushing me to tell them what really happened," said Ernie. "The current scuttlebutt is that the SWAT teams were brought down by a pack of killer rottweilers."

"And you've said—?"

"*Soy una tumba.* My lips are sealed. You think I want to lose my pension? Besides, I don't know what really happened."

"Let's put it this way: They weren't attacked by any kind of dog, were they? They weren't attacked by anything you've ever seen before. Things from hell, that's what killed them."

Ernie frowned. "You look different."

"What do you mean, I look different?"

"I don't know. Did something happen today? You look like you've got something on your mind."

"I'll tell you later, okay?" said Dan, because at that moment Lieutenant Harris walked briskly into the conference room, carrying a clipboard tucked under his arm. Lieutenant Harris was a short, tough-looking man with cropped gray hair that could have been used to polish stainless-steel saucepans. His eyes were pale green with a slightly distracting squint, and his mouth was permanently downturned, as if he believed nothing and approved of nothing and wouldn't know a frivolous remark if it stung him on the back of the neck.

Lieutenant Harris waited until the coughing and shuffling had stopped, and then he said, "Last night, during a combined operation on Rosewood Avenue in Silverlake, the Los Angeles Police Department lost eighteen good men. A night of infamy. A night of *bloody* infamy. Exactly how that disaster occurred remains, for the time being, classified, subject to a full investigation. But I have to warn you that after last night, our lives are never going to be the same again. Last night was this division's nine-eleven."

He gave a signal to a young freckle-faced officer behind him, and the officer switched on a large LCD television screen. At first the screen showed nothing but a bronze LAPD badge with the motto *to protect and to serve.* But then Chief O'Malley appeared, sitting at a conference table, with Mayor Briggs on one side of him and Deputy Chief Days on the other. An assortment of police commissioners and senior officers stood in the background, looking confused.

Dan was shocked by Chief O'Malley's appearance. His face was ashen, and his skin was strangely stretched. His eyes looked as black as two cigarette burns. His mouth appeared almost lipless, and when he spoke his voice was whispery and harsh.

"Thought the chief was still in the hospital," said Ernie.

"He should be. For our sake, as well as his. I seriously don't like the look of this."

Chief O'Malley cleared his throat. "Before I say anything else, I want to express our grief for the eighteen good men who were killed last night and our heartfelt sympathy to their families and their friends. What happened was a terrible and unexpected tragedy, and our only consolation is that all of those men died bravely, and in the line of duty.

"They went out to protect their community and to serve this great city of ours, and they died, and we shall miss them all."

There was a long silence. Chief O'Malley kept running the tip of his tongue around his lips, as if he wasn't sure what he wanted to say next. Deputy Chief Days leaned over to him and whispered something in his ear, and he nodded.

In a strained voice, he said, "Whether we like it or not, what happened last night marks the end of an era in the LAPD. Last night showed us that times have moved on, and that we can no longer enforce the law by being authoritarian and inflexible. In other words, although we are still a police force, we can no longer police by force."

"*What?*" said Ernie. "What the hell is he saying?"

"The traditional methods of keeping order in our communities have been left behind. Today, there have been so many changes in social attitudes. We have far greater moral tolerance than we used to. We are much more ethnically mixed. And more and more, people are demanding to take responsibility for their own lives—not according to the hard-and-fast rules that society lays down for them, but according to their own consciences.

"I came here to Los Angeles determined as always to impose a law-enforcement regime of zero tolerance. Never give an inch. Period. But I recognize now that this highly diverse community can make no forward progress if a stone wall is set up in its path. The way ahead is to trust the good people of Los Angeles to keep their own city in order. From now on, the name of our policing policy is *symbiosis*—that is, living together for our mutual benefit with each part of our society assisting the others.

"It's like the Egyptian plover, a bird that lives on the backs of crocodiles in the Nile, feeding on parasitic insects that infest the crocodiles' skin. The Egyptian plover protects the crocodiles from ill health, but at the same time it's protected itself because its natural predators don't dare to come too close to the crocodiles' jaws."

"Crocodiles?" said Ernie in bewilderment. "What in the name of God is he talking about?"

Chief O'Malley poured himself a glass of water, and they could hear the carafe rattling against the tumbler.

"Look at him," said Dan. "He's terrified."

Next to him, Sergeant Kennedy was shaking his head. "I thought that O'Malley was supposed to be one of the hardest cops in history. O'Malley the Mallet, that's what they used to call him."

That's before Michelange DuPriz crammed his stomach with toads, thought Dan. *That's before bufotenine turned him into a zombie—afraid of everyone and everything, especially the* manbo *who controls him.* But he could see that, in a different way, Deputy Chief Days was equally unnerved. Deputy Chief Days had seen that the human body could be turned into finely chopped tomato in a matter of minutes.

Deputy Chief Days leaned toward the microphone and said, "Chief O'Malley and I have assembled a committee of influential citizens to discuss the reorganization of law enforcement. I'd like to introduce them to you."

The camera slowly panned to the left—and there, standing on one side of the LAPD conference room were Orestes "The White Ghost" Vasquez, with Lida Siado; Vasili Krylov, with Miska; and Jean-Christophe "The Zombie" Artisson, with Michelange DuPriz; and twenty or thirty bodyguards and henchmen. All were soberly dressed in black, except Orestes Vasquez, who wore a white double-breasted suit with a black armband.

There was a roaring shout of disbelief from the assembled policemen. "No *way,* man! Those slimeballs? What the hell is he thinking, man? They're killers! Krylov? That sack of shit? Vasquez? He's got to be out of his frigging mind!"

Lieutenant Harris banged his fist on the table for order, but when the policemen saw Chief O'Malley rise from his seat and walk around to shake hands with Vasquez and Krylov and Artisson, the shouting crescendoed, and they began to stamp their feet and hammer on the desks.

Chief O'Malley was saying something, but his voice was drowned out. It was only when Lieutenant Harris bellowed, "Shut the hell up! You may not like it, but you need to frigging listen!" that the policemen finally quieted down.

Chief O'Malley was saying, ". . . these three men all have reputations some of you may find questionable. I am not going to pretend that over the years they haven't had their names linked with various activities, such as drug running, prostitution, and arms dealing.

"But in this new age of mutuality, who better to police the narcotics trade than people who know every dealer and every connection from here to Bogotá? Who better to ensure the safety and health of sex workers than people who have been running brothels for decades? These men have unparalleled influence in every field of criminal activity, and if we work *with* them rather than against them, we can harness that influence to make Los Angeles one of the most civilized cities in the world.

"I give you symbiosis, ladies and gentlemen. I give you the law enforcement of the future."

There was more shouting and more stamping. Lieutenant Harris stood with his head bowed waiting for everybody to calm down. Dan could only think of what his father had said. *Nothing good can come out of this, if witches have teamed up with mobsters.* Well, they had, and in a matter of days they had used their magic to undermine everything the LAPD stood for.

Ernie said, "What do we do now?"

"I don't know, El Gordo. Maybe we could team up with Jimmy 'The Rat' Pescano and Ruben 'Scrappy' Villa—go out working the streets together?"

"The guys—they're not going to tolerate this. Look at them now."

"If the guys don't tolerate this, they're going to wind up same way as those SWAT teams. Ground beef. Or maybe worse."

"You will have to warn them, *muchacho*. Otherwise, there could be many more killings."

"I intend to, when they simmer down."

Dan looked back at the TV screen. Although he couldn't hear what they were saying, it was obvious that Chief O'Malley was having an intense conversation with Vasili Krylov. But he could also tell by their body language that Krylov was talking in his most bombastic Russian way and making demands, and that Chief O'Malley was agreeing with him and making concessions. In the background, Mayor Briggs, usually such a mountainous presence, was standing alone with his hand pressed over his mouth, as if he had forgotten where he was.

"Okay, everybody," shouted Lieutenant Harris. "Let's put a sock in it. We need to discuss where we're going to go from here."

"Are you kidding me?" Sergeant Kennedy demanded. "The only place we need to go from here is round to the Parker Center and blow those three scumbags away."

"Kennedy, use your intelligence. Something serious has happened, and the chief is clearly under extreme pressure. It's not for us to second guess our superiors. All we can do is shut up and assess the situation before we go in with all guns blazing."

"But for Christ's sake, Lieutenant, look at him! The Mallet? More like the goddamned Marshmallow! Schmoozing with Krylov, of all people, and the Zombie, and Vasquez. Vasquez had his sister's boyfriend wrapped up in razor wire, stark naked, and dangled from the overpass at the Hollywood Split. I cut the poor bastard down myself."

Lieutenant Harris tried to settle everybody down, but the conference room remained in uproar. Dan, however, walked slowly over to the TV screen, so that he could see the pictures from the Parker Center more clearly. There was Michelange DuPriz, smiling at him as if she could sense that he was watching her, haughty and erotic and almost skeletally thin. There was Lida Siado, smiling and laughing, as if she were hosting a party. And Miska, the white-haired Russian witch, in a black puffball dress decorated with black ostrich feathers. She had a sly, cold look in her eyes, her irises as reflective as liquid mercury.

The young freckle-faced officer came over to switch off the TV, but Dan said, "Hold up!"

He had seen somebody else in the background, another strange woman. She was standing by the window with her back to the conference room, facing northeast, so that she was mostly in shadow. On her head she was wearing a floppy, wide-brimmed bonnet, almost like a nun's wimple but made of soft gray fabric. Over her shoulders she wore a long gray cloak, which was either tattered with age or deliberately torn, with feathers and knots and beads tied all over it. Dan guessed from the way that she was stooped over that she was elderly, but he couldn't see her face. He could only see a single hand in a long gray leather glove—a hand that was holding a long wooden staff with a knob on top of it about the size of a man's clenched fist.

Ernie came up to him. "What are you looking at so hard, man?"

"This old woman. What the hell is *she* doing there?"

He turned to the young officer and said, "Can you record from this TV?"

"Sure. It's fully digital. You want me to?"

Dan nodded. "You remember I told you that Annie and I located a fourth witch, an extra-powerful witch? Or at least *she* located *us*."

Ernie took his heavy-rimmed eyeglasses out of his

shirt pocket, put them on, and peered closely at the TV screen. "You think this could be her?"

"Well, she sure looks like a witch, you have to admit."

Ernie's nose was almost touching the screen when the elderly woman snapped her head around and glared at him. Ernie jolted back. The woman's eyes were milky white, like a boiled cod's, and her skin was shriveled, as if she had been hung out in the sun to dry.

She raised her staff toward him and screamed something, although they couldn't hear what she was saying. Her teeth were a jumble of brown and blackened stumps, and there were clusters of warts all around her mouth.

The clenched fist on top of her staff wasn't a fist at all, but a stuffed cat's head with empty eye sockets.

"*Madre mia*," said Ernie, crossing himself twice. "If I didn't know she couldn't see me—"

"Oh, I think she *can* see you," said Dan. "I think she can see you clear as day."

The elderly woman had turned back to the window now, but Ernie still kept his distance. "That's one real genuine witch, *muchacho*. I mean, that's like your storybook witch."

"Where do you think that storybook witches came from, man? My grade-school teacher always used to say that everything you read about in stories is based on something that really existed. Dragons, giants, demons. At one time, they were all walking the earth, and some of them still are."

Ernie said, "Now you believe in fairy stories? What happened to Dan the skeptic? Something to do with what happened today?"

"You're a perceptive man, El Gordo."

"My brother is a Capuchin monk. I know when a man has found faith."

The debriefing went on for another forty minutes. Lieutenant Harris cautioned his officers not to overreact to Chief O'Malley's announcement or his apparent truce with three of L.A.'s most notorious mobsters.

"What happened at the Vasquez joint last night— the massacre of all those men—it probably required a very diplomatic response from the chief, so as to prevent any more slaughter. We may not understand what he's doing. We may disapprove of what he's doing. But he's a very experienced chief of police, and I believe he deserves our loyalty.

Lieutenant Harris clasped his hands behind his back and lifted his chin. "All the same, I want this division to make it our business to gather as much incriminating evidence on Artisson, Vasquez, and Krylov as we possibly can. I want those scumbags followed twenty-four seven. I want to know every deal and every single act of intimidation, no matter how petty. I want to know what they eat for breakfast. I want to know what their *mothers* eat for breakfast. I want every house bugged and every phone call tapped. I want to know when they park two inches over a red line. I want to know what their shit weighs.

"As far as other felons are concerned, give them only your minimum attention. I want these three. I want so much evidence against them that all the symbiosis in the world can't keep them out of the slammer."

The room broke out into spontaneous applause, with whooping and whistling.

"Maybe as law enforcement officers we *have* fallen behind. Maybe we're not as morally tolerant as we ought to be. Maybe we don't show enough respect for ethnic groups like the Crips and the Bloods. Maybe we're too authoritarian and we enjoy kicking people too much.

"But we have eighteen of our brother officers to avenge, however they died, and that's what we're going to do. That's all, gentlemen and ladies. Get to it."

Chapter Fifteen

Dan rapped on the door of Lieutenant Harris's office.

Lieutenant Harris was talking on the phone to one of the LAPD media directors, and he gestured to Dan to sit down.

"Yes, George. No, George. We're sticking to the same line, George. All for one and one for all. Absolutely, George. Symbiosis, that's the word." He put down the phone and said, "Asshole."

Dan pulled a very tight grimace. "I'm afraid he has a point, Lieutenant, in a way."

"What, with this symbiosis shit? I don't know why we don't hand over our weapons and our patrol cars to the mobsters and go on vacation."

"I know how you feel, sir. I saw those SWAT guys, all torn to pieces. I had to wade through them, up to my ankles."

Lieutenant Harris tilted his chair back. "But? There *is* a but coming, isn't there?"

"Yes, sir. Those guys were killed by something totally unstoppable. Not men with machetes. Not rottweilers. Things from someplace else. Things that appeared, ripped them all up, and disappeared in minutes."

" 'Things'? 'Things from someplace else'?"

Dan held up both hands. "Let me tell you straight, sir. Whether you believe me or not, that has to be up to you. But so far I think there's enough evidence to prove that this is what happened. In fact I don't think there's any other explanation.

"Krylov and the Zombie and the White Ghost have all brought in women with occult powers. Witches, for want of a better word. They're using the women to take over all the criminal activity in Los Angeles and to render the police completely impotent.

"Michelange DuPriz, the Zombie's witch, burned Cusack, Knudsen, and Fusco. She put those toads in Chief O'Malley's gut, too. Those are voodoo specialties. Lida Siado, the White Ghost's witch, blinded those guests at Chief O'Malley's party, and she was the one who called up those creatures who massacred our SWAT guys. That kind of magic, that comes from Colombia.

"I don't know what Vasili Krylov's witch has been up to, but it won't be anything but mischief."

"Dan," said Lieutenant Harris. "Have you heard yourself? *Witches?*"

"I know," said Dan. "I didn't want to believe it myself. But Michelange DuPriz gave me a personal demonstration of what she can do. You remember that old slot machine routine I used to pull? Bringing up a mouthful of quarters? Well, Michelange DuPriz made me do it for real. She made me puke up thirty dollars in change."

"What?"

"I'm trying to tell you that this is *real*, Lieutenant, no matter how insane it sounds. Real witches, real magic. Chief O'Malley knows it's real, and so does Deputy Chief Days, and that's why they're giving the Zombie and Krylov and the White Ghost exactly what they want. There's no point in fighting a fight we can't possibly win. Those three women—they could wipe out the entire LAPD in minutes if they had a mind to."

Lieutenant Harris stood up and went to the window. *"Witches?"* he repeated.

"They could cremate us on the spot, Lieutenant. They could tear us to ribbons, or they could turn us all mad. They could choke us on toads or bugs or cicadas or cats or any other kind of animal they felt inclined to. The only reason they haven't is because they need us to keep the city running and keep all their rivals in order."

There was a very long silence while Lieutenant Harris stood with his hands in his pockets, thinking. Eventually, he said, "Okay, *okay*. Suppose I accept that you believe in all this?"

"I do, Lieutenant. After what I've seen."

"Suppose I accept that you believe in all this, and I ask you to find a way to take out those witches. Exorcize them, or burn them at the stake, or whatever it is you do with witches."

"I'll do it. I'll try, anyhow. I have one or two ideas already."

"Right, then. That's your assignment. Witch hunter. If there's anything you need—bells, books, or candles, just ask for them."

Dan stood up. "Lieutenant—"

"No, Dan. That's what I want you to do, just in case by some mathematically infinitesimal chance you happen to be right. Meanwhile, me and the rest of the division will work on gathering substantive evidence against Krylov, Vasquez, and Artisson in the traditional out-of-date, non-occult way."

"Sir, what I'm trying to tell you is that if you try to arrest any of those three or interfere in any of their activities, they will have their witches kill you. And I mean *wholesale*."

Lieutenant Harris came up to him and carefully adjusted Dan's flowery red necktie, the way a wife would adjust her husband's necktie before he went out to a business meeting. "In that case, Dan, you'd better make sure that you do your witch-hunting stuff pretty damned quick."

The young freckle-faced officer was waiting for Dan outside Lieutenant Harris's office. "Here's the DVD you asked for, sir."

"Thanks, officer. Appreciate it."

The officer hesitated for a moment, frowning, and then he said, "Did I hear you and the lieutenant talking about *witches?*"

"Think you misheard us. *Snitches*, that's what it was. Snitches."

It was well past 8:00 PM before he arrived back at Franklin Avenue. Annie was sitting outside on the steps, waiting for him.

"I thought you'd forgotten."

"You said you had stir-fried orchids on the menu. How could I forget?"

Annie was wearing a simple cream linen dress. Dan could almost see the dark rose smudges of her nipples, and her black hair was wound with colored beads.

"Listen," he said, "I'll just drop my stuff in my apartment, and I'll be straight back down."

"Okay . . . but don't be long. There's nothing worse than overcooked orchids."

He helped her up. As he took hold of her hand, he felt a prickle of energy, almost like an electric shock. It made the hairs on the back of his neck stand up and his shoulders tingle. "Hey," he said. "You're all full of static."

"I know. I can't touch anything without it going *snap!* When I picked up my wok I even got a spark. I thought it was the weather."

Dan looked up. The evening sky was completely clear, and a light, warm breeze was blowing. "It's not the weather. It's you. You're all charged up."

"Go dump your stuff," she told him. "There's a brewski waiting for you when you come down."

Dan went up the steps to his apartment and unlocked the door. *Please let Gayle be here*, he thought. But he was also seriously frightened in case she was. No matter how beautiful she was, no matter how tantalizing their lovemaking had been, she was dead.

He switched on the lights. There was nobody in the living room. In the kitchen, his note was still on the message board. Of course, there was no way of telling, but somehow it looked unread. He went through to the bedroom and there was nobody there either. The purple-and-blue throw was still twisted, the way he had left it when he went out.

He stood in the bedroom doorway for a long moment. *You're losing it, Dan. Why don't you face it—you had a dream or some kind of hallucination, probably brought on by post-traumatic stress. You didn't want to think of the mashed-up bodies of those two SWAT teams, so you imagined that you were making love to Gayle to blot it all out.*

He walked around the bed and switched on the bedside lamp for when he came back later. It was then that he stepped on something hard and round on the floor, right on the ball of his foot. He looked down, and beside the bed he saw a scattering of beads. Cloudy, dark blue beads, like blueberries. Beads from Gayle's necklace.

He carefully picked them up, eight or nine of them, and held them in the palm of his hand. He bent his head forward and smelled them, and they smelled like Gayle's favorite perfume, Noa by Cacharel. Without warning, his eyes filled with tears, and he had to wipe them with the heel of his hand, like a small boy. Gayle *must* have been here, dead or not, and here was the proof.

"You're very quiet," said Annie, her eyes sparkling in the candlelight. "Don't you like it?"

Dan picked up his fork. "It's terrific, all of it. The eggplant, the beansprouts, the oranges. What do you call this stuff with lentils?"

"*Sambaar.* It's Indian. Cauliflower and cabbage and carrots in a red dhal sauce."

"Terrific. I even enjoyed the orchids."

"Like I said, they're really good for the soul. If your soul is troubled by anything, especially things you should have done but didn't, orchids will always help you to see things more clearly. Have you looked inside an orchid? It always has lines, showing you which direction you should travel."

Dan said, "Listen . . . I have to talk to somebody about this. I think I'm hallucinating."

"What, now?"

"No, this morning, after I came back from Silverlake. I saw Gayle again. Well, I didn't just *see* her. She was sitting on my bed. Goddamn it, Annie, she was *alive.*"

Annie reached across the table and held his wrist. "Dan, she's *dead.* You know that."

"I know. Logically, I know. But I could see her, and more to the point, I could *feel* her. She talked to me." He hesitated for a moment and took a deep breath through both nostrils. "We had sex."

Annie didn't release her grip on his wrist. "How real did it feel?"

"What do you mean? It was *totally* real. She was warm . . . she felt like she always felt. She breathed in my ear."

"In that case, you have a serious problem."

"I don't understand."

Annie stood and walked across to her bureau. She opened it and started to rummage through the drawers, bringing out glass balls and skeins of wool and playing cards and lacquered skewers that looked like Japanese chopsticks.

"When we've finished eating, I'll do some divining. If this woman felt real, Dan, then she probably was real. But Gayle is dead, so it couldn't have been Gayle. So it was somebody else, impersonating Gayle."

"How could it have been? Come on, Annie—I'm sure it was Gayle. One hundred and thirty-eight percent. *You* get in touch with dead people, don't you? Can't they ever cross over from the other side, something like that? Can't they come back, even if it's only for twenty minutes?"

"No, Dan, they can't. Or at least they've never been known to, no matter what anybody says."

"But how can somebody make you think that they're somebody they're not?"

"It's done by a kind of hypnosis. It's like Capgras Syndrome in reverse."

"*What* syndrome?"

"Capgras Syndrome. It's a kind of paranoia, when people believe that their friends and even their family are all impersonators. Only in your case, somebody else is making you believe that she's Gayle."

"You think it could be one of those witches?"

"I don't know who else it could be. But I can't think why she's doing it."

They ate in silence for a while, and then Dan laid down his fork. "Do you mind if I use your bathroom?"

"Sure."

Unlike his own bathroom, which was starkly decorated in black and gray, Annie's looked like a Santería shrine—crowded with painted statuettes and candles and colored glass bottles and exotic seashells. He went to the washbasin and stared at his face in the mirror. He could almost believe that he was an impersonator, too—an impersonator who badly needed a shave.

He splashed cold water on his face and reached for a hand towel. When he looked in the mirror again, he gave a jolt of shock. A bald black man was standing close behind him. The man had a coronet of brown human teeth tied with twine around his forehead and pale gray ash smeared all over his face. The man grinned and revealed that his own teeth were filed into points.

"*Bon swa, mesyé,*" the man greeted him. His voice was as dry as the ash on his cheeks. "*Komon ou ye? Tout bagay anfom?*"

Dan looked around, breathing fiercely. He hadn't heard the bathroom door open, hadn't heard the man walk in. And the reason was—there was nobody in the bathroom but him.

Immediately, he turned back to the mirror. The man's reflection was still there, grinning at him, his eyes scarlet-rimmed and wildly staring.

"Don't be afraid, *mesyé.*"

"Who are you?" Dan asked unsteadily. "What are you? What the hell do you want?"

The man continued to grin, as if he were mad. "I come with a message, *mesyé.*"

"Message? What message?"

"I come to give you a warning that some of the people close to you, they are not what they seem to be."

The man was dressed in a shabby gray double-breasted suit, a funeral suit, although he was wearing no shirt underneath it, only a detached collar that was so dirty it was a waxy yellow color. Dan sniffed, and he picked up the faintest aroma of dried herbs and the smell of something else, too, something vinegary, like a very old jar of pickled cucumbers with mold on top of it.

"How come I can see you in the mirror but you're not really here?"

"There are doors everywhere, *mesyé*. In front of mirrors, and behind them. All you have to do is to walk through them."

"Did Michelange DuPriz send you?"

"Of course. She says that you must beware, *mesyé*. You will think that some of the people close to you are your friends. You will believe that they can help you. But all the time they are ready to betray you. One in particular to watch out for special."

"Who? Who are you talking about?"

"Can't say more, *mesyé*. All things pass."

"What the hell are you talking about? Who's going to betray me?"

Dan reached toward the mirror, but as he did, the man's face suddenly appeared to shudder, as if he were having a fit. He was still grinning, but brownish maggots began to drop out of his nostrils, and then he opened his mouth and inside it was seething with maggots, all over his tongue.

He opened his eyes wide, and maggots wriggled out of his eye sockets and dropped down his cheeks. Right in front of Dan, his entire head burst open and maggots poured out like a fountain.

He collapsed onto the floor and promptly disappeared from Dan's view. Dan gripped the sides of the sink and pressed his forehead as close to the mirror as he could, but all he could see on the floor of the reflected bathroom was the frayed cuff of a pair of worn-out pants with a foot protruding from it, but a foot that was made out of nothing but seething maggots.

Dan took two or three steps back. His teeth were chattering, as if he had the flu, and he couldn't stop them. The black man had been there, clearly visible in the mirror, yet he hadn't been there at all, and then he had exploded into a mess of maggots. Dan felt that he was close to the very brink of going crazy.

He was still trying to calm himself down when he heard Annie let out a low, loud moan. "Oh, God! Oh, God, *no!*"

"Annie? *Annie!*" He wrenched open the bathroom door and hurried along the passage that led to the living room.

When he pushed open the living-room door, he couldn't understand at first what he was looking at. The carpet was no longer crimson but a pale whitish color, and it appeared to be *rippling*, as if a draft were blowing underneath it. The walls were rippling, too, and now and again it looked as if small crumbs of plaster were dropping off the walls onto the floor.

Annie was standing in the middle of the room, her shoulders hunched, her hands pressed over her mouth. She was making a soft whimpering sound, like an injured animal.

It was only when he took a step forward that Dan realized the entire room was thickly carpeted with maggots, thousands and thousands of maggots, and that the walls were crawling with maggots, too, which occasionally dropped off onto the floor. Their convulsive rippling movement made the whole room look as if it were alive.

Some of the maggots were already hatching into blowflies and droning around the room or clinging to the drapes. The smell was appalling—sweet and thick— and Dan had taken only two or three breaths before his stomach knotted up like a twisted rubber band, and his mouth filled with a sour rush of half-chewed eggplant.

He spat. He had to. He wiped his mouth with the back of his hand, and then he called, "Annie! Annie, just get the hell out of there!"

"I can't— I can't— *I can't bear maggots! I can't bear maggots!*"

"It's okay! They won't hurt you. Just look me in the eyes, and walk straight toward the door. Don't look down!"

"I can't, Dan! I can't bear them! Oh God, they're crawling up my ankles!"

Dan hesitated for a moment, then said, "Wait! Don't move! I'm coming to get you!"

He stepped into the room and negotiated his way toward her, trying to avoid the deepest heaps. The maggots squashed softly as he walked on them, and some of them wriggled onto his shoes, so that he had to shake them off. He was used to the maggots that infested decomposing bodies, but he had never come across them in such overwhelming numbers, blindly crawling over one another and piling up in the corners of the room. Even the tables and chairs and bookcases looked as if they were made of maggots.

Dan reached Annie and lifted her into his arms. She weighed hardly anything, like a child. She squeezed her eyes shut and clung tightly to his neck. He carried her out of the living room and into the kitchen, then set her down. Malkin was sleeping under the kitchen counter, but when Dan and Annie came in, they woke her up. She jumped out of her basket and circled anxiously around them, mewing.

"Hey, are you feeling okay now?" Dan asked Annie.

She nodded. "Still sick. Those maggots—I can almost *taste* them."

Dan brushed the last few maggots from Annie's calves and ankles, and Malkin playfully patted them as they twisted and writhed on the floor. Dan picked them up with a paper towel, pinched them hard, and dropped them into the trash.

He said, "When I went to the bathroom, I saw somebody in the mirror. *He* turned into maggots, too. He literally fell to pieces, right in front of my eyes."

"You saw somebody in the mirror?"

"It was only a reflection. A black guy with ash on his face, like a zombie. I could see him standing right behind me, and he even talked to me, for Christ's sake. But when I turned around he wasn't there at all."

"Mirror walking," said Annie. She took a deep breath, beginning to recover. "That's not voodoo. That's more like Eastern European magic. Vampire stuff."

"Krylov's witch, maybe."

"The maggots, though—they're *definitely* voodoo. It looks like these witches are all working together, combining their different kinds of magic. This is going to be a nightmare."

"Come on," said Dan. "Let's get the hell out of here. I know a guy who can clear up all these maggots for you—Vernon Johnson. He's an exterminator."

Annie shuddered. "I'm not squeamish about anything at all except maggots. I don't mind spiders, and I don't mind snakes. I don't even mind slugs. But *maggots!*"

"Personally, they don't worry me, maggots. But I really have this thing about centipedes. Whenever I see a centipede in my bedroom, I'm always afraid that it's going to crawl across my pillow in the middle of the night and sneak into one of my ears."

Annie picked up Malkin and stroked her. "I guess the thing is, I had a dog when I was seven years old, Biffo. He was only a mongrel, but I loved him. He got caught in a barbed-wire fence, and he must have died of starvation. When I found him, I didn't realize he was dead. I picked him up and all of these maggots poured out of his stomach."

Dan put his arm around her. "Come on, you're going to be okay now. I think we could both use a drink."

"No, I think it's better if I deal with these maggots first. They were brought here by magic, so they can be sent back by magic. I don't know much about voodoo, but there have to be other ways—other kinds of magic. If those witches can do it, so can I."

"I told you—Vernon will clean them up for you. He owes me a couple of favors."

"Dan, we can't let these witches win. The more we allow them to win, the stronger they'll become. They feed on people's fear of them. We have to fight magic with magic."

"So what are you planning to do?"

"There's a book on the third shelf of the bookcase by the window, on the right-hand side. It's a thin book, bound in very dark leather. Can you get it for me?"

"You mean it's in *there*—where all the maggots are?"

Annie nodded. "It has *The Book of Flies* embossed on the front."

"*The Book of Flies*?"

"Maggots are fly larvae, aren't they? And flies are witches' familiars, as well as being messengers from Satan. *The Book of Flies* tells you how to dismiss them."

"And it's in there—where all the maggots are?"

"You said you didn't mind maggots."

"In moderation, no. But good old Vernon could be here in less than twenty minutes, and good old Vernon has a vacuum cleaner that could suck up a full-grown elephant."

"Dan, you don't understand. If we let those witches get away with this, what they do next could be so much worse."

Dan looked dubiously at the living-room door. "Third shelf, on the right-hand side?"

"That's the one."

Chapter Sixteen

He came out of the living room, his lips tightly pursed to prevent the blowflies from buzzing into his mouth, one hand flapping to keep them away from his eyes. He used the side of his shoe to push back the maggots that were spilling into the kitchen and pulled the door shut.

"*Yuck*," he said, handing Annie the book. "I hope that was worth it."

"Thanks. I never could have done that—not in a million years."

Dan bent down to smack at the cuffs of his pants in case any maggots had crawled onto them. Malkin was gleefully pouncing on the maggots that were wriggling on the kitchen floor.

Annie laid the book on the kitchen table and opened it. It had been handwritten in purplish-black ink, and its pages were water stained and discolored, so that some of them were almost illegible.

"This was originally written by Fray Angélico Benavides in the seventeenth century. Fray Benavides was a Franciscan missionary among the Pueblo tribes in New Mexico, and he was one of the first Spaniards to learn the language of the Nahbah-tóo-too-ee."

"The Nahbah-tóo-too-ee? You're not putting me on, are you?"

"That's their Indian name. They used to be well-known for practicing witchcraft and especially for changing themselves into other creatures, like hawks or coyotes or antelope or owls. There are scores of legends and stories about them."

"I never heard of them."

"Well, these days they're almost extinct. But up until the end of the seventeenth century, when the Spanish really settled New Mexico in force, the Nahbah-tóo-too-ee's council of witches was the most powerful in the Southwest. Nobody dared speak out against them or disobey them. If you challenged them, they would send swarms of flies out looking for you, all clustered together in the shape of human figures. They would come to your house, and then the figure would burst apart into thousands of separate flies, and they would crawl into your nose and your mouth, and into your lungs, and choke you."

"Thanks for telling me. As if I didn't feel nauseous enough already."

"Witches all over the world use flies in every culture—Christian or Muslim or pagan. But the Nahbah-tóo-too-ee witches were notorious for it. They killed scores of their traditional enemies with flies, mostly Zuni and Acoma, fourteen Franciscan friars, too—all of them choked. But when Fray Benavides taught himself the Nahbah-tóo-too-ee language, he was able to translate some of the magical rituals the witches used to perform in their kivas, their underground chambers. He found out that the swarms of flies could be sent away, as well as summoned, so long as you knew the right incantation for it."

Annie turned to a page of several pen-and-ink drawings of maggots and flies and densely written text.

"I need blood," she said.

"Blood? What kind of blood?"

"Human blood. Mine. Don't worry—I don't need very much."

She opened one of the kitchen drawers and took out a sharp paring knife. Dan watched her and winced as she sliced open the ball of her thumb. Dark red blood slid out, and she held it toward him.

"Here, paint it on my eyelids."

Dan hesitated, but Annie closed her eyes and said, "Hurry up—before it congeals. The flies will obey you only if you look like a devil or a demon, with blood for eyes. It's the same in every religion."

Dan rubbed blood onto the tip of his finger and carefully smeared it on Annie's eyelids. She looked horrific, as if she had lost both eyes in a serious accident. She waited for a moment until her eyelids had dried, and then she opened them.

She found the place she wanted on the page in front of her. "This is the only English-language translation I've ever seen. My mother gave it to me on my eighteenth birthday."

"Really? My mom gave me a lime-green T-shirt and a John Denver CD, God bless her."

"Well . . . my mother always wanted me to have the craft. Just like my grandmother and my great-grandmother. She said that the craft is the only thing that gives women total superiority over men."

"That's funny. I always thought it was, like, sex did that."

"No, even if they've studied magic all their lives, men don't have the same natural power as women. They're not rooted to the earth in the same way that women are."

"So, some upbringing you must have had. Didn't you ever want to go to discos, stuff like that?"

Annie looked up at him and smiled. He suddenly realized how attractive she was and how much he liked
her. Maybe it was the way the light fell across the
kitchen, giving her face a soft Renaissance shine.
Maybe it was the crisis that had suddenly confronted
them, bringing them together.

"You mean dance clubs?" she said. "Of course I did.
As a matter of fact, I still do. I went to The Vanguard
last Saturday night, for Giant."

"The Vanguard? Really?" He pulled a face to show
that he was impressed.

"We should get started," she said, "before all of
those maggots hatch into flies."

"Do you want me to open the door?"

"In a minute . . . I have to call on the *katcinas* first.
The *katcinas* are the spirits of Nahbah-tóo-too-ee ancestors who protect their witches and invest them with
their magical understanding."

"Oh. I see. Sure."

Annie raised her hands and described a fluttering
pattern in the air, like a bird's wings. She began to
chant the words from the book in a high, expressionless voice.

"I call on you, ghosts from the empty pueblos. I call
on you, the *hokomah*, the vanished ones. I call on you
to bring me your strength. I call on you to make the
foul ones shrink away and the corrupt ones to shrivel."

She was silent for more than twenty seconds, with
her blood-colored eyelids closed.

Dan cleared his throat. "*Now* should I open the
door?"

"No, Dan—wait! I can't feel the *katcinas* yet."

"Okay. Sorry."

Annie made the bird's-wing gesture again. Then she
said, "I call on the spirit of Oqwa Pi, the Red Bird. I
also call on the spirit of Tse Ye Mu, Falling in Winter.

I call, too, on the spirit of Pan Yo Pin, the Summer Mountain. I call on you to drive away the messengers of darkness, to chill their bodies and to slow their wings. I call on you to overwhelm them with your dazzling brightness and to sweep them away."

Annie paused for another twenty seconds. Dan kept a tight grip on the doorknob, waiting for her to give him a signal.

"Dismiss these minions of wickedness. Let them be dispersed by the winds. In the name of all *katcinas*, scatter them forever!"

Dan heard an extraordinary grating noise, like tons of cinderblocks being crushed; and then he felt a deep shudder go right through the foundations of the entire apartment building. At first he thought it had to be an earthquake, but it seemed to move across the floor, from one side of the kitchen to the other, as if some huge creature were slowly swimming through the solid concrete beneath their feet.

This was followed almost immediately by a sharp, complicated crackling. He looked at Annie and saw that she was surrounded by dancing blue sparks. When he had touched her earlier, he felt that she was carrying a high charge of static, but now her hair was rising vertically above her head, in elaborate black curls. Epileptic worms of electricity were crawling all over her shoulders and down her arms, and sparks were showering from the tips of her fingers. She looked like a human firework.

Her eyes were closed, but she said, "Now, Dan— open the door!"

"You're sure?"

"Open the door, Dan! Just open the door!"

Dan pushed the door open wide. He was almost deafened by the minor-key droning of thousands of newly hatched blowflies. Inside the living room, the light was flickering, and the entire carpet was in turmoil. The maggots were crawling painfully toward the far side of the room, and they were heaping themselves up higher and higher, into a swaying pillar that was almost as tall as Dan. At the same time, the blowflies were settling on them, glittering and green, until the pillar of maggots was almost entirely covered.

Annie groped her way through the open door with her eyes still closed and her eyelids black with dried blood. Now she spoke in a high-pitched, singsong scream.

"In the name of all the *katcinas*, scatter! In the name of Oqwa Pi, the Red Bird, who will devour you in your hundreds of thousands! In the name of Tse Ye Mu, Falling in Winter, who will freeze you so that you fall helpless to the earth! In the name of Pan Yo Pin, the Summer Mountain, over whose summit the blinding sun rises!"

To Dan's fascination and horror, the blowflies swarmed all over the pillar of maggots like a black billowing cloak. They left only an oval area of whitish maggots near the top. The pillar looked like a human figure with a featureless face. Like a hooded woman, standing in an unfelt wind. *Like a witch*.

Annie still hadn't opened her eyes, but Dan could see that the maggots that made up the witch's face were wriggling together to form the shape of a nose and a mouth and eye sockets. Six or seven blowflies crawled into each eye socket, to give the impression of glistening green eyes. Even the maggoty lips began to move, although no words came out.

Horrified—but fascinated, too, Dan realized that he recognized her. It was the same grotesque witch they had seen on the TV screen during their debriefing at the police station—the witch who had turned around and snarled at Ernie.

"Annie," he said. "Annie, open your eyes. You have to see this."

Annie said, "I can't. It would break the spell."

"The flies and the maggots—they've made themselves into a *person*. A witch."

"Dan, I *can't* look. I have to finish the incantation."

She raised both hands and chanted, "Scatter, and let the winds carry you far away! In the name of all the *katcinas* and the forgotten names of the vanished ones, go!"

The witch figure raised both of its arms, too, as if she were imitating Annie, and its lips began to move, but all Dan could hear was the rustling and buzzing of blowflies.

Annie repeated the chant and made a chopping gesture with her hands, like karate.

The witch figure's cloak was already flapping in a wind that Dan couldn't feel, but now the whole figure began to shudder violently. Blowflies began to break away from its hood and its shoulders, just a few at first, then more and more, and maggots tumbled away from its face.

Annie kept on chopping and chanting, and gradually the entire witch disintegrated into clouds of blowflies and showers of maggots. The unfelt wind blew them relentlessly under the door that led to the corridor, and they disappeared in their hundreds, rattling against the baseboards and the woodwork. In less than a minute, they were all gone.

"That's it," said Dan, laying his hand on Annie's shoulder. "You've done it. You're amazing."

Annie opened her eyes. She looked white, as if casting that spell had drained her of all energy. All the same, she managed a twitchy, distracted little smile. "I don't think our witch will be trying *that* one again."

"They're really gone?" Dan asked her. "I mean gone for good? They're not just heaped up on the other side of that door?"

"I sent them back where they came from, and where they came from is the bathroom mirror."

Dan went across the living room and very cautiously opened the door. The corridor was empty. No maggots, no flies. Only the faintest smell of dried herbs and vinegar. He looked up and down it, and then he crossed to the bathroom.

The bathroom was empty, too—but when he approached the sink, he saw that there were three or four blowflies still crawling across the back of the door behind him. He turned around, but they weren't there at all. They were still visible in the world of reflection, but Annie had driven them out of the real world and scattered them forever, so they would never be able to swarm again.

He returned to the living room. Malkin was sniffing under the couch, obviously disappointed that there were no more maggots left to pounce on.

Annie came out of the kitchen, wiping the dried blood from her eyelids with a wet paper towel.

"It *worked*," she said.

"You sound surprised. Didn't you think it was going to?"

"Not for a single moment."

"You made me wade through all those maggots to get that goddamned book, and you didn't even believe it was going to work?"

"I'll tell you, Dan—those maggots and blowflies were such a strong conjuration. I've never felt anything so powerful, *ever*."

"But look what you did, Annie. You're powerful, too! You drove them all away, no problem. I saw you with my own eyes, kid. You were shooting out sparks like a goddamned Roman candle!"

He came up close to her and brushed a stray hair away from her forehead. "Maybe you can't burn people alive or make them puke up toads. But you must have a whole lot more witch-type power inside of you than you ever realized."

She looked around the living room. "You're right. I *do* feel more powerful." She raised both hands and pushed them outward, as if she were pushing against an invisible force. "It's almost like there's magic everywhere . . . like the whole city's full of it."

She turned back to Dan. "I broke that spell, didn't I? I scattered all those maggots and flies. I'm sure I could never have done that before. And you know what—when one witch breaks another witch's spell, she absorbs its magic, or at least she's supposed to, and it makes her even *more* powerful."

"You mean like *Highlander*? 'There can be only one.'"

"Kind of, yes. If only we had some idea who she was, this witch."

"I recognized her," said Dan. "When those maggots and those blowflies all piled up together, they made kind of an effigy of her. I'm sure it was the same old crone I saw at Chief O'Malley's media conference, along with the Zombie and the White Ghost and Vasili Krylov and those other three witches. It wasn't a face you'd easily forget, believe me."

"The fourth witch," said Annie. "The most powerful witch of them all."

"Question is . . . why did she send those maggots after *you?*"

"How about a beer?" said Annie. "I still have this foul taste of maggots in my mouth."

Dan lifted two cold bottles of Miller out of the fridge

and unscrewed them. Annie took three deep swallows and wiped her mouth with the back of her hand. "God, that's better. I felt like I'd been chewing them."

"This witch—it almost seems like she *knows* that you have maggot-o-phobia."

"I'm pretty sure she does. I think she knew that if I was surrounded by thousands of maggots, I'd totally freeze—so that even when they hatched into blowflies and started to choke me, I wouldn't be able to move."

Dan thought for a moment, and then he said, "If she's so set on killing you, she must think that you're a serious threat."

Annie went to the kitchen door and opened it, and stepped out onto the balcony. The warm evening breeze made the city lights waver like fishing-boat lights out at sea; and it stirred her thin white linen dress, too. She closed her eyes and took two or three deep breaths. "It's the power," she said, after a while. "I can feel it. That's why she tried to choke me."

"I don't understand."

"Don't you see? She has this massive magical aura. That's how the other three witches can work such devastating magic. They're using their own spells, but they're feeding off her energy. But she can't pick and choose who taps in to her energy and who doesn't, because it's *everywhere*. It's like the wind. The wind can't decide whose kite is going to fly and whose isn't."

"So *you're* feeding off her energy, too?"

"That's what it feels like. I guess that any woman can, if she has magical sensitivity. It's just that I have much more magical sensitivity than most, and this witch can obviously sense it. Well, she must have sensed it as soon as I tried to locate her on the map. She tasted the salt. She felt the needles pricking her."

Dan said, "We're going to have to find a way to protect you. Tonight it's maggots and blowflies. Who knows what the hell she's going to send after you tomorrow."

"But I did beat her, didn't I? I did manage to break her spell."

"Yes, you beat her. But maybe she didn't realize how powerful you'd become. And maybe she didn't think that I was going to be there, to carry you out of the room. Next time, she'll be better prepared. You can bet on it."

"I wish I knew who she was. Then I would have some idea of what kind of magic she's involved in."

"I have a DVD of her. Pretty clear one, too. It was taken at Chief O'Malley's media conference this afternoon. Do you think you might recognize her?"

"I don't know. Possibly. I could take a look."

"Sure—but let's do it upstairs, in my apartment. She may not try again tonight, but you never know. And this time it might be centipedes."

Chapter Seventeen

Mayor Briggs had just opened his mouth to fork in a generous helping of Hudson Valley foie gras and rhubarb marmalade when Jean-Christophe Artisson walked into the restaurant with Michelange DuPriz, closely followed by Vasili Krylov and Miska, and then Orestes Vasquez with Lida Siado, and a much older woman in a black cloche hat and a black evening dress that looked as if she had first worn it in the 1950s.

Spago was crowded that evening because there had been a screening at Paramount of Steven Schneider's new movie, *Blood Season*. But as soon as Artisson and Krylov and Vasquez appeared, with their witches on their arms, conversation in the main dining room gradually died away. Outside in the garden, under the trees, laughter and loud conversation continued, but table by table even that began to peter out.

The maitre-d' approached Jean-Christophe Artisson with his hands clasped apologetically together. "I am *so* sorry, sir. Tonight we are completely booked."

"*Poukisa?* Why are you sorry? Nothing for you to be sorry about. Business must be good."

"Yes, sir. Maybe some other night."

"*Eskize mwen?*" said Jean-Christophe Artisson. "*Mwen grangou.* I am hungry. And my friends are also hungry. *Nou ta vle manje.*"

"I'm sorry, sir. I have explained to you already that every table is taken."

Vasili Krylov looked around the restaurant. Almost every diner had stopped eating and was staring at the mobsters with apprehension and hostility. The only noise and activity in the restaurant came from the kitchen, behind its decorative glass screen, where the clattering of saucepans and the rattling of whisks continued as normal.

"*There*," said Vasili Krylov, pointing to the table in the center of the dining room, directly under the pyramid-shaped skylight. The producer Fred Manning was sitting there with Krystie Wallis, the star of *Evil Intent*, and Leonard Shapiro, the movie financier, and Sylvia Wolpert, the casting agent. They had just been served with their wild striped bass and their grilled breasts of squab, and the sommelier had just filled their glasses with white Chateauneuf-du-Pape.

"Sir, as I have explained—" said the maitre-d', dodging between Vasili Krylov and the Manning party's table.

Vasili Krylov leaned over him, so that their noses were almost touching. "I tell you this one time only," he said in his James Bond–villain accent. "Me and my friends, we will be sitting here, at this table, in twenty seconds. How you achieve this is your difficulty."

The maitre-d' turned in desperation to Mayor Briggs. "Mr. Mayor!" Then he caught the sleeve of the nearest waiter and said, "Calvin, get Mikos and Newton in here! Do it now!"

Fred Manning stood up and said, "What the hell is going on here? Who are these people?"

Several other men stood, too, and one or two women.
A ripple of indignation went through the restaurant.
But many diners recognized at least one of the mobsters, and they stayed seated with their faces turned
away. Some of them quickly reached out and grasped
the hands of their dinner companions to prevent them
from getting to their feet.

The maitre-d' called, "Mayor Briggs! Please!"

With huge reluctance, Mayor Briggs pushed back
from his table and came across the dining room, his
napkin still tucked in his shirt collar.

"Evening, Mr. Krylov. Evening, Mr. Artisson. Evening, Mr. Vasquez. Evening, ladies."

"These bums are trying to bounce us off our table,"
said Fred Manning. "I never heard of anything like it!"

"It's a disgrace," put in Sylvia Wolpert. "We're right
in the middle of our dinner."

"Madame," said Jean-Christophe Artisson, with a
grin. "How can we help it if we are too hungry to wait
for you to finish?"

Two bulky young doormen came bustling into the
restaurant, but one of them immediately recognized
Orestes Vasquez and stopped where he was, gripping
the other doorman's shoulder to hold him back.

"Mikos!" called the maitre-d'. "Newton! Please!
Show these people out!"

The doorman shook his head.

"Mikos! You want me to fire you? Show these people
out!"

"Sorry, Mr. Sylvester, but that's not included in our
job description."

"What do you mean? You are security! So, secure
already!"

"Security, yes sir. Suicides, no way."

Mayor Briggs was about to lay a reassuring hand on
Orestes Vasquez's white-suited arm, but when he saw

the expression on Orestes Vasquez's face, he made a circling motion instead, as if he were turning round the hands of an invisible clock. Nobody ever laid a finger on the White Ghost's suits, at the high risk of losing that finger forever.

"Maybe we can come to some amicable arrangement here," Mayor Briggs suggested.

"Of course," said Orestes Vasquez. "If these folks amicably leave this table, we can amicably sit down and amicably eat."

"This is bullshit!" snapped Fred Manning. "Damon, call the police!"

"I don't think that calling the police is going to have the effect you're looking for, Mr. Manning," said Mayor Briggs.

"What are you talking about? This is Spago, for Christ's sake, not some greasy spoon. I've been eating here for twenty years. I'm not having some bunch of bozos stroll right in from the street and toss me off my table!"

Fred Manning sat down again and gripped the edge of the table with both hands. "I'm not moving, and nobody can make me move! Damon, call nine-one-one. These people don't know who they're dealing with!"

Mayor Briggs walked around to Fred Manning's chair and bent his head close to the producer's ear. "Mr. Manning, these three gentlemen are all very influential Los Angeles businessmen. I'm surprised you haven't recognized them."

"I'm surprised they haven't recognized *me*. I don't care who they are. I'm not moving from this table for nobody!"

"Mr. Manning, these three gentlemen are Vasili Krylov, Orestes Vasquez, and Jean-Christophe Artisson."

"Mr. Mayor, I don't give a rat's ass if they're the Three Wise Men. This is my table, I booked it, and me and my guests are going to stay right here."

"Mr. Manning, please. I am sure we can find a way to make this up to you. For your own sake, why don't you and your friends quietly leave and let these gentlemen have your table? We don't want any trouble, either now or later."

Fred Manning said nothing, but gripped the table even tighter, until his knuckles were spotted with white.

At that moment, the Russian witch, Miska, came up to him. This evening her feathery white hair had been tweaked up with gel, and she was wearing smudgy purple makeup around her eyes. She wore an ankle-length dress of clinging purple velvet, with one shoulder bare, and a silver necklace that looked like a collection of unusual surgical instruments—semicircular clamps to prevent patients' eyelids from closing, speculums for stretching open their body openings.

"I am Miska Vedma," she announced, her head tilted slightly to one side, almost as if she were flirting with him. But her eyes remained totally dead.

"Well, I'm Fred Manning, and don't you think for one moment that I'm moving, young lady. You and your friends need to get out of here before you get yourselves arrested."

"Oh, you don't have to move, sir," said Miska in a husky voice. "In fact, you can stay at that table for as long as you like."

Fred Manning frowned at her. "So what's all the damned fuss about? If you don't want our table, why spoil our dinner?"

"We *do* want your table, but—" she gave him a bare-shouldered shrug—"if you simply won't move—"

"You're damned tooting we won't!"

Miska raised her right hand and covered her face, so that only her eyes looked out. The restaurant had been silent, but now the diners began to whisper and murmur.

"What the hell is she doing?"

"—high on something, if you ask me."

"Maybe it's some kind of publicity stunt—"

Vasili Krylov said nothing, but turned to Orestes Vasquez and Jean-Christophe Artisson and gave them a small, smug smile.

A gilt-framed mirror hung between the tall garden doors. Inside the mirror, Miska's reflection walked with a cat's elegance around the table until she was standing close to Fred Manning's right shoulder.

In the real restaurant, however, she stayed where she was, more than ten feet away from him, her hand still covering her face.

"Crazy people," said Sylvia Wolpert, shaking her head. "Lunatics and bums! Hollywood used to have *class*."

"Let's eat," said Fred Manning. "I don't know if any of you still feel hungry. I sure don't. But I'm damned if I'm going to give these bozos the satisfaction of knowing it."

He was about to dig into his garlic-potato mash when he suddenly jerked his right arm straight up in the air, as if he were giving a Nazi salute. He looked up at his arm in surprise, but then he twisted his wrist around so that his fork was pointing downward and rammed it straight into the back of his left hand. It made a sharp, biting crunch and pinned his hand to the top of the table.

"*Aaaaahhhhh!*" he shouted, staring wildly at his fellow diners.

"Fred!" screamed Krystie Wallis. "Fred, what have you *done* to yourself?"

"Get me free!" he bellowed. "Get me free!"

Leonard Shapiro reached across the table to pull the fork out of Fred Manning's hand. As he did so, however, two knives jumped into the air and stuck themselves right through the muscle of his forearm, so that the sleeve of his cream-colored sport coat was flooded red with blood. Seconds later, both women screamed out in pain and bewilderment as Krystie Wallis slapped her left hand on top of Sylvia Wolpert's, and their hands were pinned together with a large steak knife.

In all the confusion, nobody noticed Miska's reflection, circling around the table with a smile on her face. Her reflection walked back across the restaurant until it was standing where her real self was standing, and then she took her hand away from her face.

"There!" she said. "Now you do not have to leave your table, sir! In fact, you *can't*, because you and your beloved table are joined as one. I hope you are happy together."

Michelange DuPriz stepped forward and draped a sisterly arm around her shoulders. This evening, Michelange DuPriz was wearing an indecently short cocktail dress in a vivid scarlet satin and silver earrings with scarlet beads on them that looked like drops of fresh blood. "Since you cannot move from your table," she said. "You should enjoy your dinner."

Fred Manning and his dining companions were all struggling to free themselves, but the knives and forks had been driven into the tabletop with such force that it was impossible to budge them. Leonard Shapiro had turned gray with shock, and the women were both weeping. Three or four men came across the restaurant to help them, but Lida Siado raised both hands, her fingers spread wide, and growled, "No! Leave them alone! These people have to learn their lesson."

A tall, silver-haired man shouted, "Who the hell do you think you're talking to, lady? You and your friends have caused enough trouble already. Just get the hell out of here before we throw you out!"

Mayor Briggs said to Vasili Krylov, "Please, Mr. Krylov . . . if we're going to run this city together, we can't have public scenes like these. Please, as a favor to me, let them go."

Orestes Vasquez said, "Who said anything about running the city *together*, Mr. Mayor?" Vasili Krylov let out a staccato laugh.

The silver-haired man was trying to tug out the steak knife that had pinned Krystie Wallis's and Sylvia Wolpert's hands together. "Oh my God!" Sylvia Wolpert moaned in a shaky contralto. "Oh my God, that hurts!"

"I said to leave them alone!" Lida Siado called.

"And I said for you and your friends to get the hell out of here!" the silver-haired man retorted.

Lida Siado raised her left hand again, fingers spread wide. But then she squeezed them together in a tight fist and started to tap at the little drum she wore around her neck.

The silver-haired man ignored her and kept up his efforts to pull out the steak knife. Most of the other diners had risen to their feet now and were clustered around Fred Manning's table, trying to free them. More diners were crowding in from the garden.

"You think you are brave?" Miska challenged them. "You think you can defy us? Do *you* want to learn a lesson, too?"

"I don't know who the hell you think you are," a red-headed woman shouted at her, almost screaming. "But if you know what's good for you, you'll get out of here before somebody here does you a serious mischief!"

"Oh, it's mischief you want?" said Miska. "*Serious* mischief? Me and my friends, we are very good when it comes to serious mischief!"

"Did you call the cops, Damon?" somebody asked the maitre-d'.

"I tried to call on my cell," said another man. "I can't get a signal, only static."

"Me too. Did anybody try to call for the paramedics?"

"What's happening here? Who did this? Fred, hold on, buddy. We'll get you free!"

"Sylvia, try to hold still, okay? It won't hurt so bad if you try to hold still."

"Who let these freaks in?"

"More to the point, who's going to throw them out?"

Amid the confusion, Lida Siado continued to tap at her little drum, and the tapping could clearly be heard over the shouting and the arguing and the sobbing. She began to make her way between the tables toward the silver-haired man, her hips sinuously swiveling as if she were performing some kind of erotic Colombian dance.

"Hey, keep away, lady!" one man shouted.

"Yeah, back off!" yelled another.

But she continued to glide forward, tip-*tap!* tip-*tap!* tip-*tap!* She looked so strange and intimidating that none of the diners tried to stand in her way. When she reached the silver-haired man, she stood directly in front of him and held out her fist until it was only two inches away from his chest. To begin with, the silver-haired man ignored her, but she kept her fist where it was, unwavering, and now she was tapping her drum slower and slower. Tip-*tap!* Pause. Tip-*tap!* Pause.

The silver-haired man stopped trying to pull out the fork and turned to her. Whatever he saw in her eyes, he stared at her, and kept on staring at her, as if he had recognized death.

Tip-*tapp!* Longer pause. Tip-*tapp!*

Lida Siado was still smiling, but she was smiling because the silver-haired man was beginning to realize what she was doing to him.

Tip-*tapp!* Even longer pause. Tip-*tapp!*

He stood up very straight and clamped his right hand against his chest.

"Please," he said.

"Too late," smiled Lida. "I told you to leave these people alone, but you wouldn't."

"I have a wife," said the silver-haired man, trying to maintain his dignity. Tip! "I have two—I have two beautiful daughters." *Tapp!* "Grandchildren. Five grandchildren." Tip!

Nobody in the crowd of diners understood what was happening, but most of them were producers or directors or actors, and they sensed that some kind of drama was being played out. The catcalling died away.

"John!" said one of them from the back of the crowd. "John, are you okay?"

Tapp!

"Please," repeated the silver-haired man. "Please, I'm sorry."

Even with his hand pinned to the tabletop, Fred Manning was silent. He looked at the silver-haired man, and then he looked at Lida Siado. Eventually, he said, "John? What the hell's going on?"

Lida Siado turned to Orestes Vasquez and said, "*Qué pensa, Fantasma Blanco? Debería él vivir o morir?*"

Orestes Vasquez shrugged. "*Incluso aquellos quenos desafían deberían tener su lugar en él cielo.*"

Lida Siado turned back to the silver-haired man. She was tapping her drum very, very slowly now, and he was holding on to the table for support, and his lips were turning blue.

"He said that even those who defy us should have the chance to visit heaven."

"No," said the silver-haired man. He held out his hand and cupped his fingers around her fist, as if he were trying to massage his own heart. "No . . . *please*."

But Lida stopped tapping, and he gripped his chest, and his head tilted back as if he were gargling, and he swayed.

"*John!*" said Fred Manning, but the silver-haired man let out a thin catarrhal rattle and collapsed sideways onto the floor. There were screams and cries of dismay from the crowd of diners, and Mayor Briggs roared, "Go find a paramedic—anybody—even if you have to flag down an ambulance!"

Lida Siado stalked back to stand beside Orestes Vasquez, and Miska returned to stand beside Vasili Krylov, and Michelange DuPriz stood beside Jean-Christophe Artisson. In between all of them stood the elderly woman in black, with her black cloche hat. Her face was mostly in shadow, but her skin was deathly white, and her mouth was puckered with age.

She reached out to each of the witches in turn with her wrinkled black satin gloves and patted their hands, as if she were giving them her approval.

Back at Fred Manning's table, Krystie Wallis and Sylvia Wolpert were still sobbing with pain, and Leonard Shapiro was sitting with his head slumped forward, but nobody dared to help them, not while the mobsters and their witches were still here.

Mayor Briggs said to Jean-Christophe Artisson, "Please . . . I think you've shown these good people what you're capable of."

"But you know, Mr. Mayor, we came here for dinner, and we still haven't eaten."

"Please. Don't you think they've suffered enough?"

"Okay . . . maybe you're right. It isn't good for the digestion to eat in a place where everybody is so tense. What do you think, Orestes?"

Orestes Vasquez shrugged. "We can go to the Water Grill, yes? I think anyhow I prefer the Water Grill. I feel like some of those clams in tomato sauce."

Michelange DuPriz said, "*Sekonsa*. We should let these persons finish their meal."

With that, she unfastened the clip of her red satin purse and took out her small, black enamel box. She opened it and tipped about a tablespoonful of gray powder into her hand. Stepping into the center of the dining room, she began to scatter the powder in all directions. As she did so, she sang in a high, shrill, discordant voice: "*Sel pa vante tèt il di li sale . . . nan tan grangou patat pa gen po . . .*"

Jean-Christophe Artisson leaned close to Vasili Krylov and said, "She is singing that in a time of famine, people will eat anything."

Michelange DuPriz circled around the whole dining room, scattering powder onto every table. The diners shrank away from her as she approached them. None of them made any attempt to stop her, and some even stumbled backward into their friends as they tried to keep as far away from her as possible.

At last she rejoined Jean-Christophe Artisson, and then she turned to face the dining room, her face triumphant. She raised both hands and let out a long, quavering shriek.

Most of the diners had their eyes fixed on her, so they didn't realize at first what she had done. But then one woman let out a low moan of disgust, and a man shouted, "Oh my God!"

On every plate in the restaurant, the food had been transformed into something gray and glutinous, something that moved.

Several people had to turn away, their hands clamped over their mouths.

"I thought that you must be bored with lamb and

beef and salmon," said Michelange DuPriz. "So as a special treat, I have given you a dish that is much more unusual. Unborn Siamese cats, served rare."

With that, she took Jean-Christophe Artisson's arm, and they paraded out of the restaurant, followed by Vasili Krylov and Miska, the elderly lady in black, and Orestes Vasquez and Lida Siado.

When they were gone, Spago was in an uproar, with people shouting and screaming and arguing. The maitre-d' came up to Mayor Briggs and said, "What just happened? I don't understand. I saw it with my own eyes, but it was impossible."

Mayor Briggs dragged his napkin out of his collar. "Everything's changed, Damon. Everything's different. Black is white, and women can make you cough up toads."

A weeping woman was led past them by her husband, mascara streaking her cheeks.

"If you think I'm ever coming to Spago again, you're seriously deluded," the husband told the maitre-d'. "Wolfgang Puck is going to be hearing from my lawyers."

"Please, none of this was the fault of the management."

"It was a nightmare. A *nightmare*. If my wife has to go back into therapy because of this—"

Mayor Briggs bowed his head and closed his eyes.

"Dear God," he said, and he didn't care who heard him. "Dear God, have mercy on us, please."

Chapter Eighteen

"It can't be," said Annie.

"Do you want to see it again?" Dan asked.

"Yes, please. Can you freeze it? That moment when she looks at the camera."

Dan played the DVD again. When the withered old woman turned her head and glared at them, he froze it. Annie went down on her knees in front of the television and peered at her closely.

"I'm sure it's her, especially with that cat's head on a cane. But I don't see how it's possible."

"This is a witch, Annie. Witches do impossible things all the time. You know that more than anybody."

"Yes, but even witches are mortal. They grow old like anybody else. They die like anybody else."

"What are you saying?"

"I have a picture of this woman, in a book. At least I'm pretty sure it's her. I'll go find it."

"Do you want me to come with you? You know, in case of maggots."

"If I see even a single maggot, I'll scream blue murder. I promise you."

While Annie went down to her apartment, Dan sat in front of the frozen picture of the witch he had seen at Chief O'Malley's media conference. Her face was triangular with high cheekbones and a narrow nose and a jaw as sharp as a gardener's trowel. She looked more like a rat than a woman, especially with those jagged teeth. The glitter in her eyes was one of contempt, but one of cunning, too.

Malkin went close to the television and stared at the witch. She mewed, and her white fur bristled.

"Don't like the look of her, hey?" said Dan. "Me neither. If she licked a lemon, I bet the lemon would pull faces."

Although he knew that the picture of the witch was only shuddering because he had frozen it, he had the uneasy feeling that she was breathing and alive, and that she could see him.

Annie came back into the living room carrying three books—two of them new, one of them old and bound in cracked brown leather. "Here," she said, and opened one of the new books—*An Illustrated History of Hartford*. She pointed to a small reproduction of a seventeenth-century woodcut, depicting an elderly couple, both of them shackled, standing in front of a bench of five magistrates. A jury was listening intently to what they were saying, and the court was crowded to the doors with spectators.

"This is the trial of Rebecca Greensmith and her husband Nathaniel in December 1662 for witchcraft."

Dan looked at the woodcut closely. There was no question that the woman in front of the court bore an extraordinary resemblance to the woman whose image was hovering on his television screen.

"It can't be *her*, though, can it?"

"I don't see how. This was December 1662—nearly three hundred fifty years ago. Apart from that, Rebecca and Nathaniel Greensmith were both found guilty and hanged on Gallows Hill."

"What were they supposed to have done?"

"It says here that Rebecca Greensmith saw her husband being followed through the woods by a strange red creature. He told her that it was a fox. But later, when they were out looking for a missing hog, she saw him in the company of two dark creatures, one blacker than the other. They looked like dogs walking on their hind legs.

"Her husband also brought home logs on the back of his cart that were too heavy even for two men to lift, even though he was 'a man of little body and weak.'"

"So this Rebecca Greensmith—she gave evidence against her own husband?"

"He was her second husband, and I get the impression that she didn't like him too much. I also think that she was trying to get clemency for her own dealings with the devil.

"She had already confessed that she frequently performed lewd sexual acts with the devil. At first the devil had appeared to her as a deer or a fawn, skipping all around her, so she hadn't been frightened. But then he started taking on other shapes, like a giant serpent or a black hog. She said that she would take his penis into her mouth and suck out his semen, which was black, like lamp oil. She said she used to spit the devil's semen into the loaves she baked, to poison any of her neighbors who offended her."

"Nice woman."

"She boasted to the court that the devil was so pleased with her that he gave her greater magical powers than any other witch had ever possessed. She claimed that she could appear in five different places at once, hold five different conversations at once, and eat five different meals. This is called The Quintex, from the Latin word for *five* and the Old German word *Hexe* meaning witch.

"The devil gave her other powers, too. If somebody upset her, she could turn their eyes into glass or freeze their hands and feet so that they shattered, and they would have to spend the rest of their lives with nothing but stumps.

"Mind you, it's always difficult to tell how much of what she was supposed to have done was real magic and what were the natural hazards of life in Connecticut in the seventeenth century—you know, like going blind from cataracts or frostbite."

Dan said, "All of this stuff about being in five places at once—she could have been suffering from senile dementia. My old dad's still pretty coherent, but even he finds it difficult to remember what he was doing the day before yesterday. Come to that, so do I."

He turned back to the witch's face on the TV screen. He was sure that her expression had altered slightly. She seemed to be smiling, as if she had been listening to them and was amused by how little they knew.

"Another thing . . . if she was a real witch and the devil did give her all of that power . . . they wouldn't have been able to catch her, would they? They wouldn't have been able to make her stand trial and hang her."

Annie opened the second new book, *Witchfinding in Colonial Connecticut*. A large color illustration showed Nathaniel and Rebecca Greensmith being hanged from a gallows, their eyes bulging and their tongues protruding, with several men swinging from their legs to make sure that the couple was strangulated.

"This picture was painted in 1899, but it says here that it was closely based on contemporary records. And again, look, I know her face is all contorted, but this woman does look just like the woman on the screen, doesn't she?"

"She could be a descendant," Dan suggested. "That

would make this woman—what?—about her ninth or her tenth great-granddaughter."

"Something like that—but look at this."

Now she opened the leather-bound book, where a faded silk marker had been laid, and here was a full-page woodcut, very plainly executed, of a woman who by seventeenth-century standards would have been considered elderly, maybe fifty-five to sixty years old. She was wearing a bonnet unnervingly similar to the bonnet that the woman on the TV screen was wearing, and a hooded cloak that was decorated with hooks and bows and tattered ribbons, as well as dried stalks of rue and pennyroyal.

Her face was sharp and her cheeks were drawn in, as if she were sucking on something sour. Her eyes stared out of the page with undiluted venom.

On the facing page, there was a blotchily printed text, almost illegible, describing the trial of Rebecca Greensmith and her husband Nathaniel for "familiarity with the great enemy of God and mankind and by his help having come to the knowledge of secrets in a preternatural way beyond the ordinary course of nature, to the great disturbance of several members of this commonwealth."

Annie sat cross-legged on the floor and carefully read the entire text, tracing her way down the page with her finger.

Dan nodded toward the TV. "Mind if I switch this old hag off now? She's giving me the willies."

"Oh, sure. But listen to this—this is the testimony given in court by the Reverend John Whiting, pastor of the Second Church in Hartford. I've read about him before. He was like the Eliot Ness of witch hunters.

" 'Having listened to the complaints against Goody Greensmith made by her neighbors, I went in the company of three men to Nathaniel Greensmith's farm, south of the little river. There I found Goody Greensmith at her hearth, spinning. I explained to her the accusations that had been made against her and that I had come to remove her to jail.

"'She refused to come with me and uttered several blasphemous imprecations, whereupon I instructed the men who had come with me to remove her forcibly. Two of them seized her arms, and they were good strong men, Samuel Wyllys and Richard Treat, but they were unable to move her even an inch. It was as if her feet were soundly nailed to the floor.

"'However, I had come well-prepared for such witchery, and I produced from my satchel the Enochian text, which calls upon the assistance of angels and in the face of which any associate of the devil is powerless. I had in my possession also the rose-colored stone that had been sent to our ministry from England as soon as it became apparent that the devil was so assiduously recruiting new followers in the commonwealth.

"'I spoke the words, "I reign over you in power exalted above the firmaments of wrath; in whose hands the Sun is as a sword, and the Moon as a fiery arrow. Which measureth your garments in the midst of my vestures and trussed you together as the palms of my hands."

"'Thereupon I pressed the stone against Goody Greensmith's forehead, and she collapsed to the floor, her eyes as white as two pebbles, her wrists and ankles pressed together as if tightly bound by invisible cords. Mr. Wyllys and Mr. Treat were now able to lift her, with the assistance of Walter Filer, and carry her out of the house.'"

"So that's how they caught her," said Dan. "An Enochian text and some kind of stone." He paused and sniffed. "What the hell is an Enochian text?"

"Enochian is the language of angels. It was supposed to have been spoken by Adam in Paradise."

"I see. And how does anybody know that?"

"The story is that Enochian was communicated by the angels to an English spirit medium called Edward Kelley in the late sixteenth century."

"By text message?"

Annie didn't rise to it. "They did it through mirrors, or a rose-colored crystal. Kelley was working for Dr. John Dee, who was Queen Elizabeth's astrologer, as well as being a magician and an alchemist. Dr. Dee was obsessed with the idea of talking to angels, and when Kelley said that he could do it, Dee paid him fifty pounds a year just to sit and stare at this crystal and tell him what the angels were saying, while Dee wrote it all down."

"The word *scam* comes to mind, don't you think?"

"Well . . . people have been arguing about that for centuries. But Enochian is a proper language with twenty-one distinctive letters, and it has its own consistent grammar and syntax. Not only that, each of the letters relates to a specific element and number and planetary force. Kelley was fluent in Latin and Greek, but it isn't exactly easy to make up an entire language off the top of your head."

"I don't know. You should listen to my partner Ernie."

"This could help us, though," said Annie. "If the Reverend Whiting really did manage to capture Rebecca Greensmith by using an Enochian text, maybe we could do the same to her granddaughter . . . if that's who this woman is, and if we can find out which text we need to do it with."

"Hell of a lot of ifs there," said Dan.

"I know. But it's a start, isn't it? And we can't just let these witches run riot, can we? Life in Los Angeles isn't going to be worth living."

Dan's phone burbled. It was Ernie.

"El Gordo! How's it going, man?"

"You seen the news?"

"No . . . I've been working on this witch thing. What did I miss?"

"Nothing, because this wasn't *on* the news. But the Zombie and the White Ghost and Vasili Krylov took their witches out to dinner at Spago. They couldn't get a table, so they turned the whole place upside down."

"Anybody hurt?"

"One fatality, heart attack. Apart from that, only minor injuries, but they were really weird injuries, like four people had their hands nailed to the table with cutlery."

"What?"

"Fred Manning was one of them. Oh yeah, and Krystie Wallis, her too. But nobody saw nobody do it."

"How come this wasn't on TV?"

"It's not going to be *anywhere*—TV, radio, newspapers. Our three friends have told the media that if they see one story disrespecting them in any way at all, like even criticizing the pattern on their neckties, then retaliation will be swift and strange and extremely terrible."

"Is the lieutenant still there?"

"No . . . he left about a half-hour ago."

"Okay . . . I just wanted to tell him that I've made some progress on this witch stuff. I think I've identified that old woman at Chief O'Malley's media conference. I definitely think she's the fourth witch, and all the other witches are getting their power from her. I also think that we might be able to take her out, if we go about it the right way."

"I don't like this, *muchacho*. I don't like any of this. I'm not scared of any criminal. But these witches—"

"We'll be okay, Ernie. We just have to beat them at their own game."

"Oh, for sure. You know what my father used to say? *Más vale que digan aqui comó una gallina y no aqui munó un gallo*. Better to be known as a chicken while you're alive than remembered as a brave man after you're dead."

"El Gordo, I'll catch you tomorrow. Don't have nightmares. Witches, they like you to have nightmares. They open the door to your head, man, and they can send in the scariest things you can think of, like spiders."

"You're trying to scare me? How old do you think I am? Six?"

"Of course not."

"Good," said Ernie. "I'll see you tomorrow." Then he paused, and said, "Do they really do that? Send spiders into your head, when you're asleep?"

Dan and Annie stayed up until 1:30 A.M., searching through Annie's books on witchcraft and Enochian magic. Annie found *An Enochian Dictionary*, as well as the complete text of the incantation that Rev. John Whiting had used to pinion Rebecca Greensmith, in both English and Enochian.

"*Ol sonf vorsag goho Iad Balt lonsh . . . calz vonpho sobra Z-Ol ror I ta nazps*," Annie read.

"That's it?" said Dan. "That's the language that Adam spoke in Paradise?"

"I'm not too sure I'm pronouncing it right."

"All the same—Jesus. No wonder Eve wanted to eat the fruit of the tree of knowledge. Even rap sounds better than that."

They finished a last glass of chardonnay, then decided to call it a night.

"You can stay here if you're worried about maggots," said Dan. "I can sleep on the couch."

"No . . . I think I'll risk it. But I'll keep the phone close in case I need you. Now we know what we're up against . . . I don't know, I'm beginning to feel more confident. Stronger."

"Well . . . don't hesitate to call if you need me."

"I won't." She kissed him on the lips and looked up at him and smiled. He didn't exactly know what it was that he saw in her eyes. He had never seen anything like it before in any girl. It was a recognition of her own attractiveness—but it was more than that. It was fearlessness and a farsighted sense of her own personal destiny.

In the early morning, a little after 4:00 A.M., he felt the sheet lift and somebody climb into bed beside him. A warm, naked body pressed up against his back, and fingers ruffled his hair.

In his half-awake state, he thought at first that it might be Annie, but then he remembered that his apartment door was locked and bolted, and there was no way that she could have gotten in.

He twisted around, and there was Gayle lying next to him, smiling.

"You're not here," he said, hoarsely. "You can't be here."

"Dan . . . why are you so determined not to believe in me?"

"Because you're *dead*. Because—whoever you are, you can't be Gayle, even if you look like her and sound like her."

"And *feel* like her?"

"Yes."

"But if I look like Gayle and sound like Gayle and feel like Gayle, what difference does it make?"

He climbed out of bed and reached for his blue terry bathrobe. It was still damp from last night's shower, but he put it on anyway. "Tell me the truth," he asked her. "Are you a witch?"

"A witch? What kind of a question is that?"

"My friend Annie thinks that you're a witch impersonating Gayle. She says that witches can take on any shape they want to."

"Your friend Annie? You should be very cautious about your friend Annie."

"Oh, yes? And why is that exactly?"

Gayle sat up in bed so that the sheet dropped down and bared her breasts. "Some people are not what they seem to be."

"Well, nobody could be more qualified to say that than you. Whoever you are—or whatever you are. Are you a ghost?"

"There's no such thing as ghosts, Dan. Once you're dead, you're dead."

"How can you say that? You were killed in a car wreck and cremated. Yet here you are, sitting on my bed, talking to me."

"Don't you want to make love to me?"

"No, I don't."

"Didn't you enjoy it the last time we made love?"

Dan didn't answer.

Gayle drew the sheet completely back and knelt up on the bed. "Dan, I came here to warn you. I came to protect you."

"I'm going crazy. That's it, isn't it? I'm cracking under the strain."

She took hold of his hands and pulled him toward her. Then she wrapped her arms around him and held him tight. Yes, she felt like Gayle. She even smelled like Gayle. Maybe his mind was playing tricks on him and she hadn't been killed, after all. Maybe she had finished with him, that was all, and he had rationalized his pain by pretending that she was dead.

What did it matter, so long as she was here?

"So what are you trying to tell me about Annie?" he asked her.

"All I'm saying is . . . be very careful. Don't take anything she says for granted."

Gently but firmly, Dan pried himself free from Gayle's embrace. "I want to know why."

Gayle looked at him for a long time without answering. Outside, it was growing increasingly light, and the birds were beginning to twitter.

"Why don't you make love to me?" she said. "Who knows . . . it might be the last chance we ever get."

"Tell me why I need to be cautious about Annie."

"Because magic is power, and you know what they say. Power corrupts, and absolute power corrupts absolutely."

She lay back on the bed and opened her legs wide. She reached up to him with both hands.

"Make love to me, Dan. I want you so much."

Dan looked away. Then he looked back again and tugged loose the belt of his bathrobe.

Chapter Nineteen

When he arrived at headquarters, he found Ernie already at his desk, eating a cheese burrito and talking on two phones at once, the receivers tucked under his double chins.

Dan hung his coat over the back of his chair and waited until Ernie had finished. "What's up, doc?" he asked him.

"That was Frank Quinlan from Narcotics. He's been surveilling Uncle Horrible. He has video footage of him handing over drug money to the Karim brothers, and he's picked up some real incriminating chatter from his cell phone."

"Uncle Horrible" was the nickname used by Raoul Truchaud, who was one of the Zombie's top lieutenants. Other members of the gang had equally bizarre noms de guerre, such as "Dried Meat" and "Grandfather Smoke."

"Anything that fingers the Zombie himself?"

"You bet. You remember that UPS heist at LAX last October? Uncle Horrible directly implicated the Zombie in that. He also made it one hundred percent clear that it was the Zombie who ordered the Fellini Building to be torched. And he said that the Zombie paid

Marc Bailly ten big ones to put a bullet in George Maskell. There's more than enough evidence to pull him in. And Uncle Horrible. And a few more of those Haitian dirtbags."

At that moment, Lieutenant Harris came in. He was unshaven, and his shirt was crumpled. He looked as if he hadn't slept all night.

"I've just had the ATF on the phone. Apparently they've hacked into one of Vasili Krylov's computers and uncovered a massive counterfeiting operation—designer goods mainly, but liquor, too. And the Colombian police have sent us information about a major cocaine shipment delivered to Orestes Vasquez three days ago. They gave us names, locations, everything we need."

Dan said, "And all this means what?"

"It means that we can bust all three of those bastards simultaneously."

"We're going to bust them?"

"Why not? They think this new symbiosis thing has given them some kind of immunity from the law. Well, not as far as *I'm* concerned it hasn't. And because they've gotten so goddamned overconfident, they've given us more prima facie evidence than we've ever had on them before."

"But come on, Lieutenant—what happened at the Vasquez house, that could happen all over again."

Lieutenant Harris picked up Ernie's coffee mug and took a large swallow. He grimaced and said, "Sweet Jesus, Ernie!" because Ernie always took three spoonfuls of sugar. But then he said, "Listen, Dan, we still don't know what killed those SWAT teams, not for sure. The ME hasn't even half completed his autopsies. And there's a high degree of risk with every bust. Chief O'Malley may have lost his nerve, but not me."

"Lieutenant, it was the witches," Dan insisted. "If we try to arrest those guys, I promise you, they'll rip our guys into shreds. Or worse."

"Jesus Christ, Dan. I can't run this division on superstition."

"But like I told you before, sir, this is *real*. Even by themselves, those three women have the ability to wipe out every single one of us. Burn us, tear us apart, shake us so hard that our heads fly off. But not only that, there's a fourth witch."

"A fourth witch?" said Lieutenant Harris, folding his arms. "Go on. This gets better."

"As far as we can make out, she's a descendant of the single most powerful witch ever known in America, Rebecca Greensmith. She's acting like a source of energy—like a battery charger. Every time one of those three other witches casts a spell, she gives them a huge boost of additional power. That power makes their magic a hundred times more devastating than it would be normally."

Lieutenant Harris was staring down at the floor. "Do you know where she is, this fourth witch?"

"Yes, I think we can locate her. My friend has a way of tracking witches."

Lieutenant Harris still didn't look up. "And what you're trying to tell me is that without this fourth witch, the other three witches wouldn't be so dangerous?"

"I'm pretty sure of that, yes, sir."

Lieutenant Harris at last raised his eyes. "What do you think I ought to do, Dan? Relieve you of duty on grounds of suspected insanity, or let you hunt down this witch and bring her in?"

"If I were you, sir, I'd err on the side of caution."

"Meaning?"

"I'd say to myself, 'Detective Fisher sounds as if he's gone nuts. But if he *hasn't* gone nuts, then I'd be risking a whole lot of men's lives by trying to arrest the Zombie and the White Ghost and Vasili Krylov all at the same time. So I'll give Detective Fisher a chance to put this old hag out of action, and then I'll decide what I'm going to do next.'"

"That's what you'd say to yourself?"

"Yes, sir."

"And what do you think, Detective Munoz?"

"I saw those SWAT teams, sir. They was all chopped liver. I never saw nothing like that, never. It gives me such a stupendous nightmare."

"You believe in these witches, too?"

Ernie crossed himself—twice.

"Okay," said Lieutenant Harris. "But I can't postpone these collars, even if I wanted to, which I don't. The captain's had Mayor Briggs on the phone, too. He was at Spago yesterday evening, when those three hoodlums caused all of that pandemonium. He said he felt totally helpless—humiliated."

"Oh, I see. We're going to sacrifice God knows how many officers, just to save hizzoner's dignity?"

"It's not only that. It's *our* dignity too, the LAPD. We need to take some action."

"Lieutenant, this isn't a question of politics. This is a question of saving officers' lives."

"I'm sorry, Dan. But I will make you a concession. Maybe I'm as nuts as you are, but you and Detective Munoz can carry on hunting down these witches of yours. All I ask is that you make a case against them that will stand up in court."

"How about giving us twenty-four hours' grace before you go in?"

"No can do, Dan. The warrants are on their way to us already. Our information is that the Zombie and the White Ghost and Vasili Krylov will be meeting at the West Grove Country Club at seven this evening.

Apparently they'll be having a friendly little discussion with Giancarlo Guttuso. Guttuso is more than a bit peeved that our three merry mobsters are starting to muscle in on his narcotics trade."

"I wouldn't bet on Guttuso's chances of getting any concessions out of those three," said Dan. "In fact I'll bet that by the end of the evening they'll probably have him puking up live iguanas. Or worse."

"What could be worse than puking up live iguanas?" asked Ernie.

"Puking up long-dead ones."

"So where do we start?" asked Ernie, as they climbed into Dan's SUV.

"We ask my friend Annie Conjure to find this fourth witch for us."

"Conjure? That's her real name?"

"I don't know. I don't think so. But her mother was seriously into witchcraft and her grandmother before her."

"My grandmother could tell fortunes," said Ernie. "She used these strange old cards with devils and angels on them and people with heads like animals. They used to scare the hell out of me when I was a kid. I was always worried that I would wake up one morning with a goat's head instead of my own."

When they parked outside Dan's apartment building on Franklin Avenue, they could see Annie in the backyard, pegging up pink and yellow sheets. She was wearing nothing but a man's shirt made of pale blue denim. Malkin was jumping all around her, trying to catch the drops of water as they fell on the bricks.

"Hi, Dan," said Annie, with one eye closed against the sunshine. "Hi, Ernie. How's it going?"

"Good news and bad news," Dan told her. "The bad news is, we have less than nine hours to find the fourth witch. If we don't, God knows what's going to happen. Another massacre."

He explained what had happened as they climbed the steps to Annie's apartment. "How about it?" Dan asked her. "Do you think you can find this witch for us?"

"I think so, if I'm careful. Come on in."

They followed Annie into her living room. There were seven sticks of incense burning in a copper vase, and the whole apartment smelled of musk, like a Hindu temple.

Annie said, "I've been looking up Enochian magic. I've found all of the sacred texts and all of the keys for calling the angels. I've also found the whole incantation for binding a witch—the same incantation that the Reverend Whiting must have used to capture Rebecca Greensmith."

A large leather-bound book lay open on the coffee table. On the right-hand page was a detailed hand-colored engraving of five naked women in a wood at night. They were all wearing extraordinary hats—one was embellished with ivy, one woven out of willow branches. The third had upright horns like a bull, while the fourth had curled horns like a ram. The fifth woman wore a monstrously large tricorn, from which dozens of dead mice were hanging from hooks.

Behind these five women, hidden in darkest shadow, reared a huge black serpent with yellow eyes.

"Satan," said Annie. "Satan in the guise of seduction and corruption and ultimate knowledge."

Ernie crossed himself again, three times.

"Is this Rebecca Greensmith's coven?" asked Dan.

Annie shook her head. "These five women are *all* Rebecca Greensmith, manifesting herself in five different bodies at once—The Quintex. But it also proves that she was involved in Satanic magic, as opposed to Native American magic, say, or Nganga, or Xorguinéria."

"What difference does that make? It's all magic, isn't it?"

"Not at all. Every kind of magic has different rituals and different spells and completely different chemistry. A spell that works on a Christian wouldn't necessarily have any effect on a Muslim. For instance, if you made up a charm bag to put a spell on a Christian, you would fill it with dried teasels and recently extracted teeth, to create quarrels; and ferns, to bring on thunder and lightning and heavy rain. Ferns used to be called the devil's brushes. And you'd probably add blackberry thorns, because the devil once fell into a blackberry bush, and spat on it because he was so angry.

"But if you were making a voodoo charm bag, you would put graveyard dust into it and beads and dead spiders and the coins from a corpse's eyes."

"*Brrrr!*" said Ernie. "This stuff gives me the holy creeps."

"Me too," Annie admitted. "But if we're going to go looking for this fourth witch, we have to be properly prepared. You wouldn't go looking for a dangerous gunman without wearing body armor, would you?"

"You kidding me? I wouldn't go looking for a dangerous gunman, period."

"How are you going to find her?" asked Dan. "Salt and needles, like you did before?"

"No . . . she tasted the salt, and she felt the needle pricking her, and that's how she knew we were looking for her. If we try that again, she'll be long gone before we get to where she is, or—even worse—she'll be waiting for us."

She picked up a heavy brass compass engraved with a variety of runic symbols and opened the lid. "I borrowed this from a friend of mine. She works for that occult bookstore on Melrose, you know it? The Bodhi Tree. It used to belong to one of her customers who was a clairvoyant, but who knows where *she* got it from.

"It's a witch compass. If you look under the glass you can see that it's filled with salt. The pointer is a needle that was supposed to have been used to sew the shroud of St. Francis of Assisi. It will always swing toward the nearest witch, or anybody who's had physical contact with the devil."

"Hey, right now it's pointing at *you*. You haven't been doing the wild thing with his Satanic Majesty, have you?"

"It can sense my occult aura, that's all. It's really responsive to any supernatural vibrations. You wait till we take it outside."

Dan said, "You don't have to do this, you know. It could be very dangerous."

Annie looked up at him, and again he caught that expression in her eyes.

"Okay," he conceded. "But I don't want you taking any unnecessary risks. If you suspect that something's going wrong—anything at all—you get the hell out. You understand me?"

"But not before you warn us first," Ernie put in. "I don't want to end up like mush."

Annie said, "Give me ten minutes to get dressed and to make up all the stuff we're going to need. Help yourself to a brewski, if you want."

She left them in the living room. Ernie looked around at her wands and her astrological charts and her three-barred cross with an expression of deep misgiving. He returned to the book on the coffee table and studied it for almost a minute, tugging at his mustache. "Satan, huh? I always thought that Satan was just a story. A bogeyman my mother invented to stop me from stealing her *chalupas*. You think he really looks like this? Like a snake?"

"I don't know, dude. I never believed in him either."

"You think we're making ourselves look like assholes?"

"I think we're the only ones who aren't."

Annie came out onto the sidewalk. She was still wearing the blue denim shirt, but she had put on a pair of yellow capris now, and she had a soft brown leather satchel slung across her shoulder. She was holding the witch compass in her left hand and a short dry stick in the other, tipped with a pinecone.

"What's that?" Dan asked her, tossing away his half-smoked cigarette.

"It used to belong to my grandmother. It's a thyrsus, the magic wand used by Benandanti."

"Ben and Anti?" said Ernie. "Who were they?"

"Benandanti, one word. It literally means 'good walkers.' They were Italian shamans who used to fight evil spirits in the sixteenth and seventeenth centuries. Their wands were made of fennel stalks and pinecones, like this one. If we *do* find our witch, we're going to need it."

"So? Pretty powerful piece of stick, huh?"

"Wands in themselves don't have any power at all. But they concentrate the power of the person who uses them. I guess they're like guns, in a way. On its own, a gun is just an inanimate object. Wands are the same."

"But that's a good-quality wand? Like a Smith & Wesson wand?"

"You could say that. But look—we'd better be getting on."

Annie tapped the witch compass three times with the pinecone. Then she opened the lid and began to circle slowly around, offering the compass to the north, the east, the south, and the west. Dan and Ernie shuffled respectfully out of her way.

As she circled, Annie whispered an incantation under her breath.

"Salt and needle, show the way, point toward the witch I pray. Salt and needle, spin and spin, find the one with devil's sin. Find the one who drank his seed, and on whose blackened lips did feed. Salt so white and needle bright, be my guides and be my light."

After a while she stopped circling and carefully shifted the witch compass from side to side—first to the left a little, then to the right—until its needle stopped trembling. It pointed almost due west.

Dan frowned at it, and said, "You think you've picked her up?"

"I'm sure it's her. The attraction is so amazingly strong. Hold the compass for yourself. Can you feel it? It's almost like it's *humming*. And look—the needle isn't even swinging from side to side, which it would do normally, because it would be attracted to other witches in the area, too. This witch is totally dominant."

"All right, then. Let's go."

They climbed into Dan's Torrent. Annie held the witch compass in the palm of her hand and directed them.

"Turn right onto Sunset, that's it. Keep going."

Traffic on Sunset was crawling along at its usual laidback pace, and Dan impatiently drummed his fingers on the steering wheel. "You still got her?"

"No problem. Stronger than ever. She can't be too far away."

A '73 Eldorado convertible with seven young students in it was driving in front of them at less than ten miles an hour. "Look at these bozos," Dan complained, and gave them a piercing *whup-whup-wheep* of his siren. Immediately, a scattering of hand-rolled joints were tossed out into the road. Dan overtook the students and left them looking at each other in relief and bewilderment.

They drove as far as Stone Canyon Road, and then Annie said, "Right here. Up toward the Hotel Bel-Air."

"Looks like they've given this witch a pretty ritzy place to stay," Ernie remarked, as they drove between the palms and the jacaranda and the fragrant orange-blossom bushes.

"Not the hotel, though," said Annie. "Farther up the road, to your left."

They passed the entrance to the Hotel Bel-Air. Somebody was holding a wedding by Swan Lake, and they could see a flower-decorated pavilion and the bride-groom in his white tuxedo, waiting for his bride to appear.

"Don't do it, *muchacho*," Ernie muttered under his breath. "One day for sure you will wake up and find a two-hundred-seventy pound woman lying next to you, with a long hair growing out of the mole on her chin."

"What are you talking about?" said Dan. "Your Rosa, she's absolutely beautiful."

"You never met her mother. I have seen the future, and it grows a hair on its chin and puts on weight."

Beyond the hotel, Stone Canyon Road became steeper. On the right-hand side, the houses were huge and immaculately decorated in pink and cream stucco, with sprinklers chuffing softly onto their emerald lawns. After they had taken the left branch, however, the road became narrower and overshadowed by oaks.

They found themselves driving between two gray stone walls. The roadway was unswept, and their tires crackled on dry twigs and swathes of fallen leaves.

"Are you sure this is the right way?" Dan asked Annie.

Annie held the witch compass to his ear. "No doubt about it. Can you hear it?"

Very faintly, the witch compass was giving out a high-pitched whine, like somebody circling the rim of a wineglass with a moistened fingertip. "It's actually *excited*," she said.

They turned a corner and found themselves faced by two cast-iron gates. Beyond the gates, the driveway sloped even more steeply upward until it reached a large yellow house with flaking yellow shutters and eight tall chimneys. To the left of the driveway was a thick wooded area, and it was obvious that neither the woods nor the gardens had been tended for years.

Ernie said, "Hey, I *know* this house. It used to belong to Ben Burrows when he was starring in *Friends and Family*. I had to come up here when I was a rookie because some young guy had been sexually assaulted with a snooker cue and drowned in his pool."

"I remember that," said Dan. "Pretty much finished Burrows's career, didn't it?"

"Well, people's private life, that's their own business," said Ernie. "But he always used to make out that he was so straight."

Dan climbed out of the SUV and went across to the intercom box beside the gates. He pushed the button and waited, but there was no reply. He pushed the button again. "Don't think that damned thing's working."

There was a heavy chain wound tightly around the gates to hold them together, but there was no padlock. Dan opened the Torrent's tailgate and took out his tire iron. It took him three or four minutes of wiggling and grunting to lever the chain loose, but eventually it rattled to the ground, like a thick metallic snake. He pushed the gates apart, and they drove slowly up toward the house.

"This place has such a bad aura," said Annie. "I mean, is it my imagination or is it actually *chilly?*"

"You're not imagining it, it's cold. It's these trees, blocking out the sunlight."

Dan glanced toward the woods. As he did so, he thought he glimpsed a pale fawn figure between the oaks. It flickered so quickly between the tree trunks that he couldn't be sure if he had seen it at all, but it looked tall and attenuated, kind of *stretched out*, with a pointed head or maybe horns.

"Did you see that?" he asked Ernie.

Ernie was busy peering at the house. "What's that, *muchacho?*"

"I saw somebody in the woods. Or *something.*"

Ernie turned around in his seat and stared for a while. "I don't see something. You sure you saw something?"

"Don't worry," said Dan. "I'm a little keyed up, is all. Most likely it was only a deer."

Chapter Twenty

They reached the wide-shingled turning space in front of the house and stopped. Close up, they could see how neglected the property was. The yellow stucco was flaking off the outside walls, and the chimneys were throttled with ivy. The windows were dusty and blind as an old woman's eyes, and many of the shutters were hanging at crazy angles off their hinges.

They climbed out of the Torrent and walked up to the front porch. Annie was still holding the witch compass, and she suddenly said, "She's close, Dan! She's very, very close!"

They approached the double front doors. The varnish was peeling off them in shriveled ribbons, like a skin disease.

"Dan, be careful," Annie warned. The witch compass was singing so loudly now that all of them could hear it. It set Dan's teeth on edge.

Ernie unholstered his gun and cocked it.

"Dan, she's here!" said Annie.

Dan glimpsed a quick, blurred movement on his left. He swung around and glimpsed a pale face staring at him out of one of the grimy downstairs windows. The face vanished almost at once, but he had seen who it was. The fourth witch, in her strange overhanging bonnet, her eyes narrowed with suspicion.

He strode over to the doors and furiously jiggled the handles, but they were locked.

"Ernie," he said. The two of them stood side by side, and gave the doors a hefty double kick. They heard a thunderous echo inside the house, but the doors stood firm.

"Again!" said Dan, and this time they heard one of the catches splintering and a bolt pop out of its socket, and the doors shifted inward by two or three inches.

"Again!" The doors burst apart, and the two of them nearly lost their balance.

They found themselves in a musty, high-ceilinged hallway, with a black-and-white marble floor and a wide staircase that led up to a second-floor gallery. The floor was littered with dried eucalyptus leaves and streaked with grit, which the wind had blown under the door. The black cast-iron banisters were caked with elaborate lumps of quail droppings.

"Where is she?" Dan asked Annie. He approached the first door on his left with his gun upraised. "I saw her at the window—she must have been in this room here."

Annie was slowly waving the witch compass from side to side. "No . . . she's not in there, not anymore . . . but she's definitely near."

The witch compass started to sing yet again. Annie pointed it toward the far end of the hallway and then gradually tilted it upward.

As she did so, the fourth witch materialized on the gallery overlooking them. She was silhouetted against a yellowish stained-glass window, but they could tell who she was by her bonnet and her tattered cloak and the staff with a cat's head on top of it she was holding in her left hand.

Dan pointed his gun at her and shouted, "You! Come down here! Make it real slow. I want both hands where I can see them."

"You're trespassing," said the witch. Although she was at least twenty-five feet above them, Dan felt as if she were whispering close to his ear, and he was tempted to turn around to see if she was standing right next to him, too.

"This is a private house, my friend, and you were not invited in."

"We don't need an invite. We're police. You're under arrest!"

"Under arrest? On what charge?"

"Make that 'charges'—plural. Conspiracy to commit multiple homicide, for beginners."

"Oh, yes? And what else?"

"You want the whole list? Conspiracy to commit arson, conspiracy to commit assault, conspiracy to deal in narcotics and illegal firearms. Not to mention larceny, fraud, forgery, pandering, criminal damage, and threatening behavior."

"You're going to prove that I'm guilty of such misdeeds? And how exactly are you going to do that?"

"I'm not here to discuss this with you, lady. I just want you to come down here with your hands where I can see them."

"Or what? You'll ask your pretty young friend to put a spell on me?"

"Just come down here, or I'll come up there and get you."

The witch said nothing, but she raised her cat's-head staff above her head.

"This is your last warning, lady. Come on down."

Dan crossed the hallway and started to mount the stairs. The witch swung her staff around until it was pointing at the top of the staircase, and she whispered something in a quick, guttural voice. She sounded more like a monkey chattering than a woman.

Instantly Dan heard a soft, dry, rushing noise. A huge cascade of insects surged over the top of the staircase and came gushing downward—thousands of them. Dan said, "*Shit*—" and took one step upward, but as he did so he felt a sharp crunching beneath the sole of his shoe. He looked down and saw that the creatures were centipedes, their antennae blindly waving, tumbling over one another as more and more of them came pouring down.

He jumped back down again, his heart thumping in panic. Dozens of centipedes were already swarming over his shoes, and some of them were climbing up inside the legs of his pants.

He thought, *They can't be real. This is magic, they can't be real.* But then he thought of the metallic-tasting quarters that he had puked up. They had been real enough, and so had the toads in Chief O'Malley's stomach. He stumbled back farther, frantically slapping at his ankles and gripping his pants tightly around the knees in case the centipedes scuttled up any higher.

Ernie retreated, too, stamping on any centipede that came near him, as if he were performing a heavy-footed Mexican dance. Only Annie remained serenely where she was, the witch compass still lifted in her left hand. Although a few centipedes ran over her sandaled feet, she ignored them.

"*I know what you fear the most,*" whispered the witch. "*I know what infests your nightmares. You think you can come here and arrest me? Go away, fools! Don't bother me again!*"

Ernie shouted, "You come down here, lady! I'm not scared of your centipedes!"

"*I know that!*" retorted the witch, leaning over the

banister. *"But I know what you are scared of! If I were you, fat man, I wouldn't tempt me!"*

"You got 'til the count of three to come down!"

"Very well," said the witch. She reached into her raggedy cloak and drew something out of it. From the hallway, they couldn't clearly see what it was, but it looked pendulous and heavy, and it was swinging from side to side.

Ernie turned quickly to Dan. "Are you okay?"

Dan was still crushing the last of the centipedes under his shoes. "I'm okay. Give her three, and then we'll go up there and snatch her, bugs or no bugs."

"Uno!" whispered the witch. She lifted her arm back, hesitated, and then flung down the thing that she had produced from her cloak. It circled through the air and landed with a thump right in front of Ernie's feet. Before any of them realized what it was, it scurried wildly to one side, and then back again, squealing and chittering. It was an enormous black rat, still slick with sewage, with sharp yellow teeth and a thick ringed tail.

"Mother of God!" screamed Ernie. *"Mother of God!"*

He staggered backward, his eyes bulging with terror. The rat ran toward him, then dodged toward Dan. Ernie pointed his gun at it and fired. There was a deafening bang, and the rat exploded into a bloody tangle of black fur.

"You witch!" Ernie shouted. "You witch—I'll shoot you, too!"

"Bring it all back, did it?" gloated the witch. *"That morning when you were five, in the barrio? And you opened your eyes, didn't you, and there it was, at the end of your bed? And it ran up under your blankets and bit you on the lip?"*

"I'll shoot you, too!" Ernie screamed at her. "I'll shoot you, too!"

"*Dos!*" whispered the witch. She reached into her cloak and dragged out another rat, which she tossed over the banister without any hesitation. It bounced off Dan's shoulder before it dropped to the floor.

"*Tres!*" She threw another rat over. "*Cuatro!*"

She pulled out more and more rats, and they came hurtling down from the gallery, hitting the floor all around them, wriggling and squealing and zig-zagging frantically from one side of the hallway to the other. Ernie fired again and again, until Dan was almost deafened and the hallway was thick with acrid blue smoke. Bloody fragments of rat were splattered across the black-and-white marble like a grisly parody of a Jackson Pollock painting—teeth, tails, quivering hind legs, and scarlet intestines.

At last the witch stopped throwing rats and held up her staff again. Ernie was pale and sweaty and panting like a walrus.

"*Have you had enough yet?*" the witch asked. "*I can do worse! How about* you, *young lady? What is it that terrifies you?*"

Dan glanced at Annie and realized that the witch had *asked* what frightened her. She didn't seem to know instinctively, the way she had with him and Ernie.

Annie stayed supremely calm. She dropped her witch compass into her satchel and took out a folded sheet of paper and a small white silk purse. The purse was embroidered with green petals and seed pearls, and tied at the neck with what look like silvery-gray hair.

"What's that?" Dan asked her. "What are you going to do?"

She gave him a secretive little smile. "You'll see. But get ready to run upstairs and seize her when the moment comes."

She held up the purse in her left hand and swung it from side to side. At the same time, she sang in a high, shrill voice, "Salt and juniper, marigolds and rue! Silver and primroses, red, white and blue! Balsam ash and a copper coin. Seven times shaken, seven times blessed."

The witch swept her staff in an angry, chopping pattern. *"Do you think you can catch me with garden herbs and pennies, you foolish child? Do you know who I am? Do you know where my magic comes from? It comes from the very wells of hell!"*

With that, she shouted, *"Thunder!"* and the entire house shook with a devastating clap of thunder. A chandelier dropped from the ceiling and shattered on the floor, and plaster dust came down in billowing clouds.

Annie remained where she was. She swung her little embroidered bag three more times. Then she lifted the thyrsus, the fennel stalk with the pinecone on the tip, and pointed it directly at the witch. In the other hand she held up the sheet of paper and began to read the words that she had written on it.

"Busd de yad, the glory of God."

"Lightning!" screamed the witch, and the hallway crackled with lightning. It jerked and jumped from the staircase to the front door, setting off showers of sparks. Dan was thrown back against the wall, jarring his back. Ernie's hair was standing on end, and his mustache bristled.

"Mykmah a-yal prg de vaoan!" Annie called out. *"Ar gasb tybybf doalym od telok!"*

"Storm!" the witch raged at her. At once, it was raining. Hard, cold, clattering rain that came straight out of the ceiling. They were instantly drenched, and Ernie said, "I will kill this woman! I promise you, I will personally drown her with my bare hands!" He said

something else, but his words were lost in another crackle of lightning, which dazzled all of them, and another burst of thunder.

It started to rain even more torrentially, so that water was gushing and foaming down the stairs. Yet as he turned around, Dan could see through the front doors that it was still sunny outside, with only the faintest breeze ruffling the bushes.

"*Mykmah vls de ageobofal y dluga toglo pugo a tallo!*" cried Annie, almost singing it. Then she raised the thyrsus and made the sign of the cross, three times. "I reign over you in power exalted above the firmaments of wrath!" she shouted.

"*No!*" screamed the witch, and covered her ears with her hands.

"A power in whose hands the Sun is as a sword, and the Moon as a fiery arrow!"

"*No! Stop! You don't know what you're doing!*"

"Which measureth your garments in the midst of my vestures and trussed you together as the palms of my hands!"

"*You don't know what you're doing! You don't know what you're bringing on yourself! The power of Satan and all of his demons! The legions of the night!*"

But Annie made the sign of the cross again, then again and repeated the words "*Busd de yad.* The glory of God."

A pure white light appeared on the gallery close behind the witch. It grew brighter and brighter, and it made the raindrops sparkle like diamonds and caught them in midair, as if they weren't falling at all.

The light was so brilliant that it was impossible for Dan to make out what it was, but as it shone brighter the witch let out a choking noise, as if she had a fishbone caught in her throat. She dropped to her knees, then tumbled sideways onto the floor.

"What is that?" he asked Annie. "What's happening?"

Annie kept on smiling, but she didn't answer. The expression in her eyes was almost beatific.

For a split second, Dan thought he saw a *face* in the middle of the light—a smooth, dispassionate face, like a Venetian carnival mask—but then it vanished, and the light died away. The rain gradually eased, then stopped altogether. There was one last grumble of thunder, and then the hallway fell silent, except for the witch's self-pitying moaning and the soft pattering of water drops.

"The foulest of plagues on all three of you and all of your families and all of your children, for all eternity!" whispered the witch. She tried to curse them some more, but she started to cough and couldn't stop.

"You can go get her now," said Annie. "But be careful . . . she'll probably try to bite you, and a witch's bite can make you impotent."

"You mean . . . ?" said Ernie. He held out his hand with his index finger drooping.

Annie nodded. "It's the best revenge that any woman can take on a man, don't you think?"

"I'll take her feet," said Ernie. "What? I'm a married man! I get impotent, Rosa will kill me!"

Dan and Ernie climbed the staircase, their sodden shoes squelching. When they reached the gallery, they found the witch lying on her back, coughing up strings of pale yellow phlegm and rocking from side to side. Although she wasn't tied up with cord, her wrists and her knees and her ankles were pressed tightly together, and it was clear that she was unable to pry them apart.

"I shall make the piss in your bladders boil!" she spluttered. *"I shall pull out your guts and fry them in front of you!"*

"You want to tell me your name?" Dan asked her.

"You will have to guess that, you smear of hog's excrement."

"Wouldn't be Greensmith, by any chance?"

The witch went into another coughing fit and rocked so violently that they could hear her spine making a knobbly sound against the floorboards.

"Well, whoever you are, I'm arresting you on suspicion of conspiracy to commit multiple homicide, as well as all those other crimes and misdemeanors I told you about. You have the right to remain silent. Anything you say can and will be used against you in a court of law."

"You are not fit to lick the devil's poop-hole."

Ernie raised his eyebrows. "Hey, *abuela*—I'll remember that. That should go down well at your arraignment."

Dan leaned over and forced his hands into the tattered folds of the witch's cloak, trying not to get snagged on the hooks and the dried herbs that were fastened all over it. The witch had an indescribable smell, stale urine and lavender, but something else, too, something caustic, like oven cleaner, that burned his sinuses.

"You have the right to an attorney. If you cannot afford an attorney, one will be provided for you. Do you understand what I've just said to you?"

"You think that I will stand in front of your court? Nobody can judge me except my lord and master."

Dan dug his hands deep into her bony armpits, while Ernie took hold of her ankles. "Ready?" asked Dan. "Then, *hup*."

Although she was such a skeletal old woman, the witch was surprisingly heavy. They had to carry her very slowly down the stairs, and at one point Ernie almost lost his footing and had to make a grab for the banisters to steady himself. Eventually, however, they managed to shuffle across the hallway and out of the front doors. She squeezed her eyes tightly against the sunshine, and her lips puckered.

They carried her over to the Torrent, opened the hatchback, and lowered her inside.

"You bubbles of dog snot," she sneered at them.

"Look who's talking," Ernie retorted. "You really need to blow your nose, you know?"

"How long is she going to stay helpless like this?" Dan asked Annie. "Like, do you think I should put the cuffs on her, just in case?"

"She can't get free. Not until I break the spell for her."

"What was that, all that *buzz-de-yad* stuff you were reading out? Was that Enochian?"

She nodded. "The language of the angels. That particular incantation neutralizes hexes and makes it impossible for witches to cast any spell that might do anybody harm."

"And that light?"

"What are you asking me?"

"I'm not too sure. I thought I saw some kind of face in it, that's all."

"Like you said before, you're a little keyed up."

Dan cocked his head to one side. "Annie?"

"I'm not telling you, Dan. Either you believe, or you don't."

Ernie went back to the porch and closed the front doors, wedging an old wrought-iron chair under the handles to keep them together. Then they all climbed into the Torrent, and drove back down the driveway. Dan kept glancing toward the woods, but he didn't see the pale fawn figure with the pointed head and horns.

As they turned onto Stone Canyon Road, they heard the witch kicking and moaning in the back. *"I curse you forever! You are no better than cat's vomit! I curse*

*you from the scurf in your scalp to the bunions on your
stinking feet!"*

Ernie thumped on the hatchback cover and shouted,
"Shut up, *bruja!* I've had enough of you for one day!"

Dan said, "Those other three witches are going to
be pretty pissed, don't you think, when they find out
that all of their extra power has been taken away."

"Well, yes." Annie smiled. "They won't be very
happy. But you don't want to underestimate them,
even now."

"They won't be able to do what they did to those
SWAT teams, will they?"

"No. I don't think so. It takes such an enormous
amount of magical power to raise the Night Wind,
and those *kukurpas* that follow them. And once you've
raised them, you have to be able to control them and
send them back to where they belong. Otherwise they
won't hesitate to tear *you* apart, too. They're not very
big on gratitude, creatures like that."

"How about blowing people up in midair and setting fire to them and making them cough up toads?
Can they still cast spells like that?"

"I don't know for sure. Probably. But they won't be
able to cast them at any great distance—not like they've
been doing up until now. Like I say, they're all very
skillful witches, and we still need to be careful. But
now that we've cut them off from *this* witch's magical
energy, they're going to be much easier to trap."

They drove slowly along Hollywood Boulevard and
turned into the parking lot at the back of police
headquarters. It was crowded already in anticipation
of this evening's operation at West Grove Country
Club. Four black SWAT vans, eight squad cars, three
unmarked Crown Victorias, and more than fifty officers talking and drinking coffee and checking their
equipment.

Dan climbed out of the Torrent and saluted four or five of the officers he knew. Then he turned to Ernie and said, "See all these guys here? They don't know it, but I think we've already saved their lives."

Chapter Twenty-one

Ernie climbed the steps into the station and came back out a few minutes later with two female police officers, one big and blond with hefty hips, the other black and skinny with prominent teeth. When Dan opened the Torrent's hatchback and they saw the rancid, ragged creature hunched inside, the blond officer said, "Oh my *God*," and the black officer flapped her hand in front of her face in disgust.

For her part, the witch blinked furiously into the sunlight, grinding her teeth.

"Come on, sweetheart," said Dan. "Let's get you out of there."

The witch spat and spat again, until she had long strings of saliva trembling from her lips. "*I curse you all! I curse you all forever! May your skin bubble with pustulent buboes and your tongues turn into the slimiest of slugs!*"

"Where did you find *this* charmer?" asked the blond officer.

Dan took hold of the witch's ankles. "I know she looks like a street person, but she's anything but. So treat her with caution, okay? Ernie, want to give me a hand lifting her out?"

"Hey—" Ernie reminded him. "I'm at the feet end, remember?"

The two female officers kept well back as Dan and Ernie lifted the witch out of the Torrent. The witch kept jerking and twisting and swinging herself from side to side, but they managed to carry her up the steps and through the front doors.

"Can't she walk?" asked the blond officer. "It's not like she's restrained or nothing."

"Oh, she's restrained all right. And lucky for us that she is."

As they passed the front desk, Sergeant Mullins said, "What you got there, Detectives? Last week's dirty laundry?"

"Female prisoner, name unknown. Just book her for us, will you? Conspiracy to commit homicide, plus about two dozen other offenses. I'll give you the full list later."

"You will suffer, just like these poor fools!" the witch whispered at Sergeant Mullins. *"Your fingers and toes will drop off and woodlice will crawl out of your anus!"*

Sergeant Mullins raised one eyebrow. "It's been a pleasure to meet you, too, ma'am."

Every step was a struggle, but Dan and Ernie managed to carry the witch down two flights of stairs and all the way along the gray-painted corridor to the cells. She spat and cursed and swore at them without pausing for breath, and if she had still been able to invoke her magical power, they all would have been struck down on the spot with strokes or heart attacks and a whole variety of debilitating diseases from leukemia to leprosy.

When they reached the end of the corridor, they carried her into the last cell and dropped her unceremoniously onto the bunk.

"Detective Munoz and me, we have to talk to the

lieutenant," Dan told the two female officers. "Meanwhile, we need you to strip this lady and search her. It's going to be a little awkward because she can't pry her wrists or her knees apart, but I'm sure you'll manage. Whatever she says to you—and I mean *whatever* she says to you—ignore it."

"Ignore it?" said the black officer tartly. "I wish. I never heard *nobody* with such a dirty mouth, 'specially an old lady like this."

Dan laid his hand on Annie's shoulder. "Ms. Conjure here will give you any assistance you need."

"Is she from welfare?" asked the blond officer.

"Let's just say that she's an expert in cases like these. Or as much of an expert as anybody possibly could be."

To Annie, he said, "Is she going to be safe here? She won't be able to work any you-know-what, will she?" He spun his finger around like a magic wand.

"No," said Annie. "But when these officers have finished changing her clothes, I'll put a seal on the cell door, just to make absolutely sure."

"I really appreciate what you did there, back at the house. You were amazing."

"Thanks—although it wasn't really me. I mean, I read the incantation, but the magical power that made it work . . . that came from someone much more amazing than me."

There was a challenging gleam in her eyes, as if she were daring him to ask her who it was. God? An angel? Or some other supernatural power that he had never heard of?

He looked away, then looked back again. "You did the business, that's all I care about. Listen—when you're done here, come upstairs. The desk sergeant will show you where we are."

* * *

"We got her," Dan announced. "The fourth witch—she's in custody downstairs."

Lieutenant Harris was standing at his desk, frowning at a large-scale map of West Grove Country Club. He took off his glasses and said, "You're kidding me. You found her?"

"She was hiding out in Ben Burrows's old house, up on Stone Canyon Road."

"How the hell did you find her there?"

"You wouldn't believe me if I told you, so I won't."

"Did she give you any trouble?"

"Let's put it this way—it wasn't exactly a walk in the park, but my friend Annie helped us out. The witch has been restrained now with a magical incantation."

"A magical incantation?"

"Annie did it. She's very good at magical incantations."

"Really?"

"Really. And herbal medicine. And spells. She can tell your fortune, and she can cure your back pain, and she can tell you if you're going to find the woman of your dreams. Anyhow, this magical incantation prevents the witch from casting any spells. And most important of all, it prevents her from sharing her power with those other three witches."

Lieutenant Harris pushed his fingers through his prickly gray hair. "I'm not sure what to say to you," he admitted. "You know I don't believe in any of this black magic malarkey. But . . . I have to admit to feeling kind of relieved."

"Sir, it doesn't matter if you believe in it or not. What matters is that when we go to pick up the Zombie and the White Ghost and Vasili Krylov this evening, we won't have to face the same godawful creatures that massacred those two SWAT teams.

The witches simply won't have enough power to call them up."

"You realize I won't be able to give you any kind of commendation for this? I can't even mention it in my report. Not without looking like a fruit loop, anyhow."

"That doesn't matter either," said Dan. "The most important thing is that no more officers end up getting ripped to pieces."

Annie came into Lieutenant Harris's office, and Dan introduced her.

"I gather we have something to thank you for," said Lieutenant Harris.

"I didn't really have a choice," Annie told him. "I don't know of anybody else who could have captured a witch as powerful as this one. Besides, if any witch is using her craft to do evil, I *have* to try and stop her."

"You *have* to?"

"I guess you could say it's my destiny. It's what my mother taught me to do and what my grandmother taught *her* to do. Magic is only supposed to be used for good. You know—to heal people when they're sick. To bring people love and luck and happiness. To make things grow. Magic is the greatest gift that any woman can possess."

"Well, I can understand the destiny thing," said Lieutenant Harris. "My dad was a cop and my grandfather was a cop and my great-grandfather was a U.S. marshal. I have to tell you, though, I'm still pretty skeptical about magic."

"I know you are," said Annie. "I can feel it."

"You can *feel* it?"

Annie held out both hands toward him. "Skepticism feels like thistles. Just like belief feels like polished marble, and love feels like deep, warm water."

Lieutenant Harris looked over Annie's shoulder at Dan and pulled a face.

"What can I tell you, Lieutenant?" said Dan. "Even if you don't believe in witches, you have to admit that Annie's a damn good one."

Annie said, "When you go down to the witch's cell, Lieutenant, you'll see that there's a wax medallion stuck to the door with red ribbons hanging from it. It's a sigil ... a magical seal to prevent the witch from sending any of her power out of the building to the other witches. It has some markings on it that look like forks and squiggles and triangles. Those are the signs of an angel called Cassiel, the ruler of the seventh heaven.

"Whatever you do, don't take it off. I've already told those two women officers not to remove it, and they're going to tell the desk sergeant, too."

Lieutenant Harris held up both of his hands. "If you say to leave it on the door, young lady, that's where it's going to stay. I promise you."

It was still only 3:25 P.M., so the three of them drove to Ernie's apartment building on Lincoln Boulevard to freshen up and have a late lunch. Dan hadn't felt like eating breakfast that morning, but now he was ravenous.

"You're quiet all of a sudden," he told Annie.

"I'm feeling a little strange, that's all."

"Strange in what way? Maybe you're just tired after all that incanting."

"No, I don't feel tired at all. In fact I feel really energized. Like I've drunk ten cups of espresso."

"It's that high you get after an arrest. Your system's still full of adrenaline. That's why some cops beat up on the people they've just busted. I usually tell them to go to the gym and work it all off on the rowing machine."

Ernie said, "Me, I like to eat. I book somebody, I head for the Casa Blanca Café and order the *huevos rancheros* and the pork *gorditas* and the chicken-and-cheese burrito. You can't feel aggressive with nobody after that."

"Aggressive? I'm surprised you can even walk."

They parked outside a 1960s apartment block with pale blue walls and red-painted window frames. Ernie led them to a concrete-paved courtyard into which the sun never shone. Two young boys were listlessly playing on a swingset. Ernie ruffled their hair and said, "Carlo, Sancho, say hello to your Uncle Dan. And say hello to Ms. Conjure here."

"These your boys?" asked Annie.

Ernie nodded proudly. "Carlo is nine in September, and Sancho's seven next March."

Annie took Carlo's hand between hers. "Carlo, that's a good name. Especially for an auto mechanic. You *do* want to be an auto mechanic, don't you?"

Ernie shook his head in admiration. "How did you know that? He's always been totally crazy about cars. He used to make car noises when he was sitting in his stroller."

Annie took Sancho's hand next. "And you, Sancho, you're going to grow up to be a musician. You're going to play the guitar and sing your own songs, and you'll be very famous. One day you're going to be singing a song about a white bird that comes to your window, and you'll remember this day, and me telling you about it."

Sancho shyly retrieved his hand and said nothing.

"They're terrific boys," Annie told Ernie. "They're going to make you proud."

"Uncle Dan," said Carlo, "can you do that thing with the quarter for us?"

"Hey, don't bother your Uncle Dan," Ernie scolded.

But Dan went up to him and reached down into the back of his T-shirt, so that Carlo giggled and squirmed. "Sorry, Carlo . . . there's no quarters down there today. But—wait a minute! What's this? It feels like a flower!" And he produced a dollar bill, folded into the shape of a rose.

"Me too!" said Sancho, excitedly. "Me too!"

"Kids love magic, don't they?" said Annie, as they squeezed themselves into the elevator.

Ernie pushed the button for 4. "What you said about the boys, that's really going to happen?"

Annie nodded.

Dan said, "The last time you told my fortune, you had to use tarot cards and tea leaves."

"I know. I don't really know how I did that without the tarot, but it seemed so clear. Maybe I'm just getting more sensitive."

They reached the fourth floor and walked along the red linoleum corridor. Ernie opened the door of his apartment and said, "Welcome to my home." Inside, there was a pungent smell of garlic and onions, and a woman was singing along to a Frank Corrales record on the radio, "Una Mañana de Abril."

"Rosa!" called Ernie. "Rosa, we have visitors!"

He led them through to a small living room furnished with two big couches and two big armchairs, all upholstered in rose-patterned fabric with lace antimacassars. On the walls hung oil paintings of Mexican dancers and framed photographs of Carlo and Sancho, as well as a red glass shrine to the Virgin Mary with holy water in it.

Ernie's wife came out of the kitchen wiping her hands. She was a plump, pretty young woman with curly black hair tied up with a bright red scarf, and bright red lips.

"Dan, how are you?" she said, kissing him on both

cheeks, and then once more. "Such a long time since I see you!"

"This is Annie," said Ernie. "Annie has been working with us. She has a very special gift."

Rosa shook Annie's hand. "Pleasure to meet you. Would you care for a drink? Are you hungry?"

"Hungry?" Dan told her. "I could eat a horse. In fact I could eat a whole team of horses."

"Horses I don't have—but I just baked some empanadas."

"Empanadas . . . mmm!" said Dan, in imitation of Homer Simpson. "Annie, you don't know what Mexican food is until you've eaten Rosa's empanadas. Flaky pastry filled with ground beef and chillies."

They went out onto the balcony and sat together at a glass-topped table. Rosa brought out a large jug of lemonade and a plate of empanadas and *garnachas*, little cups of tortilla dough filled with black beans and lemon-marinated slices of onion. Dan would have killed for a cold Corona, but they would be going back on duty in less than three hours.

"So what is your special gift?" Rosa asked Annie.

"She can tell fortunes," said Ernie. "She said that Carlo would be an auto mechanic and that Sancho would be a famous musician."

"Maybe you should tell Ernie's fortune," said Rosa. "He has been trying for promotion for so long."

Ernie emphatically shook his head. "No . . . never. I don't want to see what the future has in store for me. I want every day to be a surprise. Besides, you might tell me something that I don't want to hear."

Rosa said, "You're such a chicken. Annie, why don't you tell my fortune? Then I will know if I am going to be married to a captain of detectives one day."

Ernie had his mouth full of empanada, but he

pointed at Rosa and said, "Whatever you see, don't tell me what it is. I don't want to know."

Annie reached across the table and took hold of both of Rosa's hands. She stared into Rosa's eyes for nearly a minute, while Rosa sat with a shy little smile on her face. At last Annie said, "I'm sorry. I don't see anything about Ernie. All I see is you and your sons. They're all grown up and very handsome, and you're standing in a beautiful garden someplace."

"Then you *must* be getting promoted," said Rosa excitedly. "More money. A house of our own. I always wanted a garden, all my life."

"I told you I didn't want to know," Ernie protested.

"But you don't know *when*, Ernesto, do you? It will still be a surprise when it happens."

"Okay, but not so much." In spite of this show of annoyance, Dan could tell that Ernie was secretly pleased. He had talked for years of gaining a promotion, so that he could have more influence over the way that the Hispanic community was policed, and he had been studying almost every night since April for his sergeant's exam.

"Congratulations, man," said Dan. "I always knew you had it in you."

Annie said nothing, but gave Ernie a pat on his hairy forearm and smiled.

When they had finished eating, Rosa went inside to wash the plates and tidy the kitchen, and they sat for a while on the balcony, talking about what had happened up at Ben Burrows's house that morning.

"Raining, inside the hallway," said Ernie. "And lightning. And thunder. I never thought I'd ever see such a thing."

"And all those goddamned centipedes," said Dan.

"And those rats, *muchacho*. Where did she get those rats from?"

Annie said, "Out of some nearby sewer, most likely. Like I said before, witches can't *create* things like rats or toads or centipedes, but they can move almost anything from one place to another, whether it's living or not. Including themselves."

"We still don't know what her name is or where she comes from," said Ernie.

"Not for sure, no. But I'm ninety-nine percent convinced that she's a direct descendant of Rebecca Greensmith. The pictures in those old books, they're not usually very reliable when it comes to likenesses. I've seen pictures of Cotton Mather that make him look like somebody's nutty old grandma. But this woman and the woman in the Hartford witch-trial picture—they look so much alike they *must* be related somehow."

"I'm going to interrogate her when we get back to the station," said Dan. "Maybe you could come along and give me some magical support."

"Of course," said Annie. "I was going to suggest it anyhow. You never know what tricks she might try to pull on you."

They said good-bye to Rosa. Annie gave Rosa the warmest of hugs, and Ernie said, "Looks like those two have made friends."

"Annie's a great girl. And so's Rosa. Maybe when this is over, we should all go out to dinner together. Spago."

"Let's deal with those witches first. I'm not having *my* hands nailed to the table with no knife and no fork."

Chapter Twenty-two

Newton Ridley was the custody officer that afternoon. As he waddled down the stairs that led to the cells, jingling his keys, he looked back over his shoulder and said, "Maybe *you* can get her to shut up, because I can't."

"What's she been doing?"

"Making this yelping noise. On and on for hours. Sounds like a dog that can't get out of the house to do its business."

They heard her as soon as they reached the bottom of the staircase. A high, weird, ululating howl, which made Dan feel as if his scalp were shrinking. It was both frightening and depressing, and Officer Ridley was right: it sounded more like an animal in distress than a human being.

A man's voice shouted drunkenly from one of the cells, "Shut the hell up, will you? Just shut up! You're driving me nuts!"

They reached the witch's cell. The wax sigil was still in place, with its forklike symbols, and Annie touched it with her fingertips as if to reassure herself that it was firmly fixed.

"She's singing a spell," she said.

"You call that singing?"

"Well, it's singing of a sort. It's a charm to get herself out of there."

"Don't sound charming to me."

"Technically, it *is* charming. The word *charming* originally meant *singing*. In the Middle Ages, women weren't allowed to sing in church in case they cast a spell on their menfolk. Don't worry—the charm isn't working, the sigil is keeping her sealed inside."

Officer Ridley slid back the inspection panel. "She's just sitting on her bunk, rocking herself back and forth like a loony. She's been doing that nonstop since I came on duty."

"Is it safe for us to go in?" Dan asked Annie. "She won't be able to escape or anything?"

Annie peered in through the inspection panel. "She's still restrained. There's nothing she can do to us while her wrists and her ankles are still bound together."

"Okay," said Dan. "Let's go in and have a little q-and-a session."

"Rather you than me, Detective," said Officer Ridley, and unlocked the cell door for him.

The smell of the witch was even stronger than it had been before, and now it had a sourness about it, too, like turned milk. As Dan and Annie entered her cell, the witch turned and glared up at them. Her raggedy cloak had been taken away from her, and now she was wearing a plain orange smock that laced up at the back. The front was already stained dark with spittle.

"So, how it's going?" Dan asked her. "They keeping you fed and watered?"

The witch continued to howl and rock herself backward and forward.

"I guess you must know by now that this charm of yours isn't going to work. You've met your match, ma'am. Admit it."

The witch suddenly stopped howling and stared at Annie with contempt. *"You think this chit of a girl is any match for* me?" she whispered. Her voice was hoarser than ever. *"You have no idea what you have let loose, either of you."*

Dan said, "If you give us some help here, things will go a whole lot easier on you. I can promise you that."

"The only help you *need is a helping hand to hell."*

"You understand the seriousness of the charges against you? Even if you're not looking at the death penalty, you're looking at several lifetimes locked up in Valley State."

"You really think that frightens me?"

"Come on," said Dan, trying to sound reasonable. "All you have to do is tell us your name and where you come from."

"You know who I am, and you know where I come from."

"Yes, but just for the record."

The witch stared at him without saying anything, and for the first time in his life Dan felt serious dread.

"Okay, you don't want to talk. I'll come back later."

"It will do you no good, I promise you. And as for her—" She waved her bony-fingered hand at Annie and said, *"—she thinks she knows the craft, but she knows nothing. If she could truly see the future, she would cut her wrists with a broken piss-bottle."*

Annie didn't answer, but gave the witch a surprisingly indulgent smile.

"Let's get out of here," said Dan. "Maybe a few more hours in here will make her see some sense. Besides, we have some more witches to catch, don't we?"

The witch started to chuckle, and more strings of saliva slid from her lips.

"I'll tell you something," said Dan. "You really do have a serious drool issue."

At that, the witch twisted her head around and spat

directly in his face. Dan pulled out a crumpled Kleenex and wiped off the spittle in disgust, but it was clinging and viscous, and it was like trying to disentangle himself from a very wet spiderweb.

"*Do you know what happens if a witch spits on you?*" The witch grinned. "*This young girl will tell you. You will never marry, you will never have children, and you will never be happy for the rest of your life.*"

Dan took Annie's arm, and they pressed the buzzer for Officer Ridley to let them out. The witch gave them one last mocking look, and then she went back to her rocking and her ululating.

As they walked back along the corridor, Dan kept on furiously rubbing at his face. "*Yuck!* Is it true what she said?"

"About never marrying and never having children and never being happy? Oh, it will be if the curse is never lifted. But most curses can be lifted. I can lift it for you myself with a little angelica and some rose of Jericho. Oh, and maybe some rue."

"Get anything out of her?" asked Officer Ridley. "Apart from spit, I mean."

"Are you kidding me? If I hadn't seen for myself what she's capable of doing, I would have put her down as a total nutjob."

But Annie said, "The most important thing is she's sealed up in here, so she can't share her power with the other three. Once we've caught them all, and sealed *them* up, too, their sisterhood will be broken up forever. I'm not saying they'll ever be completely harmless. They're witches, after all. But they won't be able to take over a whole city again."

They climbed the stairs. The whole station was bustling, officers hurrying in all directions, carrying helmets and carbines and shrugging themselves into Point Blank Body Armor. It was ten after six, and the operation to arrest the Zombie and the White Ghost and Vasili Krylov was already under way. Outside they could hear engines starting, and there was a smell of exhaust fumes in the warm early-evening air.

"I should come with you," said Annie. "I could give you some protection in case anything goes wrong."

"We can't have civilians on a bust. Much too dangerous—and distracting, too."

"What about the staff at the country club?"

"Guttuso's booked one of their private dining rooms. He always does. He doesn't like to be seen in public these days, and he's always worried about somebody taking a potshot at him. We're going to evacuate all the waiters before we go in and move them well back out of the firing line. Now maybe you'd better get home. You have a hungry kitten who needs feeding."

"Dan—"

"Look, don't worry. At least I have a pretty good idea of what we're going to be up against. And I'll have my cell phone with me. If I need any magical advice, I'll call you."

"It's not that. It's Ernie."

Dan had taken out his gun and was checking it to make sure it was clean and fully loaded. "Ernie? What about him?"

"When I read Rosa's fortune . . . I told her that I saw her and the boys standing in a beautiful garden."

"That's right. And?"

"What I didn't tell her was that the garden was a cemetery, with headstones, and that Ernie wasn't there. Rosa was a widow."

Dan slowly holstered his gun and frowned at her. "Ernie was *dead?* Like, how far into the future are we talking about?"

"I'm not sure. It upset me, so I didn't want to continue. All I can tell you is that the boys looked much more grown up than they do now, maybe fifteen or sixteen—but who knows? Ernie might have been dead for years and they were visiting his grave."

"Shit," said Dan. Then, "Listen, when you read somebody's fortune, does it always come true? What I mean is—is there any way of changing it?"

"I think it's unavoidable. You can't alter the future any more than you can alter the past."

"Is there any way of finding out when he's going to die? If we go find him, could we do it now?"

"We could try. But I can't tell his fortune unless he wants me to."

As if he had been cued for a stage appearance, Ernie appeared through the jostling crowds of officers. "Hey, *muchacho!* How did you get on with Endora?"

"She spat on me, put a curse on me, and told us we were a couple of know-nothing losers, but apart from that—great."

"You ready to roll?"

"Sure. But there's something I wanted to ask you first. I know you weren't too happy about Annie telling your fortune for you—not in front of Rosa—but maybe you could let her do it now."

Ernie blinked at him. "You want Annie to tell my fortune? Why?"

"For fun. But she also can tell if you need to take any special precautions."

"Special precautions? You mean this evening? While we're doing this bust?"

"Not necessarily. Just, you know, in general. After all, you have Carlo and Sancho to think of, as well as Rosa."

"What do you mean by special precautions?"

"Well, like maybe wearing body armor."

"Are *you* wearing body armor?"

"No . . . but we're not front line, are we? It won't be us kicking the doors down."

"So, if *you're* not wearing body armor, why should I?"

"Because you should. That's all I can tell you. Better yet, why don't you tell the lieutenant you're sick? Go home. Drink lots of Corona. Play dominos with your boys."

Ernie turned to Annie. His expression was very serious. "When you were telling Rosa's fortune, did you *see* something?"

"I'm not going to lie to you, Ernie. I can't be sure. But I think it would be a good idea if I told *your* fortune, too, so that you know what to look out for, and when."

"No. I told you before. If each day is not a surprise, then what is the point in living at all? This is a dangerous job we do. Any day we could get hurt or maybe killed. I know that. I could die from eating too many burritos. I could die from a Russian space satellite falling on my head. It's not up to me what happens. It's up to God."

"El Gordo," Dan appealed. "You're making no sense, man. Look, suppose you stepped off the curb and there was a truck barreling toward you at sixty miles an hour, and I shouted, 'Look out!' Would you carry on walking because it wasn't my responsibility to stop you from getting squished, it was God's?"

"I don't care. You don't tell my fortune. That's it. That's my decision, okay?"

"Okay, if you won't do it, you won't do it. But if you get killed, don't come whining to me."

They drove out of the police station and headed west on Sunset. The sun was dazzling, so Dan put on his mirrored sunglasses. Ernie had sat on his sunglasses last week, and so he had a monstrous lump of grubby

Band-Aid right between his eyes to hold them to-gether.

They made up an informal motorcade. Ahead of them there were five squad cars, and behind them came two black SWAT vans.

"I'd love to know how the captain got himself the green light for this little caper," said Dan. "I thought the chief wanted us to leave these sleazebags to their own devices."

He stopped for a red traffic signal and watched ap-preciatively as a girl with very long blond hair and a very short checkered skirt crossed the road in front of them.

"Now *there's* the kind of woman I should be chasing tonight," he said, raising his sunglasses and giving the girl his special toothy grin. "Not some crabby old gang of witches." The girl turned around as she reached the opposite side of the road and gave him the finger.

Ernie shook his head. "If I were you, *muchacho*, I would stick to witches. And don't grin like that. It's terrible."

"What do you mean? It never fails, that grin."

"Sure. It never fails to make you look like you just arrived from the Ozarks."

They followed the squad cars as they turned up Laurel Canyon. After a while, Ernie said, "From what I was hearing back at the station, the chief is pretty much a basket case. Stays in his office all day and won't talk to nobody. Scared of his own reflection, that's what they say. The only reason they haven't replaced him is because Artisson and Vasquez and Krylov have insisted that he stay. Deputy Chief Days isn't much better, but he seems to have gotten at least one of his balls back."

They drove along Mulholland until they reached

the entrance to West Grove Country Club. Two sandstone pillars supported a wrought-iron arch with the club's insignia in the center of it—a coronet and two crossed golf clubs. Beyond the arch, a red asphalt drive curved up toward a collection of low, art-deco style buildings. The main clubhouse had an entrance like a 1930s movie theater, and the steps that led up to it were built on top of a reflecting pool with ducks and a fountain.

To the left of the clubhouse, around a shady courtyard, there was a complex of conference rooms and private dining rooms. It was in here that the Zombie and the White Ghost and Vasili Krylov were meeting with Giancarlo Guttuso.

Dan parked at an angle outside the country club entrance and climbed out of his SUV. Lieutenant Harris was already there, talking to the SWAT commander—a squat barrel-chested man with a prickly ginger mustache.

"Looks like we're dead on schedule," said Lieutenant Harris. "We have twenty-seven plainclothes officers inside the club, posing as members and guests, and they've gradually been extracting all the civilians and most of the staff. The last of them will be coming out any minute now.

"We have another thirty-six officers dressed as waiters and kitchen staff, and as soon as the place is clear, they'll split up into teams of six. Six of them will go for each of the witches, and six of them will go for each of the mobsters. We have another team to get Guttuso and his bodyguards out of there. Detective Scott's in charge of that because Guttuso knows him and trusts him."

He looked around. The golf course that surrounded the country club was emerald green and peaceful, and a cool evening breeze was blowing from the west. The parking lot was full of gleaming black SUVs—Cadillac Escalades, BMWs, and Porsche Cayennes. A groundsman in an orange baseball cap was sweeping the front steps of the clubhouse as if he had been given the rest of his natural life to do it, but apart from that, the club looked deserted.

Dan, however, could see the black-uniformed officers lying in the shadow of the bunkers, concealed in the alcoves beside the main entrance to the clubhouse, and crouching behind the ornamental flower planters and the wide-spreading cedar trees.

"I'm assuming that you've briefed these guys about the witches?" he asked Lieutenant Harris.

"They've been told that they're something different from your garden-variety gangster's arm candy, if that's what you mean."

"I mean have you told them that they have supernatural powers? Have you told them that they can shake people to death without even touching them and make them puke up the most disgusting stuff that you can think of?"

"Hey, come on, Detective. You told me that you'd taken most of their power away from them."

"I have. But these officers still need to be aware that these women can work magic spells."

"They've been warned that all three women have unusual abilities in unarmed combat. If I had told them about 'magic spells,' do you honestly think they would have believed me? I told them to go in very hard and very fast and to physically restrain the women before anybody else. Gag them, too."

"Well, I guess that's good advice. At least they won't be able to do any whispering or charming or incantations."

Lieutenant Harris gave him a long, sober look. "When this is over, Dan, I want you to take a psych evaluation and a long vacation someplace normal, where 'spell' means 'a short period of time,' and nothing else."

Chapter Twenty-three

It was 6:58 P.M. when one of Vasili Krylov's heavies came out of the main entrance to the country club in his dark designer suit and his floral designer necktie and lit a cigarette.

He leaned on the railing overlooking the reflecting pool, blowing smoke. Lieutenant Harris said, "Some fricking timing."

They waited tensely while the Russian continued to smoke.

"We can bring him down," said the SWAT commander.

"In total silence? Before he has the chance to shout out or let off a shot?"

"Sure. Officer Lefkowitz over there can blow off a mosquito's left nut from a mile and a half away."

"We can't just kill him in cold blood, Sergeant. So far he's presenting us with no threat whatsoever, let alone a deadly threat."

"He's a goddamned inconvenience. That's good enough for me."

"Have two of your guys jump him. Then we'll go in."

The SWAT commander gave a complicated hand

signal to one of the officers hiding in the alcoves beside the main entrance. There was a moment's pause, and then two officers came running toward the Russian while he was still leaning against the railing with his back turned.

But he must have heard their composition-soled boots drumming across the decking because he half turned around, and when he saw them coming toward him he rolled over the top of the railing and dropped into the pool. He made a loud splash, and he startled the ducks, but the pool was only seven or eight inches deep, and he recovered his balance and started to run diagonally across it, leaping and bounding like a champion hurdler. He ran straight through the fountain in a burst of spray.

"Goddamn it to hell!" cursed the SWAT commander. "Get in after him, you clowns!"

The two SWAT officers clambered over the railing and jumped into the water, but the Russian was already screaming on his walkie-talkie. "Police! *Police!*"

As he reached the far side of the pool, more SWAT officers rose from the nearby sand bunkers, and he shouted, *"Chyort voz'mi!* Police everywhere!"

"Go!" said Lieutenant Harris, and the SWAT commander echoed, "Go!"

But instantly, with a thunderous bang, the doors to the country club's main entrance slammed shut. Every other door and window slammed shut, too, dozens of them, one after the other, like tumultuous applause.

"They've locked the whole place down!" crackled a voice over Lieutenant Harris's walkie-talkie. "We'll have to use the breaching ram!"

Ernie looked at Dan uneasily. "How did they do that? Shut all those doors and windows, all at once? I thought they couldn't hardly do nothing no more."

"I don't know," said Dan, but he wasn't at all happy

about it. He began to feel that something was about to go badly wrong. "Lieutenant!" he shouted. "Maybe the men need to pull back."

"Too late now!" Lieutenant Harris responded. "Come on, you guys, let's get in there! Hard and fast!"

The SWAT teams came pouring out of concealment and ran toward the country club buildings from all directions. Five men started to batter down the main doors, while the other teams swarmed around the conference center and the private dining rooms. They quickly set up mobile floodlights and swung them around to shine on the dining-room windows—although the shutters were all closed, and they couldn't see the mobsters inside. The double oak doors were firmly closed, too.

"Okay—*go!*" yelled the SWAT commander.

Four men ran forward, carrying a breaching ram between them, while a dozen others covered them. But they hadn't even reached the first step when the doors were flung open, and three figures appeared, calm and unblinking in the brilliant floodlight.

On the left was Michelange DuPriz, wearing a clinging scarlet dress and a necklace of shining copper disks. Her snakelike hair appeared to be writhing like a Gorgon's. On the right was Miska Vedma in a very short dress of metallic bronze satin and a bronze satin cap that completely covered her head, like a swimmer.

In the center, her arms spread wide, was Lida Siado in a filmy yellow dress that looked like flames, and her hair tied up in a yellow chiffon scarf. Her eyes were staring and her white teeth were bared in a furious grimace. She could have been a madwoman on the steps of an asylum.

"*Have you no ears?*" she screamed at the SWAT team. "*Did you not hear our agreement, that we should live together in harmony?*"

Lieutenant Harris made his way through the SWAT officers and up to the steps. "Harmony means exactly that, ma'am. Harmony. But you and your friends have been acting anything but harmonious. You're all under arrest for homicide, conspiracy to commit homicide, and too many other offenses than I have time to tell you. So let's see you come with us quietly. We have vans ready."

"*Eskize mwen, msyé*, you don't understand," said Michelange DuPriz, stepping forward on very high heels. She was smiling at Lieutenant Harris in the way a hooker smiles at a potential client—teasing him, daring him, but deeply contemptuous of him, too. "You have to leave us alone. You have no choice."

"Oh, you think so?" Lieutenant Harris retorted. "Not only do I have a choice, I have a duty, and I have more than a hundred heavily armed police officers who are going to assist me in carrying it out. So let's go, shall we?"

"Treating three innocent women in such a way!" Michelange DuPriz scolded him, strutting down the steps until she was less than three feet away from him. "Such behavior should make you *malad!*"

With that, she opened the palm of her hand and blew a shower of fine gray dust at him. Lieutenant Harris backed away, flapping at the dust with his left hand.

"That's it!" he snapped. "I want these women restrained. Sergeant!"

"Yes, sir!" said the SWAT sergeant, and unclipped the cuffs from his belt.

But at that moment, Lieutenant Harris abruptly dropped to his knees, and said, "*Gahh!*"

"Lieutenant?"

"*Gaahhhhh!*" gargled Lieutenant Harris. His eyes

were bulging, and he was clutching his neck with both hands, as if trying to strangle himself.

"Paramedics!" Dan called out. "Paramedics, now!"

He hurried over to Lieutenant Harris and knelt down beside him. As he did so, he glanced up at Michelange DuPriz, and she was grinning at him.

"Mwen regret sa," she said. "But I did advise you to warn them, didn't I?"

Lieutenant Harris was bent double, his face gray, whining for breath. Dan said, "What is it? What have you put inside him? For Christ's sake, you witch, he's choking!"

The SWAT sergeant advanced on Michelange DuPriz, but now Lida Siado stepped forward, too, pointing at him with one finger and flicking the little drum that she wore around her neck. Tap-*flick*-tap-*flick*!

"Rete!" said Michelange DuPriz. "You do not want to come any closer, police, else worse bad thing happen to you!"

Lieutenant Harris was shuddering now, his mouth stretched wide open.

"What the hell have you put inside him?" Dan shouted.

Half a dozen more SWAT officers approached the witches, but Lida Siado pointed at each of them, one by one, as if she were placing a curse on them individually, and they all held back, even though it was obvious from the confused looks on their faces that they didn't understand why.

Lieutenant Harris gave one last convulsion, and out of his mouth came a bulging mass of worms, hundreds of them, pink and brown and some still streaked with dirt. He vomited again and again, until there was a whole tangle of worms wriggling on the steps in front of him.

"Oh, God," he moaned, spitting out the last stray worms. "Oh, God, help me!"

The SWAT commander shielded his eyes in disgust, and one of the younger officers turned away and retched.

"Worms!" sang Michelange DuPriz, gleefully. "But not just any worms! These worms came from Forest Lawn Cemetery, where your father was buried! These worms came out of his casket! Don't you remember what you said after his funeral? 'I always hated his guts. I hope the worms make a good meal out of him.' Well, they did—and now *you* have, too. Although, what a pity, it doesn't look as if it agreed with you!"

Dan helped Lieutenant Harris to his feet. Lieutenant Harris was still sweaty and ashen, but he jabbed one finger at Michelange DuPriz and rasped, "You, lady—you're finished!"

"Finished, Mesyé Police? We have not even begun!"

Lida Siado took out two clamshells and pressed them over her eyes, as she had at Chief O'Malley's house. Then she quickened the tapping on her drum. *Tap*—flick—*tapp!* and it seemed to Dan that the ferocious woman's face painted on the drumskin slowly opened her eyes and stared at him just as madly as Lida had herself.

"Night Wind! Come blow for me! Night Wind! Rise up for me! Bring me your darkness! Bring me your children! Bring me your fear! Night Wind! Come blind this company!"

Dan gripped Lieutenant Harris's sleeve. "Lieutenant, we have to get out of here. Everybody! *Now!*"

Lieutenant Harris spat and spat again. He was shaking with rage. "If you think I'm letting these bitches get away with this, Detective, you're making a serious mistake! Sergeant, get the bracelets on them! And let's get inside and collar the rest of them! Let's move!"

The SWAT commander shouted into his r/t mike: "Inside team! This is it! Go! Go! Go!"

They heard three deafening explosions from inside the dining rooms and a stuttering volley of submachine-gun fire. Then there was another explosion and shouting and three or four shots from a .45 automatic.

The SWAT team mounted the steps to seize the three witches, but as they did so there was a catastrophic bellow of thunder, and the sky turned instantly black, as if the sun had been switched off.

"Cuff them!" yelled Lieutenant Harris, before he broke into a coughing fit. But there was another rumble of thunder, followed by a low howling sound, which quickly developed into a high-pitched scream.

A gale rose up, and the courtyard was filled with dust and grit and whirling leaves. It blew harder and harder, until Dan could hardly stay on his feet. The SWAT officers were staggering about in confusion, shouting at each other, but the wind was so loud that they couldn't even hear the headphones in their helmets. One man was blown against a low wall and tumbled over backward, firing his carbine into the air.

With his hand raised to protect his eyes, Dan looked toward the witches. All three were completely unruffled by the wind. Not even their dresses were stirring. Yet hundreds of rose petals were flying all around them, and chairs were tipping over, and shutters were being ripped away from the country club windows to career off into the darkness.

"Retreat!" shouted the SWAT commander. "Retreat and regroup!"

Not many of his men could hear what he was saying, but his hand signals made it clear. With the wind screaming at their backs, they battled their way out of the courtyard toward the front of the country club, trying to keep their balance, as if they had only just learned to walk.

Suddenly one of the officers spun around, holding his arms out and groping at the air. He tripped and fell heavily onto his back, but instead of trying to get up, he stayed where he was, his hands pressed over his eyes. Two more officers struggled across the driveway to help him, but then they lost their footing, too. By the time Dan and Ernie reached them, twenty or thirty more officers had fallen to the ground. Some of them were attempting to get to their feet, but most were kneeling or lying where they were, shouting desperately for help.

"What's wrong with them?" shouted Ernie.

Lieutenant Harris gave him his answer. He came toward them with his eyes staring wide, but from the jerky way that he was walking and the way that he was waving his arms around in front of him, it was obvious that he had lost his sight.

"She's blinded them!" Dan shouted back. "That Night Wind spell! She's blinded them!"

He tried to take Lieutenant Harris's arm, to guide him toward the country club driveway, but Lieutenant Harris screamed, "Get away! Get away from me!"

With that, he went zig-zagging off in the direction of the golf course.

Dan and Ernie looked around, their eyes narrowed against the gale. Everywhere they looked, SWAT and police officers were wandering around like marionettes with their strings cut. Several of them waded straight into the reflecting pool, and others blundered into the sand bunkers. Occasional bursts of gunfire flickered in the darkness, as submachine guns were accidentally let off.

"This is all my fault!" Dan shouted.

"What? I can't hear you!"

He leaned close to Ernie's right ear. "This is all my fault! I didn't realize the witches had so much power. I didn't think they could do anything much, not on their own. Not without that fourth witch."

"How were you supposed to know that? You can't go blaming yourself. None of this is natural, is it? It's *blasfemia!*"

Dan took out his cell phone and punched in Annie's number. He held it to his ear, but he could hear nothing but fizzing. Whatever had brought on the wind and the darkness had blotted out phone reception, too.

Ernie yelled, "We can see!"

"What do you mean?"

"All of these other guys—they're all blind! But you and me, we can *see!*"

"Well, let's get the hell out of here while we still can!"

"We should help these guys. Lookit—even the paramedics have gone blind!"

"What do you think you and me can do? There's over a hundred guys here!"

Ernie turned around and around in desperation. "I don't know! But why haven't you and me gone blind?"

"Who knows? Let's just be grateful, shall we, and get going, before we do."

They had nearly reached the decking at the front of the country club, and they clung on to the railings for support. The wind was shrieking so loudly that they gave up trying to shout at each other, but as they reached the reflecting pool, Ernie turned around and frantically jabbed his finger at the water.

Dan looked down. In spite of the wind, which must have been blowing at nearly ninety miles an hour, the surface of the pool was absolutely still, and three floodlights were shining across it so that it looked like a mirror. The ducks had either flown away or been blown away, but the fountain was still playing as if there were no wind at all.

All that disturbed the water were the floating bodies of seven or eight SWAT officers, lying facedown.

Dan and Ernie were still staring at them when two more officers appeared on the opposite side of the pool, blindly weaving their way toward them.

"Stop!" Ernie screamed at them, waving his arms. "Stop!"

Dan leaned close to him. "It's no use! They can't hear you and they can't see you!"

Ernie tried to pull himself along the railings to the end of the pool, but he was too late. The first of the two officers stumbled into the pool, closely followed by his companion. They started to splash across it, slipping from time to time, but still managing to keep going. They bumped into some of the floating bodies, and stopped, and bent over, fumbling around to find out what they were. When they felt their water-logged uniforms, one of them began to panic and wade wildly around in circles. The other officer stepped slowly backward, blindly trying to retrace his steps.

The first officer slipped and fell into the water on his hands and knees. He stayed there, his head lowered as if he had lost the will to get up and try to climb out of the pool.

"Let's go get him!" Ernie shouted. But before they could reach the end of the railings, Dan saw a dark shape approaching the officer underneath the surface of the water.

"Ernie! What's that?"

Ernie peered at it hard. "It's a guy," he said, at last.

"He's upside down, like a reflection. But—there's no guy there!"

Ernie was right. Reflected in the water, his image wobbling slightly in the ripples, was a man wearing a dark suit. His reflection was standing directly in front of the crouching officer's reflection, but in reality there was nobody there.

"Come on!" said Dan, but Ernie crossed himself and held back, the wind whipping up his necktie.

"This is more black magic!"

"This is *all* black magic! Come on!"

There was another rumble of thunder, right over their heads, and then an ear-splitting crackle of lightning.

In the reflecting pool, the man in the dark suit leaned forward and grasped the crouching officer by the back of his neck. The officer struggled and thrashed his arms and tried to twist himself free, but the reflected man pushed his head upward, toward the surface. In reality, the officer's head was forced *downward*, under the water—although there was nobody anywhere near him, and it looked as if he were trying to drown himself.

Dan tugged out his gun and pointed it at the reflected man.

"It's a reflection!" Ernie shouted at him. "What is the point?"

All the same, Dan fired twice, and the gun kicked in his hands. The bullets broke up the reflection for a few seconds, but they didn't have any effect on the reflected man at all. He continued to hold the officer's head under the water, until the officer had stopped struggling and floated inertly on the surface.

Ernie had reached the end of the railings now, and he clambered down into the water. He waded over to the drowned officer and dragged him to the edge of the pool. Dan stepped into the water after him, his gun still raised, searching the pool for any sign of the reflected man. He thought he saw a shadow moving through the water toward the country club, but the floodlights were shining so brightly on the surface that he could have been mistaken.

He went over to join Ernie, who had taken off the officer's helmet and his body armor and was giving him CPR. He tried for over five minutes, but it was clear that the officer was dead. Without his helmet, he looked so young, freckled and snub-nosed like somebody's kid brother.

In the end, Dan said, "Forget it, Ernie. He's gone. The best thing we can do for these guys is get the hell out of here and find some other way of beating these goddamned witches."

Here, in the pool, it was eerily still, even though the wind was furiously blowing all around them, and SWAT officers were stumbling everywhere, blinded and hysterical. The country club was in chaos, like some medieval vision of hell. The sky was still black, and the driveway was crowded with abandoned vans and squad cars, their red lights flashing.

Dan made his way to the edge of the pool and was about to climb out when he saw something running diagonally across the driveway toward the dining rooms. It was tall and light-colored, with an attenuated head. It looked more like a huge insect than a man, and yet it ran upright, like a man, and it appeared to have arms and legs like a man.

For a moment it disappeared behind a row of yew bushes, but then it reappeared, and it was heading directly for a SWAT officer who was kneeling on the driveway with his head lifted as if he were praying, which he probably was.

"Ernie," he said, as Ernie reached the edge of the pool, "what the hell do you think *that* is?"

But before Ernie could answer, the man-insect collided with the kneeling SWAT officer, sending him flying. The SWAT officer tried to climb to his feet, but the man-insect was on him instantly, with teeth and claws and feet. There was a blizzard of blood and ripped-apart clothing and ribbons of scarlet flesh. Then there were loops of yellowish intestines and bones. Half of the SWAT officer's rib cage was tossed out of the carnage, and it rolled across the driveway.

Even though they were blinded, the officers around him must have sensed that something was seriously wrong because they scattered in different directions. But the man-insect caught hold of another one and clawed at his clothes with even more ferocity.

"Holy Mother of God," said Ernie. "That's what must have happened at the White Ghost's house. Look at that thing!"

Dan said, "*Things*, plural. Look."

Out of the woods appeared at least ten more man-insects, running toward the blinded SWAT officers, their legs moving like pistons.

"Let's go," said Dan, and lifted himself out of the pool. He turned around and offered Ernie his hand, but as he did so, Ernie's eyes widened, and he shouted, "Behind you, *muchacho!*"

Chapter Twenty-four

Dan slowly heaved Ernie out of the water. Then, without turning around, he drew out his gun. The wind was moaning and screaming like a chorus of damned souls. They could barely hear each other shouting.

"How far behind me?"

"Five yards! Not much more!"

Dan found himself breathing deeply and steadily. Every time he woke up in the morning, it was always in the back of his mind that he might be killed or seriously injured before the day was over. But he had always imagined that he would be hit by a stray bullet as he drove along Olympic or stabbed at random by some crackhead Crip on Eighty-third Street. He had never thought that his whole body might be ripped apart and his bones scattered like sticks.

He cocked his gun and swung around. The man-insect was standing so close to him that he took an involuntary step backward and then another and almost fell back into the pool.

It was nearly seven and a half feet tall with a narrow, elongated head that was more like the skull of an antelope than the head of an insect. It appeared to be fleshless, with skin that was parchment colored and very dry. It didn't have horns on top of its head, but a kind of jagged crown made of cracked shards of bone.

Its eyes were a dull red, and when it blinked, its eyelids rolled upward.

A *kukurpa*, a hungry spirit from the mythology of the Uitoto Indians in the depths of the Amazon rain forest. Except that it was real and could be summoned with the Night Wind to tear apart the enemies of those who had called it up.

It had skeletal shoulders, raised up like wings, and spindly arms with terrifying claws. Its body was covered in fine, tawny hair, similar to a dog's coat, and its skin was loose. Between its thighs hung a long pale brown penis like a braided bell rope, and testicles like dried fruit.

There were claws on its feet, too, and curved spurs of bone protruded from its heels.

It took one spastic step toward them, and Dan fired twice. The first bullet thumped into the creature's chest, leaving an inch-wide hole. The second blasted a spray of bone fragments from the crown on top of its head.

The *kukurpa* barely flinched. It raised its left arm, and Dan fired again, hitting it in the side of its chest. As it jerked toward him, he fired twice more, at point-blank range. The next thing he knew, it struck him on the shoulder. Its arm was as hard as a pickax handle, and he was knocked off his feet onto the decking. His gun tumbled into the pool.

He bunched himself up in the fetal position, his eyes shut tight, expecting at any second to have the clothes ripped off his back and the flesh pulled away from his ribs.

God forgive me. Gayle forgive me. Please don't let it hurt too much.

But then he was suddenly drenched with something wet and warm, and he heard a hoarse, despairing shout.

He rolled over to find that he was plastered with blood and to see the *kukurpa* attacking Ernie.

"No!" he shouted. He grabbed hold of the railings and pulled himself onto his feet. "Get off him, you freak! *Get off him!*"

But the *kukurpa*'s claws were lashing at Ernie in a frenzy, and when Dan tried to pull it away, it knocked him over again, onto his back, so hard that all the wind was jolted out of him.

Ernie lifted his left arm to protect his face, but the *kukurpa* tore his entire arm out of its socket and tossed it away into the darkness. Blood was spurting everywhere, and even as he climbed to his feet again, Dan knew that Ernie didn't stand a chance of survival. Ernie glanced up at him, and there was an expression in his eyes worse than agony and worse than dread. It was resignation.

The *kukurpa* tore into him like a threshing machine, relentless and unstoppable. Dan turned away as it lashed into Ernie's chest and stomach, and slashed his intestines into bloody rags.

He limped up the decking, back toward the country club's main entrance. His head felt empty, like a gas-filled balloon, and he could hardly manage to keep his balance. He passed one ripped-apart SWAT officer after another. There were so many body parts in the gardens outside the convention center that it could have been the scene of an air crash.

He saw two or three *kukurpas* moving in their strange stilted way through the shadows behind the trees, but he no longer cared. If they wanted to tear him apart, too, there was nothing he could do to stop them. He walked straight to the steps outside the private dining rooms, where the three witches were still standing.

As he approached them, the wind began to falter, and the leaves and rose petals whirling in the air began to sink to the ground. By the time he reached the steps, there was nothing but a soft breeze blowing, and the glittering lights of West Hollywood had reappeared out of the darkness.

Dan stood in front of the witches and pointed back toward the pool. "One of your things just killed my partner."

"The perils of police work," said Lida Siado. "You can't tell us that you we didn't warn you."

"You've massacred these men. Do you really think that you're going to get away with this? They'll bring in the National Guard."

"They can bring in whoever they wish," said Miska. "All will meet the same fate."

Just then, the White Ghost appeared in a dazzling white tuxedo, followed by the Zombie in a green velvet smoking jacket, and Vasili Krylov in a pinstriped Bill Blass suit.

"*Bonswa*, Detective." The Zombie grinned, showing his golden teeth. "Sorry for what just happened here, but you knew what our lady friends would do to you if you tried to pull us in."

"There were more than a hundred officers here tonight," Dan told him. He was so shaken that he could hardly speak.

"You can send a thousand if you like," said Vasili Krylov. "You can send ten thousand. We have the power of hell behind us, my friend. All hell, let loose."

"That thing killed my partner! He was my friend. He was a husband and a father. He had two little boys. And that thing tore him to pieces!"

"We are deeply sorry for your loss," said the White Ghost. "We never wanted violence, believe me. We simply came to have a friendly dinner with Signor Guttuso. We had an arrangement with the police department. We never expected you to interrupt us."

At that moment, Giancarlo Guttuso came out, accompanied by four bodyguards with shiny black hair and shiny black suits. Giancarlo Guttuso was at least seventy years old, with wobbly jowls and a face the color of liverwurst. He made his way between the mobsters and the witches, and pushed past Dan without even looking at him.

When he saw the carnage in the garden, however—the bones and the blood and the long hose reels of intestines—he stopped and looked around, and his face was distraught. His bodyguards took hold of his arms and quickly led him away, and even they were coughing in disgust.

"I don't think that Signor Guttuso will be making any more complaints about us," the Zombie remarked. "In a way, Detective, you and your friends saved us a great deal of unpleasant wrangling. Once Signor Guttuso saw a live demonstration of what we are capable of doing to protect our interests, he accepted that we could take over as much of his business as we wanted."

"You won't get away with this," Dan repeated.

"You don't think so?" asked the White Ghost. "How will you prove in court that we had anything to do with this? Hah? A natural disaster, that's all. It was a freak of the weather that killed all these men—a localized hurricane. A tragedy, for sure. But an act of God."

"That creature of yours killed my partner!"

"But it didn't kill *you*, did it, *msyé?*" said Michelange DuPriz. "Has it occurred to you to ask *poukisa?*"

"*I* can tell him why!" called out a thin, shrill voice. "*I* can tell him why he's still alive and why he can still see out of his peepers!"

Michelange DuPriz and Lida Siado both stepped to one side. From behind them, Dan was stunned to see the fourth witch appear in her wide felt hat and her raggedy cloak covered with hooks and dried herbs. As always, she was carrying her staff with the cat's head on top.

"Surprised to see me, my good sir?" the fourth witch mocked. "Thought I was locked up in the choky, did you? You can't keep one of his majesty's favorites confined like that!"

Dan dropped to his knees, defeated. Now this evening's tragedy made sense. He couldn't imagine how the fourth witch had broken Annie's sigil and escaped from her cell, but here she was, with her overwhelming magical power. It seemed as if she and her three sister witches were unbeatable.

"Don't be depressed, Detective!" said the fourth witch, hobbling down the steps. "If we all learn to rub along together, there won't be any further need for blood to be shed!"

Dan looked up at her wearily and said nothing.

"If we all treat each other with a little more respect, we won't have to tear each other's lights out, shall we, or roll our heads around like bowling balls."

"Go to hell," Dan told her.

"I probably shall! And pay my respects to his majesty and then return! Come on, my good sir, I know you're grieving for your friend, but all of us have to meet death one day or another, and at least his death was quick, and dare I say heroic in its own insignificant way?"

Dan didn't know what to say. The pain he felt for Ernie's death was almost too much for him to bear. The fourth witch stood very close to him—so close that he could smell her rancid odor, dried urine, and lavender. But there was an extraordinary expression on her face—thoughtful, almost tender, as if she could feel how grief stricken he was.

"You mustn't hate me," she said. "I shall be around

for a very long time now, and hating me will get you nowhere." She laid one of her bony hands on his shoulder. He tried to twist away, but she dug in her fingernails, gripping him tight. "You will never be free of me, my good sir, not until you go to meet your friend."

"So why am I still alive now?"

"You are alive because I *want* you alive. You are alive because you are useful to me. You have something that is shared by no other man in the world."

"Oh, yes. And what the hell is that?"

"If you *knew*, my good sir, you would no longer be useful. And if you were no longer useful, I should have to kill you, too. With centipedes, perhaps, or lightning, or I would ask my sister Lida to conjure up one of her *kukurpas* for you."

"If I really thought that I was any use to you, I would kill myself anyhow," Dan told her.

"No, you wouldn't. It's not in your nature. You are the kind of man who will fight death to the bitter end. Just as you will try to fight *me* to the bitter end. But you will never succeed in besting me, I am happy to say."

"So what happens now?" Dan asked.

"You may go. You have to tell your surviving colleagues what happened here this evening, don't you? And you have to tell your unfortunate friend's wife and children that he has met with a sticky end. And you have to go back to your young lady friend and discuss how you can get your revenge on us."

She gripped his shoulder even tighter, until it felt as if her fingernails were going to break his skin. "You should rest, too, my good sir, and try to have pleasant dreams. When your waking life is a nightmare, what other escape can you find?"

She released him, and he stiffly stood up. He looked at Michelange DuPriz and Lida Siado and Miska

Vedma and their smugly smiling employers, and pointed
his finger at each of them in turn, the same way that
Lida Siado had pointed at the SWAT officers when
they attempted to arrest her.

He said nothing, but he left no doubt that he was
making each of them a promise: that he would come
back for them, as soon as he could, and punish them
for what they had done here tonight, whether he did it
legally or not.

He weaved his way between the empty squad cars and
SWAT vans, their lights still flashing, and climbed into
his Torrent. He swerved away, back along Mulholland,
but after he had driven less than a mile he pulled to the
side of the road and took out his cell phone.

He called Captain Friendly, back at the station.

"Fisher? What the hell is going on? We've totally
lost contact with Lieutenant Harris."

"There's been a problem, sir."

"Problem? What kind of a problem?"

"Maybe *problem* is the wrong word."

"All right. So what's the right word?"

"Massacre. They've all been killed. All of them except for me."

"Fisher, are you drunk?"

"No, sir. You need to alert Deputy Chief Days and
the coroner and maybe the governor, too. I'm not too
sure what the procedure is when a hundred officers
get torn to pieces."

"Where are you now, Fisher?"

"On Mulholland about a mile east of West Grove.
Listen, have we lost any prisoners from the cells? Any
of them escaped?"

"Not to my knowledge. Why?"

"I just need to know if any prisoners have gotten
out, that's all."

"Listen, Fisher—come on in. Don't talk to anybody else. And I mean *nobody*."

"Yes, sir."

Before he switched off, he heard Captain Friendly say, "—Fisher . . . sounds like he's smashed—"

He called Annie. She took a long time to answer, and when she did she sounded as if she had her mouth full.

"Annie? It's me."

"Dan! Are you okay?"

"Not really. The whole thing's been a disaster. The witches have killed all of them—the same way they did the last time, at Orestes Vasquez's house."

"Oh my God. How could they?"

"The fourth witch was there, that's how. Somehow she managed to get out of her cell."

"But she *couldn't*. Not even a grand wizard could have gotten past that sigil."

"I'm telling you, Annie, she was there. I saw her, and I talked to her. I was the only survivor."

"I don't understand it. I simply don't. Her wrists and her knees and her ankles were bound by that Enochian incantation. Even if she'd persuaded somebody to take the sigil off the door, she still couldn't have escaped."

"Seeing is believing, Annie. I'm going back to the station now, and I'm going to check for myself. Why don't you meet me there?"

"Okay. My friend Sally's here, so she'll give me a ride." She paused for a moment, and then she said, "You *are* all right? You're not hurt or anything?"

"Physically, no," he told her, but it was all he could do to hold back his tears.

The station was grim and quiet when he arrived. News of what had happened at West Grove Country Club must have spread through the building already. Annie was waiting for him by the front desk, wearing pink jeans and a loose long-sleeved T-shirt.

The desk sergeant said, "Detective? Captain Friendly wants to see you up in his office right away."

"There's something I have to check on first. Who's on lockup duty?"

"Manson. He just went for coffee. Is it true what they're saying about that country club bust?"

Dan nodded.

"Lieutenant Harris?"

"All of them. Ernie, too."

"Ernie!" said Annie, and her eyes filled with tears. "Oh no, not Ernie!"

The desk sergeant said, "Shit, man. I can't believe it. And they was armed to the frigging teeth."

"Listen, I'm not supposed to talk about it, not yet."

"But how did it happen? Don't tell me those mobsters have *that* much of an army?"

"Oh, they do, believe me."

Officer Manson came back along the corridor with two Styrofoam cups of coffee.

"It's true," said the desk sergeant.

Officer Manson put the cups down on the desk. "Shit," he said, shaking his head.

"All of them," said the desk sergeant. "Lieutenant Harris, Ernie Munoz—all of them. Except for Detective Fisher here."

"What the hell happened?"

"I can't tell you yet," Dan said. "Right now, I urgently need to take a look at that old bag lady downstairs."

"She didn't have nothing to do with this, did she?"

"I just need to see her, that's all."

"Okay, Detective. But you must be some kind of masochist. That woman stinks like a rotten chicken."

He led Dan and Annie down the stairs and along the

corridor to the end cell. "The sigil's still in place," said Annie, wiping her eyes.

"That wax thing?" asked Officer Manson. "I was told to leave it on there, no matter what. Looks like some kind of hex to me."

"Well, you're almost right," said Dan. He slid back the inspection hatch and peered inside the cell. But the witch wasn't sitting on her bunk. She wasn't standing in the corner, either.

"She's not there. I can't see her, anyhow."

"Hey, come on—she *must* be there. She was there at five when I gave her a peanut-butter sandwich, and this door hasn't been opened since. Not by me, not by anybody."

"Well, let's take a look."

Officer Manson fumbled with his keys and unlocked the door. He and Dan stepped into the cell and looked around. The smell was nauseating—worse than rotten chicken, more like rotten chicken stuffed with rotten mackerel heads. Officer Manson said, "Jesus H. Christ," and clamped his hand over his mouth and nose. Dan felt his mouth flooding with bile.

In one corner of the cell there was a heap of maggots—enough maggots to have made a witch. They squirmed and writhed and tumbled over each other, as if they were trying to climb up the wall.

"What the hell happened to her?" said Officer Manson, behind his hand. "Nobody decomposes that quick. Not even a stinky old bat like her."

"Let's just get out of here," said Dan.

They left the cell and Officer Manson locked the door behind them. "That is totally disgusting. That isn't *her*, is it?"

Annie nodded. "In a way, that's what's left of her."

"How come she went all maggoty so quick?"

"I don't know. I really don't."

"I'd better call the coroner's department. That's if they have any MEs to spare."

Dan and Annie went back upstairs. They walked together to the elevators, but before he pressed the button, Dan said, "You *do* know what happened to her, don't you?"

"Yes, I think so."

"So are you going to share it with me?"

Annie said, "The witch didn't escape. She couldn't have. Instead, she killed herself."

"She *killed* herself? But I saw her up at West Grove, and she sure wasn't dead then!"

"That's because there's more than one of her. The Quintex. Not only did she have five lives, but unless those five lives were brought to an end by execution or murder or suicide, they would carry on forever. Rebecca Greensmith went to the gallows, as we know. We saw the picture of those men hanging from her legs to make sure she was dead. But that was only one Rebecca Greensmith. The other four must have left Hartford and gone to live secretly elsewhere."

"Annie, we're talking three hundred fifty years old."

"And after everything you've witnessed, you don't think that's possible? The fourth witch isn't a descendant of Rebecca Greensmith. She *is* Rebecca Greensmith."

Dan pressed the heel of his hand against his forehead and squeezed his eyes shut. This was all too much. The fourth witch had been right: all he wanted to do now was forget about the nightmare of reality, and go to sleep and dream. Except that he would probably have that dream about Gayle and the scaffolding pole.

Annie said, "Don't you understand? That's why she turns maggoty so quickly. She's probably full of maggots already, just bursting to get out."

"Those maggots in your apartment—were *they* her, too?"

"I'm sure of it. She came into my living room and deliberately killed herself so that I would be surrounded by maggots. She hoped that she would intimidate me so much that I would stop trying to find her."

"That's kind of extreme. Losing one of her lives, just to scare you off."

"But that tells me that *she's* more scared of *me* than I am of her. It also tells me that I'm much more powerful than I thought I was. She can't hurt me, Dan, not directly. Otherwise she would have done it by now. And she must have thought that it was worth losing one of her lives, just to get rid of me."

"Well . . . that means that she only has two lives left. Unless she's lost another one that we don't know about."

He checked his watch. "Listen, I have to report to the captain, tell him what happened. I don't know when I'll be home, but I'll give you a knock, okay? We need to talk about this a whole lot more."

Annie gave him a kiss. "I'm so sorry about Ernie," she said. "You must be devastated."

"Devastated doesn't even come close. We were like brothers, Ernie and me." He kissed her back, and said, "I'll see you later, okay?"

Chapter Twenty-five

It was well past 2:30 A.M. before he made it back to Franklin Avenue. Annie's lights were out, so he decided not to disturb her. He went up to his own apartment and tugged off his shirt as he walked across the kitchen.

He was exhausted. Apart from the trauma of what had happened at West Grove Country Club, there had been a five-hour debriefing with all of the emergency services, including the police, the Highway Patrol, the fire department, and the FBI.

The LAPD's press officer announced that there had been several "climate-related" fatalities at the country club and that a "thorough and searching" investigation was under way. Until its findings were complete, there would be no further official comment. Most of the press already knew that the Zombie and the White Ghost and Vasili Krylov had been meeting Giancarlo Guttuso at the country club. After the threats they had received, they were quite happy to report the official version and not dig too deeply into what might really have happened.

Dan went to the fridge, took out a two-liter bottle of Mountain Dew, and drank several large mouthfuls.

Then, burping loudly, he went into the bedroom and stripped off the rest of his clothes. He knew that he needed a shower, but he collapsed facedown on the bed and lay there with his eyes open, feeling as if he had been beaten up by professionals.

"Ernie," he said out loud. "Ernesto Munoz. Wherever you are, El Gordo, rest in peace."

He knew that his first call in the morning would be to see Rosa and tell her that she and the boys would never see Ernie again. Why the hell hadn't Ernie taken Annie's advice and stayed at home?

He closed his eyes. He slept. He dreamed that he was walking toward the three witches with half a dozen pale *kukurpas* stalking beside him. As he came nearer, the witches drew back, and a figure in a black veil appeared, holding up a staff with a cat's head on top of it. The figure came gliding toward him, and he was suddenly seized with a terrible sense of dread. He knew, however, that he couldn't turn and run. He was surrounded by *kukurpas*, and they would rip him to shreds if he tried to escape.

The figure in the black veil came right up to him. It was impossible to see her face, but he could see her eyes glittering through the layers of chiffon. "I have spared you," she whispered. "I have protected you and taken care of you. There is one favor you can do for me, in return."

"You killed my friend," he replied, and his voice was shaking. "I'll see you in hell before I do you any favors."

"You don't understand," the figure told him. "You look, you see, but you don't understand. Nothing is what it seems to be."

"I understand that Ernie's dead and that you and your fellow bitches were responsible for it."

The figure lifted her right hand and drew back her veil. It wasn't Rebecca Greensmith at all: it was Gayle.

She was looking pale but still perfect, and she was smiling at him gently.

"Gayle? *You're* protecting me?"

"Of course. Who else did you think it was?"

"I don't know. You're not a witch, are you?"

She glided right up to him and took hold of his hand. Her fingers were cool, but she didn't feel as if she were dead. "I'm the memory of somebody who loved you very much."

He looked down at her. His eyes were filled with tears—not just for her, but for Ernie, too, and all the men who had died that night, and whose wives would be widowed, and whose children would be left without a father.

"Ssh," said Gayle, and stood on tiptoe so that she could brush his lips with hers. "Life is always full of grief. It is only the end of life that brings peace and understanding and the longest sleep of all."

Dan was about to kiss her again when he was woken up by his bedside telephone ringing. He scrabbled to pick it up and said, "Whuh? What time is it?"

"Morning, son! It's just gone seven-thirty. I thought you would have been up by now and working out."

"Dad, what the hell do you want?"

"I hear there's been some funny stuff going on."

"Funny stuff?" Dan sat up in bed and ruffled his hair.

"That's right. Funny stuff. Like the sky going inky black and the wind getting up and police officers getting killed."

"Where'd you hear that?"

"I'm seventy-seven years old, Dan, I have plenty of friends. In fact, I had a call from Jake Harriman at CNN. He and I go way back. He wanted to know if we were talking black magic here. Strictly off the record. Apparently, the media have been told that it was a freak electric storm."

"I can't tell you anything, Dad. I'm sorry."

His father cleared his throat. "This is something to do with these witches you were telling me about, isn't it?"

"I'm sorry, Dad. I'm not allowed to say."

"Dan—you listen to me—I may be getting on in years, but I'm not stupid. I was years in the business, and like I told you before, I knew some genuine practitioners of voodoo and hoodoo and who-knows-who-do. I've seen people who can work black magic, and I know that it's real."

Dan took a deep breath, and then he said, "Okay. It was those witches. About a hundred officers got killed, including my partner Ernie Munoz."

Briefly, haltingly, he told his father about Rebecca Greensmith and her five lives, and what the four witches had done up at West Grove Country Club.

"Come see me," said his father.

"What?"

"You heard me. Come see me just as soon as you can. And bring that Annie Conjure along with you."

"Dad—"

"For once in your life, Dan, don't argue with me. You lost your partner. I don't want to lose *you*."

"Okay," Dan conceded. "I'll see you around eleven."

He filled the coffeemaker, and then he took a shower. As he came back into the kitchen with a towel wrapped around his waist, the TV news was showing pictures of downtown L.A. and bodies lying in the street.

"Early this morning, seven members of the Eighty-third Street Gangster Crips were found dead in the street in what police could only describe as 'mysterious circumstances.' All the victims suffered broken necks.

"The Eighty-third Street Gangster Crips, known as the Eight-Tray, have been notorious since 1979 for their drug trafficking, particularly, in recent years, their selling of highly addictive crack cocaine.

"They have made huge profits out of their drug business, and they have been involved in almost constant gang warfare with several other Crip sets, especially the Rollin' 60s. But eyewitness accounts of this morning's carnage indicate that rival Crip gangs may *not* have been responsible for the deaths of these seven young men."

A black youth appeared on the screen, with his back to the camera so that he could not be identified. He said, "They was standing on the sidewalk together outside of the Bubble Club when they just went kind of jerky and dropped down dead. At first we thought that maybe some other gang was shooting at us with silencers or something, but there wasn't nobody there."

Another youth said, "I was talking to my friend Eazy-P in front of this store window, and I swear I seen some white dude in a suit come up behind him and grab him round the neck and kind of twist his head around. Eazy-P's head twisted around for real and I heard his neck break, but when I turn around there was no white dude there. Like, you can't have your neck broke by a reflection, can you?"

The news anchorwoman added, "Whoever was responsible for these inexplicable fatalities, the Eighty-third Street Gangster Crips released a surprise statement about an hour ago saying that they would no longer involve themselves in any kind of drug trafficking. An LAPD spokesperson gave this statement 'a cautious welcome.'"

Dan poured himself a cup of black coffee. It looked as if Vasili Krylov wasn't wasting any time in expanding his drug empire. The crack cocaine industry in south Los Angeles was worth millions. He wondered which Crip set would be next on Miska Vedma's hit list—the Grape Street Crips or the PJ Crips. If it wasn't simply a case of one bunch of drug traffickers being taken over by another, he would have given it a "cautious welcome," too.

He dressed and went downstairs to see Annie. He found her in her kitchen wearing a Doris Day–style blouse with the collar turned up and pale green capris. She was boiling a sticky green liquid in a saucepan, while Malkin was sitting on the windowsill, trying frantically to catch a mosquito.

"That smells interesting."

"Sea holly. Some people call it erengoes. It's an aphrodisiac. You boil it in sugar until it caramelizes. I sell boxes and boxes of it, especially at my book circle."

She came up to him and laid her hands on his shoulders. "I just needed to do something normal. I was so upset by last night, I couldn't sleep."

Dan grimaced. "I have to go see Rosa. I don't know what I'm going to say to her. Maybe you could come along. A woman's touch, if you know what I mean."

"Sure. I can bring her something to calm her down, too—some white bean and orange cake."

Dan said, "I had a call from my dad this morning. He wants to me to visit him, and he'd like you to come along. I think he has some angle on how we can deal with these witches."

"In that case, what are we waiting for? Hey, Malkin—leave that poor mosquito alone. Even insects have a right to life. Well, apart from maggots."

They spent more than an hour and a half with Rosa. She trembled, but she didn't shed a single tear. All the same, Dan could tell how deeply shocked she was. The crying would come later, when they had left. The crying would probably go on for the rest of her life.

At about a quarter of eleven, Rosa's cousin Carilla came around, a gentle young woman with wavy black hair and a dark crimson dress. She was just as shocked as Rosa to hear that Ernie had been killed, but she told Dan and Annie that she would take Rosa to stay with her aunt for a while, and collect Carlo and Sancho from school.

"That was pretty grim," said Annie, as they drove to Pasadena.

"Tell me about it. Poor Rosa. I don't know how she's going to manage without Ernie. They first met when they were in high school." He paused, and then he said, "I don't know how *I'm* going to manage without Ernie."

Dan's father was sitting out on his balcony when they arrived at the Stage Performers' Retirement Home, feeding millet to his canary. He was wearing a maroon-and-green striped bathrobe, and a maroon-spotted cravat.

"So this is Annie! You told me how clever she was, but you didn't tell me how pretty she was!"

"I didn't want you getting ideas, you old dog."

They sat down together in white basketwork chairs, and Dan's father rang his bell for fruit juice and sodas. "That was a hell of a business last night. At least they haven't been stupid enough to send in the National Guard."

"They don't have a clue what to do," Dan told him. "I think the governor wanted to send in the troops, but the mayor warned him not to. The mayor's seen those witches in action first hand, and I think he'd prefer to negotiate."

"Wise man. No good trying to put a fire out with gasoline."

Dan watched him feeding his canary for a while. Then he said, "So . . . you've thought of a way we can get rid of these witches?"

"I think so. I said I *think* so. I can't give you any guarantee, but it's worth a try. It mainly depends on how much of a risk you're prepared to take and how proficient this young lady is at working any kind of genuine magic."

"Like I told you, Dad, Annie managed to catch at least *one* Rebecca Greensmith out of the four of them. And we think that Annie may possess some kind of magical power that even *she* isn't aware of, because Rebecca Greensmith seems pretty damn anxious to put her out of the picture."

"All the same," said Dan's father, "I wouldn't like anything to happen to you. *Either* of you."

"I don't think that any of the witches can do me any harm," Annie reassured him. "Not directly, anyhow. And I think I have a duty to try to stop them. It was what my grandmother and my mother would have expected of me. Being able to work magic—it's not just a parlor trick. It's a calling."

"You mean, unlike sawing women in half and pulling bunches of chrysanthemums out of your ass."

Annie smiled. "I didn't mean that at all, Mr. Fisher. I know what a great illusionist you are."

Dan's father shrugged. "Thanks for the compliment. But you and me both know that it's trickery and not genuine magic."

"So what's the deal for getting rid of the witches?" asked Dan.

"Part trickery and part genuine magic. I was giving it all some serious thought, when it suddenly came back to me the time I spent in New Orleans, back in the early 1960s, playing at the Saenger Theater on North Rampart Street. Backstage I got talking to a healer and a shaman named Dr. Henry, who showed me one or two tricks in exchange for one or two tricks of mine. The cut-your-own-head-off trick, that was nifty.

"I was curious about voodoo, and Dr. Henry told me that he had broken up a coven of voodoo witches in the mid-1950s in Terrebonne Parish, west of New Orleans. There were seven of them, so he said, and they were kicking up all kinds of trouble, setting fire to people's houses and stealing money and jewelry, and if anybody tried to stop them the witches would stop their hearts with a pendulum or choke them on their own blood.

"This Dr. Henry was unofficially asked by the local sheriff to see what he could do to get rid of these witches. So he took his stage assistant, who was a very pretty girl called Emmeline, if I recall correctly, and they hunted this coven down one at a time. That was the secret, he said. Pick them off individual-like, because together they have a combined power that is far too much for any one person to overcome."

"So what did he do?" asked Dan.

"He and Emmeline followed each of the witches until they got them alone. Then Emmeline would distract the witch with one of her conjuring tricks, while Dr. Henry would work a voodoo spell on her. I don't see any reason why you and Annie here couldn't do the same—except that you could do the distracting, while Annie worked the spell."

Dan looked dubious. "I'm pretty rusty when it comes to magic. I haven't done any serious tricks for years."

"Then let me bring you back up to speed," said his father. "Witches are human beings, after all—they're just as impressed by conjuring tricks as anybody else. You only need to capture their attention for a couple of seconds—just long enough for Annie to get her spell in first."

"I don't know," said Dan. "Do you honestly believe it will work?"

"I think it might," Annie put in. "So long as I use

the right magic for each witch. I can use voodoo against Michelange DuPriz, but I need to use Uitoto magic against Lida Siado and Russian mirror magic against Miska Vedma. Otherwise, my spells won't have any effect. It would be like trying to exorcize a Roman Catholic demon with a Hindu incantation."

"Here, let me show you this one," said Dan's father. He unfastened the catch on his canary's cage and reached inside. "Come on, Sylvester. Come on, boy. I call him boy, but for all I know he could be a girl. I've never been prurient enough to look."

He took the canary off its perch and cupped it in his hand. He tucked its head under its wing and started to stroke it with his finger, very gently.

"You know something—in France in the fifteenth century, they used to pluck chickens when they were still alive. Pluck them, take all their feathers off. Then they used to paint them with butter and cold basting juices, tuck their heads under their wings like I've done with Sylvester here, and turn them around and around until they fell asleep.

"Then they brought these sleeping chickens to the dinner table surrounded by real roast chickens. They'd give them a prod, and the birds would jump up and run down the table, upsetting everybody's drinks. Pretty hilarious, huh?"

The canary's eyes closed in less than a minute. Dan's father held it up so that Dan and Annie could see it. Then he pulled off his cravat and loosely covered Sylvester.

"Poor little canary. At least he's going to die in his sleep."

He gently closed his fingers around his cravat. Then he raised his arm and began to crush it in his fist, tighter and tighter.

Annie said, "Oh my God. That poor little bird."

"Ex-bird," Dan's father corrected. His fist was clenched so tightly that there were white spots on his knuckles.

He kept his fist uplifted for a moment longer. Then he suddenly opened his fingers and whipped away the cravat. The canary flew up into the air, chirping, and he snatched at it and caught it, and placed it tenderly back on its perch.

"So how did you do that?" Dan asked.

"Easy. Sylvester was asleep, so when I lifted my arm up, I dropped him straight down my sleeve. I only had to shake him a little to wake him up. The point is, people always want to think the worst. They *want* to believe that I crushed him."

"And you really think that these witches are going to fall for tricks like that?"

"Why not? You did, didn't you—both of you, and you're much more skeptical than your average person in the street about conjuring tricks and magic."

Dan looked at Annie, and she gave him a shrug, as if to say, *What do we have to lose?*

"Okay then, Dad," he conceded. "I'll come back tomorrow morning, and you can give me a refresher course."

The tricks that his father taught him were more difficult than he had expected, and even after three hours of practice, he still wasn't entirely confident that he could carry them off.

"But that's not the point," said his father. "All you're trying to do is create a distraction. Not a threatening distraction, like taking out your gun, because your witches will retaliate immediately, which is just what you're trying to avoid. You're trying to catch their eye, that's all, and amuse them. So it doesn't matter if you don't pull the tricks off perfectly."

"I hope this works," Dan said.

His father took hold of his hand and squeezed it. "Just remember one thing: stage magic, it's all about *belief*. So long as you believe that what you're doing is real magic, then your audience will, too. I never once met a stage magician who wasn't totally serious about his craft, even the comic magicians who pretended to mess up everything they did."

"Thanks, Dad."

"It's been a pleasure, son. Take care of yourself and take care of that pretty girlfriend of yours." He picked up Sylvester's cage and handed it over. "And take care of Sylvester, okay? I want this little fellow back in one piece. That's if he *is* a fellow."

When he returned to Franklin Avenue, he found Annie sitting cross-legged in the middle of her living room, with incense smoldering in a curvy brass pot. Her laptop was open, and books and magazines were scattered all around her.

"Voodoo," she said. "I think we should go for Michelange DuPriz first, because she's the one who can debilitate her victims the quickest."

Dan set the canary cage down on the table, and Malkin immediately jumped up and tried to poke her paw through the bars. But Sylvester seemed oblivious to her, and carried on twittering and bouncing on his perch.

"Malkin!" Annie snapped. "That's our new assistant, not your lunch!"

Dan picked up one of her books and flicked through it. There were recipes for spells and potions and gris-gris bags, as well as drawings of voodoo dolls and diagrams of *veves*—magical designs for summoning the *loua*, or voodoo spirits.

"Are you sure you can do this?" asked Dan.

"Dan, I feel more than ready, believe me. Ever since that third Rebecca Greensmith turned all maggoty in her cell, I feel even more powerful than ever. *I* trapped her. *I* restrained her. It's the natural order of magic. All of the influence that particular manifestation of Rebecca Greensmith used to possess—it's mine now."

"Okay. Then I'll tell you what I'm going to do. I'm going to ask a couple of uniforms to sit on the Zombie's house on Laurel Canyon and to give us a head's up any time that Michelange DuPriz goes out on her own. Meantime, I think I'm going to do some more practicing. That goddamned stabbing-yourself-in-the-eyes trick, that really takes some precision. There must be thousands of magicians out there who never got it right, all walking around with guide dogs."

Annie took hold of his hands and kissed him. "We'll do it, Dan. I know we can do it. We have to, because nobody else can."

Chapter Twenty-six

Two officers in an unmarked police car kept watch on Jean-Christophe Artisson's mansion on Laurel Canyon until well past midnight, but there was no sign of Michelange DuPriz—either with or without her sister witches.

Dan was still trying to stab himself in the eyes when the officers called him.

"Sorry, Detective. Looks like a bust for today."

"Okay, thanks. We'll make an early start in the morning. She has to come out of the house sometime."

He opened a last bottle of stout and went out onto the balcony. The night was unnaturally quiet, as if everybody had realized that there were magical forces at work in the city and was trying not to disturb them. But in reality only those who had been unfortunate enough to confront the witches knew what was happening. He had watched the news bulletins about the SWAT officers who had been killed at West Grove Country Club, and he could hardly believe how successfully the story had been suppressed. Meteorological experts were still sitting in the TV studios talking about "highly localized tornado conditions."

It made him wonder how many other news stories were suppressed and how many disasters and conspiracies and official foul-ups went unreported—or distorted beyond recognition.

He fed Sylvester and filled his water bowl. Then he showered and went to bed. He lay in the dark for almost an hour with his eyes open. Then he slept and started to dream.

He was speeding southward along 101, at over 120 mph. Gayle was sitting beside him, singing "Comfortably Numb" in a weird, off-key falsetto.

"When I was a child—I had a fever! Eee—eee—eee!"

"Hey, this time we're going to be okay," he told her.

She turned to stare at him, her blond hair fluffing in the slipstream. "What do you mean?"

"This time we're not going to crash. You're not going to be killed."

"This time? How much did you and Gus have to drink? I've never been killed. Do I *look* like I've been killed?"

"You died, Gayle, and it was all my fault. But I'm not going to let it happen again."

"Dan, what are you talking about? I'm alive!"

He opened his eyes. Gayle was lying in bed next to him, naked, her bare shoulder silhouetted against the window. He could feel her breath on his cheek.

"Are you real?" he asked her, a catch in his throat.

She kissed him on the forehead, then on the tip of his nose. "Of course I'm real. Don't I feel real?"

"Yes. You feel real. But I don't know whether you're really you."

"Who else could I be?"

He sat up. She snuggled up behind him and traced patterns on his back with her fingertips.

"Who else could I be, Dan?"

"I don't know. I'm not so sure that I want to know."

"Has that friend of yours been talking to you again? That Annie?"

"What does Annie have to do with us?"

"You tell me. Just so long as she doesn't come between us."

Dan twisted around and stared at her in the darkness. "How can she come between us, Gayle? You're dead!"

She put her arms around him and drew him down on top of her. "Do I *feel* dead?"

At 10:07 A.M., his cellphone rang. He was sitting on a stool in the kitchen drinking coffee. The blinds were pulled down tight to keep out the morning sunshine.

"Detective Fisher? Officer McNab. We have movement. Your lady friend just left the property in a black Escalade."

"Anybody with her?"

"One of the Zombie's musclemen, that's all."

"Okay, great. Keep on her. And keep me posted on her progress."

"You got it."

Dan had not directly told the officers that their surveillance on Michelange DuPriz was part of his investigation into the mass slaughter at West Grove Country Club and at the White Ghost's house at Silverlake, but everybody at the station knew that he was involved in some of the weirder events of the past few days— starting with the three detectives burned to death outside the Palm—and they gave him their unquestioning support.

He called Annie. "Are you ready to go? Michelange DuPriz has left the Zombie's house, and so far she only has a single bodyguard with her."

"I'm ready. I've had all my stuff packed since six o'clock this morning."

He went into the bedroom. Gayle was lying there, still asleep. He walked around the bed and gently shook her shoulder.

"Gayle?"

"What time is it?"

"I have to go work. Are you still going to be here when I get back, or are you going to disappear again?"

Her eyes were misted, as if she had been crying. "It depends if you want me here."

"I don't know. I'm finding this very difficult to deal with."

"You mean you don't love me anymore?"

"No, of course not. But how can I love you if I'm not sure that you're not really you?"

She lay back on the pillow and smiled up at him. "Now *there's* a question."

He picked up Sylvester's cage and went downstairs to Annie's apartment, holding the cage high like a lantern.

"I've had an update," he told Annie when she opened the door. "Michelange DuPriz is on Rodeo Drive in Bijan, of all places."

"Bijan—you're not serious! The Zombie must be paying her a fortune if she's shopping there. Their perfume's—what—about three grand a bottle."

"Okay . . . you got everything you need?"

Annie lifted a loose-weave bag, embroidered with gray and scarlet beads. "Everything's in here. How about you?"

"I'm ready, yes. But I can't say that I'm not scared shitless."

They climbed into Dan's Torrent and headed for Rodeo Drive. It was a bright, warm morning and

Beverly Hills looked its normal, affluent self. They drove slowly past the House of Bijan, with its arched entrance and its squiggly Bijan signature above the door. One of the Zombie's shiny black Escalades was parked outside, and an unmarked Crown Victoria was parked three or four cars away, two cops in shirtsleeves sitting in it.

Dan steered the Torrent in a U-turn and parked behind the police car. He reached over to the backseat and lifted Sylvester out of his cage. The canary fluttered furiously, but Dan carefully closed his fingers around it and stowed it in the right-hand pocket of his sport coat.

He climbed out of his SUV and walked up to the two officers in the Crown Victoria.

"Thanks, fellows. You did good. How long has she been in there?"

"Twenty minutes. Long enough to spend about three years' salary. *My* salary, anyhow."

"How about the bodyguard?"

"He's been in and out. Look, here he comes again."

One of the Zombie's black-suited heavies emerged from Bijan and walked across the sidewalk to open the Escalade's passenger door. Through the boutique's tinted window, Dan could see Michelange DuPriz in a pale gray dress, talking to two Bijan assistants who were carrying several shopping bags for her.

Dan pointed to Annie. "This young lady and me, we're going to be apprehending the woman. She may look like a thin streak of nothing, but believe me she's extremely dangerous and you two guys shouldn't go anywhere near her. *Capiche?* She was responsible for Cusack and Fusco and Knudsen getting cremated. You don't want the same thing to happen to you."

The two officers looked up at him, and he could tell that they desperately wanted to ask him what this was all about.

"Listen," he said, "if we can pull this off, I'll explain it all to you later. Right now, it's probably better that you don't know. All I want you to do is go for the bodyguard. Disarm him, get him down on the ground, and cuff him. I'm going to repeat myself and say—whatever happens, stay well clear of the woman."

"Okay, Detective. Got you."

At that moment, the front door of Bijan opened and Michelange DuPriz stepped out, putting on a large pair of Chanel sunglasses. Dan heard the door of his Torrent slam as Annie climbed out, and now she was walking toward the front of the store at a quick, determined pace. As she approached, she reached into her bag, and Dan saw her take out a large red candle and a small brown pouch.

He started walking toward Michelange DuPriz himself, obscuring his face with his hand as if he were trying to keep the sun out of his eyes. But Michelange DuPriz was too concerned with organizing her shopping bags, and she didn't even look at him until he was only three or four feet away from her.

"*Hey!*" he shouted, and threw Sylvester up into the air, right in front of her. She took a step back in surprise. Without any hesitation, Dan smacked his hands together so that the canary appeared to explode in a burst of feathers.

"*Kisa ou ap fe?*" said Michelange DuPriz. It was all the distraction that Annie needed. With her left hand she pointed the candle at Michelange DuPriz and with her right hand she shook the small brown pouch so that a fine ash was blown all over her. Then she took out a tiny silver whistle and started blowing it in shrill, staccato bursts.

The bodyguard yelled, "Get away from her, lady!" and started to cross the sidewalk toward her. But he was less than halfway before the two police officers called out, "Police! Freeze!" and cut across in front of him with their guns drawn. "Facedown on the sidewalk, sir! Do it now!"

Annie continued to shrill her whistle, faster and faster, and Michelange DuPriz staggered backward and collided with Bijan's window. She looked as if she were drunk or somebody had hit her very hard. She waved her right arm like a chicken's wing and Dan guessed that she was attempting to cast a spell to protect herself. The ash that Annie had thrown over her was zombie dust, which had numbed her and thrown her off balance. By whistling, Annie was calling up a *rada*, a sweet and powerful spirit from the Haitian netherworld. The ash candle was engraved with a *veve*, which made the spirit welcome and willing to help her.

Michelange DuPriz must have known that, too, because she tried to scream out a voodoo curse. But she had lost the initiative, and it was too late for her to start an incantation. All she could do was splutter and spit. She dropped onto her knees, and her sunglasses clattered across the sidewalk. Her face was contorted with frustration.

Annie stopped whistling and took out a stick with a plume of feathers tied to the end. She started to tap the side of the candle, using the same staccato rhythm.

"Rada Ye, I ask with all my heart to end this evil for me. Rada Ye, bring this witch the punishment that she deserves for all of her wickedness. *Souple, souple.*"

She approached Michelange DuPriz until she was standing right over her, and she touched her forehead three times with the tip of the candle. Meanwhile, the two police officers had forced the bodyguard to lie spreadeagle on the ground, and one of them was cuffing him. The bodyguard wasn't trying to wrestle himself free: he knew better than that.

"Rada Ye, I pray to you. Rada Ye, I will reward you well for your strength and your kindness. You may take this witch's spirit as your prize. Hear me, Rada Ye, and bring her the pain that she has brought to so many others. *Mesi, mwen sinyur.*"

Michelange DuPriz started to shake. Her eyes rolled up so that Dan could only see the whites, and her face turned a dirty white color. One shiny black stiletto shoe began to click repeatedly against the sidewalk, almost in synchronization with Annie's tapping.

Annie glanced toward Dan and said, "*Now*, Dan!"

Dan hunkered down close to Michelange DuPriz and held out his loose fist so that it was right in front of her face. Michelange DuPriz's eyes rolled back into focus, and she stared at him in hatred and bewilderment. Dan gave her a humorless grin and said, "Abracadabra, Ms. DuPriz!"

He opened his fist and there was Sylvester, completely unhurt. The canary cheeped and twittered and fluttered his wings in annoyance, but Dan had trapped the bird's feet between his fingers so that he couldn't fly off.

Michelange DuPriz raised both of her angular arms to cover her eyes, but again she was too late. Annie tapped the *veve* candle again and again, ti-*tappa*-ti-*tappa*-ti-*tappa*, and Dan became aware of a ripple in the air, like the ripple from a hot summer highway, and he was conscious of a resonance, too, so deep that it was almost below the range of human hearing.

Michelange DuPriz went rigid, and her arms dropped stiffly by her sides. She raised her axelike profile upward, her eyes bulging wide, and her neck began to swell. She let out a terrible choking noise, as if she had a fishbone caught in her windpipe.

Ti-*tappa*-ti-*tappa*-ti-*tappa!*

Her lips stretched wide, and a gray and greasy shape began to emerge from her mouth, so large that she couldn't entirely regurgitate it. At first Dan couldn't understand what it was. It looked anvil-shaped, and it seemed to be covered with fur. Then it opened its yellow eyes, and he realized with shock what Michelange DuPriz was painfully bringing up. Not cockroaches, or toads, or quarters.

It was a cat, and it was trying to force its way out of her mouth so that it could come after Sylvester.

Dan, still hunkered down, took two crablike steps backward. "Jesus Christ, Annie!"

The cat managed to push its head out, and then one paw, but then it got stuck and started to wriggle and yowl in frustration.

"Annie!" Dan protested.

"I can't help it, Dan! I didn't choose this! This was what the *loua* decided she deserved."

"Jesus, can't you stop it?"

But Michelange DuPriz dropped sideways onto the ground, jerking and juddering and whining through her nostrils. Her dreadlocks shriveled and turned gray, and all the beads that she had worn in her hair dropped onto the sidewalk and rolled away. Underneath her pale gray dress, her body appeared to collapse, as if she were crumbling to dust in front of their eyes. The skin of her face tautened, and then wrinkled, and then broke away from her skull like cellophane burned by a naked flame.

The cat kept on wriggling and struggling. At last, with a loud crack, it managed to dislocate Michelange DuPriz's jaw. It forced its way out of her mouth, its fur still slick with mucus. It shook itself, and then it scurried away, its belly low to the ground.

Dan looked down at what remained of Michelange DuPriz. There was scarcely anything left except her bones and her dress and her black stiletto shoes. A warm breeze was blowing down Rodeo Drive, and it started to lift her dust away.

In the House of Bijan, the horrified staff had their faces pressed to the window, and even when Dan tried to wave them away they stayed where they were, wide-eyed. One of the police officers came up to Dan and said, "Holy shit."

Annie used her feathered stick to lift the hem of Michelange DuPriz's dress. There was nothing underneath but bones and ash.

The police officer shook his head. "Unbelievable. I saw a nine-year-old kid who fell into a pig-feed machine. I saw a woman who got herself plastered all over in burning asphalt. But I never saw nothing like this before."

Dan laid a hand on his shoulder. "With any luck, officer, you'll never see anything like this again."

They went for Miska Vedma next. The following day, at about a quarter to one, two detectives spotted Vasili Krylov's Porsche Cayenne parked outside Traktir, a Russian restaurant on Santa Monica Boulevard in West Hollywood. One detective took a quick look inside, then called Dan.

"Bill McNab here, sir. Vedma and Krylov are having lunch. The Zombie was there for a couple of minutes, but he split. The White Ghost is there, too, along with that other woman we're supposed to be looking out for. Black hair, red dress, big tits. And some other old crow, looks about a hundred, wearing a hat like a turkey vulture just landed on her head."

"Go on."

"It's hard to tell, but they're definitely riled up about something. Krylov keeps stabbing his finger at the woman with the turkey vulture on her head, and the one with the black hair keeps flinging her arms around."

"Anything else?"

"Vedma's having the Darnitsky salad, and Krylov's ordered the *kharcho*. Well, so the owner told me."

"Okay, just sit on them, will you, and keep me posted. Most of all, I want to know if Krylov and Vedma leave the place alone, without the other two women, and where they go."

Dan turned to Annie. "Our witches are having a council of war. Sounds like they're pretty upset, too."

Annie was eating a bowl of homemade muesli with nasturtium leaves in it and reading *Russian Word Charms*. "Good," she said. "We need to rattle them. They'll be more inclined to make mistakes."

"Do you think they know it was us who took out Michelange DuPriz?"

"Oh, they must. Rebecca Greensmith will have scried it by now."

"Scried it? What does that mean?"

"Well, Michelange DuPriz wouldn't have come home, would she, and neither would her bodyguard, so Rebecca Greensmith would probably have tried to find out where she was. Most likely she looked into a mirror or a bowl of water. That's called scrying. You can do it with crystal balls, too.

"She would have discovered that Michelange DuPriz is dead—but more than that, she would have found out that a *loua* has taken her spirit off to the nether-world as his reward for killing her. The only person who could have done *that* to her is me."

She lifted another spoonful of muesli. "The thing is, Michelange DuPriz belongs to the *rada* now, in eternal servitude and eternal silence—so Rebecca Greensmith wouldn't have been able to ask her what I did to her or how."

* * *

Dan's cell phone rang at 3:25 P.M.

"Detective Fisher? They're still at Traktir, but the White Ghost has split, and so have the woman with the black hair and the other old biddy. Krylov's sitting at the table with five of his Russian buddies, drinking vodka. Vedma's in the bar talking to some younger guy."

"Any idea who he is?"

"He looks like some kind of entrepreneur to me. Expensive suit. Purple silk necktie. One of these Russians who can fix you anything from a Ferrari to a front-row seat for the Dodgers."

"Listen to me carefully—is there a mirror in the bar?"

"Sure . . . all along the back wall."

"Where she's sitting now, is Miska Vedma reflected in that mirror?"

"Er . . . yes, she is. How is that relevant, if you don't mind my asking?"

"I'll tell you later. Meantime, I'm on my way. Krylov doesn't look like he's leaving anytime soon, does he?"

"He just ordered another bottle of Stolichnaya, so I doubt it."

Dan put down the phone and said, "Okay, Annie. Action stations. Operation Vedma is a go."

Annie picked up her bag. "You're happy with your trick?" she asked.

"Not really. But even if it goes wrong, it should distract her, shouldn't it?"

"Try and do it right, please. Miska Vedma is a highly accomplished witch, and she can probably use all kinds of Russian magic that I've never read about and won't be prepared for."

"You still don't have to do this," Dan told her. "You can back out anytime you like."

"You know that I can't. More than that, you know that I *won't*."

Dan looked at her narrowly. "This is more than just a crusade for you, isn't it? You're loving it, beating those witches at their own game."

Annie picked up Malkin and gave her a kiss on her tiny pink nose. "Maybe," she admitted. "See you later, Malkin. Don't do any uh-uhs on the rug this time."

Chapter Twenty-seven

When they walked into Traktir, they immediately saw Vasili Krylov and his friends sitting around a table in the left-hand corner, knocking back shots of Stolichnaya and talking loudly in Russian. Dan knew at least two of them: a pimp from West Hollywood with criss-cross scars on his cheeks and a hairy-handed drug dealer from the Fairfax District.

On the opposite side of the restaurant, perched at the bar, was Miska Vedma, wearing a short silver dress. Her hair was brushed up and gelled, like blond flames. She was listening intently to the young man in the smart suit and the purple necktie. Dan recognized him as Boris Slutsky, not an entrepreneur at all, but a particularly vicious and sadistic enforcer for Vasili Krylov's extortion rackets.

The detective who had alerted him to Miska Vedma's presence here was sitting by himself in the right-hand corner with a plate of grilled pork chops and boiled potatoes in front of him, pretending to read a copy of the Russian-language newspaper *Panorama*. Dan and Annie sat down opposite him.

"Good work, Detective McNab. How's the food here?" Dan asked.

"Terrific. Pity you got here before I had the chance to finish it."

Dan looked around the restaurant, sizing up distances and lines of fire. "This young lady and I are going to be taking out Miska Vedma. Or trying to. What I need you to do is cover us—so that means looking out for Vasili Krylov over there and also the guy Vedma is talking to. His name's Boris Slutsky, and he's probably armed and certainly dangerous.

"In other words, if there's any sign of trouble, I don't want you thinking twice. Just ice the bastards."

Detective McNab raised his eyebrows, but he said, "Okay. If that's the way you want to play it."

Dan looked toward the bar. Miska Vedma was half turned away from him, so she couldn't see him, but she suddenly sat up very straight and frowned, as if she could sense that something was wrong.

"Just hope she hasn't made us," said Dan.

"She might have sensed my aura," Annie whispered. "Remember, I have Michelange DuPriz's aura in me now, as well as two of Rebecca Greensmith's."

"In that case, we'd better go in now. Do you have everything ready?"

Annie lifted up her bag. "It's all in here. Let's do it."

Dan stood up. A waiter was crossing the restaurant, holding a tray of *razguiya* sandwiches and chicken *taboka*. Dan fell into step with him and walked beside him toward the bar, so that Miska Vedma wouldn't be able to see him coming.

As the waiter passed behind her, Dan stopped and tapped her on the shoulder. She turned around and snapped, "What?"

Dan held up his right fist and then opened his fingers. There was an ear-splitting explosion, and a cloud of white smoke rolled out of his hand. Everybody in the restaurant gasped, and some of them ducked for cover. Dan held up his left fist, and Miska Vedma said, "What are you doing? What is this? Idiot! Go away!"

Dan opened his left fist, and there was another explosion and another cloud of white smoke.

Miska Vedma pointed at him angrily, and her eyes were as colorless as cold water. But even as she did so, she jolted, as if somebody had pushed her from behind. She jerked her head from side to side, trying to see what had struck her, but then she jolted again and almost fell over.

Boris Slutsky stood up and reached under his coat. Dan went for his gun, too, but Detective McNab was even quicker. There was a deafening shot and Boris Slutsky was knocked off his bar stool onto the floor and lay there with his legs quivering like a fallen pony.

Two of Vasili Krylov's party stood up, too, but Detective McNab shouted, "Police! Hands where I can see them! Don't even breathe!"

Miska Vedma was shuddering violently, as if she were freezing cold. She kept looking from left to right, her eyes darting from side to side, but it was only when Annie appeared that she realized what was happening to her.

Annie's face was covered by an expressionless white mask. It had a slit for a mouth and two almond-shaped holes for eyes, and it was surrounded by dry gingery hair with white silk poppies woven into it. She slowly approached Miska Vedma, both hands raised in front of her, and as she came nearer Dan could hear her whispering.

"*Mirror, glass, and water bright. Take this woman from my sight. Mirror, glass, and water clear. Take her far away from here. Take her far beyond your face. To that cold and soulless place. Skin and bone and fleshly matter. Take her, break her, make her shatter.*"

Miska Vedma let out a scream and flailed her arms.

The mask that Annie was wearing was the face of a Rusalka, a Russian water witch who could trap her victims behind any shiny surface—a pool, a window, or a mirror.

But while Miska Vedma appeared to be helpless, her reflection in the mirror behind the bar had swiftly walked away from the position where her real self was standing and circled around the tables until she was coming up behind Dan with both of her hands raised to seize him around the neck.

"*Dan!*" Annie warned.

Dan swung around, but there was nobody there—nobody he could see, anyhow. But Annie shouted, "Take a step sideways, now!"

He did as he was told and dodged and feinted, as he used to do in college football. He actually felt Miska Vedma stumble past him, and when he turned toward the mirror he could see that her reflection was only two feet away from his, and that she was reaching out with her clawlike fingers as if she wanted to scratch out his eyes.

He ducked again and again, but then he felt fingernails rake across his lips, and a hand snatching at his hair. He twisted around, striking at the air with his gun, but there was no point in shooting at a witch he couldn't see.

Annie came toward him as he struggled with his invisible opponent. She was carrying two blue glass globes in her hands, and she held them up in front of him. Miska Vedma had jumped onto his back now and was biting at his ears and wrenching out his hair and digging her bony knees into his sides.

"*Go, witch, go, from out my sight! Where right is left and left is right! Join the wicked and perverse! In the world where all's reversed!*"

Miska Vedma screamed so shrilly in Dan's ear that

he was almost deafened. "You think you can play with *me*, child? You think you can pretend to be a Rusalka? My grandmother was a Rusalka!"

She clutched Dan's throat and clawed at his Adam's apple. The strangest thing was that the real Miska Vedma was nowhere near him. The real Miska Vedma was standing furious but motionless beside the bar, at least eight feet away, with her fists clenched. Only her reflection was wrestling with him and tearing at his face.

But Annie half turned and lifted one of the blue glass globes. She drew her arm back, and Dan realized that she was going to throw it.

"*Nooooo!*" cried Miska Vedma, and as Annie hurled the globe toward the mirror, she scrambled off Dan's back, and Dan could see her reflection diving toward the globe with one hand desperately outstretched.

Miraculously, when it was only a few inches away from the mirror's surface, she caught it. She didn't turn around, but she raised the globe high and shook her fist, and her reflection stared out at them in utter triumph. Just as the second globe hit the mirror right next to her.

The mirror was twenty feet wide by six feet high, and it exploded as if it had been hit by a bomb. Thousands of shards of silvered glass flew everywhere, glittering and sparkling. Diners in the restaurant raised their hands to protect their eyes, but even so Dan saw one woman with a coronet of splinters stuck in her forehead.

Dan heard a sharp, crackling voice. It sounded like a radio message from very far away—from Russia, from the steppes, from the coldest reaches of a country where magic ran with the whitest of wolves.

Miska Vedma, standing beside the bar, began to break into pieces, as if she were made of nothing but glass. One of her arms dropped to the floor and then half her face. Her legs snapped in half just below the knees, and the rest of her body fell backward onto the floor and smashed into smithereens.

Traktir went very quiet. Detective McNab was already on his radio calling for backup and at least three busses. Annie untied her mask and stood over Miska Vedma's remains, and—strangely—the expression on her face was almost regretful.

Vasili Krylov came over with two of his bodyguards close behind him.

"You don't think you're going to get away with this, Detective?"

"I was under the impression we just did. RIP witch number two."

"Vasili Krylov never forgets, Detective."

"Give you something to remember, then, when you're sitting in San Quentin."

"I will kill you, Detective. I promise."

He went down on one knee on the floor and picked up one of Miska Vedma's broken-off fingers. It was actually made of milk-white glass, with a silver ring on it.

"This woman, I was going to make her my bride." He looked up, and Dan actually saw tears in his eyes.

"Not a good idea, marrying witches," Dan told him. "Didn't you ever see *Charmed*?"

Lida Siado was more difficult to find on her own. Dan had two uniforms sitting outside Orestes Vasquez's mansion round the clock, but she didn't appear until the following morning, and when she did, she was accompanied by Rebecca Greensmith and four heavies.

Annie wasn't concerned about the heavies—she knew plenty of spells for gnarling their muscles into agonizing knots. But she was worried about Rebecca Greensmith.

"She knows what we're doing, and she's constantly scrying to find out where we are. It wouldn't surprise me if she tried to lay some kind of a trap for us."

Dan had been peering into a circular mirror framed with tiny seashells, inspecting the livid red scratches on his neck. He nodded toward the book she was reading, a large illustrated treatise on *Uitoto Myths & Legends*. "How were you thinking of offing Lida Siado?"

Malkin came padding across the rug and started to lick Annie's fingers with her tiny pink tongue. "It's the salt," she said. "She always comes and licks my fingers after I've been witch testing."

"It's those goddamned creatures that Lida Siado conjures up—those are what really scare me. Like the one that killed poor Ernie."

"*Kukurpas*, yes. They're horrible. But the Uitoto magic men found ways of destroying them."

"Such as?"

"Well, one way was to feed them poisoned babies. Another way was to trick them into a hut and then set fire to it, but the hut had to be smeared with anaconda fat, so that the fire was very fierce."

Dan pulled a face. "I don't think either of those alternatives is very practical, do you?"

Annie said, "With any luck, we won't need them. But I have to neutralize Lida Siado before she has a chance to drum up the Night Wind."

"And you're going to do that how?"

"I'm going to try to drum up a spirit of my own. A Uitoto spirit. I'm not sure that it's going to work. Even if I can manage to make it appear, it won't be easy to handle or to dismiss. But Lida Siado is so powerful, even without Rebecca Greensmith, and I can't think of any other way."

"Okay," said Dan. "After Miska Vedma, I think I'm game for anything."

It was 6:47 P.M. when the phone rang.

"Officer Stavrianos here, Detective. Lida Siado and the White Ghost just left the house with three body-guards and three albino Great Danes."

"No old lady?"

"That's why I called you, sir. No old lady, for defi-nite. Looks like they're headed due west."

"Thanks, officer. Keep a tail on them, and keep me updated."

Dan said, "Orestes Vasquez and Lida Siado are driv-ing westward with three large dogs but *without* Re-becca Greensmith."

"Oh, God," said Annie.

"I'll bet you fifty bucks I know where they're going. One of the White Ghost's favorite restaurants is Ocean Avenue Seafood, in Santa Monica. They'll take the dogs for a run on the beach, and then they'll have dinner."

Annie stood up and straightened her short black linen dress. "I just hope I'm ready for this. The sum-moning ritual . . . it's very complicated, and I don't even know if I can pronounce the words right."

Dan shrugged on his sand-colored coat and picked up his gun from the side table. "Only one way to find out."

Annie took her soft woven bag and a small split-drum, similar to the drum that Lida Siado wore around her neck, except that this one had a single eye painted on the front, and the back was curved and tapered and scaly like an alligator's tail. It must have had dried beans or beads inside it, because it made a maracas-like rattle when she slung it around her shoulders.

"That's all you're taking?" Dan asked.

"Hopefully, that's all I'm going to need."

"No poisoned babies? No inflammable huts?"

Annie smiled and shook her head, but Dan suddenly said, "Maybe that gives me an idea. Let's call in at the station before we head for the beach."

"You're going to pick up a couple of poisoned babies?"

"Just some extra protection, that's all—in case Uitoto magic doesn't quite cut it."

They sped westward with the sinking sun in their eyes. Annie was unusually quiet, and Dan had the impression that she was more anxious about this encounter than any of the others—even their capture of Rebecca Greensmith up at Ben Burrows's old house.

"Everything's going to work out fine," he reassured her as he steered around the double-hairpin curve past Will Rogers State Park, and the orange sunlight rotated around the inside of the SUV.

Annie squeezed her hands together as if she were washing them. "I feel strong," she told him. "I feel very confident. I feel the power of Moma."

"Moma?"

"The Uitoto god of all things. He was made like a stick, with no anus."

"Really? I used to have a captain of detectives like that."

They had reached the Pacific Coast Highway. The ocean was dazzling, like liquid bronze, and the silhouettes of walkers and joggers on the beach looked as if they were being melted in a blast furnace.

Dan turned left and crawled slowly southward. He had only driven two hundred yards before he saw Orestes Vasquez's Porsche Cayenne parked by the side of the highway, two of his bodyguards standing beside it. He pulled in behind a lime-green Jeep and switched off the Torrent's engine. "There," he said and pointed down to the shoreline.

The White Ghost and Lida Siado were standing close to each other, watching the three albino Great Danes as they bounded around in the surf, barking. Lida Siado was wearing a loose red kaftan, which billowed in the warm evening breeze. The White Ghost was wearing a white linen suit and a Panama hat, and carrying a cane.

A third bodyguard was standing to their left, about twenty yards away from them, with his hands cupped between his legs.

"Think we can take her?" asked Dan.

"I'm not sure. I'm worried about innocent bystanders, too," said Annie. "When I drum this spirit up—"

Dan looked around. The sun was already touching the horizon, and there were only six or seven other people on the beach.

"We'll have to risk it," said Dan. "God knows when we'll get another chance like this."

Annie took off her sunglasses. "All right. Let's see if I'm any good at Uitoto magic, shall we?"

"If you're not, we'll soon know about it."

They climbed out of the SUV, but stayed behind the lime-green Jeep so that they were out of Lida Siado's line of sight. Annie swung her drum around so that it was angled across her breasts, and she immediately started to tap it with her fingertips. The rhythm she played was completely different from Lida Siado's. Instead of a regular systolic heartbeat, it was quick and complicated, with an insistent, underlying *bomma-da-bomma-da-bomma-da-bomma*. It sounded like an animal running through the undergrowth.

"That's terrific," Dan told her. "Let's hope your spirit digs it, too."

Two young Rollerbladers cruised past and circled around so that they could listen to Annie drumming.

"Hey, that is really cool, lady! You can really play that thing! What is it? Looks like a giant pickle!"

"Beat it!" Dan hissed at them.

"Hey, come on, dude, we're not doing nothing."

"I said, beat it, asshole!" Dan repeated, and he drew back his coat so that they could see the butt of his gun.

"Sure, dude, whatever," they said, and went Rollerblading away as fast as they could, until they were almost out of sight.

Annie kept on drumming and drumming, and after two or three minutes, she started to chant—a soft, low incantation that sounded like "Da-*dot*-da! da-*dit*-da!" interspersed with tongue clicks.

Dan looked around them. Toward the northwest, along the coastline, the sky was beginning to grow black, as if a storm were boiling. He could see snakes'-tongue flickers of lightning in the clouds and hear a very low rumbling. The wind began to rise, too, and sand began to sizzle across the sidewalk.

He wanted to ask Annie what was happening, but she was concentrating so hard on her drumming and her chanting that he didn't dare interrupt. Whatever she was doing, it appeared to be working. There was more lightning and thunder, and he could see sheets of silvery rain, high in the air, like curtains.

Instead of the fresh ozone smell that usually preceded a rainstorm, however, Dan smelled heat and humidity and tangled vegetation. He smelled *jungle*.

Lida Siado, standing on the beach, looked up at the sky. She said something to Orestes Vasquez, and Orestes Vasquez whistled for his dogs to come out of the surf, but both he and Lida Siado remained where they were.

Annie stopped drumming, but she continued to chant and click her tongue. Then she stopped chanting, too. She closed her eyes, waited, and then she said, *"Now!"*

Dan went back to the Torrent and lifted out a black canvas satchel. Then he crossed the sidewalk and began to walk toward Lida Siado, although he kept slightly to her left so that it didn't look as if he were approaching her directly. The sand was dry and very soft, and he couldn't walk too fast, but it took him less than fifteen seconds to reach her.

As he neared her, she slowly turned around, as if she could sense him. But it was Orestes Vasquez who recognized him first.

"Madre mia! Detective Fisher, isn't it? What do you do here on the beach, Detective Fisher? Not following us, I hope? Not interfering with our human rights?"

Dan stopped, frowned at them, and staggered a little, as if he were drunk. "Human rights? Didn't anybody ever tell you? You have to be human to have human rights!"

Chapter Twenty-eight

Orestes Vasquez pointed a finger at him. "You think you can talk to me like that? I'll have them take away your badge for that!"

There was another rumble of thunder, much closer this time, and Lida Siado touched Orestes Vasquez's arm.

"Something is wrong here, Orestes, I'm sure. This storm—it does not look natural. It does not *smell* natural."

"Seems like you and the storm got a couple of things in common, Mr. White Ghost, sir," said Dan. "It don't look natural, and it don't smell natural, just like you."

Orestes Vasquez took two steps toward Dan, his fist raised. "You want me to have my bodyguard beat you up?"

But Lida Siado said, "Something is wrong, Orestes! He's playing you!" She turned around and around, frantically looking for the danger that she could feel but not identify.

Dan, however, had seen Annie coming toward them, although she was keeping herself hidden behind a silvery-haired couple strolling along the shoreline hand in hand.

Dan lurched toward Orestes Vasquez and said, "You know something, Mr. White Ghost, sir, you make me sick to my stomach. You and this piece of Colombian trash. In fact, I detest you so much, I would rather go blind than ever set eyes on you again."

"Hey, Detective, I can arrange that."

"I'm sure you can, sir. I'm sure you can. But I would much prefer to do it myself."

With that, Dan pulled two steel knives out of his coat pocket and held them up in front of Orestes Vasquez's face. His bodyguards immediately began to hurry toward them, but Orestes Vasquez raised his hand and called out, "Stop! I want to see what this gentleman intends to do!"

Dan looked up at the thundery sky, and said, "God, give me the strength to do this, so that I don't have to look at this scumbag for a single second longer."

The expression on Orestes Vasquez's face was extraordinary: he was elated; he was aroused; he was almost salivating. Lida Siado, however, was frowning, and she began to step away from him. "Orestes, I think we should go—"

At that moment, however, Dan lifted both knives in front of his face.

"*Orestes—!*"

Lightning flickered, and there was a deafening burst of thunder right over their heads. Raindrops began to patter onto the sand. But Orestes stayed where he was, staring at Dan and his upraised knives, his eyes bright with anticipation.

"Come on, Detective Fisher! What kind of a man are you, who cannot keep a promise?"

But Lida Siado started tapping at her drum. "Night Wind!" she called. "Night Wind!"

Dan stood with his face tilted upward, the two knives only inches away from his eyes. Orestes Vasquez shouted, "Do it, Detective! Do it! Don't disappoint us!" Even though she was panicking, Lida Siado had to stop chanting and drumming to see whether Dan would actually blind himself.

Dan hesitated for a moment. Then he screamed, "*Aaaahhhhh!*" and stabbed himself straight in both eyes. He staggered backward in the sand, spinning around off balance. Then he bent forward, still holding both knife hilts. He stayed there, shuddering, as if trying to summon the courage to do what he had to do next.

Orestes Vasquez looked at Lida Siado in excitement, but also in horror. "Did you see him? He is mad! He is totally loco!"

Lida Siado said, "This is not right. Believe me, Orestes. Something is wrong."

But then Dan shouted, "Christ! Oh, Christ! Oh, holy Christ!" and tugged both knives out again.

He turned to face Orestes Vasquez and Lida Siado, and he held up the knives so that they could see for themselves that there was a glistening eyeball on the point of each of them. His eyelids were closed tight, and thin streams of blood were trickling down his cheeks. Orestes Vasquez and Lida Siado stared at him in shock.

"For the love of God," said Orestes Vasquez. "When I said to do it—I didn't actually mean to *do* it!"

But now, only fifteen yards behind them, Annie had broken cover and was running noiselessly toward them over the sand. It was only when she had almost reached them that she started to shake her split-drum like a rattle and sing out, "Come to me! Ik'ib'alam! Come to me! Bring me your darkness, Ik'ib'alam! Bring me your grace! Bring me the power of darkness and evil!"

Lida Siado suddenly realized what was happening, and she held up one hand to deter Annie from coming any closer, while at the same time she began tapping on her drum again. "Night Wind! Night Wind! Send me your scavengers! Send me your *kukurpas*!"

She was too late. The lightning crackled, and the thunder rumbled again, but as the thunder subsided they heard a heavy, loping sound, like a large animal running fast. Lida Siado dropped to her knees in the sand, her eyes wild, although she kept tapping her drum and crying out her incantation to the Night Wind and the *kukurpas*.

Annie spread her arms wide and threw back her head, as if she were having a religious revelation. "Ik'ib'alam! Ik'ib'alam! Ik'ib'alam!"

"What the hell is going on?" shouted Orestes Vasquez. "José! Hilario! Round up the dogs! We're getting out of here right now!"

But the loping noise grew louder, until it was a gallop, and then there was a roar that sounded like three tons of gravel being emptied into a truck. Out of the gloom, as fast as an express train, came an enormous black jaguar with burning red eyes. It collided with Orestes Vasquez with an audible *thump!* and sent him hurtling sideways into the sand.

One of the bodyguards hauled out his automatic, but he didn't even have time to aim before the jaguar jumped and knocked him over, too. It stood on his chest, glaring down at him with its incandescent eyes. Then it gave another roar and bared its fangs and bit into the side of his neck.

The bodyguard let out a pathetic, childlike cry, but then the jaguar shook its head from side to side and tore away the side of his neck as far as his ear, and a thick triangular piece of his shoulder muscle. Afterward, it looked up, strings of flesh and sinew hanging from its jaws, and roared again. The other two bodyguards didn't even attempt to draw their guns: they started running toward the highway.

Dan edged his way over to Annie, keeping his eyes on the jaguar the whole time.

"What is it?" he asked her. "Is this the spirit you were drumming up?"

She nodded. "Ik'ib'alam, sometimes known as Balam, the black jaguar god of the Amazon rain forest. Some say he is evil through and through; but some say he *commands* evil, and everyone evil has to obey him or suffer the consequences."

Orestes Vasquez was trying to get back onto his feet, but he was obviously concussed. Meanwhile the black jaguar had finished tearing at the bodyguard's remains and had turned toward Lida Siado.

Lida Siado was screaming now, although it was thundering again, right overhead, and they could hardly hear her. Off to the west, on the horizon, all that remained of the sun was a molten golden ingot.

"Night Wind! Night Wind! Bring me your messengers!"

The black jaguar was huge, over six feet from shoulder to claw, but it moved with a terrible fluid grace. Beneath its gleaming black fur, its bones and muscles slid together in a complicated ballet of tension and impending death.

It approached Lida Siado until its nose was almost touching her forehead, and Dan could see its nostrils flaring. Lida Siado was in a state of hysteria, sobbing and begging and tapping furiously at her drum.

"Look!" said Annie.

Dan narrowed his eyes. Out of the gathering darkness, a *kukurpa* was stalking toward them through the surf, pale and skeletal. Only one *kukurpa*, but one was more than enough.

Lida Siado turned her head and saw the *kukurpa* too. "Night Wind!" she shrieked out, triumphantly. *"Night Wind!"*

Ik'ib'alam lifted its head to the clouds and roared so loudly that it drowned out the thunder. Then, without any hesitation, it buried its teeth in Lida Siado's face.

She let out a muffled scream, and thrashed her arms and legs. But the jaguar's jaws were locked into her cheekbones, and no matter how frantically she struggled, it wouldn't release her. Every desperate breath she took came straight from the jaguar's lungs, and her face must have been slathered with the jaguar's saliva.

The jaguar picked her up, and then it swung her violently from side to side, as if she were a child's doll.

Annie covered her face with her hands, but Dan watched in dreadful fascination as the jaguar gradually tore Lida Siado's head from her body, inch by inch, sinew by sinew, until she was lolling at an impossible angle and her limbs were flopping lifelessly across the sand.

But now the *kukurpa* had reached them, and it came toward the jaguar with its claws upraised. The jaguar dropped Lida Siado's body and circled the *kukurpa*, snarling. The *kukurpa* moved jerkily, but it lashed at the jaguar and caught it with its claw. The jaguar had to spring backward to avoid being lashed a second time.

"I think this is where I give magic a helping hand!" Dan shouted, trying to make himself heard over the thunder.

"What?"

He lifted the black canvas bag that he had collected from the station and took out a Very pistol. "It's not exactly a hut covered in ananaconda fat, but it'll have to do."

The jaguar and the *kukurpa* were ripping and tearing and lunging at each other now, and the jaguar was roaring almost continuously. Dan made his way around them and approached as close as he dared. It began to rain, hard, and the sky was flickering with forests of lightning trees.

The jaguar ripped at the *kukurpa*'s skull-like face, and the *kukurpa* lurched back and dropped onto one knee. That was Dan's chance. He held the Very pistol in both hands and aimed it at the *kukurpa*'s abdomen. There was a sharp crack, and a dazzling scarlet flare shot into the *kukurpa*'s body, bursting its way through papery skin and lodging itself, sizzling, in the creature's pelvis.

The *kukurpa* screamed and tried to pluck the flare out of its insides, but the flare was burning at nearly three thousand degrees Celsius, and the *kukurpa*'s pelvis acted like a natural fireplace, so that it burned hotter and hotter every second.

The jaguar gradually backed away into the darkness. But Dan stayed where he was, watching the *kukurpa* burn.

The creature didn't fall over. It burned upright, crackling and popping and pouring out showers of brilliant sparks. All the time it burned, it appeared to be staring at Dan in resentment and hatred, but Dan knew that he had beaten it and that he had taken at least a token revenge for Ernie's killing. There were probably thousands more *kukurpas* in the Uitoto spirit world, but that no longer mattered because Lida Siado was dead, too, and she couldn't call up any more.

The *kukurpa*'s left claw dropped off, shriveling and clutching at nothing at all, and then its rib cage collapsed, and its skull-like head rolled across the sand and lay burning at Dan's feet. In the distance he could hear the wailing and honking of fire trucks.

Annie came up to him and took hold of his hand.

"Where's Icky?" he asked her.

"Ik'ib'alam? Melted away. I didn't even see where he went."

"He was damned good, that Icky, as gods of evil go."

The sky was beginning to clear, and the rain had stopped. All along the Pacific Highway, emergency lights were flashing, and crowds were gathering to find out what had happened.

The last flame was dwindling on the *kukurpa*'s charred collarbone. Dan reached down and scooped up a handful of sand and put out the fire.

"This is for Ernie."

They walked back up the beach. Orestes Vasquez was being helped away by his bodyguards, but he didn't even look at Dan and Annie. His three Great Danes jumped up into the back of his Porsche Cayenne, and then he was gone with an exhibitionistic squeal of tires.

"Good trick with the sheep's eyes," said Annie as they climbed into Dan's SUV.

"Sheep's eyes? What do you mean, sheep's eyes? They were pickled onions."

They should have felt like celebrating that evening, but they were both very tired, and somehow there didn't seem to be anything much to say. But they sat in Annie's living room for an hour together and shared a bottle of pinot grigio, while Malkin purred on Annie's lap and the Scissor Sisters played in the background.

"Gayle used to love the Scissor Sisters," said Dan. "She used to sing all their songs. Well, let's put it this way: she *tried* to sing all their songs."

"Malkin's purring," said Annie. "Did you know that jaguars can't purr? They don't have the vocal cords for it."

"No, I didn't know that. I never really *needed* to

know that. Come to think of it, I'm not even sure I need to know that now."

Annie said, "We only have Rebecca Greensmith to go for now. With any luck, she may decide that we've beaten her, and she'll quietly disappear."

"Either that, or she'll want to take some hideous witch-type revenge on us."

"Don't be such a pessimist."

"I'm a detective. I went to detective school. They give you a special course in Advanced Pessimism."

Annie leaned against his shoulder. "Dan," she said, "what am I going to do with all of this magical power?"

"Something good, I hope. Like clearing the smog or mixing up the perfect tequila sunrise."

"It makes me feel strange. I almost feel like I don't know myself anymore."

Dan kissed her hair. "Don't worry. I know you. If you're ever in any doubt, just come up and ask me."

It was well past 2:00 AM before Dan finished his wine and went back up to his apartment. He took a long shower and almost fell asleep standing up. Then he brushed his teeth and heaved himself into bed.

He fell asleep within a few minutes and started to dream almost at once. He dreamed that he was walking along the beach with Ik'ib'alam, the black jaguar, walking beside him. Off to his left, a dozen strange figures were walking on the surface of the ocean, keeping pace with him, although they were more than a hundred yards away, and they kept their distance. They wore a variety of masks—white, expressionless masks like the Rusalka and bony staglike masks like the *kukurpa*—but apart from that they were naked, both men and women.

At first he couldn't understand what they were trying

to tell him. But then he thought: *They're all wearing masks. Maybe they're trying to show me that none of this battle against the witches has been magic at all. It was all a charade, but I was tricked into believing it.*

If that were true, though, who was tricking him and why?

He turned around. The black jaguar had disappeared, and he realized that it had only been a shadow.

He turned back toward the ocean. One of the figures was approaching him through the surf, a woman wearing a mask that looked like a cat's head. She was young and slim with rounded breasts, and the ocean breeze had stiffened her nipples. Her vulva was waxed, but it was elaborately decorated with henna flowers. Around her forehead she wore a narrow cord of tightly braided hair that had a heart-shaped silver clasp.

"You've been deceived," she said, and her voice sounded very close to his ear. "Didn't I tell you that some people are not what they pretend to be?"

She came up very close to him, and then she took off her mask. It was Gayle, and she was smiling at him benignly.

"This has all been a trick? All of this witch stuff? Michelange DuPriz and Lida Siado and Miska Vedma? What about Rebecca Greensmith?"

Gayle turned back to look at the other figures on the ocean. "Oh, Rebecca Greensmith is real enough. Rebecca Greensmith is the only one who is real. But the witch you think is Rebecca Greensmith—that isn't Rebecca Greensmith at all."

"I'm totally confused. If *she* isn't Rebecca Greensmith, then who is?"

Gayle stood on tiptoe and kissed him, and it was then that he found he wasn't walking along the beach at all; he was lying in bed, and Gayle was lying on top of the sheet beside him. She had one leg across his, and he could feel the weight of it and the warmth.

"Who do you think Rebecca Greensmith really is? Who's the most powerful witch you know? Who's the *only* witch you know?"

Dan sat up. "You're talking about *Annie?*"

"Think about it, Dan. Doesn't it all fit into place? When she saw how those four witches were taking control of the whole of the city, Annie persuaded you to help her destroy them and to steal their powers, one after another. Who better to have as her familiar than a police detective? A police detective can open all kinds of doors that even magic can't open."

"So what's she going to do now?"

"Who knows what dark plans she has? She now possesses all the magical powers that once belonged to her sister witches, and without that power, none of those three mobsters can survive for even a day. They are beholden to her now, completely, and that means she personally holds sway over more than half the organized crime in Los Angeles. Drugs, extortion, prostitution. These are the devil's delights, and Rebecca Greensmith has acquired them all, in homage to her master."

Dan switched on the bedside lamp and climbed out of bed. Gayle sat up, and in the lamplight she was just as beautiful as she had ever been. Her green eyes, her glistening lips, the curve of her hip.

"What the hell can I do to stop her?" asked Dan.

"There's only one way. You'll have to kill her."

"Kill her? I can't do that."

"She helped the Colombian witch kill your friend Ernie, didn't she? She's helped kill scores of police officers, too."

"How do you *know* all this?"

Gayle knelt up on the bed. "I know it because I have been sent as an agent from the one who opposes Satan."

"You've been sent by *God?* Oh, come on. Of all the people in the world who can help Him fight the devil, God chose *me?* Talk about scraping the barrel."

"Of course He chose you. It makes absolute sense. You are the only one Annie trusts to come close to her, and you are the only one who can kill her."

Dan picked up his pants from the floor and pulled them on. Then he opened his closet and took out a black polo shirt.

"How do I know that *you're* not deluding me?"

She climbed off the bed and came across to him and linked her arms around his waist. "I'm Gayle, Dan. You know it's me."

"Yes, my dead girlfriend. My very dead girlfriend."

"Ssh. God has it in His power to give me back to you, alive, as your reward for vanquishing Satan. If you kill Annie, He will breathe life back into me, and we can be lovers again."

Dan looked down at her for a very long time, biting his lip in indecision. Then he said, "I'll tell you what I'll do. I'll go down and talk to Annie about this, confront her with it."

"No! You can't do that. You have to surprise her, or she'll destroy you on the spot. Suffocate you or burn you or shake off your arms and legs. You won't stand a chance."

"So how do I kill her?"

"You walk straight into her apartment and you take this cord and you strangle her with it." She reached up and untied the braided cord around her head. "It's woven from the hair of sacrificed witches. It's the only way you can kill her."

She gave him the cord, and he held it up. It was very tightly braided—blond hair and titian hair and silver hair, too. It was fastened at one end with a silver clasp, which at first glance looked like a heart, but on closer inspection turned out to be the face of a horned demon.

"I can't do this. Are you sure I'm not dreaming?"

Gayle took his left hand in hers, and drew it down between her legs, guiding two of his fingers up inside her. "You could have me, Dan, just as I was. But if you don't do this for me, you won't ever see me again. Ever."

"But *Annie*—"

"Don't you understand? She's *not* Annie! She never has been Annie! Did you ever meet her parents? Did she ever tell you where she came from? She's a three-hundred-year-old witch who lives only to give sacrifices to Satan. She's lewd and she's sadistic and she's blasphemous. She's evil incarnate. You have to kill her!"

Dan felt as if his skull were shrinking. He lifted the braided cord again, and then he thought: *yes, this does make sense.* Why had Annie been so determined to destroy all those other witches, even though it was so dangerous? It had nothing to do with her destiny or what her mother and her grandmother had taught her about always fighting evil. She had wanted their magical power for herself.

"Okay," he said. "Let's finish this witch business, once and for all."

When they went down to Annie's apartment, they found that the lights were still on, and music was still playing. Dan turned to Gayle and said, "She hasn't gone to bed yet."

Gayle was loosely wrapped in his dark blue satin bathrobe, and she looked even prettier and more vulnerable than ever. "You can still surprise her. Just be quick, and don't give her any time to realize what you're doing."

Dan nodded and nervously sniffed. Then he rang Annie's door chime.

At first she didn't answer. Maybe she was in bed, after all. But then he heard her slippers flip-flapping on the floor, and she opened up.

"Dan! Can't you sleep, either?"

Without a word, Dan pushed her back into her hallway and manhandled her into the living room. Malkin jumped out of the way with a squeak and scurried behind the couch.

"Dan! What are you *doing?* Dan, you're hurting me!"

Dan didn't say anything, but forced Annie facedown onto the couch, with his knee in the small of her back, and deftly looped the braided cord around her neck.

"Dan! What are you doing! You're crazy! Stop it! You're really hurting me! *Dan!*"

Gayle came into the living room and stood close by, watching and biting at her thumbnail. "Do it, Dan! Do it now! Strangle the witch before she can cast one of her evil spells on you! Do it! *Do* it! *Do-it-do-it-do-it-do-it-do-it!*"

Dan twisted the braided cord so that it cut into Annie's neck. She let out a guttural choking noise and clawed at the cord in a futile effort to pull it free, but Dan tightened it even more.

"Strangle the witch!" Gayle repeated. "Strangle the witch!"

There was a moment when time stopped. When the incense from Annie's joss sticks hung suspended in midair. When there was no sound, no music, no clocks ticking. This was the moment when Annie had only one breath left.

Then suddenly, Dan heard the Scissor Sisters on Annie's CD player.

"When I was a child I had a fever . . . my hands swelled up like two balloons . . . eee! eee! eee!"

He heard a hollow, metallic sound, like somebody blowing down a metal pipe. He slowly turned and saw to his horror that Gayle was standing in the middle of the living room with a sawed-off scaffolding pole embedded in her face, her eyes staring at him in desperation like the eyes of a flatfish.

"You're not Gayle!" he shouted at her. "Jesus Christ! You're not Gayle! *Annie!*"

With fumbling fingers he unwound the braided cord and dragged it away from Annie's neck. He turned her over onto her back. Her eyes were closed, and her lips were pale blue.

Gayle came stiffly toward him, both hands held out like a zombie.

Dan said, "Get away! I don't know who the hell you are or *what* the hell you are, but get away!"

He took a deep breath, opened Annie's mouth, and blew into it. He did it again and then again, and then Annie coughed and opened her eyes.

"Dan—" she gasped. "Dan, what's—"

She caught sight of Gayle, and her eyes widened. Dan said, "It's okay. Somebody nearly made me do something terrible."

He stood up and faced Gayle. She stayed where she was, swaying slightly, the front of her dress plastered in blood.

"I don't know any magic incantations," said Dan. "I don't know any spells, and I don't have any magic dust. But you're not Gayle. Gayle is dead, and you are nothing but a mockery of Gayle, and I dismiss you."

Gayle blinked once, and she uttered that strange piping sound again, and bubbles of blood crawled out of the end of the scaffolding pole.

"If you're Rebecca Greensmith—go back to the place where you belong, and don't ever come back. If you're not, then whoever you are, rest in peace. But if you see the spirit of the real Gayle, you can tell her this:

"Tell her that Dan begs her to forgive him. Tell her that Dan was drunk and careless and arrogant and failed to protect her. Tell her that he still grieves for her every day, and that he's sorry."

Gayle listened to this, still swaying slightly. Then, suddenly, her head erupted, like a huge geyser of boiling oil, and her body burst open. She reared up in front of him, a seething column of glossy black, and within the space of a few seconds he was confronted by a giant snake, like a python, with a flat head and a flickering tongue and the deadest of eyes.

"*This is my master,*" said a thin, half-strangulated voice. "*My master curses you forever.*"

The snake's head veered from side to side, the tip of its tongue almost licking Dan's face. He stood rigid, unable to coordinate his muscles. He was so terrified that he had forgotten how to move. He was so terrified that he had almost forgotten how to think. *Almost*—because he could see the name imprinted in his mind's eye, as if it had been branded there and was still smoking. *Satan.*

Behind him, Annie sat up on the couch. She picked up a thin dried root from the table, and pointed it directly at the snake.

"*Busd de yad!*" she said, hoarsely. "*Mykmah a-yal prg de vaoan, ar gasb tybylf doalyn od telokh!*"

The snake reared up to the ceiling, its shining skin rippling as if it had swallowed scores of living creatures.

"My master curses you!" it hissed. "My master will never let you rest until your final damnation!"

"*Mykmah vls de ageobofaly dluga toglo pugo a talho! Busd de yad!* The glory of God! *Busd de yad!* The glory of God!"

The room was abruptly filled with a brilliant white light—so bright that Dan had to shield his eyes with his hand. The snake writhed and hissed, and its tail swung from side to side across the floor, scattering books and candles and cushions. But the light continued to grow more intense, and the snake's glossy skin seemed to break up and crumble.

Something buzzed toward Dan and stung him on the cheek. A blowfly. And that was when he realized what was happening to the snake—it was disintegrating into millions of blowflies. The servant of Satan, the lord of the flies.

For a few seconds, Dan was confronted by an entire snake made out of blue, glittering blowflies. But then there was a sharp crack, and the snake was blown apart, until the whole room was thick with a whirlwind of blowflies. Dan tried to beat them away, but they pattered against his face like hailstones and caught in his hair, and even tried to crawl into his mouth. He spat and spat again and pinched them out from between his lips.

Through the hail of blowflies, he saw for a single heart-stopping second the same face that he had seen on the landing of Ben Burrows's house when they had captured Rebecca Greensmith. Calm, placid, knowing, and so powerful that it was almost like staring into the sun.

Busd de yad, the glory of God.

The blowflies started to flare up and burn, then fall to the floor as tiny clouds of white ash. For a moment, the room was filled with thousands of sparks.

Dan felt an extraordinary swelling of emotion. He was filled with hope, with love, and a huge surge of pride that brought tears to his eyes. At the same time, though, he felt painfully aware of his own mortality, that he would have to die one day, and of the mortality of those he loved, like Gayle and Ernie and all the officers who had been slaughtered by The Quintex.

Annie got up from the couch and came over to him. Her face was alight with the same radiance. It shone from her eyes, and it seemed to give her a flickering halo. She put her arms around him and pressed her head against his chest, and the two of them stayed like that, holding each other until the last blowfly flared and vanished, and the light had died away.

"I could have killed you," said Dan.

"It wasn't your fault. Rebecca Greensmith had enormous magical influence. After you had strangled me, she probably would have persuaded you to kill yourself, too."

Dan looked down at her. "It's over, isn't it? We've gotten rid of her—all five of her."

Annie nodded. He kissed her hair, then her forehead, then her lips.

Outside, it was gradually beginning to grow light.

He came back home that evening and rang her door bell. She came out, smiling and wiping her hands on a cloth. "Sorry, I've been mixing up some dried cicadas and black pepper. It's a wonderful cure for indigestion."

"Think I'll stick to Pepto-Bismol, thanks."

"How about a brewski?" she asked him.

"Sure. I have some very excellent news. It won't be announced officially until tomorrow morning, but the Zombie and the White Ghost and Vasili Krylov have all been arrested, along with twenty or thirty of their accountants and lawyers and other assorted goons."

He followed her into the kitchen, and she took two cans of Coors out of the fridge. "Another update that's going to come out tomorrow—Chief O'Malley has retired for health reasons, and Deputy Chief Days is taking over until they can find a replacement."

"And what about all those men who were killed? Are they going to say how that happened?"

Dan shook his head. "I think they're going to stick to the freak tornado story. The Quintex came to town, but now she's gone, so I don't think there's any need to frighten Joe Public more than we have to."

"Would you like some supper? I have a chicken-and-thyme pie in the oven."

"Great. Love some."

He took off his coat and hung it over the back of one of the kitchen chairs. As he did so, a jet-black kitten came into the room, looked up at him, and mewed.

"Hey—" he said. "Who's *this* little feller?"

Annie had started to peel potatoes. She turned and looked at him, and her eyes were curiously dark, as if she had no eyes at all. "That's Malkin, of course."

"*Malkin?* But Malkin's—"

JACK KETCHUM

Burned again. Men never treated Dora well. This latest cheated on her and dumped her. The last decent guy she knew was her old high school boyfriend, Jim. He'd said that he loved her. Maybe he did. So with the help of Flame Finders, Dora's tracked him down. Turns out he's married with two kids. But Dora isn't about to let that stand in her way…

OLD FLAMES

Includes the novella,
RIGHT TO LIFE

ISBN 13: 978-0-8439-5999-4

☐ **YES!**

Sign me up for the Leisure Horror Book Club and send my FREE BOOKS! If I choose to stay in the club, I will pay only $8.50* each month, a savings of $7.48!

NAME: _____

ADDRESS: _____

TELEPHONE: _____

EMAIL: _____

☐ I want to pay by credit card.

☐ VISA   ☐ MasterCard.   ☐ DISCOVER

ACCOUNT #: _____

EXPIRATION DATE: _____

SIGNATURE: _____

Mail this page along with $2.00 shipping and handling to:

Leisure Horror Book Club
PO Box 6640
Wayne, PA 19087

Or fax (must include credit card information) to:

610-995-9274

You can also sign up online at **www.dorchesterpub.com**.

*Plus $2.00 for shipping. Offer open to residents of the U.S. and Canada only. Canadian residents please call 1-800-481-9191 for pricing information.

If under 18, a parent or guardian must sign. Terms, prices and conditions subject to change. Subscription subject to acceptance. Dorchester Publishing reserves the right to reject any order or cancel any subscription.

GET FREE BOOKS!

You can have the best fiction delivered to your door for less than what you'd pay in a bookstore or online. Sign up for one of our book clubs today, and we'll send you *FREE* BOOKS* just for trying it out...**with no obligation to buy, ever!**

As a member of the Leisure Horror Book Club, you'll receive books by authors such as **RICHARD LAYMON, JACK KETCHUM, JOHN SKIPP, BRIAN KEENE** and many more.

As a book club member you also receive the following special benefits:
- **30% off all orders!**
- **Exclusive access to special discounts!**
- **Convenient home delivery and 10 days to return any books you don't want to keep.**

Visit **www.dorchesterpub.com** or call **1-800-481-9191**

There is no minimum number of books to buy, and you may cancel membership at any time.
*Please include $2.00 for shipping and handling.